DANGEROUS WOMEN

DANGEROUS WOMEN

EDITED BY **OTTO PENZLER**

NEW YORK   BOSTON

Compilation copyright © 2005 by Otto Penzler
Introduction copyright © 2005 by Otto Penzler
"A Thousand Miles from Nowhere" by Lorenzo Carcaterra. Copyright © 2005 by Lorenzo Carcaterra. • "Cielo Azul" by Michael Connelly. Copyright © 2005 by Michael Connelly. • "Mr. Gray's Folly" by John Connolly. Copyright © 2005 by John Connolly. • "What She Offered" by Thomas H. Cook. Copyright © 2005 by Thomas H. Cook. • "Born Bad" by Jeffery Deaver. Copyright © 2005 by Jeffery Deaver. • "Rendezvous" by Nelson DeMille. Copyright © 2005 by Nelson DeMille. • "Witness" by J. A. Jance. Copyright © 2005 by J. A. Jance. • "Her Lord and Master" by Andrew Klavan. Copyright © 2005 by Andrew Klavan. • "Louly and Pretty Boy" by Elmore Leonard. Copyright © 2005 by Elmore Leonard, Inc. • "Dear Penthouse Forum (A First Draft)" by Laura Lippman. Copyright © 2005 by Laura Lippman. • "Improvisation" by Ed McBain. Copyright © 2005 by Hui Corporation. • "Third Party" by Jay McInerney. Copyright © 2005 by Bright Lights, Big City, Inc. • "Karma" by Walter Mosley. Copyright © 2005 by Walter Mosley. • "Give Me Your Heart" by Joyce Carol Oates. Copyright © 2005 by Joyce Carol Oates. • "Sneaker Wave" by Anne Perry. Copyright © 2005 by Anne Perry. • "Soft Spot" by Ian Rankin. Copyright © 2005 by John Rebus Ltd. • "The Last Kiss" by S. J. Rozan. Copyright © 2005 by S. J. Rozan.

All rights reserved.

Mysterious Press
Warner Books

Time Warner Book Group
1271 Avenue of the Americas, New York, NY 10020
Visit our Web site at www.twbookmark.com.

The Mysterious Press name and logo are registered trademarks of Warner Books.

Printed in the United States of America

First Printing: January 2005

10 9 8 7 6 5 4 3 2 1

Library of Congress Cataloging-in-Publication Data

Dangerous women / edited by Otto Penzler.
    p. cm.
  ISBN 0-89296-004-3
    1. Detective and mystery stories, American. 2. Detective and mystery stories, English. 3. Women—Fiction. I. Penzler, Otto.

PS648.D4D365 2005
813'.0872083522—dc22   2004049870

For Lisa Michelle Atkinson
Whose perfection
makes her dangerous

CONTENTS

INTRODUCTION

What makes a woman dangerous? No doubt there are any number of opinions, depending upon the experience of the man or woman who responds.

Personally, I think the most dangerous women are those who are irresistible. Each of us may have a unique weakness, an Achilles' heel that is unfathomable to others, or we may share universal sensibilities that everyone understands. It may be a woman's great beauty that wins our hearts, or her charm, or intelligence. It may be the way she brushes her hair back from her eyes, or the way she laughs, or the way she sneezes.

She may be acutely aware of her power, or utterly innocent of it. One will use it as a steel-edged weapon, another as a fuzzy security blanket. The intent neither increases nor diminishes the power, and that is the terrible danger to those who may be in thrall to it.

Power is dangerous. We may know it, even fear it, but if we want the heat from that flame, we will risk everything to get as close to it as possible.

Dangerous women have always been with us. Remember

Delilah? Authors have understood the ferocious attraction of dangerous women and used them as literary devices relentlessly. Most of the great women of history, as well as most significant female literary figures, have been dangerous. Perhaps not to everyone, but frequently to those who have fallen in love with them. Men have killed for dangerous women, betrayed their countries, their loved ones and themselves, given up thrones and committed suicide. Sometimes the dangerous women may even be worth it—worth risking everything and giving up all one holds dear.

Many literary detectives have been aware of the dangerous woman. Sam Spade fell for one, Brigid O'Shaughnessy, while Philip Marlowe and Lew Archer are often chased by them; they have been known to allow themselves to be caught.

Sherlock Holmes, although he allowed himself to be enamored of Irene Adler ("the daintiest thing under a bonnet on this planet"), had a famously powerful aversion to most members of the opposite sex. "Women are never to be entirely trusted—not the best of them," Holmes stated in *The Sign of the Four*. "I assure you that the most winning woman I ever knew was hanged for poisoning three little children for their insurance money."

Although Archie Goodwin loves women, his boss, Nero Wolfe, generally speaks and behaves like a misogynist. "You can depend on women for anything except constancy," he said. Further, while in a particularly foul mood, he declared, "The vocations for which they [are] best adapted are chicanery, sophistry, self-advertisement, cajolery, mystification and incubation."

And neither Holmes nor Wolfe ever met the dangerous women on these pages. They would have been shocked and appalled. But, as I predict you, too, will be, they would have been fascinated. They would have been helpless in their desire to know what they were up to, where they would lead, what adorable little tricks they had up their sleeves.

It is clear from the enduring success of Hammett, Chandler, Macdonald, Doyle and Rex Stout that they understood much, including the appeal, of a kind, of dangerous women. The authors in this book have proven to be no less accomplished in providing an array of *femmes fatale* to delight you—and cause you to shudder in relief that they are not women who matter in your life. At least, for your sake, it is to be hoped that they don't.

Lorenzo Carcaterra is the author of six books, including the controversial *Sleepers*, which became a *New York Times* number one best seller both in hardcover and paperback, as well as a major motion picture starring Brad Pitt, Robert DeNiro, Dustin Hoffman, Kevin Bacon and Minnie Driver. He is currently a writer and producer for the NBC series *Law and Order*.

After a successful career as a journalist, Michael Connelly turned to fiction writing and produced *The Black Echo*, which introduced his LAPD detective Hieronymous Bosch and won an Edgar Allan Poe Award from the Mystery Writers of America. He followed this with three more Bosch novels, *Black Ice*, *The Concrete Blonde* and *The Last Coyote*, then wrote a stand-alone thriller, *The Poet*. As one of the world's most beloved authors, his books have become automatic best sellers in many countries.

The young Irish writer John Connolly has worked as a bartender, a local government official, a waiter, a dogsbody at Harrods department store and a journalist. The former policeman Charlie Parker was introduced in 1999 in *Every Dead Thing*, and followed in *Dark Hollow*, *The Killing Kind* and *The*

White Road. Connolly's most recent novel, *Bad Men,* is a stand-alone thriller. No writer working today better combines the detective novel with elements of the supernatural.

When the Mystery Writers of America gave Thomas H. Cook the Edgar Allan Poe Award for *The Chatham School Affair* in 1997, it was an overdue honor for one of America's finest crime writers. He had been previously nominated for Edgars in two other categories, Best First Novel and Best Fact Crime, and had won the Herodotus Award for Best Historical Short Story of the Year for "Fatherhood."

Jeffery Deaver was working as a journalist when he decided to go to law school so that he could become a legal writer. Instead, he practiced law for several years and, while taking long commutes, began writing suspense fiction with extraordinary success. He has been nominated for four Edgars and won the Ellery Queen Reader's Award for best short story of the year three times. His Lincoln Rhyme novels are staples on the bestseller lists; *The Bone Collector* was filmed with Denzel Washington as the paralyzed former forensic officer and Angelina Jolie as the young cop who helps bring a serial killer to justice.

Few writers sell as many books as Nelson DeMille, whose blockbuster thrillers have sold more than 30 million copies worldwide. Notable for their impeccable plotting and distinguished literary style, his best sellers include *The Lion's Game, Plum Island, Spencerville, Gold Coast, Word of Honor* and *The General's Daughter,* a pure detective novel successfully filmed starring John Travolta, with a screenplay by William Goldman. "Rendezvous" is his first short story in twenty-five years.

J. A. Jance did not have an easy time becoming a bestselling author. She was denied entry to a creative writing program because the professor thought women should be teachers or nurses, and her alcoholic husband agreed. After her divorce and his death at the age of forty-two from acute alcohol poisoning, she wrote from 4:00 to 7:00 a.m. before sending her kids off to school. Her series about Detective J. P. Beaumont began modestly as paperback originals but now are regulars on bestseller lists.

Writing as Andrew Klavan and using the pseudonym Keith Peterson, the author has won two Edgars but has somehow failed to make the best-seller list, though he has had great success in Hollywood. Clint Eastwood directed and starred in *True Crime*, about a journalist trying to save an innocent man; it also featured Isaiah Washington, James Woods, Denis Leary and Lisa Gay Hamilton. Two years later, Michael Douglas and Famke Janssen starred in another film based on a Klavan novel, *Don't Say a Word*.

Often regarded as the finest crime writer alive (*Newsweek* said maybe the best ever), Elmore Leonard has had twenty consecutive best sellers, including *Mr. Paradise, Tishomingo Blues, Pagan Babies* and the short story collection *When the Women Come Out to Dance*. Numerous films have been made from his work: *Hombre, 3:10 to Yuma, The Moonshine War, Stick, The Big Bounce, Get Shorty, Out of Sight* and *Jackie Brown*. He has been named a Grand Master by the Mystery Writers of America for lifetime achievement.

Three of the first four books Laura Lippman wrote were nominated for Edgar Allan Poe Awards, a feat unmatched in the history of the Mystery Writers of America; *Charm City* won. The series of detective fiction novels featuring Tess Monaghan also won Shamus, Agatha and Anthony awards from the Private Eye Writers of America, and the Malice Domestic and Bouchercon conventions respectively.

Evan Hunter and Ed McBain are two best-selling novelists living in the same body. Hunter's first adult novel, *The Black-*

board Jungle, shocked a nation, as did the wildly successful film made from it. As McBain, he has written more than fifty novels, including the iconic 87th Precinct novels, which essentially defined the police procedural for a half-century. Hunter also wrote the screenplay for Alfred Hitchcock's *The Birds*. He is a Grand Master and was the first American to be given a Diamond Dagger for lifetime achievement by the (British) Crime Writers Association.

If a single writer could be held up to the light as the personification of cool and hip in the 1980s, it was Jay McInerney, who rode to instant stardom with his first book, *Bright Lights, Big City*. While he has seldom ventured into the world of crime fiction (unless you count drug use and abuse), his short story "Con Doctor" was selected for *Best American Mystery Stories 1998*.

Even if Bill Clinton had not told the media that Walter Mosley was his favorite mystery writer, the Easy Rawlins series would have been successful. It made its debut with *Devil in a Blue Dress*, which was nominated for an Edgar and then filmed with Denzel Washington and Jennifer Beals. As one of the most original voices in the world of crime fiction, Mosley has seen such Rawlins novels as *Black Betty* and *A Little Yellow Dog* make the *New York Times* best-seller list. He is a former president of the Mystery Writers of America.

Among the world's most distinguished living authors, surely Joyce Carol Oates ranks as the greatest not to have won the Nobel Prize, although rumors abound that she has been short-listed several times. She has produced a wide variety of work at a prodigious rate, and it seems unlikely that any living American writer has received more accolades and awards, far too many to list here, but including six National Book Award nominations (including the winner, *Them*, in 1970) and three finalists for the Pulitzer Prize. Among her most recent books are *Take Me, Take Me With You*, *Rape: A Love Story* and *The Tattooed Girl*.

After writing and being rejected for twenty years, Anne Perry's first novel, *The Cater Street Hangman*, was published in 1979. Since then, she has averaged more than a book a year, mainly the beloved Victorian-era detective novels that have put her on the best-seller list. The first series was about Inspector Thomas Pitt and his wife Charlotte, while the second is a darker series about Inspector William Monk. She won an Edgar for her short story, "Heroes," which featured college professor and chaplain Joseph Reavley, now featured in a new series beginning with *No Graves As Yet*.

Not many crime writers make it into *The Guinness Book of World Records*, but Ian Rankin did when he had seven best sellers on the *London Times* list at the same time. He has won three Daggers from the (British) Crime Writers Association, two for short stories and one for *Black and Blue*, which was also nominated for an Edgar. His Inspector Rebus novels, beginning with *Knots and Crosses* in 1987, have served as the basis for a BBC television series. He was also one of the first winners of the prestigious Chandler-Fulbright Award.

S. J. Rozan's novels about Lydia Chin and Bill Smith are among the most honored of recent years, winning Shamus, Anthony, Macavity and Edgar awards, with *Winter and Night* winning the Edgar for Best Novel in 2003 to join the statue of Poe she won for best short story. Lydia is a young American-born Chinese private eye whose cases mainly originate in the Chinese community, while Smith is an older, experienced PI who lives above a bar in Tribeca. They work together smoothly in carefully constructed (the author is, after all, an architect) plots, essentially taking turns as the dominant figure from book to book.

These giants of the mystery writing world have put to-gether a bevy, a veritable harem, of dangerous women of all kinds. The gentler sex? Don't make me laugh. And stay on guard, lest they win your heart, because they'd like to have it. Perhaps with some fava beans and a nice Chianti.

Otto Penzler

DANGEROUS WOMEN

IMPROVISATION

ED McBAIN

Why don't we kill somebody?" she suggested.

She was a blonde, of course, tall and willowy and wearing a sleek black cocktail dress cut high on the leg and low at the neckline.

"Been there," Will told her. "Done that."

Her eyes opened wide, a sharp blue in startling contrast to the black of the dress.

"The Gulf War," he explained.

"Not the same thing at all," she said, and plucked the olive from her martini and popped it into her mouth. "I'm talking about murder."

"Murder, uh-huh," Will said. "Who'd you have in mind?"

"How about the girl sitting across the bar there?"

"Ah, a random victim," he said. "But how's that any different from combat?"

"A *specific* random victim," she said. "Shall we kill her or not?"

"Why?" he asked.

"Why not?" she said.

Will had known the woman for perhaps twenty minutes at most. In fact, he didn't even know her name. Her suggestion that they kill someone had come in response to a standard pickup line he'd used to good effect many times before, to wit: "So what do we do for a little excitement tonight?"

To which the blonde had replied, "Why don't we kill somebody?"

Hadn't whispered the words, hadn't even lowered her voice. Just smiled over the rim of her martini glass, and said in her normal speaking voice, "Why don't we kill somebody?"

The *specific* random victim she had in mind was a plain-looking woman wearing a plain brown jacket over a brown silk blouse and a darker brown skirt. There was about her the look of a harried file clerk or lower-level secretary, the mousy brown hair, the unblinking eyes behind what one had to call spectacles rather than eyeglasses, the thin-lipped mouth and slight overbite. A totally unremarkable woman. Small wonder she was sitting alone nursing a glass of white wine.

"Let's say we *do* actually kill her," Will said. "What'll we do for a little excitement afterward?"

The blonde smiled.

And crossed her legs.

"My name is Jessica," she said.

She extended her hand.

He took it.

"I'm Will," he said.

He assumed her palm was cold from the iced drink she'd been holding.

• • •

On this chilly December evening three days before Christmas, Will had no intention whatever of killing the mousy little file clerk at the end of the bar, or anyone else for that matter. He had killed his fair share of people a long time ago, thank you, all of them *specific* random victims in that they had been wearing the uniform of the Iraqi Army, which made them the enemy. That was as specific as you could get in wartime, he supposed. That was what made it okay to bulldoze them in their trenches. That was what made it okay to *murder* them, whatever fine distinction Jessica was now making between murder and combat.

Anyway, Will knew this was merely a game, a variation on the mating ritual that took place in every singles bar in Manhattan on any given night of the year. You came up with a clever approach, you got a response that indicated interest, and you took it from there. In fact, he wondered how many times, in how many bars before tonight, Jessica had used her "Why don't we kill somebody?" line. The approach was admittedly an adventurous one, possibly even a dangerous one—suppose she flashed those splendid legs at someone who turned out to be Jack the Ripper? Suppose she picked up a guy who really *believed* it might be fun to kill that girl sitting alone at the other end of the bar? Hey, great idea, Jess, let's do it! Which, in effect, was what he'd tacitly indicated, but of course she knew they were just playing a game here, didn't she? She certainly had to realize they weren't planning an actual murder here.

"Who'll make the approach?" she asked.

"I suppose I should," Will said.

"Please don't use your 'What'll we do for a little excitement tonight?' line."

"Gee, I thought you liked that."

"Yes, the first time I heard it. Five or six years ago."

"I thought I was being entirely original."

"Try to be more original with little Alice there, okay?"

"Is that what you think her name is?"

"What do you think it is?"

"Patricia."

"Okay, I'll be Patricia," she said. "Let me hear it."

"Excuse me, Miss," Will said.

"Great start," Jessica said.

"My friend and I happened to notice you sitting all alone here, and we thought you might care to join us."

Jessica looked around as if trying to locate the friend he was telling Patricia about.

"Who do you mean?" she asked, all wide-eyed and wondering.

"The beautiful blonde sitting right there," Will said. "Her name is Jessica."

Jessica smiled.

"Beautiful blonde, huh?" she said.

"*Gorgeous* blonde," he said.

"Sweet talker," she said, and covered his hand with her own on the bar top. "So let's say little Patty Cake decides to join us. Then what?"

"We ply her with compliments and alcohol."

"And then what?"

"We take her to some dark alley and bludgeon her to death."

"I have a small bottle of poison in my handbag," Jessica said. "Wouldn't that be better?"

Will narrowed his eyes like a gangster.

"Perfect," he said. "We'll take her to some dark alley and poison her to death."

"Wouldn't an apartment someplace be a better venue?" Jessica asked.

And it suddenly occurred to him that perhaps they weren't discussing murder at all, jokingly or otherwise. Was it possible that what Jessica had in mind was a three-way?

"Go talk to the lady," she said. "After that, we'll improvise."

• • •

Will wasn't very good at picking up girls in bars.

In fact, aside from his "What'll we do for a little excitement tonight?" line, he didn't have many other approaches in his repertoire. He was emboldened somewhat by Jessica's encouraging nod from where she sat at the opposite end of the bar, but he still felt somewhat timid about taking the empty stool alongside Alice or Patricia or whatever her name was.

It had been his experience that plain girls were less responsive to flattery than were truly knockout beauties. He guessed that was because they were expecting to be lied to, and were wary of being duped and disappointed yet another time. Alice or Patricia or Whoever proved to be no exception to this general Plain-Jane observation. Will took the stool next to hers, turned to her, and said, "Excuse me, Miss," exactly as he'd rehearsed it with Jessica, but before he could utter another word, she recoiled as if he'd slapped her. Eyes wide, seemingly surprised, she said, "What? What is it?"

"I'm sorry if I startled you . . ."

"No, that's all right," she said. "What is it?"

Her voice was high and whiney, with an accent he couldn't quite place. Her eyes behind their thick round lenses were a very dark brown, still wide now with either fright or suspicion, or both. Staring at him unblinkingly, she waited.

"I don't want to bother you," he said, "but . . ."

"That's all right, really," she said. "What is it?"

"My friend and I couldn't help noticing . . ."

"Your friend?"

"The lady sitting just opposite us. The blonde lady at the other end of the bar?" Will said, and pointed to Jessica, who obligingly raised her hand in greeting.

"Oh. Yes," she said. "I see."

"We couldn't help notice that you were sitting here, drinking alone," he said. "We thought you might care to join us."

"Oh," she said.

"Do you think you might care to? Join us?"

There was a moment's hesitation. The brown eyes blinked, softened. The slightest smile formed on her thin-lipped mouth.

"I think I would like to, yes," she said. "I'd like to."

• • •

They sat at a small table some distance from the bar, in a dimly lighted corner of the room. Susan—and not Patricia or Alice, as it turned out—ordered another Chardonnay. Jessica stuck to her martinis. Will ordered another bourbon on the rocks.

"No one should sit drinking alone three days before Christmas," Jessica said.

"Oh, I agree, I agree," Susan said.

She had an annoying habit of saying everything twice. Made it sound as if there were an echo in the place.

"But this bar is on my way home," she said, "and I thought I'd stop in for a quick glass of wine."

"Take the chill off," Jessica agreed, nodding.

"Yes, exactly. Take the chill off."

She also repeated *other* people's words, Will noticed.

"Do you live near here?" Jessica asked.

"Yes. Just around the corner."

"Where are you from originally?"

"Oh dear, can you still tell?"

"Tell what?" Will asked.

"The accent. Oh dear, does it still show? After all those lessons? Oh my."

"What accent would that be?" Jessica asked.

"Alabama. Montgomery, Alabama," she said, making it sound like "Mun'gummy, Alabama."

"I don't hear any accent at all," Jessica said. "Do you detect an accent, Will?"

"Well, it's a regional dialect, actually," Susan said.

"You sound like you were born right here in New York," Will said, lying in his teeth.

"That's so kind of you, really," she said. "Really, it's so very kind."

"How long have you been up here?" Jessica asked.

"Six months now. I came up at the end of June. I'm an actress."

An actress, Will thought.

"I'm a nurse," Jessica said.

An actress and a nurse, Will thought.

"No kidding?" Susan said. "Do you work at some hospital?"

"Beth Israel," Jessica said.

"I thought that was a synagogue," Will said.

"A hospital, too," Jessica said, nodding, and turned back to Susan again. "Would we have seen you in anything?" she asked.

"Well, not unless you've been to Montgomery," Susan said, and smiled. "*The Glass Menagerie*? Do you know *The Glass Menagerie*? Tennessee Williams? The play by Tennessee Williams? I played Laura Wingate in the Paper Players' production down there. I haven't been in anything up here yet. I've been waitressing, in fact."

A waitress, Will thought.

The nurse and I are about to kill the plainest waitress in the city of New York.

Or worse, we're going to take her to bed.

· · ·

Afterward, he thought it might have been Jessica who suggested that they buy a bottle of Moët Chandon and take it up to Susan's apartment for a nightcap, the apartment being so close and all, just around the corner, in fact, as Susan herself had earlier pointed out. Or perhaps it was Will himself who'd made the suggestion, having consumed by then four hefty shots of Jack Daniels, and being somewhat bolder than he might ordinarily have been. Or perhaps it was Susan who invited them up to her place, which was in the heart of the theatrical district, right around the corner from Flanagan's, where she herself had consumed three or four glasses of Chardonnay and had begun performing for them the entire scene in which the Gentleman Caller breaks the little glass unicorn and Laura pretends it's no great tragedy, acting both parts for them, which Will felt certain caused the bartender to announce last call a full ten minutes earlier than he should have.

She was some terrible actress.

But oh so inspired!

The minute they hit the street outside, she raised her arms to the heavens above, her fingers widespread, and shouted in her dreadful Southern accent, "Just look at it! Broadway! The Great White Way!" and then did a little sort of pirouette, twirling and dancing up the street, her arms still high over her head.

"My God, let's kill her *quick*!" Jessica whispered to Will.

They both burst out laughing.

Susan must have thought they were sharing her exuberance.

Will guessed she didn't know what lay just ahead.

Or maybe she did.

At this hour of the night, the hookers had already begun their stroll up Eighth Avenue, but none of them so much as lifted an eyebrow to Will, probably figuring he was a John already occupied twice over, one on each arm. In an open liquor store, he bought a bottle of not Moët Chandon but Veuve Clicquot, and they went walking up the avenue together again, arm in arm.

Susan's apartment was a studio flat on the third floor of a walk-up on Forty-ninth and Ninth. They climbed the steps behind her, and she stopped outside apartment 3A, fiddled for her keys in her handbag, found them at last, and unlocked the door. The place was furnished in what Will called Struggling Young Actress Thrift. A tiny kitchen to the left of the entrance. A double bed against the far wall, a door alongside it leading to what Will supposed was a bathroom. A sofa and two easy chairs and a dresser with a mirror over it. There was a door on the entrance wall, and it opened onto a closet. Susan took their coats and hung them up.

"Mind if I make myself comfortable?" she asked, and went into the bathroom.

Jessica waggled her eyebrows.

Will went into the kitchen, opened the refrigerator, and emptied two of the ice cube trays into a bowl he found in the overhead cabinets. He also found three juice glasses he supposed would have to serve. Jessica sat on the sofa watching him while he started opening the champagne. A loud pop exploded just as another blonde stepped out of the bathroom.

• • •

It took him a moment to realize this was Susan.

"Makeup and costume go a long way toward realizing a character," she said.

She was now a slender young woman with short straight blonde hair, a nice set of jugs showing in the swooping neckline of a red blouse, a short tight black skirt, good legs in very high-heeled black pumps. She held dangling from her right hand the mousy brown wig she'd been wearing in the bar, and when she opened her left hand and held it out to him, palm flat, he saw the dental prosthesis that had given her the overbite. Through the open bathroom door, he could see her frowzy brown suit hanging on the shower rod. Her spectacles were resting on the bathroom sink.

"Little padding around the waist thickened me out," she said. "We have all these useful props in class."

No Southern accent anymore, he noticed. No brown eyes, either.

"But your eyes . . ." he said.

"Contact lenses," Susan said.

Her *real* eyes were as blue as . . . well, Jessica's.

In fact, they could pass for sisters.

He said this out loud.

"You could pass for sisters," he said.

"Maybe 'cause we are," Jessica said. "Sure had you going, though, didn't we?"

"I'll be damned," he said.

"Let's try that champagne," Susan said, and swiveled into the kitchen where the bottle was now resting in the bowl of ice. She lifted it, poured into the juice glasses, and carried back into the other room the three glasses in a cradle of fingers and thumbs. Jessica plucked one of the glasses free. Susan handed one to Will.

"Here's to the three of us," Jessica toasted.

"And improvisation," Susan added.

They all drank.

Will figured this was going to turn into one hell of a night.

• • •

"We're in the same acting class," Jessica told him.

She was still sitting on the sofa, legs crossed. Splendid legs. Will was in one of the easy chairs. Susan was in the easy chair opposite him, her legs also crossed, also splendid.

"We both want to be actors," Jessica explained.

"I thought you were a nurse," Will said.

"Oh, sure. Same way Sue is a waitress. But our ambition is to act."

"We're gonna be stars one day."

"Our names up in lights on Broadway."

"The Carter Sisters," Jessica said.

"Susan and Jessica!" her sister said.

"I'll drink to that," Will said.

They all drank again.

"We're not really from Montgomery, you know," Jessica said.

"Well, I realize that now. But that certainly was a good accent, Susan."

"Regional dialect," she corrected.

"We're from Seattle."

"Where it rains all the time," Will said.

"Oh, that's not true at all," Susan said. "Actually it rains less in Seattle than it does in New York, that's a fact."

"A statistically proven fact," Jessica said, nodding in agreement, and draining her glass. "Is there any more bubbly out there?"

"Oh, lots," Susan said, and shoved herself out of the easy chair, exposing a fair amount of thigh as she got to her feet. Will handed her his empty glass, too. He sure hoped the ladies wouldn't be drinking too much here. There was some serious business to take care of here tonight, some serious improvisation to do.

"So how long have you been living here in New York?" he asked. "Was it true what you said in the bar? Is it really only six months?"

"That's right," Jessica said. "Since the end of June."

"We've been taking acting classes since then."

"Were you really in *The Glass Menagerie*? The Paper Players? Is there such a thing as the Paper Players?"

"Oh yes," Susan said, coming back with their replenished glasses. "But in Seattle."

"We've never been to Montgomery."

"That was part of my character," Susan said. "The character I was assuming in the bar. Little Suzie Sad Ass."

Both girls laughed.

Will laughed along with them.

"I played *Amanda* Wingate," Jessica said.

"In *The Glass Menagerie*," Susan explained. "When we did it in Seattle. Laura's mother. Amanda Wingate."

"Actually I am the older one," Jessica said. "In real life."

"She's thirty," Susan said. "I'm twenty-eight."

"Here all alone in the big bad city," Will said.

"Yep, here all alone," Jessica said.

"Is that where you girls sleep?" Will asked. "The bed across the room there? The two of you all alone in that big bad bed?"

"Uh-oh," Jessica said. "He wants to know where we sleep, Sue."

"Better be careful," Susan said.

Will figured he ought to back off a little, play it a bit more slowly here.

"So where's this acting school you go to?" he asked.

"Right on Eighth Avenue."

"Near the Biltmore," Susan said. "Do you know the Biltmore Theater?"

"No, I don't," Will said. "I'm sorry."

"Well, near there," Jessica said. "Madame D'Arbousse, do you know her work?"

"No, I'm sorry, I don't."

"Well, she's only famous," Susan said.

"I'm sorry, I'm just not familiar with . . ."

"The D'Arbousse School? You've never heard of the D'Arbousse School of Acting?"

"I'm sorry, no."

"It's only world-famous," Susan said.

She seemed to be pouting now, almost petulant. Will figured he was losing ground here. Fast.

"So . . . uh . . . what was the idea of putting on the costume tonight?" he asked. "Going to that bar as a . . . well . . . I hope you'll forgive me . . . a frumpy little file clerk, was what I thought you were."

"It was that good, huh?" Susan said, smiling. Her smile, without the fake overbite, was actually quite lovely. Her mouth didn't look as thin-lipped anymore, either. Amazing what a little lipstick could do to plump up a girl's lips. He imagined those lips on his own lips, in the bed across the room there. He imagined her sister's lips on his, too. Imagined all their lips entangled, intertwined . . .

"That was part of the exercise," Susan said.

"The exercise?"

"Finding the place," Jessica said.

"The *character's* place," Susan said.

"For a private moment," Jessica explained.

"Finding the place for a character's private moment."

"We thought it might be the bar."

"But now we think it might be here."

"Well, it *will* be here," Jessica said. "Once we create it."

They were losing Will. More important, he felt he was losing them. That bed, maybe fifteen feet away across the room, seemed to be receding into an unreachable distance. He had to get this thing back on track. But he didn't know how quite yet. Not while they were rattling on about . . . what were they saying, anyway?

"I'm sorry," he said, "but *what* exactly is it you're trying to create?"

"A character's private moment," Jessica said.

"Is this the place we're going to use?" Susan asked.

"I think so, yes. Don't you think so? Our own apartment. A real place. It feels very real to me. Doesn't it feel real to you, Sue?"

"Oh, yes. Yes, it does. It feels *very* real. But I don't feel private yet. Do you feel private?"

"No, not yet."

"Excuse me, ladies . . ." Will said.

"Ladies, ooo hoo," Susan said, and rolled her eyes.

". . . but we can get a lot *more* private here, if that's what you ladies are looking for here."

"We're talking about a private *moment*," Jessica explained. "The way we behave when no one's watching."

"No one's watching us right now," Will said encouragingly. "We can do whatever we wish to do here, and no one will ever . . ."

"I don't think you understand," Susan said. "A *character's* private feelings and emotions are what we're trying to create here tonight."

"So let's *start* creating all these feelings and emotions," Will suggested.

"These feelings have to be *real*," Jessica said.

"They have to be *absolutely* real," Susan said.

"So that we can apply them to the scene we're doing."

"Ah-ha!" Will said.

"I think he's got it," Jessica said.

"By George, he's got it."

"You're rehearsing a scene together."

"Bravo!"

"What scene?" Will asked.

"A scene in *Macbeth*," Susan said.

"Where she tells him to screw his courage to the sticking point," Jessica said.

"Lady Macbeth."

"Tells Macbeth. When he's beginning to waver about killing Duncan."

"Screw your courage to the sticking point," Jessica said again, with conviction this time. "And we shall not fail."

She looked at her sister.

"That was very good," Susan said.

Will figured maybe they were back on track again.

"Screw your courage, huh?" he said, and smiled knowingly, and took another sip of champagne.

"She's telling him not to be such a wuss," Susan said.

"The thing is they're plotting to kill the king, you see," Jessica said.

"This is a private moment for both of them."

"Where they're both examining what they're about to do."

"They're planning a *murder*, you see."

"What does that *feel* like?" Susan asked.

"What is that like inside your *head*?" Jessica said.

"That private moment inside your *head*."

"When you're actually contemplating someone's death."

The room went silent for an instant.

The sisters looked at each other.

"Would anyone like some more champagne?" Susan asked.

"I'd love some," Jessica said.

"I'll get it," Will said, and started to rise.

"No, no, let me," Susan said, and took his glass and carried all three empty glasses into the kitchen. Jessica crossed her legs. Behind him, in the kitchen, Will could hear Susan refilling their glasses. He watched Jessica's jiggling foot, her pump half-on, half-off, held only by her toes.

"So that stuff in the bar was all part of the exercise, right?" Will said. "Your suggesting we kill somebody? And then choosing your sister as the victim?"

"Well, sort of," Jessica said.

Her pump fell off. She bent over to retrieve it, spreading her legs, the black dress high on her thighs. She crossed one leg over the other, put the pump back on, smiled at Will. Susan was back with the full glasses.

"Still some more out there," she said, and passed the glasses around. Jessica held hers up in a toast.

"From this time such," she said, "I account thy love."

"Cheers," Susan said, and drank.

"Meaning?" Will said, but he drank, too.

"That's in the scene," Jessica said. "Actually, it's at the start of the scene. Where he's beginning to waver. By the end of the scene, she's convinced him the king must die."

"False face must hide what the false heart doth show," Susan said, and nodded.

"That's Macbeth's exit line. At the end of the scene."

"Is that why you were dressed as a file clerk? False face must hide . . . whatever it was you just said?"

"What the false heart doth show," Susan repeated. "But no, that's not why I was in costume."

"Then why?"

"It was my way of trying to create a character."

"Maybe he hasn't got it, after all," Jessica said.

"A character who could kill," Susan said.

"You had to become a *frump*?"

"Well, I had to become someone *else*, yes. Someone not like myself at all. But it turned out that wasn't enough. I had to find the right place, too."

"The place is *here*," Jessica said.

"And *now*," Will said. "So, ladies, if no one minds . . ."

"Ooo hoo, ladies again," Susan said, and again rolled her eyes.

". . . can we get off all this acting stuff for a moment . . . ?"

"How about *your* private moment?" Susan said.

"I don't have any private moments."

"Don't you ever fart alone in the dark?" Jessica asked.

"Don't you ever jack off alone in the dark?" Susan asked.

Will's mouth fell open.

"Those are private moments," Jessica said.

For some reason, he could not close his mouth again.

• • •

"I think it's beginning to work," Susan said.

"Take the glass from his hand before he drops it," Jessica said.

Will watched them with his eyes and his mouth wide open.

"I'll bet he thinks it's curare," Jessica said.

"Where on earth would we get curare?"

"The jungles of Brazil?"

"Venezuela?"

Both girls laughed.

Will didn't know if it was curare or not. All he knew was he couldn't speak and he couldn't move.

"Well, he *knows* we didn't go all the way down to the Amazon for any poison," Jessica said.

"That's right, he knows you're a nurse," Susan said.

"Beth Israel, you bet," Jessica said.

"Access to lots of drugs there."

"Even *synthetic* curare drugs."

"Plenty of those around."

"List them for him, Jess."

"Don't want to bore him, Sue."

"You have to *inject* curare, Will, did you know that?"

"The natives dip their darts in it."

"Shoot the darts from blowpipes."

"The victims are paralyzed."

"Helpless."

"Death comes from asphyxia."

"That means you can't breathe."

"Because the respiratory nerve muscles get paralyzed."

"Are you having trouble breathing yet, Will?"

He did not think he was having trouble breathing. But what were they saying? Were they saying they'd poisoned him?

"The synthetics come in tablet form," Susan told him.

"Easy to pulverize."

"Easy to dissolve."

"Lots of legitimate uses for synthetic curare drugs," Jessica said.

"Provided you're careful with the dosage."

"We weren't particularly careful with the dosage, Will."

"Did your champagne taste a little bitter?"

He wanted to shake his head no. His champagne had tasted just fine. Or had he been too drunk to know just *how* it had tasted? But he couldn't shake his head, and he couldn't talk.

"Let's watch him," Susan said. "Study his reactions."

"Why?" Jessica asked.

"Well, it could be helpful."

"Not for the scene we're doing."

"Killing someone."

"Killing someone, yes. Duh, Susan."

Killing *me*, Will thought.

They are actually killing me here.

But, no . . .

Girls, he thought, you're making a mistake here. This is not the way to go about this. Let's go back to the original plan, girls. The original plan was to pop a bottle of bubbly and hop into the sack together. The original plan was to share this lovely night three days before . . . actually only two days now, it was already well past midnight . . . *two* days before Christmas, share this sweet uncomplicated night together, a sister act with a willing third partner is all this was supposed to be here. So how'd it get so serious all of a sudden? There was no reason for you girls to get all serious about acting lessons and private moments, really, this was just supposed to be fun and games here tonight. So why'd you have to go drop poison in my champagne? I mean, *Jesus*, girls, why'd you have to go do that when we were getting along so fine here?

"Are you feeling anything?" Susan asked.

"No," Jessica said. "Are you?"

"I thought I'd feel . . ."

"Me, too."

"I don't know . . . sinister or something."

"Me, too."

"I mean, *killing* somebody! I thought it would be something special. Instead . . ."

"I know what you mean. It's just like watching somebody, I don't know, getting a *haircut* or something."

"Maybe we should have tried something else."

"Not poison, you mean?"

"Something more dramatic."

"Something scarier, I know what you mean."

"Get some kind of reaction out of him."

"Instead of him just *sitting* there."

"Sitting there like a dope and dying."

The girls leaned over Will and peered into his face. Their faces looked distorted, so close to his face and all. Their blue eyes looked as if they were popping out of their heads.

"Do something," Jessica told him.

"Do something, asshole," Susan said.

They kept watching him.

"It's not too late to stab him, I suppose," Jessica said.

"You think?" Susan said.

Please don't stab me, Will thought. I'm afraid of knives. Please don't stab me.

"Let's see what's in the kitchen," Jessica said.

He was suddenly alone.

The girls were suddenly gone.

Behind him . . .

He could not turn his head to see them.

. . . behind him he could hear them rummaging through what he guessed was one of the kitchen drawers, could hear the rattle of utensils . . .

Please don't stab me, he thought.

"How about this one?" Jessica asked.

"Looks awfully big for the job," Susan said.

"Slit his fuckin' throat good," Jessica said, and laughed.

"See if he sits there like a dope then," Susan said.

"Get some kind of *reaction* out of him."

"Help us to *feel* something."

"Now you've got it, Sue. That's the whole point."

Will's chest was beginning to feel tight. He was beginning to have difficulty breathing.

In the kitchen, the girls laughed again.

Why were they laughing?

Had they just said something he couldn't hear? Were they going to do something *else* with that knife, other than slit his throat? He wished he could take a deep breath. He knew he would feel so much better if he could just take a deep breath. But he . . . he . . . he didn't seem to be . . . to be able to . . .

"Hey!" Jessica said. "You! Don't poop out on us!"

Susan looked at her.

"I think he's gone," she said.

"Shit!" Jessica said.

"What are you doing?"

"Taking his pulse."

Susan waited.

"Nothing," Jessica said, and dropped his wrist.

The sisters kept looking at Will where he sat slumped in the easy chair, his mouth still hanging open, his eyes wide.

"He sure as hell *looks* dead," Jessica said.

"We'd better get him out of here."

"Be a good exercise," Jessica said. "Getting rid of the body."

"I'll say. I'll bet he weighs at least a hun' ninety."

"I didn't say good *exercise*, Sue. I said *a* good exercise. A good *acting* exercise."

"Oh. Right. What it feels like to get rid of a dead body. Right."

"So let's do it," Jessica said.

They started lifting him out of the chair. He was, in fact, very heavy. They half-carried him, half-dragged him to the front door.

"Tell me something," Susan said. "Do you . . . you know . . . *feel* anything yet?"

"Nothing," Jessica said.

CIELO AZUL

MICHAEL CONNELLY

On the way up, the car's air conditioner gave up shortly after Bakersfield. It was September and hot as I pushed through the middle of the state. Pretty soon I could feel my shirt start to stick to the vinyl seat. I pulled off my tie and unbuttoned my collar. I didn't know why I had put a tie on in the first place. I wasn't on the clock and I wasn't going anywhere that required a tie.

I tried to ignore the heat and concentrate on how I would try to handle Seguin. But that was like the heat. I knew there was no way to handle him. Somehow, it had always been the other way around. Seguin had the handle on me, made my shirt stick to my back. One way or the other that would end on this trip.

I turned my wrist on the steering wheel and checked the date on my Timex. Exactly twelve years since the day I had met Seguin. Since I had looked into the cold green eyes of a killer.

· · ·

The case began on Mulholland Drive, the winding snake of a road that follows the spine of the Santa Monica Mountains. A group of high schoolers had pulled off the road to drink their beer and look down upon the smoggy city of dreams. One of them spotted the body. Nestled among the mountain brush and the beer cans and tequila bottles tossed down by past revelers, the woman was naked, her arms and legs stretched outward in some sort of grotesque display of sex and murder.

The call went to me and my partner, Frankie Sheehan. At the time we worked out of the LAPD's Robbery-Homicide Division.

The crime scene was treacherous. The body was snagged on an incline with a better than sixty-degree grade. One slip and a person could tumble all the way down the mountainside, maybe end up in somebody's hot tub down below or on somebody's concrete patio. We wore jumpsuits and leather harnesses and were lowered down to the body by firemen from the 58th Battalion.

The scene was clean. No clothes, no ID, no physical evidence, no clues but the dead woman. We didn't even find any fibers that were going to be useful. This was unusual for a homicide.

I studied the victim closely and realized she was barely a woman—probably still a teenager. Mexican, or of Mexican descent, she had brown hair, brown eyes and a dark complexion. I could tell that in life she had been beautiful to look at. In death she was heartbreaking. My partner always said the most dangerous women were the ones like her. Beautiful in life, heartbreaking in death. They could haunt you, stick with you even if you found the monster that took everything from her.

She had been strangled, the indentations of her killer's thumbs clear on her neck, the petechial hemorrhaging putting a murderous rouge around her eyes. Rigor mortis had come and gone. She was loose. That told us she had been dead more than twenty-four hours.

The guess was that she had been dumped the night before, under cover of darkness. That meant she had been lying dead somewhere else for twelve hours or more. That other place was the true crime scene. It was the place we needed to find.

• • •

When I turned the car inland toward the bay the air finally began to cool. I skirted the east side of the bay up to Oakland and then went across the bridge into San Francisco. Before crossing the Golden Gate I stopped for a hamburger at the Balboa Bar & Grill. I get to San Francisco two or three times a year on cases. I always eat at the Balboa. This time I ate at the bar, glancing occasionally up at the television to see the Giants playing in Chicago. They were losing.

But mostly I rolled the old case back and forth in my head. It was a closed case now and Seguin would never hurt another person again. Except himself. His last victim would be himself. But still the case stuck with me. A killer was caught, tried and convicted, and now stood to be executed for his crimes. But there was still an unanswered question that stuck with me. It was what put me on the road to San Quentin on my day off.

• • •

We didn't know her name. Fingerprints from the body matched no prints contained in computerized records. Her description matched no description on an active missing persons case anywhere in Los Angeles County or on national crime computer systems. An artist's rendering of her face put on the TV news and in the papers brought no calls from a loved one or an acquaintance. Sketches faxed to five hundred police agencies across the southwest and to the State Judicial Police in Mexico drew no responses. The victim remained unclaimed and unidentified, her body reposing in the refrigerator at the coroner's office while Sheehan and I worked the case.

It was tough. Most cases start with the victim. Who that person was and where she lived becomes the center of the wheel, the grounding point. Everything comes from the center. But we didn't have that and we didn't have the true crime scene. We had nothing and we were going nowhere.

All that changed with Teresa Corazon. She was the deputy coroner assigned to the case officially known as Jane Doe # 90-91. While preparing the body for an autopsy she came across the lead that would take us first to McCaleb and then to Seguin.

Corazon found that the victim's body had apparently been washed with an industrial strength cleaner before being discarded on the hillside. It was an attempt by the killer to destroy trace evidence. This in itself, however, was both a solid clue and trace evidence. The cleaning agent could help lead to the killer's identity or help tie him to the crime.

However, it was another discovery made by Corazon that turned the case for us. While photographing the body the deputy coroner noticed an impression in the skin on the rear left hip. Post-mortem lividity indicated the blood in the body had settled on the left half, meaning the body had been lying on its left side in the time between the stilling of the heart and the dropping of the body down the hillside off of Mulholland. The evidence indicated that during the time that the blood settled the body had been lying on top of the object that left the impression on the hip.

Using angled light to study the impression, Corazon found

that she could clearly see the number 1, the letter J and part of a third letter that could have been the upper left stem of an H, a K or an L.

"A license plate," I said when she called me to the autopsy suite to view the discovery. "He put her down on a license plate."

"Exactly, Detective Bosch," said Corazon.

Sheehan and I quickly formed the theory that whoever had killed the woman with no name had hidden the body in the trunk of a car until it was nighttime and safe to take it up to Mulholland and dump it. After carefully cleaning the body the killer put it into the trunk of his car, mistakenly putting it down on part of a license plate that had been taken off the car and also placed in the trunk. That part of the theory was that the license plate had been removed and possibly replaced with a stolen plate as one more safety measure that would help the killer avoid detection if his car happened to be spotted by a suspicious passerby at the Mulholland overlook.

The skin impression gave no indication of what state issued the license plate. But the use of the Mulholland outlook gave us the idea that we were looking for someone familiar with the area, a local. We began with the California Department of Motor Vehicles and obtained a list of every car registered in Los Angeles County that carried a plate beginning 1JH, 1JK and 1JL.

The list contained over one thousand names of car owners. We then cut forty percent of those names by discounting the female owners. The remaining names were slowly fed into the National Crime Index computer and we came up with a list of thirty-six men with criminal records ranging from minor to the extreme.

The first time I studied the list of thirty-six I knew. I felt certain that one of the names on it belonged to the killer of the woman with no name.

. . .

The Golden Gate lived up to its name in the afternoon sun. It was packed with cars going both ways and the tourist turnoff on the north side had the LOT FULL sign up. I kept moving, into the rainbow-painted tunnel and through the mountain. Soon enough I could see San Quentin up on the right. A foreboding-looking place in an idyllic spot, it housed the worst criminals California had to offer. And I was going to see the worst of the worst.

. . .

"Harry Bosch?"

I turned from the window where I had been looking down at the white stones of the veterans cemetery across Wilshire. A man in a white shirt and maroon tie stood holding open the door to the FBI offices. He looked like he was in his mid-thirties with a lean build and healthy look about him. He was smiling.

"Terry McCaleb?"

"That's me."

We shook hands and he invited me back, leading me through a warren of wood-paneled hallways and offices until we came to his. It looked like it might have been a janitor's closet at one time. It was smaller than a solitary confinement cell and had just enough room for a desk and two chairs.

"Guess it's a good thing my partner didn't want to come," I said, squeezing into the room.

Frankie Sheehan alternately referred to criminal profiling as "bur-oh bullshit" and "Quantico quackery." When I had chosen a week earlier to contact McCaleb, the resident profiler in the bureau's L.A. office, there had been an argument about it. But I was lead on the case; I made the call.

"Yeah, things are kind of tight here," McCaleb said. "But at least I get a private space."

"Most cops I know like being in a squad room. They like the camaraderie, I guess."

McCaleb just nodded and said, "I like being alone."

He pointed to the guest chair and I sat down. I noticed a photo of a teenaged girl taped to the wall above his desk. She looked to be just a few years younger than my victim. I thought that if maybe it were McCaleb's daughter it would be a little plus for me. Something that would make him put a little extra drive into my case.

"She's not my daughter," McCaleb said. "She's from an old case. A Florida case."

I just looked at him. It wouldn't be the last time he seemed to know my thoughts like I was saying them out loud.

"So, still no ID on yours, right?"

"No, nothing yet."

"That always makes it tough."

"So on your message you said you'd reviewed the file?"

"Yes, I did."

I had sent copies of the murder book and all crime scene photographs the week before. We had not videotaped the crime scene and this distressed McCaleb. But I had been able to get tape of the scene from a television reporter. His station's chopper had been in the air over the crime scene but had not aired any footage because of the graphic nature of its contents.

McCaleb opened a file on his desk and referred to it before speaking.

"First of all, are you familiar with our VICAP program—Violent Criminal Apprehension?"

"I know what it is. This is the first time I ever submitted a case."

"Yes, you're a rarity in the LAPD. Most of you guys don't want or trust the help. But a few more guys like you and maybe I can get a bigger office."

I nodded. I wasn't going to tell him that it was institutional distrust and suspicion that stopped most LAPD detectives from seeking the help of the bureau. It was an unspoken dictate that came from the police chief himself. It was said that the chief could be heard cursing loudly in his office every time news of an FBI arrest within city limits was reported. It was well known in the department that the bank robbery squad routinely monitored the radio transmissions of the bureau's bank squad and often moved in on suspects before the feds got the chance.

"Yeah, well, I just want to clear the case," I said. "I don't really care if you're a psychic or Santa Claus; if you've got something that will help me I'll listen."

"Well, I think maybe I do."

He turned the page in the file and picked up a stack of crime scene photographs. These were not the photos I had sent him. These were 8x10 blowups of the original crime scene photos. He had made these on his own. It told me that McCaleb had certainly spent some time with the case. It made me think that maybe it had hooked him the way it had hooked me. A woman with no name left dead on the hillside. A woman no one had come forward to claim. A woman no one cared about. The dangerous kind. In my secret heart I cared and I had claimed her. And now maybe McCaleb had, too.

"Let me just start with my overview of what I think you've got here," McCaleb said.

He shuffled through the photos for a moment, ending with a still that had been made off of the news video. It showed an aerial shot of the naked body, arms and legs stretched wide on the hillside. I took out my cigarettes and shook one out of the pack.

"You may have already arrived at these same conclusions. If so, I apologize. I don't want to waste your time. By the way, you can't smoke in here."

"Don't worry about it," I said, putting the smokes away. "What have you got?"

"The crime scene is very important in that it gives us an avenue to the killer's thinking. What I see here suggests the work of what we call an exhibition killer. In other words, this is a killer who wanted his crime to be seen—to be very public— and by virtue of this to instill horror and fear in the general population. From this reaction by the public he draws his gratification. He is somebody who reads the newspapers and watches the news for any information or update on the investigation. It is a way of keeping score. So when we find him, I think we will find newspaper clippings and maybe even videos containing television reports on the case. These will probably be in his bedroom because they would be useful to him in carrying out masturbatory fantasies."

I noticed he had said "we" in reference to the case investigators but I didn't react. McCaleb went on as if he was talking to himself and there was no one else in the office.

"A component of the exhibition killer's fantasy is the duel. Exhibiting his crime to the public includes exhibiting it to the police. In effect, he is throwing down a challenge. He is saying, 'I am better than you, smarter and more clever. Prove me wrong, if you can. Catch me, if you can.' You see? He is dueling with you in the public media arena."

"With me?"

"Yes, you. In this case in particular you appear to be the media front man. It is your name in the newspaper stories included in the file."

"I'm lead on the case. I've been the one talking to the reporters."

McCaleb nodded.

"Okay," I said. "All this is good in terms of understanding what a nut job this guy is. But what do you have that will help point us to the right guy?"

McCaleb nodded.

"You know how the Realtors say, location, location, location? It's the same with me. The place he chose to leave her is significant in that it plays into his exhibitionistic tendencies. You have the Hollywood Hills here. You have Mulholland Drive and the view of the city. This victim was not dropped here randomly. This place was chosen, perhaps just as carefully as she was chosen as a victim. The conclusion is that the drop site is a place our killer may be familiar with because of the routines of his life, but nonetheless was not chosen because of reasons of convenience. He chose this spot, he wanted this spot, because it was the best spot to announce his work to the world. It was part of the canvas. It means he could have come from a long distance to leave her there. He could have come a few blocks."

I noticed the use of "our" as in our killer. I knew if Frankie had come with me he would've blown a gasket by now. I let it go.

"Did you look at the list I gave you of the names?"

"Yes, I looked at everything. And I think your instincts are good. The two potential suspects you highlighted both fit into the profile I constructed for this killing. Late twenties with a history of crimes of escalating nature."

"The Woodland Hills janitor has routine access to industrial cleaners—we could match something to the cleaning agent used on the body. He's the one we like best."

McCaleb nodded but didn't say anything. He seemed to be studying the photographs, which were now spread across the desk.

"You like the other guy, don't you? The stage builder from Burbank."

McCaleb looked up at me.

"Yes, I like him better. His crimes, though minor, fall more into line with the sexual predator maturation models we have seen. I think when we talk to him we have to make sure we do it in his home. We'll get a better feel for him. We'll know."

"We?"

"Yes. And we need to do it soon."

He nodded to the photos covering his desk.

"This wasn't a one shot deal. Whoever he is, he's going to do it again . . . if he hasn't already."

• • •

I had been responsible for many men going to San Quentin but I had never been there myself before. At the gate I showed ID and was given a printout with instructions that directed me to a fenced lot for law enforcement vehicles. At a nearby door marked LAW ENFORCEMENT PERSONNEL ONLY I was ushered through the great wall of the prison and my weapon was taken and locked in a gun vault. I was given a red plastic chit with the number 7 printed on it.

After my name was put into the computer and the prearranged clearances were noted, a guard who didn't bother introducing himself walked me through an empty recreation yard to a brick building that had darkened over time to a fireplace black. It was the death house, the place where Seguin would get the juice in one week's time.

We moved through a man trap and a metal detector and I was passed off to a new guard. He opened a solid steel door and pointed me down a hall.

"Last one on the right," he said. "When you want out wave at one of the cameras. We'll be watching."

He left me there, closing the steel door with a thunderous bang that seemed to reverberate through my marrow.

• • •

Frankie Sheehan wasn't happy about it but I was the lead and I made the call. I allowed McCaleb to come with us on the interviews. We started with Victor Seguin. He was first on McCaleb's list, second on mine. But there was something about the intensity in McCaleb's eyes and words that made me defer and go with Seguin first.

Seguin was a stage builder who lived on Screenland Drive in Burbank. It was a small house with a lot of woodwork you might expect to find in a carpenter's house. It looked as though when Seguin wasn't finding movie work he was home building handsome window boxes and planters for the house.

The Ford Taurus with the license plate containing 1JK on it was parked in the driveway. I put my hand on the hood as we walked up the driveway to the door. It was cold.

At 8:00 p.m., just as the light was leaving the sky, I knocked on the front door. Seguin answered in blue jeans and a T-shirt. No shoes. I saw his eyes go wide when he looked at me. He knew who I was before I held up the badge and said my name. I felt the cold finger of adrenaline slide down my back. I remembered what McCaleb had said about the killer tracking the police while they tracked him. I had been on TV talking about the case. I had been in the papers.

Giving nothing away, I calmly said, "Mr. Seguin, I am Detective Harry Bosch with the LAPD. Is that your car in the driveway?"

"Yeah, it's mine. What about it? What's going on?"

"We need to ask you about it, if you don't mind. Can we come in for a few minutes?"

"Well, no, I'd first like to know what—"

"Thank you."

I moved through the threshold, forcing him to step back. The others followed me in.

"Hey, wait a minute, what is this?"

We had worked it out before we'd arrived. The interview was mine to conduct. Sheehan was second seat. McCaleb said he just wanted to observe.

The living room was carpenter overkill. Built-in bookshelves on three walls. A wooden mantel that was too big for the room had been built around the small, brick fireplace. A floor to ceiling television cabinet was built in place as a divider between the sitting area and what looked like a little office space.

I nodded approvingly.

"Nice work. You get a lot of downtime with your work?"

Seguin reluctantly nodded.

"Did most of this when we had a strike a couple years ago."

"What do you do?"

"Stage builder. Look, what is this about my car? You can't just push your way in here like this. I have rights."

"Why don't you sit down, Mr. Seguin, and I'll explain. We believe your car was possibly used in the commission of a serious crime."

Seguin dropped into a soft chair positioned for best viewing of the television. I noticed that McCaleb was moving about the outer edges of the room, studying the books on the shelves and the various knickknacks displayed on the mantel and other surfaces. Sheehan sat down on the couch to Seguin's left. He stared at him coldly, wordlessly.

"What crime?"

"A murder."

I let that sink in. But it appeared to me that Seguin had recovered from his initial shock and was hardening. I had seen this before. He was going to try to ride it out.

"Does anyone drive your car besides you, Mr. Seguin?"

"Sometimes. If I loan it to somebody."

"What about three weeks ago, August fifteenth, did you lend it to anybody?"

"I don't know. I'd have to check. I don't think I want to answer any more questions and I think I want you people to leave now."

McCaleb slid into the seat to Seguin's right. I remained standing. I looked at McCaleb and he nodded slightly and only once. But I knew what he was telling me; he's the guy.

I looked at my partner. Sheehan had missed the sign from McCaleb because he had not taken his eyes off Seguin. I had to make a call. Go with McCaleb's signal or back out. I looked back at McCaleb. He looked up at me, his eyes as intense as any I had ever seen.

I signaled Seguin to stand up.

"Mr. Seguin, I need you to stand up for me. I am placing you under arrest on suspicion of murder."

Seguin slowly came to his feet and then made a sudden move toward the door. But Sheehan was ready for it and was all over him and had his face down in the carpet before he had gotten three feet. Frankie pulled his arms behind his back and cuffed them. I then helped him pull Seguin to his feet and we walked him out to the car, leaving McCaleb behind.

Frankie stayed with the suspect. As soon as I could I came back inside. I found McCaleb still sitting in the chair.

"What was it?"

McCaleb reached out his arm to the nearest bookshelf.

"This is his reading chair," he said.

He pulled a book off the shelf.

"And this is his favorite book."

The book was badly worn, its spine cracked and its pages weathered by repeated readings. As McCaleb thumbed the pages I could see paragraphs and sentences had been underlined by hand. I reached over and closed the book so I could read the cover. It was called *The Collector.*

"Ever read it?" McCaleb asked.

"No. What is it?"

"It's about a guy who abducts women. He collects them. Keeps them in his house, in the basement."

I nodded.

"Terry, we need to back out of here and get a search warrant. I want to do this right."

"So do I."

. . .

Seguin was sitting on the bed in his cell looking at a chessboard set up on the toilet. He didn't look up when I came to the bars, though I could tell my shadow had fallen across the game board.

"Who are you playing?" I asked.

"Somebody who died sixty-five years ago. They put his best moment—this game—in a book. And he lives on. He's eternal."

He looked up at me then, his eyes still the same—cold, green killer's eyes—in a body turned pasty and weak from twelve years in small, windowless rooms.

"Detective Bosch. I wasn't expecting you until next week."

I shook my head.

"I'm not coming next week."

"You don't want to see the show? To see the glory of the righteous?"

"Doesn't do it for me. Back when they used the gas, maybe that'd be worth seeing. But watching some asshole on a massage table get the needle and then drift off to Never-Never Land? Nah, I'm going to go see the Dodgers play the Giants that day. Already got my ticket."

Seguin stood up and approached the bars. I remembered the hours we had spent in the interrogation room, close like this. The body was worn but not the eyes. They were unchanged. Those eyes were the signature of all the evil I had ever known.

"Then what is it that brings you to me here today, Detective?"

He smiled at me, his teeth yellowed, his gums as gray as the walls. I knew then that the trip had been a mistake. I knew then that he would not give me what I wanted and release me.

• • •

Two hours after we put Seguin in the car two other detectives from RHD arrived with a signed search warrant for the house and car. Because we were in the city of Burbank, I had routinely notified the local authorities of our presence and a Burbank detective team and two patrol officers arrived on scene. While the patrol officers kept a vigil on Seguin, the rest of us began the search.

We spread out. The house had no basement. McCaleb and I took the master bedroom and Terry immediately noticed wheels had been attached to the legs of the bed. He dropped to his knees, pushed the bed aside and there was a trapdoor in the wood floor. There was a padlock on it.

While McCaleb went off into the house to find the key I took my picks out of my wallet and worked the lock. I was alone in the room. As I fumbled with the lock I banged it against the metal hasp and I thought I heard a noise from beyond the door in response. It was far away and muffled but to me it was the sound of terror in someone's voice. My insides seized with my own terror and hope.

I worked the lock with all my skill and in another thirty seconds it came open.

"Got it! McCaleb, I got it!"

McCaleb came rushing back into the room and we pulled open the door revealing a sheet of plywood below with finger latches at the four corners. We raised this next and there beneath the floor was a young girl. She was blindfolded, gagged and her hands were shackled behind her back. She was naked beneath a dirty pink blanket.

But she was alive. She turned and pushed herself into the soundproofing padding that lined the coffinlike box. It was as if she were trying to get away. I realized then that she thought the opening of the door had been him coming back to her. Seguin.

"It's okay," McCaleb said. "We're here to help."

McCaleb reached down into the box and gently touched her shoulder. She startled like an animal but then calmed.

McCaleb then lay down flat on the floor and reached into the box to start removing the blindfold and gag.

"Harry, get an ambulance."

I stood up and stepped back from the scene. I felt my chest growing tight, a clarity of thought coming over me. In all my years I had spoken for the dead many times. I had avenged the dead. I was at home with the dead. But I had never so clearly had a part of pulling someone away from the outstretched hands of death. And in that moment I knew we had just done that. And I knew that whatever happened afterward and wherever my life took me, I would always have this moment, that it would be a light that could lead me out of the darkest of tunnels.

"Harry, what are you doing? Get an ambulance."

I looked at him.

"Yeah, right away."

• • •

The woodworker's cell was all concrete and steel. It had been a decade since he had run his fingers over the grain of wood. I stepped closer to the bars and looked in at him.

"You're running out of time. You've exhausted your appeals, you've got a governor who needs to show he's tough on crime. This is it, Victor. A week from today you take the needle."

I waited for a reaction but there was nothing. He just looked at me and waited for what he knew I would ask.

"Time to come clean. Tell me who she was. Tell me where you took her from."

He moved closer to the bars, close enough for me to smell the decay in his breath. I didn't back away.

"All these years, Bosch. All these years and you still need to know. Why is that?"

"I just need to."

"You and McCaleb."

"What about him?"

"Oh, he came to see me, too."

I knew McCaleb was out of the life. The job had taken his heart. He got a transplant and moved to Catalina. He was running a fishing charter.

"When did he come?"

"Oh, let me see. Time is so hard to track here. A few months ago. Dropped by for a chat with his new heart, Terry did. Said he was in the neighborhood. He didn't like my review of the film. What did you think of it?"

He was talking about the film in which Clint Eastwood portrayed McCaleb.

"I didn't see it. What did he want when he came here?"

"He wanted to know the same thing. Who was the girl, where did she come from? He told me you gave her a name back then, during the trial. *Cielo Azul.* That's really very pretty, Detective Bosch. Blue Sky. Why did you choose that?"

"He told you that?"

"Yes, standing right where you are standing. That's unprofessional, isn't it, Detective Bosch? To get close like that. That could be dangerous to let a woman in like that. Dead or alive."

I wanted to go, to get away from him.

"Look, Seguin, are you going to tell me or not? Or are you just going to take it with you?"

He smiled and stepped back from the bars. He walked over to the chessboard and seemed to look down at it to consider a move.

"You know, they used to let me keep a cat in here. I miss that cat."

He picked up one of the plastic game pieces but then hesitated and returned it to the same spot. He turned and looked at me.

"You know what I think? I think that you two can't stand the thought of that girl not having a name, not coming from a home with a mommy and a daddy and a little baby brother. The idea of no one caring and no one missing her, it leaves you hollow, doesn't it?"

"I just want to close the case."

"Oh, but it is closed. You're not here because of any case. You are here on your own. Admit it, Detective. Just as McCaleb came on his own. The idea of that pretty little thing—and by the way, if you thought she was beautiful in death then you should have seen her before—the idea of her lying unclaimed in an unmarked grave all this time undercuts everything you do, doesn't it?"

"It's a loose end. I don't like loose ends."

"It's more than that, Detective. I know."

I said nothing, hoping that if he kept on talking he would make a mistake.

"Her face was like an angel's," he said. "And that long brown hair . . . I was always a sucker for that kind of hair. I can still remember its smell. She told me she used a strawberry and cream shampoo. I didn't even know they put that stuff in shampoo, man."

He was taunting me. The whole idea I had of getting him to tell me her name seemed absurd now.

"She was one of those women, you know."

"No, I don't know. Why don't you tell me?"

"Well, she had that thing, that power. That was why I chose her."

"What power?"

"You know, she could wound you with just a look. Face like

an angel but a body like . . . Have you ever noticed how red cars look like they're going fast even if they're just sitting still? She was like that. She was dangerous. She had to go. If I didn't do it, she would've done it to us. A lot of us."

He smiled at me and I knew he was still pulling the strings. He was giving me nothing, just trying to get a rise out of me.

"Hey, Bosch?"

"What?"

"If a tree falls in the forest and nobody hears it, does it make a sound?"

His smile opened even broader.

"If a woman is murdered in the city and nobody cares, does it matter?"

"I care."

"Exactly."

He came back to the bars.

"And you need me to relieve you of that burden by giving you a name, a mommy and daddy who care."

He was a foot away from me. I could reach through the bars and grab his throat if I wanted to. But that would be what he'd want me to do.

"Well, I won't release you, Detective. You put me in this cage. I put you in that one."

He stepped back and pointed at me. I looked down and realized both my hands were tightly gripped on the steel bars of the cage. My cage.

I looked back up at him and his smile was back, as guiltless as a baby's.

"Funny isn't it? I remember that day—twelve years ago today. Sitting in the back of the car while you cops played hero. So full of yourselves for saving her. Bet you never thought it would come to this, did you? You saved one but you lost the other."

I lowered my head to the bars.

"Seguin, you're going to burn. You are going to hell."

"Yes, I suppose so. But I hear it's a dry heat."

He laughed loudly and I looked at him.

"Don't you know, Detective? You have to believe in heaven to believe in hell."

I abruptly turned from the bars and headed back toward the steel door. Above it I saw the mounted camera. I made an open up gesture with my hand and picked up my speed as I got closer. I needed to get out of there.

I heard Seguin's voice echoing off the walls behind me.

"I'll keep her close, Bosch! I'll keep her right here with me! Eternally together! Eternally mine!"

When I got to the steel door I hit it with both fists until I heard the electronic lock snap and the guard began to slide it open.

"All right, man, all right. What's the hurry?"

"Just get me out of here," I said as I pushed past him.

I could still hear Seguin's voice echoing from the death house as I crossed back across the open field.

GIVE ME YOUR HEART

JOYCE CAROL OATES

Dear Dr. K——,

It's been a long time, hasn't it! Twenty-three years, nine months and eleven days.

Since we last saw each other. Since you last saw, "nude" on your naked knees, me.

Dr. K——! The formal salutation isn't meant as flattery, still less as mockery—please understand. I am not writing after so many years to beg an unreasonable favor of you (I hope), or to make demands, merely to inquire if, in your judgment, I should go through the formality, and the trouble, of applying to be the lucky recipient of your most precious organ, your heart. If I may expect to collect what is due to me, after so many years.

I've learned that you, the renowned Dr. K——, are one who has generously signed a "living will" donating his organs to those in need. Not for Dr. K—— an old-fashioned, selfish funeral and burial in a cemetery, nor even cremation. Good for you, Dr. K——! But I want only your heart, not your kidneys, liver or eyes. These, I will waive, that others more needy will benefit.

Of course, I mean to make my application as others do, in medical situations similar to my own. I would not expect favoritism. The actual application would be made through my cardiologist. *Caucasian female of youthful middle age, attractive, intelligent, optimistic though with a malfunctioning heart, otherwise in perfect health.* No acknowledgment would be made of our old relationship, on my part at least. Though you, dear Dr. K——, as the potential heart donor, could indicate your own preference, surely?

All this would transpire when you die, Dr. K——, I mean. Of course! Not a moment before.

(I guess you might not be aware that you're destined to die soon? Within the year? In a "tragic"—"freak"—accident as it will be called? In an "ironic"—"unspeakably ugly" end to a "brilliant career"? I'm sorry that I can't be more specific about time, place, means; even whether you'll die alone, or with a family member or two. But that's the nature of *accident*, Dr. K——. It's a surprise.)

Dr. K——, don't frown so! You're a handsome man still, and still vain, despite your thinning gray hair which, like other vain men with hair loss, you've taken to combing slantwise over the shiny dome of your head; imagining that, since you can't see this ploy in the mirror, it can't be seen by others. *But I can see.*

Fumbling, you turn to the last page of this letter to see my signature—"Angel"—and you're forced to remember, suddenly . . . With a pang of guilt.

Her! She's still . . . alive?

That's right, Dr. K——! More alive now than ever.

Naturally you'd come to imagine I had vanished. I had ceased to exist. Since you'd long ago ceased to think of me.

You're frightened. Your heart, that guilty organ, has begun to pound. At a second-floor window of your house on Richmond Street (expensively restored Victorian, pale gray shingles with dark blue trim, "quaint"—"dignified"—among others of its type in the exclusive old residential neighborhood east of the Theological Seminary) you stare out anxiously at—what?

Not me, obviously. I'm not there.

At any rate, I'm not in sight.

Yet, how the pale-glowering sky seems to throb with a sinister intensity! Like a great eye staring.

Dr. K——, I mean you no harm! Truly. This letter is in no way a demand for your (posthumous) heart, nor even a "verbal threat." If you decide, foolishly, to show it to police, they will assure you it's harmless, it isn't illegal, it's only a request for information: should I, the "love-of-your-life" you have not seen in twenty-three years, apply to be the recipient of your heart? What are Angel's chances?

I only wish to collect what's mine. What was promised to me, so long ago. *I've* been faithful to our love, Dr. K——!

You laugh, harshly. Incredulously. How can you reply to "Angel," when "Angel" has included no last name, and no address? *You will have to seek me. To save yourself, seek me.*

You crumple this letter in your fist, throw it onto the floor.

You walk away, stumble away, you mean to forget, obviously you can't forget, the crumpled pages of my handwritten letter on the floor of—is it your study?—on the second floor of the dignified old Victorian house at 119 Richmond Street?—where someone might discover them, and pick them up to read what you wouldn't wish another living person to read, especially not someone "close" to you. (As if our families, especially our blood-kin, are "close" to us in the true intimacy of erotic love.) So naturally you return, with badly shaking fingers you pick up the scattered pages, smooth them out and continue to read.

Dear Dr. K——! Please understand: I am not bitter, I don't harbor obsessions. That is not my nature. I have my own life, and I have even had a (moderately successful) career. *I am a normal woman of my time and place.* I am like the exquisite black-and-silver diamond-headed spider, the so-called "happy" spider; the sole sub-species of *Araneida* that is said to be free to spin part-improvised webs, both oval and funnel, and to roam the world at will, equally at home in damp grasses and the dry, dark, protected interiors of man-made places; rejoicing in (relative) free will within the inevitable restrictions of *Araneida* behavior; with a sharp venomous sting, sometimes lethal to human beings, and especially to children.

Like the diamond-head, I have many eyes. Like the diamond-head, I may be perceived as "happy"—"joyous"— "exulting"— in the eyes of others. For such is my role, my performance.

It's true, for years I was stoically reconciled to my loss, in fact to my losses. (Not that I blame you for these losses, Dr. K——. Though a neutral observer might conclude that my immune system has been damaged as a result of my physical and mental collapse following your abrupt dismissal of me from your life.) Then, last March, seeing your photograph in the paper—DISTINGUISHED THEOLOGIAN K—— TO HEAD SEMINARY—and, a few weeks later, when you were named to the President's Commission on Religion and Bioethics, I reconsidered. *The time of anonymity and silence is over,* I thought. *Why not try, why not try to collect what he owes you.*

Do you remember Angel's name, now? That name that, for

twenty-three years, nine months and eleven days you have not wished to utter.

Seek my name in any telephone directory, you won't find it. For possibly my number is unlisted, possibly I don't have a telephone. Possibly my name has been changed. (Legally.) Possibly I live in a distant city in a distant region of the continent; or possibly, like the diamond-head spider (adult size, approximately that of your right thumbnail, Dr. K——), I dwell quietly within your roof, spinning my exquisite webs amid the shadowy rafters of your basement, or in a niche between your handsome old mahogany desk and the wall, or, a delicious thought, in the airless cave beneath the four-poster brass antique bed you and the second Mrs. K—— share in the doldrums of late middle age.

So close am I, yet invisible!

Dear Dr. K——! Once you marveled at my "flawless Vermeer" skin and "spun gold" hair rippling down my back, which you stroked, and closed in your fist. Once I was your "Angel"—your "beloved." I basked in your love, for I did not question it. I was young, I was virginal in spirit as well as body, and would not have questioned the word of a distinguished elder. And in the paroxysm of lovemaking, when you gave yourself up utterly to me, or so it seemed, how could you have . . . deceived?

Dr. K—— of the Theological Seminary, biblical scholar and authority, protege of Reinhold Niebuhr and author of "brilliant"—"revolutionary"—exegeses of the Dead Sea Scrolls, among other esoteric subjects.

But I had no idea, you are protesting. *I'd given her no reason to believe, to expect . . .*

(That I would believe your declarations of love? That I would "take you at your word"?)

My darling, you have my heart. Always, forever. Your promise!

. . .

These days, Dr. K——, my skin is no longer "flawless." It has become the frank, flawed skin of a middle-aged woman who makes no effort to disguise her age. My hair, once shimmering strawberry-blond, is now faded, dry and brittle as broom sage; I keep it trimmed short, like a man's, with a scissors, scarcely glancing into a mirror as I *snip! snip-snip!* away. My face, though reasonably attractive, I suppose, is, in fact, a blur to most observers, including especially middle-aged American men; you've glanced at me, and through me, dear Dr. K——, upon more than one recent occasion, no more recognizing your "Angel" than you would have recognized a plate heaped with food you'd devoured twenty-three years ago with a zestful appetite or an old, long-exhausted and dismissed sexual fantasy of adolescence.

For the record: I was the woman in a plain, khaki-colored trench coat and matching hat who waited patiently at the university bookstore as a line of admirers of yours moved slowly forward, for Dr. K—— to sign copies of *The Ethical Life: 21st Century Challenges.* (A slender theological treatise, not a mega-bestseller of course but a quite respectable bestseller, most popular in university and upscale suburban communities.) I knew your "brilliant" book would disappoint, yet I purchased it and eagerly read to discover (yet another time) the puzzling fact: you, Dr. K——, the man, are not the individual who appears in your books; the books are clever pretenses, artificial structures you've created to inhabit temporarily, as a crippled, deformed individual might inhabit a structure of surpassing beauty, gazing out its windows, taking pride in posing as its owner, but only temporarily.

Yes? Isn't this the clue to the renowned "Dr. K——"?

For the record: several Sundays ago, you and I passed closely by each other in the State Museum of Natural History; you were gripping the hand of your five-year-old granddaughter ("Lisle," I believe?—lovely name) and took no more notice of me than you'd have taken of any stranger passing you on the steep marble steps, descending from the Hall of Dinosaurs on the gloomy fourth floor as you were ascending; you'd stooped to smilingly speak to Lisle, and it was at that moment I noted the silly, touching ploy of you hair-combing (over the spreading bald spot), I saw Lisle's sweet, startled face (for the child, unlike her myopic granddaddy, had seen me and "knew" me in a flash); I felt a thrill of triumph: for how easily I might have killed you then, I might have pushed you down those hard marble steps, my hands firm on your now rather rounded shoulders, the force of my rage overcoming any resistance you, a puffy, slack-bellied two-hundred-pound man of late middle age, might have mustered; immediately you'd have been thrown off balance, falling backward, with an expression of incredulous terror, and still gripping your granddaughter's hand you'd have dragged the innocent child backward with you, toppling down the marble steps with a scream: concussion, skull fracture, brain hemorrhage, death!

Why not try, why not try to collect what he owes me.

Of course, Dr. K——, I didn't! Not that Sunday afternoon.

Dear Dr. K——! Are you surprised to learn that your lost love with the "spun gold" hair and the "soft-as-silk breasts" managed to recover from your cruelty, and by the age of twenty-nine had begun to do well in her career, in another part of the country? Never would I be renowned in my field as you, Dr. K——, in yours, that goes without saying, but through diligence and industry, through self-deprivation and cunning, I made my way in a field traditionally dominated by men and achieved what might be called a minor, local "success." That is, I have nothing to be ashamed of, and perhaps even something to be proud of, if I were capable of pride.

I won't be more specific, Dr. K——, but I will hint: my field is akin to yours though not scholarly or "intellectual." My salary is far less than yours, of course. I have no public identity, no reputation and no great wish for such. I'm in a field of *service*, I've long known how to *serve*. Where the fantasies of others, primarily men, are involved, I've grown quite adept at *serving*.

Yes, Dr. K——, it's possible that I've even served you. Indirectly, I mean. For instance: I might work in, or even oversee a medical laboratory to which your physician sends blood samples, biopsy tissue samples, etcetera, and one day he sends our laboratory a specimen extracted from the body of the renowned Dr. K——. *Whose life may depend upon the accuracy and good faith of our laboratory findings.*

Just one example, Dr. K——, among many!

No, dear Dr. K——, this letter is no threat. How, stating my position so openly, and therefore innocently, could I be a *threat*?

Are you shocked to learn that a woman can be a "professional"—can have a career that's fairly rewarding—yet still dream of justice after twenty-three years? Are you shocked to learn that a woman might be married, or might have been married, yet remain haunted still by her cruel, deceitful first love, who ravaged not only her virginity but her faith in humankind?

You'd like to imagine your cast-off "Angel" as a lonely embittered spinster, yes? Hiding away in the dark, spinning ugly sticky webs out of her own poisonous guts, yet the truth is the reverse: just as there are "happy" spiders, observed by ento-mologists as exhibiting a capacity for (relative) freedom, spinning webs of some variety and originality, so too there are "happy" women who dream of justice, and will make sure that they taste its sweetness, one day. Soon.

(Dr. K——! How lucky you are, to have a little grand-daughter like Lisle! So delicate, so pretty, so . . . angelic. I have not had a daughter, I confess. I will not have a granddaughter. If things were otherwise between us, "Jody," we might share Lisle.)

"Jody"—what a thrill it was for me, at the age of nineteen, to call you by that name! Where others addressed you formally, as Dr. K——. That it was secret, illicit, taboo—like calling one's own father by a lover's name—was part of the thrill, of course.

"Jody," I hope your first, anxious wife E—— never discovered certain bits of incriminating evidence in your trouser pockets, wallet, briefcase where, daringly, I secreted them. Love notes, childlike in expression. *Love love love my Jody. My BIG JODY.*

You're not BIG JODY very often now, are you, Dr. K——?

"Jody" has faded with the years, I've learned. With the thick wiry gypsy-black hair, those shrewd clear eyes and proud posture and the capacity of your stubby penis to rejuvenate, reinvent itself with impressive frequency. (At the start of our affair, at least.) For any nineteen-year-old girl-student to call you "Jody" now would be obscene, laughable.

Now you most love being called "Granddaddy!"—in Lisle's voice.

Yet in my dreams sometimes I hear my own shameless whisper, *Jody please don't stop loving me, please forgive me, I want only to die, I deserve to die if you don't love me* as in the warm bath blood-tendrils seeped from my clumsily lacerated forearms; but it was Dr. K——, not "Jody," who spoke brusquely on the phone informing me *This is not the time. Good-bye.*

(You must have made inquiries, Dr. K——. You must have learned that I was found there in the bloody bathwater, unconscious, nearing death, by a concerned woman friend who'd tried to call me. You must have known, but prudently kept your distance, Dr. K——! These many years.)

• • •

Dr. K——, not only have you managed to erase me from your memory, but I would guess you've forgotten your anxious first wife E——, "Evie." The rich man's daughter. A woman two years older than you, lacking in self-confidence, rather plain, with no style. Loving me, you were concerned about making "Evie" suspicious, not because you cared for her but because you would have made the rich father suspicious, too. And you were very beholden to the rich father, yes? *Few members of the Seminary faculty can afford to live near the Seminary. In the elegant old East End of our university town.* (So you boasted in your bemused way. As if contemplating an irony of fate, not a consequence of your own maneuvering. As, smiling, you kissed my mouth, and drew a forefinger along my breasts, across my shivery belly.)

Poor "Evie"! Her hit-and-run "accidental" death, a mysterious vehicle swerving on a rain-lashed pavement, no witnesses . . . I would have helped you mourn, Dr. K——, and been a loving stepmother to your children, but by then you'd banished me from your life.

Or so you believed.

(For the record: I am not hinting that I had anything to do

with the death of the first Mrs. K———. Don't bother to read and reread these lines, to determine if there's something "between" them—there isn't.)

And then, Dr. K———, a widower with two children, you went away, to Germany. A sabbatical year that stretched into two. I was left to mourn in your place. (Not luckless "Evie," but you.) Your wife's death was spoken of as a "tragedy" in certain circles, but I preferred to think of it as purely an accident: a conjunction of time, place, opportunity. *What is accident but a precision of timing?*

Dr. K———, I would not accuse you of blatant hypocrisy (would I?), still less of deceit, but I can't comprehend why, in such craven terror of your first wife's family (to whom you felt so intellectually superior), you nonetheless remarried, within eighteen months, a woman much younger than you, nearly as young as I, which must have shocked and infuriated your former in-laws. Yes? (Or did you cease caring about what they thought? Had you siphoned enough money from the father-in-law, by that time?)

Your second wife, V———, would be spared an accidental death, and will survive you by many years. I have never felt any rancor for voluptuous—now rather fattish—"Viola," who came into your life after I'd departed it. Maybe, in a way, I felt some sympathy for the young woman, guessing that, in time, you would betray her, too. (And haven't you? Numberless times?)

I have forgotten nothing, Dr. K———. While you, to your fatal disadvantage, have forgotten almost everything.

Dr. K———, "Jody," shall I confess: I had secrets from you even then. Even when I seemed to you transparent, translucent. Deep in the marrow of my bones, a wish to bring our illicit love to an end. An end worthy of grand opera, not mere melodrama. When you sat me on your knees naked—"nude" was your preferred term—and gobbled me up with your eyes, "Beautiful! Aren't you a little beauty!"—even then, I exulted in my secret thoughts. You seemed at times drunken with love—lust?—for me, kissing, tonguing, nuzzling, sucking . . . sucking nourishment from me like a vampire. (The stress of fatherhood and maintaining a dutiful son-in-law pose as well as the "renowned theologian" were exhausting you, maddening you in your masculine vanity. Of course, in my naiveté I had no idea.) Yet laying my hand on the hot-skinned nape of your neck I "saw" a razor blade clenched in my fingers, and the first astonished spurts of your blood, with such vividness I can "see" it now. I began to faint, my eyes rolled back in my head, you caught me in your arms . . . and for the first time (I assume it was the first time) you perceived your spun-gold angel as something of a concern, a liability, a burden not unlike the burden of a neurotic, anxiety-prone wife. *Darling, what's the matter with you? Are you playing, darling? Beautiful girl, it isn't amusing to frighten me when I adore you so.*

Gripping my chilled fingers in your hot, hard fingers and pressing my hand against your big powerfully beating heart.

Why not? why not try? try to collect?—that heart.

That's owed me.

How inspired I am, composing this letter, Dr. K——! I've been writing feverishly, scarcely pausing to draw breath. It's as if an angel is guiding my hand. (One of those tall leathery-winged angels of wrath, with fierce medieval faces, you see in German woodcuts!) I've reread certain of your published works, Dr. K——, including the heavily footnoted treatise on the Dead Sea Scrolls that established your reputation as an ambitious young scholar in his early thirties. Yet it all seems so quaint and long-ago, back in the twentieth century when "God" and "Satan" were somehow more real to us, like household objects . . . I've been reading of our primitive religious origins, how "God-Satan" were once conjoined but are now, in our Christian tradition, always separated. Fatally separated. For we Christians can believe no evil of our deity, we could not love Him then.

Dr. K——, as I write this letter my malfunctioning heart with its mysterious "murmur" now speeds, now slows, now gives a lurch, in excited knowledge that you are reading these words with a mounting sense of their justice. A heavy rain has begun to fall, drumming against the roof and windows of the place in which I am living, the identical rain (is it?) that drums against the roof and windows of your house only a few (or is it many?) miles away; unless I live in a part of the country thousands of miles distant, and the rain is not identical. And yet *I can come to you at any time. I am free to come, and to go; to appear, and to disappear.* It may even be that I've contemplated the charming facade of your precious granddaughter's Busy Bee Nursery School even as I've shopped for shoes in the company of V——, though the jowly-faced, heavily made-up woman with the size ten feet was oblivious of my presence, of course.

And, just last Sunday: I revisited the Museum of Natural History, knowing there was a possibility that you might return. For it had seemed to me possible that you'd recognized me on the steps, and sent a signal to me with your eyes, without Lisle noticing; you were urging me to return to meet with you, alone. The deep erotic bond between us will never be broken, you know: you entered my virginal body, you took from me my innocence, my youth, my very soul. *My angel! Forgive me, return to me, I will make up to you the suffering you've endured for my sake.*

I waited, but you failed to return.

I waited, and my sense of mission did not subside but grew more certain.

I found myself the sole visitor on the gloomy fourth floor, in the Hall of Dinosaurs. My footsteps echoed faintly on the worn marble floor. A white-haired museum guard with a paunch like yours regarded me through drooping eyelids; he sat on a canvas chair, hands on his knees. Like a wax dummy. Like one of those trompe l'oeil mannequins. You know: those uncanny, lifelike figures you see in contemporary art collections, except this slouching figure wasn't bandaged in white. Silently I passed by him as a ghost might pass. My (gloved) hand in my bag, and my fingers clutching a razor blade I'd learned by this time to wield with skill, and courage.

Stealthily I circled the Hall of Dinosaurs looking for you, but in vain; stealthily I drew up behind the dozing guard, feeling my erratic heartbeat quicken with the thrill of the hunt . . . but of course I let the moment pass, it was no museum guard but the renowned Dr. K—— for whom the razor blade was intended. (Though I had not the slightest doubt that I could have wielded my weapon against the old man, simply out of frustration at not finding you, and out of female rage at centuries of mistreatment, exploitation; I might have slashed his carotid artery and quickly retreated without a single blood drop splashed onto my clothing; even as the old man's life bled out onto the worn marble floor, I would have descended to the near-deserted third floor of the museum, and to the second, to mingle unnoticed with Sunday visitors crowded into a new computer graphics exhibit. So easy!) I found myself adrift amid rubbery dinosaur-replicas, some of them enormous as Tyrannosaurus rex, some the size of oxen, and others fairly small, human-sized; I admired the flying reptiles, with their long beaks and clawed wings; in a reflecting surface over which one of these prehistoric creatures soared I admired my pale, hot-skinned face and floating ashy hair. *My darling,* you whispered, *I will always adore you. That angelic smile!*

Dr. K———, see? I'm smiling, still.

Dr. K———! Why are you standing there, so stiffly, at an upstairs window of your house? Why are you cringing, overcome by a sickening fear? *Nothing will happen to you that is not just. That you do not deserve.*

These pages in your shaking hand, you'd like to tear into shreds—but don't dare. Your heart pounds, in terror of being snatched from your chest! Desperately you're contemplating—but will decide against—showing my letter to police. (Ashamed of what the letter reveals of the renowned Dr. K———!) You are contemplating—but will decide against—showing my letter to your wife, for you've had exhausting sessions of soul-baring, confession, exoneration with her, numerous times; you've seen the disgust in her eyes. No more! And you haven't the stomach to contemplate yourself in the mirror, for you've had more than enough of your own face, those stricken guilty eyes. While I, the venomous diamond-head, contentedly spin my gossamer web amid the rafters of your basement, or in the niche between your desk and the wall, or in the airless cave beneath your marital bed, or, most delicious prospect!—inside the very mattress of the child's bed in which, when she visits her grandparents in the house on Richmond Street, beautiful little Lisle sleeps.

Invisible by day as by night, spinning my web, out of my guts, tireless and faithful—"happy."

KARMA

WALTER MOSLEY

eonid McGill sat at his desk, on the sixty-seventh floor of
the Empire State Building, filing his nails and gazing at
New Jersey. It was three-fifteen. Leonid had promised himself that he'd exercise that afternoon but now that the time had
come he felt lethargic.

It was that pastrami sandwich, he thought. *Tomorrow I'll
have something light like fish and then I can go to Gordo's and
work out.*

Gordo's was a third-floor boxer's gym on Thirty-first
Street. When Leonid was thirty years younger, and sixty
pounds lighter, he went to Gordo's every day. For a while
Gordo Packer wanted the private detective to go pro.

"You'll make more money in the ring than you ever will
panty sniffin'," the seemingly ageless trainer said. McGill liked
the idea but he also loved Lucky Strikes and beer.

"I can't bring myself to run unless I'm being chased," he'd
tell Gordo. "And whenever somebody hurts me I wanna do

him some serious harm. You know if a guy knocked me out in the ring I'd probably lay for him with a tire iron out back'a Madison Square when the night was through."

The years went by and Leonid kept working out on the heavy bag two or three times a week. But a boxing career was out of the question. Gordo lost interest in Leonid as a prospect but they remained friends.

"How'd a Negro ever get a name like Leonid McGill?" Gordo once asked the P.I.

"Daddy was a communist and Great-Great-Granddaddy was a slave master from Scotland," Leo answered easily. "You know the black man's family tree is mostly root. Whatever you see aboveground is only a hint at the real story."

Leo got up from his chair and made a stab at touching his toes. His fingers made it to about midshins but his stomach blocked any further progress.

"Shit," the P.I. said. Then he returned to his chair and went back to filing his nails.

He did that until the broad-faced clock on the wall said 4:07. Then the buzzer sounded. One long, loud blare. Leonid cursed the fact that he hadn't hooked up the view-cam to see who it was at the door. With a ring like that it could have been anyone. He owed over forty-six hundred dollars to the Wyant brothers. The nut was due and Leonid had yet to collect on his windfall. The Wyants wouldn't pay any attention to his cash flow problems.

It might have been a prospective client at the door. A real client. Someone with an employee stealing from him. Or maybe a daughter being influenced by a bad crowd. Then again it could be one of thirty or forty angry husbands wanting revenge for being found out at their extramarital pastimes. And then there was Joe Haller—the poor schnook. But Leonid had never even met Joe Haller. There was no way that that loser could have found his door.

The buzzer sounded again.

Leonid got up from his chair and walked into the long hall that led to his reception room. Then he came to the front door.

The buzzer blared a third time.

"Who is it?" McGill shouted in a southern accent that he used sometimes.

"Mr. McGill?" a woman said.

"He's not here."

"Oh. Do you expect him back today?"

"No," Leonid said. "No. He's away on a case. Down in Florida. If you tell me what it is you want I'll leave him a note."

"Can I come in?" She sounded young and innocent but Leonid wasn't about to be fooled.

"I'm just the building janitor, honey," he said. "I'm not allowed to let anybody in any office in this here building. But I'll write down your name and number and leave it on his desk if you want."

Leonid had used that line before. There was no argument against it. The janitor couldn't be held responsible.

There was silence from the other side of the door. If the girl had an accomplice they'd be whispering about how to get around his ploy. Leonid put his ear against the wall but couldn't hear a thing.

"Karmen Brown," the woman said. She added a number with the new 646 prefix. Probably a cell phone, Leonid thought.

"Hold on. Let me get a pencil," he complained. "Brown, you say?"

"Karmen Brown," she repeated. "Karmen with a K." Then she gave the number again.

"I'll put it on his desk," Leonid promised. "He'll get it the minute he gets back to town."

"Thank you," the young woman said.

There was hesitation in her voice. If she was a thinking girl she might have wondered how a janitor would know the whereabouts of the private detective. But after a moment or two he could hear her heels clicking down the hall. He returned to his office to stay awhile just in case the girl, and her possible accomplice, decided to wait until he came out.

He didn't mind hanging around in the office. His sublet apartment wasn't nearly as nice, or quiet, and at least he could be alone. Commercial rents took a nosedive after 9-11. He picked up the ESB workspace for a song.

Not that he'd paid the rent in three months.

But Leonid Trotter McGill didn't worry about money that much. He knew that he could pull a hat trick if he had to. Too many people had too many secrets. And secrets were the most valuable commodity in New York City.

At 5:39 the buzzer sounded again. But this time it was two long blasts followed by three short. Leonid made his way down the hall and opened the front door without asking who it was.

The man standing there was short and white, balding and slim. He wore an expensive suit with real cuff links on a white shirt that had some starch in the collar and cuffs.

"Leon," the small white man said.

"Lieutenant. Come on in."

Leonid led the dapper little man through the reception area, along the hallway (that had three doors down its length), and finally into his office.

"Sit down, Lieutenant."

"Nice office. Where's everybody else?" the visitor asked.

"It's just me right now. I'm in a transition phase. You know, trying to develop a new business plan."

"I see."

The slender white man took the chair in front of Leonid's desk. From there he could see the long shadows across New Jersey. He shifted his gaze from the window to his host. L. T. McGill, P.I.

Leonid was short, no taller than five seven, with a protruding gut and heavy jowls. His skin was the color of dirty bronze and covered with dark freckles. There was a toothpick jutting out from the right side of his mouth. He wore a tan suit that had been stained over time. His shirt was lime green and the thick gold band on his left pinky weighed two or three ounces.

Leonid McGill had powerful hands and strong breath. His eyes were suspicious and he would always appear to be a decade over his actual age.

"What can I do for you, Carson?" the detective asked the cop.

"Joe Haller," Carson Kitteridge said.

"Come again?" Leonid let his face wrinkle up, feigning ignorance if not innocence.

"Joe Haller."

"Never heard that name before. Who is he?"

"He's a gigolo and a batterer. Now they're trying to tell me he's a thief."

"You wanna hire me to find something on him?"

"No," the cop said. "No. He's in the Tombs right now. We caught him red-handed. He had thirty thousand right there in his closet. In the briefcase that he carried to work every day."

"That makes it easy," Leonid said. He concentrated on his breathing, something he had learned to do whenever he was being questioned by the law.

"You'd think so, wouldn't you?" Carson asked.

"Is there a problem with the case?"

"You were seen speaking to Nestor Bendix on January four."

"I was?"

"Yeah. I know that because Nestor's name came up in the robbery of a company called Amberson's Financials two months ago."

"Really?" Leonid said. "What does all that have to do with Joe whatever?"

"Haller," Lieutenant Kitteridge said. "Joe Haller. The money he had in the bag was from the armored car that had just made a drop at Amberson's."

"An armored car dropped thirty thousand dollars at the place?"

"More like three hundred thousand," Kitteridge said. "It was for their ATM machines. Seems like Amberson's had got heavy into the ATM business in that neighborhood. They run sixty machines around midtown."

"I'll be damned. And you think Joe Haller and Nestor Bendix robbed them?"

Lieutenant Carson Kitteridge stayed silent for a moment, his gray eyes taking in the rough-hewn detective.

"What did you and Nestor have to say to each other?" the cop asked.

"Nothing," Leonid said, giving a one-shoulder shrug. "It was a pizza place down near the Seaport, if I remember right. I ducked in there for a calzone and saw Nestor. We used to be friends back when Hell's Kitchen was still Hell's Kitchen."

"What did he have to say?"

"Not a thing. Really. It was just a chance meeting. I sat

down long enough to eat too much and find out that he's got two kids in college and two in jail."

"You talk about the heist?"

"I never even heard about it until you just said."

"This Joe Haller," the policeman said. "He practices what you call an alternative lifestyle. He likes married women. It's what you might call his thing. He finds straight ladies and bends them. They say he's hung like a horse."

"Yeah?"

"Yeah. What he does is gets the ladies to meet him at hotels near where he works and goes in to teach them about how the other eight inches live."

"You've lost me, Lieutenant," Leonid said. "I mean unless one of the she-guards at Amberson's is Haller's chicken."

The elegant policeman shook his head slightly.

"No. No. This is how I see it, Leon," the policeman said. He sat forward in his chair and laced his fingers. "Nestor pulled off the robbery but somebody let it slip and me and my crew got on his ass. So he calls on you to find him a pigeon and you give him Haller. Don't ask me how. I don't know. But you set up the Romeo and now he's looking at twenty years in Attica."

"Me?" Leonid said, pressing all ten fingers against his breast. "How the hell you think I could do something like that?"

"You could pluck an egg out from under a nesting eagle and she'd never even know it was gone," Kitteridge said. "I got a man in jail and his alibi girlfriend saying that she never even heard his name. I got an armed robber laughing at me and a P.I. more crooked than any crook I ever arrested lyin' in my face."

"Carson," Leonid said. "Brother, you got me wrong. I did see Nestor for a few minutes. But that's all, man. I've never been to this Amberson's place and I never heard of Joe Haller or his girlfriend."

"Chris," Kitteridge said. "Chris Small. Her husband has already left her. That's what our investigation has accomplished so far."

"I wish I could help you, man, but you got me wrong. I wouldn't even know how to set up some patsy for a crime after it was committed."

Carson Kitteridge stared mildly at the detective and the darkening neighbor state. He smiled and said, "You can't get away with it, Leon. You can't break the law like that and win."

"I don't know nuthin' about nuthin', Lieutenant. Maybe the man you caught really is the thief."

• • •

Katrina McGill was a beauty in her day. Svelte and raven-haired, from Latvia or Lithuania—Leonid was never sure which one. They had three kids, of which at least two were not Leonid's. He'd never had them tested. Why bother? The east European beauty had left him early on for a finance lion. But she got fat and the sugar daddy went broke so now the whole crowd (minus the sugar daddy) lived on Leonid's dime.

"What's for dinner, Kat?" he asked, breathing hard after scaling the five flights to their apartment door.

"Mr. Barch called," she answered. "He said that either you pay up by Friday or he's going to start eviction."

It was the square shape of her face and the heaviness around her eyes that made her ugly. When she was young gravity was in suspense but he should have seen the curtain coming down.

The kids were in the living room. The TV was on but no one was watching. The oldest boy, the red-headed Dimitri, was reading a book. He had ochre skin and green eyes. But he had

Leonid's mouth. Shelly, the girl, looked more Chinese than anything else. They used to have a Chinese neighbor when they lived on Staten Island. He worked at an Indian jewelers' center in Queens. Shelly was sewing one of Leonid's jackets. She loved her father and never questioned her mother or the face in the mirror.

Shelly and Dimitri were eighteen and nineteen. They went to City College and lived at home. Katrina would not hear of them moving out. And Leonid liked having them around. He felt that they were keeping him anchored to something, keeping him from floating away down Forty-second Street and into the Hudson.

Twill was the youngest boy. Sixteen and self-named. He'd just come home after a three-month stay at a youth detention center near Wingdale, New York. The only reason he was still in high school was that that was part of his release agreement.

Twill was the only one who smiled when Leonid entered the room.

"Hey, pop," he said. "Guess what? Mr. Tortolli wants to hire me at his store."

"Hey. Good." Leonid would have to call the hardware man and tell him that Twill would open his back door and empty out the storeroom in three weeks' time.

Leonid loved him but Twill was a thief.

"What about Mr. Barch?" Katrina said.

"What about my dinner?"

• • •

Katrina knew how to cook. She served chicken with white wine sauce and the flakiest dumplings he had ever eaten. There was also broccoli and almond bread, grilled pineapples, and a dark fish sauce that you could eat with a spoon.

Cooking was difficult for Katrina since her left hand had become partially paralyzed. The specialist said that it was probably due to a slight stroke. She worried all the time. Her boyfriends had stopped calling years before.

But Leonid took care of her and her kids. He even asked to have sex with her now and then because he knew how much she hated it.

"Did anybody else call?" he asked when the college kids were in their rooms and Twill was back out in the street.

"A man called Arman."

"What he say?"

"There's a little French diner on Tenth and Seventeenth. He wants to see you there at ten. I told him I didn't know if you could make it."

When Leonid moved to kiss Katrina she leaned away and he laughed.

"Why don't you leave me?" he asked.

"Who would raise our children if I did that?"

This caused Leonid to laugh even harder.

•   •   •

He reached Babette's Feast at nine-fifteen. He ordered a double espresso and stared at the legs of a mature woman seated at the bar. She was at least forty but dressed as if she were fifteen. Leonid felt the stirrings of the first erection he'd had in over a week.

Maybe that's why he called Karmen Brown on his cell phone. Her voice had sounded as if it should be clad in a dress like that.

When the call was answered Leonid could tell that she was outside.

"Hello?"

"Miss Brown?"

"Yes."

"This is Leo McGill. You left a message for me?"

"Mr. McGill. I thought you were in Florida." The roar of an engine almost drowned out her words.

"I'm sorry if it's hard to hear me," she said. "There was a motorcycle going down the street."

"That's okay. How can I help you?"

"I'm having a problem and, and, well it's rather personal."

"I'm a detective, Miss Brown. I hear personal stuff all the time. If you want me to meet with you then you'll have to tell me what it's about."

"Richard," she said, "Mallory. He's my fiancé and I think he's cheating on me."

"And you want me to prove it?"

"Yes," she said. "I don't want to marry a man who will treat me like that."

"How did you get my name, Miss Brown?"

"I looked you up in the book. When I saw where your office was I thought that you must be good."

"I can meet you sometime tomorrow."

"I'd rather meet tonight. I don't think I'll get any sleep until this thing is settled."

"Well," the detective hesitated. "I have a meeting at ten and then I'm going to see my girlfriend." It was a private joke, one that the young Miss Brown would never understand.

"Maybe I can meet you before you see your girlfriend," Karmen suggested. "It should only take a few minutes."

They agreed on a pub on Houston two blocks east of Elizabeth Street, where Gert Longman lived.

Just as Leonid was removing the hooked earphone from his ear Craig Arman entered the bistro. He was a large white man with a broad, kind face. Even the broken nose made him seem more vulnerable than dangerous. He wore faded blue jeans and a T-shirt under a large loose knit sweater. There was a pistol hidden somewhere in all that fabric, Leonid knew that. Nestor Bendix's *street accountant* never went unarmed.

"Leo," Arman said.

"Craig."

The small table that Leonid had chosen was behind a pillar, removed from the rest of the crowd in the popular bistro.

"Cops got their package," Arman said. "Our guy was in and out of his place in ten minutes. A quick call downtown and now he's in the Tombs. Just like you said."

"That means I can pay the rent," Leonid replied.

Arman smiled and Leonid felt a few ounces being placed on his thigh under the table.

"Well, I got to go," Arman said then. "Early to bed, you know."

"Yeah," Leonid agreed.

Most of Nestor's boys didn't have much truck with the darker races. The only reason Nestor ever called was that Leonid was the best at his trade.

• • •

Leonid caught a cab on Seventh Avenue that took him to Barney's Clover on Houston.

The girl sitting at the far end of the bar was everything Katrina had once been except she was blonde and her looks would never fade. She had a porcelain face with small, lovely features. No makeup except for a hint of pale lip gloss.

"Mr. McGill?"

"Leo."

"I'm so relieved that you came to meet me," she said.

She was wearing tan riding pants and a coral blouse. There was a white raincoat folded over her lap. Her eyes were the kind of brown that some artist might call red. Her hair was cut short—boyish but sexy. Her tinted lips were ready to kiss babies' butts and laugh.

Leonid took a deep breath and said, "I charge five hundred a day—plus expenses. That's mileage, equipment rentals, and food after eight hours on the job."

He had just received twelve thousand dollars from Craig Arman but business was business.

The girl handed him a large manila envelope.

"This is his full name and address. I have also included a photograph and the address of the office where he works. There's also eight hundred dollars in it. You probably won't need more than that because I'm almost sure that he'll be seeing her tomorrow evening."

"What you drinkin', guy?" the bartender, a lovely faced Asian boy, asked.

"Seltzer," the detective asked. "Hold the rocks."

The bartender smiled or sneered, Leonid wasn't sure which. He wanted a scotch with his fizzy water but the ulcer in his stomach would keep him up half the night if he had it.

"Why?" Leonid asked the beautiful girl.

"Why do I want to know?"

"No. Why do you think he's going to see her tomorrow night?"

"Because he told me that he had to go with his boss to see *The Magic Flute* at Carnegie Hall. But there is no opera scheduled."

"You seem to have it all worked out yourself. Why would you need a detective?"

"Because of Dick's mother," Karmen Brown said. "She told

me that I wasn't worthy of her son. She said that I was common and coarse and that I was just using him."

The anger twisted Karmen's face until even her ethereal
beauty turned into something ugly.

"And you want to rub her face in it?" Leonid asked. "Why
wouldn't she be happy that her boy found another girl?"

"I think that the woman he's seeing is married and older,
way older. If I could get pictures of them then when I leave at
least she won't be so smug."

Leonid wondered if that would be enough to hurt Dick's
mother. He also wondered why Karmen suspected that Dick
was seeing an older married woman. He had a lot of questions
but didn't ask them. Why question a cash cow? After all, he had
two rents to pay.

The detective looked over the information and glanced at
the cash, held together by an oversized paper clip, while the
young bartender placed the water by his elbow.

The photograph was of a man whom he took to be Richard
Mallory. He was a young white man whose face seemed unfin-
ished. There was a mustache that wasn't quite thick enough
and a mop of brown hair that would always defy a comb. He
seemed uncomfortable standing there in front of the Rocke-
feller Center skating rink.

"Okay, Miss Brown," Leonid said. "I'll take it on. Maybe
we'll both get lucky and it'll be over by tomorrow night."

"Karma," she said. "Call me Karma. Everybody does."

· · ·

Leonid got down to Elizabeth Street a little after ten-thirty. He
rang Gert's bell and shouted his name into the security micro-
phone. He had to raise his voice to be heard over the roar of a
passing motorcycle.

Gert Longman lived in a small studio on the third floor of a stucco building put up in the fifties. The ceiling was low but the room was pretty big and Gert had set it up nicely. There was a red sofa and a mahogany coffee table with cherry wood cabinets that had glass doors along the far wall. She had no kitchen but there was a miniature refrigerator in one corner with a coffee percolator and a toaster on top. Gert also had a CD player. When Leonid got there she was playing Ella Fitzgerald singing Cole Porter tunes.

Leonid appreciated the music and said so.

"I like it," Gert said, somehow managing to negate Leonid's compliment.

She was a dark-skinned woman whose mother had come from the Spanish side of Hispaniola. Gert didn't speak with an accent, though. She didn't even know the Spanish tongue. Actually Gert knew nothing about her history. She was proud to say of herself that she was just as much an American as any Daughter of the American Revolution.

She sat on the southern end of the sofa.

"Did Nestor pay you yet?" Gert asked.

"You know I been missing you, Gertie," Leonid said, thinking about her satin skin and the fortyish woman in the teeny-bopper dress from the French bistro.

"That's done, Leo," Gert said. "That was over a long time ago."

"You must still have needs."

"Not for you."

"One time you told me you loved me," Leonid replied.

"That was after you told me that you weren't married."

Leonid sat down a few inches away from her. He touched her knuckle with two fingers.

"No," Gert said.

"Come on, baby. It's hard as a boil down there."

"And I'm dry to the bone."

. . . but to a woman a man is life, Ella sang.

Leonid sat back and shoved his right hand into his pants pocket.

After Karmen Brown had left him at Barney's Clover Leonid ducked into the john and counted out Gert's three thousand from the twelve Craig Arman had laid on his lap. He took the wad from his pocket.

"You could at least give me a little kiss on my boil for all this," he said.

"I could lance it too."

Leonid chuckled and Gert grinned. They'd never be lovers again but she liked his ways. He could see that in her eyes.

Maybe he should have left Katrina.

He handed her the roll of hundred-dollar bills and asked, "Could anybody find a trail from you to Joe Haller?"

"Uh-uh. No. I worked in a whole 'nother office from him."

"How did you find out about his record?"

"Ran off a list of likely employees for the company and did a background search on about twenty."

"From your desk?"

"From the public library computer terminal."

"Can't they trace you back on that?" Leonid asked.

"No. I bought an account with a Visa number I got from Jackie P. It's some poor slob from St. Louis. There's no tracing that. What's wrong, Leo?"

"Nuthin'," the detective said. "I just want to be careful."

"Haller's a dog," Gert added. "He'd been doin' them girls around there for months. And when Cynthia Athol's husband found out and came after him Joe beat him so bad that he had to go to the hospital. Broke his collarbone. He beat Chris Small with a strap just two weeks ago."

When Nestor asked Leonid to find him a patsy for a mid-day crime Leonid came to Gert and she went to work as a temp for Amberson's Financials. All she had to do was come up with a guy with a record who might have been part of the heist; a guy who no one could connect with Nestor.

She did him one better. She came up with a guy that no one liked.

Haller had robbed a convenience store twelve years before, when he was eighteen. And now he was a gigolo with some kind of black belt in something. He liked to overwhelm the silly office secretaries with his muscles and his big thing. He didn't mind if their significant others found out because he believed he could take on almost any man one on one.

Gert had been told that he once said, "Any woman with a real man wouldn't let me take her like that."

"Don't worry," Gert said. "He deserves whatever happens to him and they'll never follow it back to me."

"Okay," Leonid said.

He touched her knuckle again.

"Don't."

He let his fingers trail up toward her wrist.

"Please, Leo. I don't want to wrestle with you."

Leonid's breath was shallow and the erection was pressing against his pants. But he moved away.

"I better be going," he said.

"Yeah," Gert agreed. "Go home to your wife."

• • •

It didn't take long to get past security at the Empire State Building. Leonid worked late at least three nights a week.

He didn't want to go home after Gert had turned him down.

He never knew why he took Kartrina back in.

He never knew why he did anything except if it had to do with the job.

Leonid became a P.I. because he was too short to qualify for the NYPD when he was eligible. They changed the requirements soon after that but by then he'd already been busted for unlawful entry.

He didn't care. The private sector was more lucrative and he could work his own hours.

•   •   •

He found a Richard Mallory in the phone book that had the same address that Karmen Brown had typed out on her fiancé's fact sheet. Leonid dialed the number. Someone answered on the third ring.

"Hello?" a tremulous man's voice asked.

"BobbiAnne there?" Leonid asked in one of his dozen accents.

"What?"

"BobbiAnne. She there?"

"You have the wrong number."

"Oh. All right," Leonid said and then he hung up.

For a dozen minutes by the big clock on the wall Leonid thought about the voice of the man who might have been Richard Mallory. Leonid thought that he could tell the nature of anyone if he could talk to him just when he was roused out of a deep sleep.

It was 2:34 a.m. And Richard, if that was Richard, sounded like a straightforward guy, a working stiff, somebody who didn't cross the line over into the Life.

This was important to Leonid. He didn't want to get involved following some guy who might turn around and blow his head off.

• • •

At half past three he called Gert.

"Six-two-oh-nine," the recording of her voice said after five rings. "I'm not available right now but if you leave a message I'll be sure to call you back."

"Gertie, it's Leon. I'm sorry about before. I miss you, honey. Maybe we can have dinner tomorrow night. You know—I'll make it up to you."

He didn't hang up for a few seconds more, hoping that Gert was listening and would decide to pick up.

• • •

The buzzer woke him. The clock had it just past nine. The window was filled with cloud—just a pillowy white gauze that didn't give three inches' visibility.

The buzzer jangled his dull mind again. Another long ring. But this time Leonid wasn't awake enough to have fear. He stumbled down the hall in the same suit he'd been wearing for over twenty-four hours.

When he opened the front door the two thugs pushed in.

One was black with a bald head and golden-rimmed glasses while the other was white with thick greasy hair.

They each had five inches on Leonid.

"The Wyants want forty-nine hundred," the black man said. His mouth on the inside was the color of gingivitis. His eyes behind the lenses had a yellowy tint.

"Forty-six," Leonid corrected groggily.

"That was yesterday, Leo. That interest is a motherfucker."

The black man closed the door and the white one moved to Leonid's left.

The white hooligan grinned and Leonid felt a hatred in his heart that was older than his communist father's father.

The white man had coarse chestnut hair that had been hacked rather than cut. His eyes were bisected between blue and brown and his lips were ragged, as if he had spent a portion of his earlier life soul-kissing a toothy leopard.

"We wake you up?" the black collector asked, just now remembering his manners.

"Li'l bit," Leonid said, stifling a yawn. "How you been, Bilko?"

"Okay, Leon. I hope you got the money, 'cause if you don't they told us to bust you up."

The white man snickered in anticipation.

Leonid reached into his breast pocket and came out with the thick brown envelope he'd received the night before.

While counting out the forty-nine hundred-dollar bills Leonid had a familiar sensation: the feeling of never having as much money as he thought he did. After his debt and interest to the Wyants, this month's rent and last on his apartment, after his wife's household expenses and his own bills, he would be broke and still three months behind on his office rent.

This made him even angrier. He'd need Karmen Brown's money and more if he was going to keep his head above water. And that white fool just kept on grinning, his head like a wobbling tenpin begging to fall down.

Leonid handed the money to Bilko, who counted it slowly while the white goon licked his ragged lips.

"I think you should tip us for havin' to come all the way up here to collect, Leon," the white man said.

Bilko looked up and grinned. "Leon don't tip the help, Norman. He's got his pride."

"I knock that outta him right quick," Norman said.

"I'd like to see you try it, white boy," Leonid dared. Then he looked at Bilko to see if he had to take on two at once.

"It's between you two," the black capo said, holding up one empty hand and one filled with Leonid's green.

Norman was faster than he looked. He laid a beefy fist against Leonid's jaw, knocking the middle-aged detective back two steps.

"Whoa!" Bilko cried.

Norman's frayed lips curved into a smile. He stood there looking at Leonid, expecting him to fall down.

That was the mistake all of Leonid's sparring partners had made at Gordo's gym. They thought the fat man couldn't take a punch. Leonid came in low and hard, hitting the big white man three times at the belt line. The third punch bent Norman over enough to be a sucker for a one-two uppercut combination. The only thing that kept Norman from falling was the wall. He hit it hard, putting his hands up reflexively to ward off the attack he knew was coming.

Leonid got three good blows to Norman's head before Bilko pushed him away.

"That's enough now, boy," Bilko said. "That's enough. I need him on his feet to get back out on the street."

"Take the asshole outta here then, Bilko! Take him outta here before I kill his ass!"

Dutifully Bilko helped the half-conscious, bleeding white man away from the wall. He pointed him at the door and then turned to Leonid.

"See you next month, Leon," he said.

"No," Leonid replied, breathing hard from the exertion. "You won't be seeing me again."

Bilko laughed as he led Norman toward the elevators.

Leonid slammed the door behind them. He was still in a rage. After all his pay he was still broke and hard-pressed by fools like Bilko and Norman. Gert wouldn't take his calls and he didn't even have a bed that he could sleep in alone. He would have killed that ugly fool if it wasn't for Bilko.

Leonid Trotter McGill let out a roar and kicked a hole in the paneled veneer of his nonexistent receptionist's cubicle wall. Then he picked up the phone, called Lenny's Delicatessen on Thirty-fifth Street and ordered three jelly doughnuts and a large cup of coffee with cream.

He called Gert again but she still wasn't answering.

• • •

It was a small office on the third floor above a two-story Japanese restaurant called Gai. There was no elevator so Leonid took the stairs. Just those twenty-eight steps winded him. If Norman had fought back at all, Leonid realized, he would be broken and broke.

The receptionist weighed less than ninety-eight pounds fully dressed and she was nowhere near fully dressed. All she had on was a black slip trying to pass as a dress and flat paper sandals. Her arms had no muscle. Everything about the girl was preadolescent except her eyes, which regarded the bulky P.I. with deep suspicion.

"Richard Mallory," Leonid said to the brunette.

"And you are?"

"Looking for Richard Mallory," Leonid stated.

"What business do you have with Mr. Mallory?"

"No business of yours, honey. It's man-talk."

The young woman's four-ounce jaw hardened as she stared at Leonid.

He didn't mind. He didn't like the girl; dressed so sexy and talking to him as if they were peers.

She picked up a phone and whispered a few angry words, then she walked away from her post into a doorway behind her chair, leaving Leonid to stand there at the waist-high barrier-desk. In the mirror on the wall Leonid could see through the window behind his back and out onto Madison Avenue. He could also see the swelling on the right side of his head where Norman had hit him.

A few moments later the tall man with a sparse mustache strode out. He wore black trousers and a tan linen jacket and the same uncomfortable expression he had on the photograph in Leonid's pocket.

Leonid hated him too.

"Yes?" Richard Mallory said to Leonid.

"I'm looking for Richard Mallory," Leonid said.

"That's me."

The P.I. took a deep breath through his nostrils. He knew that he had to calm down if he wanted to do his job right. He took another, deeper breath.

"What happened to your jaw?" the handsome young man asked the amateur boxer.

"Edema," Leonid said easily. "Runs on my father's side of the family."

Richard Mallory was stymied by this. Leonid thought that he probably didn't know the definition of the word.

"I want to talk business with you, Mr. Mallory. Something we can both make money on."

"I don't see what you mean," Mallory said with the blandest of bland expressions on his face.

Leonid produced a card from his breast pocket. It read:

Van Der Zee Domestics and In-Home Service Aides
Arnold DuBois, Agent

"I don't understand, Mr. DuBois," Mallory said, using the French pronunciation of McGill's alias.

"Du *boys*," Leonid said. "I represent the Van Der Zee firm. We're just establishing ourselves here in New York. We're from Cleveland originally. What we want is to get our people in as domestics, care for the aged, dog walkers, and nannies in the upper-crust buildings. All of our people are highly presentable and professional. They're bonded too."

"And you want me to help you get in?" Mallory asked, still a little leery.

"We'll pay fifteen hundred dollars for every exclusive presentation you get us in for," Leonid said. By now he had forgotten his dislike of the receptionist and Mallory. He wasn't even mad at Norman anymore.

The mention of fifteen hundred per presentation (whatever that meant) moved Dick Mallory to action.

"Come with me, Mr. DuBois," he said, pronouncing the name the way Leonid preferred.

The real estate agent led the fake employment agent down a hall of cubicles inhabited by various other agents.

Mallory took Leonid to a small conference room and closed the door behind them. There was a round pine table that had three matching chairs. Mallory gestured and they both sat down.

"Now what is it exactly that you're saying, Mr. DuBois?"

"We have a young girl," Leonid said. "A pretty thing. She sets up a small table in the entry hall of any building you say.

She talks to the tenants about all the various types of in-home labor they might need. Somebody might want an assistant twice a week to help with filing and shopping. They might already have an assistant but still need somebody to walk their pets when they're away. Once somebody hires one of our people we're confident that they will hire others as needs arise. All we want is your okay to install the young lady and we pay you fifteen hundred dollars."

"For every building I get you into?"

"Cash."

"Cash?"

Leonid nodded.

The young man actually licked his lips.

"If you can guarantee us a lobby in an upscale building, I can pay you as early as tonight," Leonid said.

"Does it have to be that soon?"

"I'm an agent on commission for Van Der Zee Enterprises, Mr. Mallory. In order to make a profit I have to produce. I'm not the only one out here trying to make contacts. I mean, you can call me whenever you want, but if you can't promise me a lobby by the end of today then I will have to go farther down my list of contacts."

"But—"

"Listen," Leonid said, cutting off any logic that Richard Mallory might have brought to bear. He reached into his pocket and brought out three one-hundred-dollar bills. These he placed on the table between them. "That's one-fifth up front. Three hundred dollars against you finding me one lobby that I can send Arlene to tomorrow morning."

"Tomorrow—"

"That's right, Richard. Van Der Zee Enterprises will give me control over the whole Manhattan operation if I'm the first one to bring in a lobby."

"So I get to keep the money?"

"With twelve hundred more coming to you at eight this evening if you have the lobby set for me."

"Eight? Why eight?"

"You think you're the only guy I'm talking to, Richard? I have four other meetings set up this afternoon. Whoever gets to me when it's all done, at eight o'clock, will get at least part of the prize. Maybe he'll get the whole thing."

"But I have a date tonight—"

"Just call me on the phone, Richard. Tell me where you are and I'll bring you the money and the letter confirming to the super that Arlene can set up her table."

"What letter?"

"I hope you don't think I'm going to be handing you fifteen hundred dollars a week in cash without getting a letter for the super to show my boss," Leonid said blandly. "Don't worry, we won't mention the money, just that Van Der Zee Enterprises can set up in the lobby offering our services."

"But what if somebody complains?"

"You can always tell your bosses that you were thinking on your own, trying to offer a service. They won't know about the money changing hands. At the very least we'll be thrown out, but that'll take a couple'a days, and Arlene is very good at handing out those brochures."

"That's fifteen hundred in cash a week?"

"Twice that if we can find another Arlene and you can hook us up like I been told."

"But I'm going to be out tonight," Mallory complained.

"So? Just call me. Give me the address. And I'll drop by with the form. We're talkin' ten minutes for twelve hundred dollars."

Richard fingered the money. Then he tentatively picked it up.

"I can just take this?"

"Take it. And take the rest tonight and then that much again once a week for the next four or five months." Leonid grinned.

Richard folded the money and put it in his pocket.

"What's your phone number, Mr. DuBois?"

• • •

Leonid called his wife and told her to have his brown suit ready and pressed by the time he got home.

"Am I your maid now?" she asked.

"I got the rent and the expenses here in my pocket," Leonid growled. "All I'm asking from you is a little cooperation."

The private eye then called his cell phone service. When the voice on the line said to record a new message, Leonid said, "Hello. This is Arnold DuBois, employment agent for Van Der Zee Enterprises. At the tone leave me what you got."

• • •

When he got home he found the suit folded on the bed and Katrina gone. Alone in the house, he drew a bath and poured himself a glass of ice water. He wanted a cigarette but the doctors had told him his lungs could barely take New York air.

He sat back in the old-fashioned tub, turning the hot water on and off with his toes. His jaw ached and he was almost broke again. But still he had a line on Richard Mallory and that made the detective happy.

"At least I'm good at what I do," he said to no one. "At least that."

• • •

After the bath Leonid called Gert again. This time the phone rang and rang with no interruption. That was very odd. Gert had it set up so that her service picked up when she was on the line.

Sometimes he didn't talk to Gert for months at a time. She had made it clear that they could never be intimate again. But he still felt something for her. And he wanted to make sure that she was okay.

• • •

When Leonid got to Gert's near four he found the downstairs door had been wedged open.

Her front door was crisscrossed with yellow police ribbon.

"You know her?" a voice asked.

It was a small woman standing at a doorway down the hall. She was old and gray and wore gray clothes. She had watery eyes and mismatched slippers. There was a low-grade emerald ring on the index finger of her right hand and the left side of her mouth lagged just a bit.

Leonid noticed all of this in a vain attempt to work away from the fear growing in his stomach.

"What happened?"

"They say he must'a come in last night," the woman said. "It was past midnight, the super says. He just killed her. Didn't steal anything. Just shot her with a gun no louder than a cap pistol, that's what they said. You know you're not safe in your own bed anymore. People out here just get some crazy idea in their head and you find yourself dead with no rhyme or reason."

Leonid's tongue went dry. He stared at the woman so intensely that she stopped rambling, backed into her apartment, and closed the door. He leaned against the doorjamb, dry-eyed but stunned.

Leonid had never cried. Not when his father left home for the revolution. Not when his mother went to bed and never came out again. Never.

• • •

There was a different bartender serving drinks at Barney's Clover that afternoon. A woman with faded blue-green tattoos on her wrists. She was thin and brown-eyed, white and past forty.

"What you have, mister?"

"Rye whiskey. Keep 'em comin'."

• • •

He was on the sixth shot when his cell phone sounded. The ring had been programmed by his son Twill. It started with the sound of a lion's roar.

" 'lo?"

"Mr. DuBois? Is that you?"

"Who is this?"

"Richard Mallory. Are you sick, Mr. DuBois?"

"Hey, Dick. Sorry I didn't recognize you. I got some bad news today. An old friend of mine died."

"I'm so sorry. What happened?"

"It was a long illness," Leonid said, finishing one shot and gesturing for another.

"Should I call you later?"

"You got me a lobby, Dick?"

"Um, well yes. A fairly large building on Sutton Place South. The super is a friend of mine and I promised him five hundred."

"That's the way to do business, Dick. Share the wealth. That's what I've always done. Where are you?"

"It's a Brazilian place on West Twenty-six. Umberto's. On the second floor, between Sixth and Broadway. I don't know the exact address."

"That's okay. I'll get it from information. See you about nine. Looks like we're gonna be doing some business, you and me."

"Okay, um, all right. I'm sorry about your loss, Mr. DuBois. But please don't call me Dick. I hate that name."

•   •   •

Umberto's was an upscale restaurant on a street filled with wholesalers of Indian trinkets, foods, and clothing. Leonid sat across the street in his 1963 Peugeot.

It was after ten and the fat detective was drinking from a pint bottle of bourbon in the front seat. He was thinking about the first time he had met Gert, about how she knew just what to say.

"You're not such a bad man," the sultry New Yorker had said. "It's just that you been making your own rules for so long that you got a little confused."

They spent that night together. He really didn't know that she'd be upset about Katrina. Katrina was his wife but there was no juice there. He remembered the hurt look on Gert's face when she finally found out. After that came the cold anger she treated him with from then on.

They'd remained friends but she would never kiss him again. She would never let him into her heart.

But they worked well together. Gert had been in private security for a dozen years before they met. She enjoyed his *shady cases*, as she called them. Gert didn't believe that the law was fair and she didn't mind getting around the system if that was the right thing to do.

Maybe Joe Haller didn't rob Amberson's, but he'd beaten and humiliated both men and women pursuing his perverse sexual appetites.

Leonid wondered if Nestor Bendix could have had something to do with Gert's killing. But he'd never told anyone her name. Maybe Haller got out and somehow traced his problem back to her. Maybe.

A lion roared in his pocket.

"Yeah?"

"Mr. McGill? This is Karma."

"Hey. I'm on the case. He *is* on a date but I haven't seen her yet. I'll have the pictures for you by tomorrow afternoon. By the way, I had to lay out three hundred to get this address."

"That's all right, I guess," she said. "I'll pay for it if you can bring me proof about his girlfriend."

"All right. Let me off now. I'll call you when I have something for sure."

When Leonid folded the phone a colony of monkeys began chattering.

"Yeah?"

"You knew Gert Longman, didn't you?" Carson Kitteridge asked.

Ice water formed in Leonid's lower intestine. His rectum clenched.

"Yeah."

"What's that supposed to mean?"

"You asked me if I knew someone and I told you. Yeah. We were close there for a while."

"She's dead."

Leonid remained silent for a quarter face sweep of his Timex's second hand. That was long enough to seem as if he was shocked by the news.

"How did it happen?"

"Shot."

"By who?"

"A man wielding a long-barreled .22 pistol."

"Do you have a suspect?"

"That's the kinda pistol you like to use, isn't it, Leon?"

For a moment Leonid thought that the lieutenant was just blowing smoke, trying to get under his skin. But then he remembered a gun that he'd lost. It was seventeen years before. Nora Parsons had come to him scared to death that her husband, who was out on bail before sentencing in his embezzlement trial, was going to come kill her. Leonid had given her his pistol, and after her husband, Anton, was sentenced, she'd told him that she was afraid to have the pistol in the house so she threw it into a lake.

It was a cold piece. Nothing to it.

"Well?" Detective Kitteridge asked.

"I haven't owned a gun in twenty years, man. And even you can't think that I'd use my own piece if I wanted to kill somebody."

But still he thought he might give Nora Parsons a call. Maybe.

"I'd like you to come in for voluntary questioning, Leon."

"I'm busy right now. Call me later," Leonid said, and then he disconnected the call.

He didn't want to be so rude to a member of New York's Finest but Richard was coming out of the front door of Umberto's Brazilian Food. He was accompanied by the haughty receptionist from the real estate company. Now she was wearing a red slip and black pumps with a gossamer pink shawl around her bare shoulders. Her limp brown hair was up.

Richard glanced around the street, probably looking for Mr. DuBois, then hailed a cab.

Leonid turned over the engine. He watched as a cab swooped down to pick them up. The driver wore a Sikh turban.

They went up to Thirty-second Street, headed east over to Park and then up to the Seventies.

They got out at a building with big glass doors and two uniformed doormen.

Almost as if they were posing, the two stopped on the street and entwined their lips in a long soul kiss. Leonid had been taking photographs since he'd hung up on the cop. He had shots of the taxi's numbers, the driver, the front of the building and the couple talking, holding hands, dueling tongues, and grasping at skin.

They reminded Leonid of Gert, of how much he wanted her. And now she was dead. He put down his camera and bowed his head for a moment. When he raised it again Richard Mallory and the receptionist were gone.

• • •

"You awake?" Leonid whispered in bed next to Katrina.

It was early for him, only one-thirty. But she had been asleep for hours. He knew that.

In the old days she was always out past three and four. Sometimes she wouldn't come in till the sun was up—smelling of vodka, cigarettes, and men.

Maybe if he had left her and gone to Gert. Maybe Gert would still be alive.

"What?" Katrina said.

"You wanna talk?"

"It's almost two."

"Somebody I been working with the last ten years died tonight," Leonid said.

"Are you in trouble?"

"I'm sad."

For a few moments Leonid listened to her hard breath.

"Will you hold hands with me?" the detective asked his wife.

"My hands hurt," she said.

For a long time after that he lay on his back staring at the darkness before the ceiling. There was nothing he could think that did not damn him. There was nothing he had done that he could remember with pride.

Maybe an hour later Katrina said, "Are you still up?"

"Yeah."

"Do you have a life insurance policy? I'm just worried for the kids."

"I got better than that. I got a life insurance philosophy."

"What's that?" Katrina asked.

"As long as I'm worth more alive than dead I won't have to worry about banana peels and bad broth."

Katrina sighed and Leonid climbed out of the bed.

Just as he got to the small TV room Twill came in the front door.

"It's three in the morning, Twill," Leonid said.

"Sorry, Dad. But I got into this thing with the Torcelli sisters and Bingham. It was their parents' car so I had to wait until they were ready to go home. I told them that I was on probation but they didn't care—"

"You don't have to lie to me, boy. Come on, let's sit."

They sat across from each other over a low coffee table. Twill lit up a menthol cigarette and Leonid enjoyed the smoke secondhand.

Twill was thin and on the short side but he carried himself with understated self-importance. The bigger kids left him alone and the girls were always calling. His father, whoever he was, had some Negro in him. Leonid was grateful for that. Twill was the son he felt closest to.

"Somethin' wrong, Dad?"

"Why you ask that?"

" 'Cause you're not ridin' me. Somethin' happen?"

"An old friend died today."

"A guy?"

"No. A woman named Gert Longman."

"When's the funeral?"

"I, I don't know," Leonid said, realizing that he never wondered who would bury his ex-lover. Her parents were dead. Her two brothers were in prison.

"I'll go with you, Dad. Just tell me when it is and I'll cut school."

With that Twill got up and headed for his bedroom. At the door he stopped and turned.

"Hey, Dad."

"What?"

"What happened to the guy slammed you in the jaw?"

"They had to carry him out."

Twill gave the father of his heart a thumbs-up and then moved into the darkness of the doorway.

• • •

Leonid was at work at five. It was dark in Manhattan and in New Jersey across the river. He'd put twenty-five hundred dollars in Katrina's wallet, dropped the film off at Krome Addict Four Hour Developing Service, and bought an egg sandwich with Bermuda onions and American cheese. He didn't turn on the lights. As the morning wore on the dawn slowly invaded his room. The sky cleared and then opened—after a while it turned blue.

Carson Kitteridge came to the door a little before seven.

Leonid ushered him to the back office where they took their regular seats.

"Did you and Gertie have a fight, Leo?" the cop asked.

"No. Not really. I mean I might'a got a little fresh and she had to show me the door but I was sorry. I wanted to take her out to dinner. You're not dumb enough to think that I would have killed Gert?"

"If somebody gave me information that you were involved with John Wilkes Booth I'd take the time to check it out, Leon. That's just the kind of guy I think you are."

"Listen, man. I have never killed anybody. Never pulled a trigger, never ordered a job done. I didn't kill Gert."

"You called her," Kitteridge said. "You called her from that phone on your desk just about when she was getting killed. It speaks to your innocence but one wonders what you had to talk to her about at that hour, on that night? What were you apologizing for?"

"I told you—I got a little fresh."

"And here I thought you had a wife."

"Listen. She was my friend. I liked her—a lot. I don't know who did that to her but if I find out you can be sure that I'll let you know."

Kitteridge made a silent clapping gesture.

"Get the fuck out of my office," Leonid said.

"I have a few more questions."

"Ask 'em out in the hall." Leonid stood up from his chair. "I'm through with you."

The policeman waited a moment. Maybe he thought that

Leonid would sit back down. But as the seconds ticked by on the wall clock it began to dawn on him that Leonid's feelings were actually hurt.

"You're serious?" he asked.

"As a heart attack. Now get your ass outta here and come back with a warrant if you expect to talk to me again."

Kitteridge stood.

"I don't know what you're playing here, Leon," he said. "But you can't put out the law."

"But I can put out an asshole who doesn't have a warrant."

The lieutenant delayed another moment and then began to move.

Leonid followed him down the hall and to the door, which he slammed behind the lawman. He kicked another hole in the wall and marched back to his office, where his gut began to ache from whiskey and bile.

• • •

"Yes, Ms. Brown," Leonid was saying to his client on the telephone later that afternoon. "I have the photographs right here. It wasn't an older woman like you suspected."

"But it was a woman?"

"More like a girl."

"Is there any question about their, um . . . their relationship?"

"No. There's no doubt of the intimate nature of their relationship. What do you want me to do with these pictures and how will we settle accounts?"

"Can you bring them to me? To my apartment? I'll have the money you put out and there's one more thing that I'd like you to do."

"Sure I'll come by to you if that's what you want. What's the address?"

• • •

Karmen Brown lived on the sixth floor. He pressed the number she gave him, sixty-two, and found her waiting at the door.

The demure young thing had on a dark brown leather skirt that wouldn't keep her modest if she sat without crossing her legs. Her blouse had the top three buttons undone. She wasn't a large-breasted girl but what she had was mostly visible.

Her delicate features were serious but Leonid wouldn't have called her brokenhearted.

"Come in, Mr. McGill."

The apartment was small—like Gert's.

There was a table in the middle with a brown manila folder on it.

Leonid held a similar folder in his right hand.

"Sit down," Karmen said, gesturing toward a blue sofa.

In front of the couch was a small table holding up a decanter half-filled with an amber fluid and flanked by two squat glasses.

Leonid opened the folder and reached for the photographs he'd taken.

She held up a hand to stop him.

"Will you join me in a drink first?" the young siren asked.

"I think I will."

She poured and they both slugged back hard.

She poured again.

After three stiff drinks and with a new one in her glass Karmen said, "I loved him more than anything, you know."

"Really?" Leonid said, his eyes drifting between her cleavage and her crossed legs. "He seemed like kind of a loser to me."

"I would die for him," she said, gazing steadily into Leonid's eyes.

He brought out the dozen or so pictures.

"For this louse? He doesn't even respect you or her." Leonid felt the whiskey behind his eyes and under his tongue. "Look at him with his hand under her dress like that."

"Look at this," she replied.

Leonid looked up to see her ample mound of pubic hair. Karmen had pulled up her skirt, revealing that she wore nothing underneath.

"This is my revenge," she said. "You want it?"

"Yes, ma'am," Leonid answered, thinking that this was the other *thing* she wanted him to take care of.

He had been half-aroused since the last night he saw Gert. Not sexy but prey to a sexual hunger. The whiskey set that hunger free.

She got down on her knees on the blue sofa and Leonid dropped his pants. He didn't remember the last time he'd been that eager for sex. He felt like a teenager. But push as he would he couldn't press into her.

Finally she said, "Wait a minute, Daddy," and reached around to lubricate his erection with her own saliva.

After his first full thrust he knew he was going to come. He couldn't do anything about it.

"Do it, Daddy! Do it!" she cried.

Leonid thought about Gert, realizing at that moment that he had always loved her, and about Katrina who he was never good enough for. He thought about that poor child so much in love with her man that she had to have revenge on him by giving her love away to an overweight, middle-aged gumshoe.

All of that went through his mind but nothing could stand in the way of the pulsing rhythm. He was slamming against Karmen Brown's slender backside. She was yelling. He was yelling.

And then it was over—just like that. Leonid didn't even feel the ejaculation. It all blended into his violent, spasmodic attack.

Karmen had been thrown to the floor. She was crying.

He reached to help her up but she pulled away.

"Leave me alone," she said. "Let me go."

She was in a heap with her skirt up around her waist and the slick sheen of spit on her thighs.

Leonid pulled up his pants. He felt something like guilt about having had sex with the girl. She was only just a few years older than his wife's girl, the daughter of the Chinese jeweler.

"You owe me three hundred dollars," he said.

Maybe sometime in the future he'd tell someone that the best tail he ever had paid him three hundred dollars for the privilege.

"It's in the envelope on the table. There's a thousand dollars there. That and the ring and the bracelet he gave me. I want you to give them back to him. Take it and go. Go."

Leonid tore open the envelope. There he found the money, a ring with a large ruby in it, and a tennis bracelet lined with quarter-karat diamonds.

"What do you want me to tell him?" Leonid asked.

"You won't have to say a word."

Leonid wanted to say something but he didn't.

He went out the door, deciding to take the stairs rather than wait for the elevator.

On the first flight down he thought about Karmen Brown begging for sex and then crying so bitterly. On the third flight he started thinking about Gert. He wanted to reach out and touch her but she was gone.

On the first floor he passed a tattooed young man waiting at the elevator doors.

When Leonid glanced at the young man he looked away.

He was wearing leather gloves.

Leonid went out the door and turned westward.

He took four steps, five.

He made it all the way to the end of the block and it was then, when he had the urge to take off his jacket, because of the heat, that he wondered why somebody would be wearing leather gloves on a hot day. He thought about the tattoos and the image of a motorcycle came into his mind.

It had been parked right outside Karmen Brown's front door.

• • •

He pressed every buzzer on the wall until someone let him in. He was even ready to run up the stairs but the elevator was there and open.

On the ride he was trying to make sense out of it.

The doors slid open and he lurched toward Karmen's apartment.

The young man with the tattooed arms was coming out. He jumped back and reached for his pocket but Leonid leaped and hit him. The young man took the punch hard but he held on to the pistol. Leonid grabbed his hand and they embraced, performing an intricate dance that revolved around their strengths and that gun. When the kid wrenched the pistol from Leonid's hand the heavier man let his weight go dead and they fell to the floor. The gun went off.

Leonid felt a sharp pain at just about the place that his liver was situated. He leaped back from the motorcycle man, grabbing at his belly. There was blood on the lower half of his shirt.

"Shit!" he cried.

His mind went to November 1963. He was fifteen and devastated at the assassination of Kennedy. Then Oswald was shot by Ruby. Shot in the liver and in excruciating pain.

That's when Leo realized that his pain had passed. He turned toward his opponent and saw that he was lying on his back, gasping for air. And then, midgasp, he stopped breathing.

Realizing that the blood on him was the kid's, Leo stood up.

Karmen lay on the floor in the corner, naked. Her eyes were open and very, very bloodshot. Her throat was dark from strangulation.

But she wasn't dead.

When Leonid leaned over her those destroyed eyes recognized him. A deep gurgling went off in her throat and she tried to hit him. She croaked a loud inarticulate curse and actually sat up. The exertion was too much. She died in a sitting position, her head bowed over her knees.

There was no blood under her nails.

Why was she naked? Leonid wondered.

He went into the bathroom to check the tub—but it was dry.

He thought about calling the hospital but . . .

The kid had used a .22 caliber long-barrel pistol. Leonid was sure that it was the pistol Nora Parsons said that she lost seventeen years before.

In her wallet the dead girl's license had the name Lana Parsons.

It was then that Leonid felt the heat from her jewelry and cash in his own pocket.

The killer had a backpack. It contained two stamped envelopes. One was addressed to a lawyer named Mazer and the other to Nora Parsons in Montclair, New Jersey.

The letter to her mother included one of the photographs that Leonid had taken of Richard Mallory and his girlfriend.

Dear Mom,

While you were in the Bahamas with Richard last year I went to your house looking for anything that might have belonged to dad. You know that I loved him so much. I just thought you might have something I could remember him by.

I found a rusty old metal box in the garage. You still had the key in the hardware drawer. I guess it shouldn't surprise me that you hired a detective to prove that daddy was stealing from his company. He must have told you and you figured you could keep his money and your boyfriends while he was dying in prison.

I waited for a long time to figure out what to do about it. Finally I decided to use the man you used to kill daddy to break your heart. Here's a picture of your precious Richard and his real girlfriend. The boy you say you love. The boy you sent through college. What do you think about that?

And I took the report Leonid McGill made about daddy. I'm sending it to my lawyer. Maybe he can prove some kind of conspiracy. I'm sure you framed daddy and if the lawyer can prove it then maybe they'll send both of you to prison. Maybe even Mr. McGill would testify against you.

See you in court.

Your loving daughter,
Lana

To the lawyer she sent a yellowing and frayed report that Leonid had made many years before. It detailed how Nora's husband kept a secret account with money that he'd embezzled from a discretionary fund he controlled. Leonid remembered the meeting with Mrs. Parsons. She'd said that she couldn't trust a man who was a thief. Leo didn't argue. He was just there to collect his check.

Lana had included a copy of the letter to her mother in the lawyer's envelope. She asked him to help her get justice for her father.

Leonid washed his hands carefully and then removed any sign that he had been in the girl's apartment. He rubbed down every surface and the glass he drank from. He gathered the evidence he'd brought and the unmailed letters, then buttoned his coat over the bloody shirt and hurried away from the crime scene.

• • •

Twill was wearing a dark blue suit with a pale yellow shirt and maroon tie that had a wavering blue line orbiting its center. Leonid wondered where his son got such a fine suit but he didn't ask.

They were the only two in the small funeral parlor chapel where Gert Longman lay in an open pine coffin. She looked smaller than she had in life. Her stiff face seemed to be fashioned from wax.

The Wyant brothers fronted him fifty-five hundred dollars for the funeral. They gave him their preferential rate of two points a week.

Leonid lingered at the casket while Twill stood to the side—half a step behind him.

Behind the pair two rows of folding chairs sat like a mute crowd of spectators. The director had set the room for a service but Leonid didn't know if Gert was religious. Neither did he know any of her friends.

After the forty-five minutes they were allotted Twill and

Leonid left the Little Italy funeral home. They came out onto the bright sun shining on Mott Street.

"Hey, Leon," a voice called from behind them.

Twill turned but Leonid did not.

Carson Kitteridge, dressed in a dark gold suit, walked up.

"Lieutenant. You met my son Twill."

"Isn't it a school day, son?" the cop asked.

"Grief leave, Officer," Twill said easily. "Even prison lets up in cases like that."

"What you want, Carson?" Leonid said.

He looked up over the policeman's head. The sky was what Gert used to call blue-gorgeous. That was back in the days when they were still lovers.

"I thought that you might want to know about Mick Bright."

"Who?"

"We got an anonymous call five days ago," Carson said. "It was about a disturbance in an apartment building on the Upper East Side."

"Yeah?"

"When the officers got there they found a dead girl named Lana Parsons and this Mick Bright—also dead."

"Who killed 'em?" Leonid asked, measuring his breath.

"Looks like a rape and robbery. The kid was an addict. He knew the girl from the Performing Arts high school."

"But you said that he was dead too?"

"I did, didn't I? Best the detectives could tell the kid was high and fell on his own gun. It went off and nicked his heart."

While saying this Carson stared deeply into McGill's eyes.

Twill glanced at his father and then looked away.

"Stranger things have happened," Leonid said.

Leonid had long since realized that Lana found the pistol in her mother's metal box too. He knew why she'd killed Gert and had Bright kill her. She wanted to hurt him and then send him off to prison like he'd done to her father.

It was as good a frame as he would have thought up himself. The lawyer would make the letters available to the cops. Once they suspected Leonid they'd match his semen inside her. She would expect him to have kept the expensive jewelry. Robbery, rape, and murder and he would have been as innocent as Joe Haller.

I'd die for him, she'd said. She was talking about her father.

"I been knowing about the case for days," Kitteridge said. "The girl's name stuck in my head and then I remembered. Lana Parsons was the daughter of Nora Parsons. You ever hear of her?"

"Yeah. I brought her information about her husband. She was considering a divorce."

"That's right," Kitteridge said. "But he wasn't fooling around. He was embezzling money from their own company. They sent him to jail on the dirt you dug up."

"Yeah."

"He died in prison, didn't he?"

"I wouldn't know."

. . .

Leonid burned the letters Lana had intended to incriminate him.

His work for Lana's mother had driven the girl to murder and suicide. For a while he considered sending the photograph of Richard and his girlfriend to Lana's mother. At least he could accomplish one thing that she intended to do. But he decided against it. Why hurt Nora when he was just as guilty?

He kept the picture, though, in the top drawer of his desk.

The shot of Richard with his hand up under the receptionist's red dress, out on Park Avenue after a spicy Brazilian feast. Next to that he had placed an item from the *New York Post*. It was a thumbnail article about a prisoner on Ryker's Island named Joe Haller. He'd been arrested for robbery. While waiting to stand trial he hung himself in his cell.

DEAR PENTHOUSE FORUM (A FIRST DRAFT)

LAURA LIPPMAN

Y ou won't believe this, but this really did happen to me just last fall, and all because I was five minutes late, which seemed like a tragedy at the time. "It's only five minutes," that's what I kept telling the woman behind the counter, who couldn't be bothered to raise her gaze from her computer screen and make eye contact with me. Which is too bad, because I don't need much to be charming, but I need *something* to work with. Why did they make so many keystrokes, anyway, these ticket clerks? What's in the computer that makes them frown so? I had the printout for my E-ticket, and I kept shoving it across the counter, and she kept pushing it back to me with the tip of a pen, the way I used to do with my roommate Bruce's dirty underwear, when we were in college. I'd round it up with a hockey stick and stash it in the corner, just to make a pathway through our dorm room. Bruce was a Goddamn slob.

"I'm sorry," she said, stabbing that one key over and over. "There's just nothing I can do for you tonight."

"But I had a reservation. Andrew Sickert. Don't you have it?"

"Yes," she said, hissing the "s" in a wet, whistling way, like a middle-school girl with new braces. God, how did older men do it? I just can't see it, especially if it really is harder to get it up as you get older, not that I can see that either. But if it does get more difficult, wouldn't you need a *better* visual?

"I bought that ticket three weeks ago." Actually, it was two, but I was seeking any advantage, desperate to get on that plane.

"It says on your printout that it's not guaranteed if you're not at the gate thirty minutes ahead of departure." Her voice was oh-so-bored, the tone of a person who's just loving your pain. "We had an overbooked flight earlier in the evening and a dozen people were on the standby list. When you didn't check in by 9:25, we gave your seat away."

"But it's only 9:40 now and I don't have luggage. I could make it, if the security line isn't too long. Even if it's the last gate, I'd make it. I just have to get on that flight. I have . . . I have . . ." I could almost feel my imagination trying to stretch itself, jumping around inside my head, looking for something this woman would find worthy. "I have a wedding."

"You're getting married?"

"*No!*" She frowned at the reflexive shrillness in my voice. "I mean, no, of course not. If it were my wedding, I'd be there, like, a week ago. It's my, uh, brother's. I'm the best man."

The "uh" was unfortunate. "Is the wedding in Providence?"

"Boston, but it's easier to fly into Providence than Logan."

"And it's tomorrow, Friday?"

Shit, no one got married on Friday night. Even I knew that. "No, but there's the rehearsal dinner, and, you know, all that stuff."

More clicks. "I can get you on the 7:00 a.m. flight if you

promise to check in ninety minutes ahead of time. You'll be in Providence by 8:30. I have to think that's plenty of time. For the rehearsal and *stuff*. By the way, that flight is thirty-five dollars more."

"Okay," I said, pulling out a Visa card that was dangerously close to being maxed out, but I was reluctant to give up my cash, which I would need in abundance Friday night. "I guess that's enough time."

And now I had nothing but time to spend in the dullest airport, Baltimore-Washington International, in the dullest suburb, Linthicum, on the whole Eastern Seaboard. Going home was not an option. Light Rail had stopped running, and I couldn't afford the thirty-dollar cab fare back to North Baltimore. Besides, I had to be in line at 5:30 a.m. to guarantee my seat, and that meant getting up at four. If I stayed here, at least I couldn't miss my flight.

I wandered through the ticketing area, but it was dead, the counters all on the verge of closing down. I nursed a beer, but last call was 11:00 p.m., and I couldn't get to the stores and restaurants on the other side of the metal detectors because I didn't have a boarding pass. I stood by the stairs for a while, watching the people emerge from the terminals, their faces exhausted but happy because their journeys were over. It was almost as if there were two airports—"Departures," this ghost town where I was trapped, and "Arrivals," with people streaming out of the gates and onto the escalators, fighting for their baggage and then throwing themselves into the gridlocked lanes on the lower level, heading home, heading out. I should be doing the same thing myself, four-hundred-some miles away. My plane would be touching down by now, the guys would be looking for me, ready to go. I tried to call them, but my cell was dead. That was the kind of night I was having.

I stretched out on one of the padded benches opposite my ticket counter and essayed a little catnap, but some old guy was pushing a vacuum cleaner right next to my head, which seemed a little hostile. Still, I closed my eyes and tried not to think of what I was missing in Boston. The guys would probably be at a bar by now, kicking back some beers. At least I'd make it to the major festivities the next night. It hadn't been a complete lie, the wedding thing. I was going to a friend's bachelor party, even though I wasn't invited to the wedding proper, but that's just because there's bad blood between the bride and me. She tells Bruce I'm a moron, but the truth is we had a little thing, when they were sorta broken up junior year, and she's terrified I'm going to tell him. And, also, I think, because she liked it, enjoyed ol' Andy, who brought a lot more to the enterprise than Bruce ever could. I'm not slagging my friend, but I lived with the guy for four years. I know the hand he was dealt, physiologically.

Behind my closed eyes, I thought about that week two years ago, how she had come to my room when she knew Bruce was at work, and locked the door behind her, and, without any preamble, just got down on her knees, and—

"Are you stranded?"

I sat up with a start, feeling as if I had been caught at something, but luckily I wasn't too disarranged down there. There was a woman standing over me, older, somewhere between thirty and forty, in one of those no-nonsense suits and smoothed-back hairdos, toting a small rolling suitcase. From my low vantage point, I couldn't help noticing she had nice legs, at least from ankle to knee. But the overall effect was prim, preternaturally old-ladyish.

"Yeah. They overbooked my flight, and I can't get another one until morning, but home's too far."

"No one should have to sleep on a bench. A single night could throw your back out of alignment for life. Do you need money? You probably could get a room in one of the airport motels for as little as fifty dollars. The Sleep-Inn is cheap."

She fished a wallet out of her bag, and while I'm not strong on these kind of details, it looked like an expensive purse to me, and the billfold was thick with cash. Most of the time, I don't angst over money—I'm just twenty-three, getting started in the world, I'll make my bundle soon enough—but it was hard, looking at all those bills, and thinking about the gap between us. Why shouldn't I take fifty dollars? She clearly wouldn't feel it.

But, for some reason, I couldn't. "Naw. Because I'd never repay you. I mean, I *could*, I've got a job. But I know myself. I'll lose your address or something, never get it back to you."

She smiled, which transformed her features. Definitely between thirty and forty, but closer to the thirty end now that I studied her. Her eyes were gray, her mouth big and curvy, fuller on top than on the bottom, so her teeth poked out just a little. I go for that overbite thing. And the suit was a kind of camouflage, I realized, in a good way. Most women dress to hide their flaws, but a few use clothes to cover up their virtues. She was trying to hide her best qualities, but I could see the swells beneath her outfit—both on top, and in the back, where her ass rose up almost in defiance of the tailored jacket and straight skirt. You can't keep a good ass down.

"Don't be so gallant," she said. "I'm not offering a loan. I'm doing a good deed. I like to do good deeds."

"It just doesn't seem right." I don't know why I was so firm on this, but I think it was because she was basically sweet. I couldn't help thinking we'd meet again, and I wouldn't want to be remembered as the guy who took fifty dollars from her.

"Well—" that smile again, bigger this time. "We have a stand-off."

"Guess so. But you better get down to that taxi stand if you want to get home tonight. The line's twenty-deep." We glanced out the windows, down to the level below, which was just chaos. Up here, however, it was quiet and private, the man with the vacuum cleaner having finally moved on, the counters all closed.

"I'm lucky. I have my own car."

"I think the lucky person is the man who's waiting at home for you."

"Oh." She was flustered, which just made her sexier. "There's no one—I mean—well, I'm single."

"That's hard to believe." The automatic bullshit thing to say, yet I was sincere. How could someone like that ticket-clerk crone have a ring on her finger, while this woman was running around loose?

"It's a chicken-or-egg problem."

"Huh?"

"Am I single because I'm a workaholic, or am I a workaholic because I'm single?"

"Oh, that's easy. It's the first one. No contest."

Her faced seemed to light up and I swear I saw her eyes go filmy, as if she were about to cry. "That's the nicest thing anyone's ever said to me."

"You need to hang out with better people, then."

"Look—" She put her hand on mine, and it was cool and soft, the kind of hand that gets slathered in cream on a regular basis, the hand of a woman who's taking care of every part of herself. I knew she'd be waxed to a fine finish beneath that conservative little suit, with painted toenails and nothing but good smells. "I have a two-bedroom apartment on the south side of the city, just a few blocks from the big hotels. You can spend the night in my guest room, catch the first airport shuttle from the Hyatt at five. It's only fifteen dollars, and you'll get where you're going rested and unkinked."

Funny, but I felt protective of her. It was almost as if I were two people—a guy who wanted to keep her from a guy like me, the guy who wanted to get inside her apartment and rip that suit off, see what she was keeping from the rest of the world.

"I couldn't do that. That's an even bigger favor than giving me fifty dollars for a hotel room."

"I don't know. It seems to me there are ways you could pay me back, if you put your mind to it."

She didn't smile, or arch an eyebrow, or do a single thing with her face to acknowledge what she had just offered. She simply turned and began pulling her bag toward the sliding glass doors. But I was never more certain in my life that a woman wanted me. I got up, grabbed my own suitcase, and followed her, our wheels thrumming in unison. She led me to a black BMW in the short-term lot. Neither one of us said a word, we could barely look at each other, but I had her skirt halfway up her thigh even as she handed the parking lot attendant two bucks. He never even bothered to look down, just handed her the change, bored with his life. It's amazing what people don't see, but after all—people didn't see *her*, this amazing woman. Because she was small and modest, she passed through the world without acknowledgment. I was glad I hadn't made the mistake of not seeing what was there.

Her apartment was only twenty minutes away, and if it had been twenty-five, I think I would have made her pull over to the side of the road or risked bursting. I had her skirt above her waist now, yet she kept control of the car and leveled her eyes straight ahead, which just made me wilder for her. Once she parked, she didn't bother to pop the trunk, and by that time I wasn't too worried about my suitcase. I wasn't going to need any clothes until the morning. She ran up the stairs and I followed.

The apartment building was a little shabby, and in an iffier neighborhood than I expected, but those warehouse lofts usually are in odd parts of town. She pulled me into the dark living room and locked the door behind me, throwing on the dead bolt as if I might change my mind, but there was no risk of that. I didn't have the time or the inclination to take in my surroundings, although I did notice that the room was sparsely furnished—nothing more than a sofa, a desk with an open laptop, and this huge credenza of jars with gleaming gold tops, which looked sort of like those big things of peppers you see at some delis, although not quite the same. I couldn't help thinking it was a project of hers, that maybe they were vases distorted by the moonlight.

"You an artist?" I asked as she backed away and began pulling her clothes off, revealing a body that was even better than I had hoped.

"I'm in business."

"I mean, as a hobby?" I inclined my head toward the credenza, as I was trying to get my trousers off without tripping.

"I'm a pickler."

"What?" Not that I really cared about the answer, as I had my hands on her now. She let me kiss and touch what I could reach, then sank to her knees, as if all she cared about was pleasing me. Well, she had said she was into good deeds, and I had done pretty well by her in the car.

"A pickler," she said, her breath warm and moist. "I put up

fruits and vegetables and other things as well, so I can enjoy them all winter long." And then she stopped talking because she had—

. . .

Maureen stops, frowning at what she has written. Has she mastered the genre? This is her sixth letter, and while the pick-ups are getting easier, the prose is becoming harder. Part of the problem is that the men bring so little variation to their end of the bargain, forcing her to be ever more inventive about their lives and their missions. Even when they do tell her little pieces of their back stories, like this one, Andy, it's so boring, so banal. Late to the airport, a missed connection, not enough money to do anything but sleep on a bench, blah, blah, blah. Ah, but she doesn't have the luxury of picking them for material. She has to find the raw stuff and mold it to her needs.

So far, the editors of *Penthouse* haven't printed any of her letters—too much buildup, she supposes, which is like too much foreplay as far as she's concerned. Ah, but that's the difference between men and women, the unbridgeable gap. One wants seduction, the other wants action. It's why her scripts never sell, either. Too much buildup, too much narrative. And, frankly, she knows her sex scenes suck. Part of the problem is that in real life Maureen almost never completes the act she's trying to describe in her fiction; she's too eager to get to her favorite part. So, yes, she has her own foreplay issues.

No, she definitely has voice problems in this piece. Would a young man remember that whistling sound that braces make, or is she simply giving too much away about her own awkward years? Would a twenty-three-year-old man recognize an expensive purse? Or use the word "preternatural"? Also, she probably should be careful about being too factual.

The two-dollar parking fee—a more astute person, someone who didn't have his hand up a woman's skirt, fumbling around as if he's looking for spare change beneath a sofa cushion, might wonder why someone returning from a business trip paid for only an hour of parking. She should recast her apartment as well, make it more glamorous, the same way she upgraded her Nissan Sentra to a gleaming black BMW. Speaking of which, she needs to get the car to Wax Works, just in case, and change Andy's name in the subsequent drafts. She doesn't worry that homicide detectives read *Penthouse Forum* for clues to open cases, but they almost certainly read it. Meanwhile, his suitcase is gone, tossed in a Dumpster behind the Sleep-Inn near the airport, and Andy's long gone, too.

Well—she looks up at the row of gleaming jars, which she needs to lock away again behind the credenza's cupboards, but they're so pretty in the moonlight, almost like homemade lava lamps. Well, she reminds herself. *Most* of Andy is long gone.

RENDEZVOUS

NELSON DeMILLE

A s I learned in high school biology, the female of the species
is often more dangerous than the male. Maybe that was
true in the animal kingdom, I remember thinking, but
with human beings, the male was more dangerous.

I changed my mind about this when I crossed paths with a
very deadly lady with a rifle, who was intent on killing me and
everyone around me.

I was a young infantry officer doing a tour of duty in Vietnam in 1971–72. After a few months of combat, I mistakenly
volunteered for a crappy job. I found myself leading a ten-man
Long Range Reconnaissance Patrol, known as the Lurps.

I was near the end of my tour, with twelve patrols under my
belt, and all I could think about was getting home alive.

We were patrolling near the Laotian border west of Khe
Sanh, a hilly area of dense, semitropical rainforest broken up
now and then by expanses of head-high elephant grass and
bamboo thickets. The local population of indigenous Montag-

nard tribespeople had long since fled this free-fire zone for the safety of fortified compounds to the west.

I had the feeling—which was total illusion—that I and my nine men were the only human beings in this Godforsaken place. The reality was that there were thousands of enemy soldiers moving around us, but we hadn't seen them, and they hadn't seen us, which was the name of the game.

Our mission was not to engage the enemy, but to find and map the elusive Ho Chi Minh Trail—actually a network of narrow roads used by the enemy to infiltrate troops and supplies into South Vietnam. We were also to report such movements via radio so that American artillery, helicopter gunships, and fighter bombers could deliver appropriate disincentive to the enemy.

It was July, it was hot, humid, and buggy. Snakes and mosquitoes loved the weather. At night, we could hear the chattering of monkeys and the growl of tigers.

Long-range reconnaissance patrols usually lasted about two weeks. Beyond two weeks, the carried rations ran low and the patrol's nerve ran out. You can only take so much time in the jungle, deep in enemy-controlled territory, outnumbered by hostile forces, who could snuff out a ten-man patrol in a heartbeat if they discovered you.

We carried two radios—PRC-25s, called Prick Two Fives—so that we could keep in contact with our headquarters far, far away, to make reports, call in artillery or bombs, and ultimately arrange our extraction by helicopter when the mission was completed, or when the mission was compromised, i.e., if and when Charlie was breathing down our necks.

Radios sometimes fail. Or get damaged. Radio frequencies sometimes don't work. Sometimes Charlie is listening to you on *his* radio, so there is a contingency plan if the radios are no longer an option. There were three prearranged pickup sites marked on my terrain map, with three prearranged times of helicopter rendezvous. These are called Rendezvous Alpha, Bravo, and Charlie. If you don't see your helicopter at Alpha at the designated time, you move to Bravo, and if that meeting fails, you move to Charlie. If that fails, you move back to Alpha. Then you're on your own. And as our Viet friends say, *Xin Loi*. Good luck.

Things that caused a missed prearranged rendezvous were weather and enemy activity in the area. So far, the weather was clear, and we hadn't seen or heard the enemy. But he was there. We saw fresh ruts and footprints in the network of trails, and we came upon recently abandoned camps, and we smelled cooking fires at night. He was all around us, but he was invisible, and so, too, I hoped, were we.

That all changed on Day Ten.

We were patrolling an area that gave me some concern; it was a place that had once been lush woodland, but was now an expanse of napalm-charred tree trunks, compliments of the U.S. Air Force. Our job here was to report on the effects of the recent air strike, and I was trying to comprehend and evaluate what I was seeing: black ash, charred trucks, and dozens of grotesquely contorted and incinerated bodies, white teeth protruding from charcoal faces. We needed to do a vehicle and body count.

The problem with this place, other than the obvious, was that it offered little or no cover and concealment to me and my men.

I spoke in a whisper to my radio operator behind me, a guy named Alf Muller. "Radio." I put my hand out behind me to take the radiophone, but it wasn't slapped into my hand as it should have been.

I turned to see Alf lying facedown in the black ash, his radio strapped to his back and his arms thrown out from his sides, one hand holding the phone at the end of the wire.

It took me half a second to realize he'd been hit.

I yelled "Sniper!" and dove to the ground and did a roll in the ash with everyone else. We lay there, hoping to look like something inanimate among the blackened debris of the blasted earth.

Sniper. The scariest thing on the battlefield, where scary things abound. I hadn't heard the shot, and I wouldn't hear the next one either. Nor would I see the sniper even if I was still alive after the next shot. The sniper operates from a long distance—about a hundred or two hundred meters—and he has a very good rifle, equipped with a telescopic sight, a silencer, and a flash suppressor. He wears camouflage clothing and his face is blackened like the ash I was lying in. He is the Grim Reaper who harvests the living.

No one moved, because movement meant death.

There was no way to tell where the shot had come from, so we couldn't get behind something because we could actually be putting ourselves in the direct line of fire. We couldn't run because we could be running right toward the sniper.

I turned my head slowly toward Alf. His face lay in the ash, and there was no sign of breathing.

To the extent that I had any thoughts at all except terror, I wondered why the sniper had taken Alf, the radio man, rather than me; the guy next to the radio man is the officer or the sergeant, who is the prime target in combat, like taking out the quarterback. Strange. But I wasn't complaining.

There is no best thing to do in this situation, but the second best thing to do is nothing. My guys were trained, and they knew to keep their nerve and stay motionless. If the sniper fired again, and someone got hit—assuming we knew someone was hit—then we'd have no choice but to scatter and take a chance that the sniper could only hit so many moving targets before some of us were out of range.

I get paid to make decisions, so I decided that the sniper was too far off to hear us. I needed a head count, and I called out, "Dawson. Report."

My patrol sergeant, Phil Dawson, called back, "Landon is hit. He was moving, but I think he's dead."

The patrol medic, Peter Garcia, called out, "I'll try to get to him."

"No!" I shouted. "Stay put. Everyone report."

The men reported in order of their assigned patrol numbers. "Smitty here," then "Andolotti here," followed by "Johnson here," then after a few long seconds, Markowitz and Beatty reported.

Sergeant Dawson, whose job it is to count heads, reported to me, "Nine accounted for, Lieutenant. You got Muller with you?"

I called back, "Muller is dead."

"Shit," said Dawson.

So we had the two radio operators dead, which was not a coincidence. But it was puzzling.

I needed to get on the radio and ask for observation helicopters and gunships to form a ring of fire around us and maybe flush out the son of a bitch. I glanced toward Muller, who was about five feet from me. He had the radiophone in his right hand, which was farthest away from me.

Well, I thought, we could stay here and get picked off one by one, we could wait until sundown and hope the sniper didn't have a nightscope, or I could earn some of that extra combat pay. I had a thought, based on a year of this kind of crap, that the sniper was gone. I thought this because all this possum playing didn't amount to much, considering how exposed we were in this burned-out terrain. So, if the sniper was still there, he'd have taken a few more shots by now. I called out, "Report."

Everyone who was alive a few minutes ago was still alive.

I took a deep breath and rolled twice, then a third time over Alf's body and came to a motionless stop on top of his outstretched arm. I snatched the radiophone out of his stiffening fingers and put it to my ear, waiting for the shot that would blow my brains out. I squeezed the send button and said in the mouthpiece, "Royal Duck Six, this is Black Weasel." I released the send button, and I pressed the earpiece hard against my ear, but there was dead silence. I tried again, but there wasn't even a radio hum or the sound of breaking squelch coming through the earpiece. The radio was as dead as Alf Muller.

I waited for the impact of a bullet somewhere in my body. I could almost feel the hot steel tearing into me.

I waited. I got pissed off. I stood and called out to my patrol, "If I go down, you scatter!"

I stood there and nothing happened.

I ordered again, "Report."

The seven other survivors reported again.

I looked down at Alf Muller and saw now the bullet hole in his radio. I walked along the line of the patrol and saw my men lying in the black ash, their heads turning toward me, and some of them saying, "Get down, Lieutenant! You crazy?"

You get this sixth sense that it's not your turn that day, that you're okay now, that fate has spared you for something worse later.

I found Landon facedown like Muller, and like Muller there was a single hole in the top of his radio. The battery is in the bottom; the guts are in the top. The sniper knew that and was able to put a single round through the electronics and into the spine of both radio operators.

What I didn't understand was why the sniper didn't take out at least a few other guys. He certainly had the time, had the range, had a clear field of fire, and obviously was a good shot.

Actually, I knew the answer. This guy was playing with us. There was no other reason for his actions. A little psychological warfare, played with a deadly rifle instead of propaganda leaflets or Radio Hanoi broadcasts. A message to the Americans. And the game wasn't over.

Snipers think and act differently from normal people, and our own snipers, some of whom I'd met, liked to play games, too. It gets boring waiting for hours or days or weeks for a target. The sniper's mind does weird things during the long, lonely waits, so when a target finally shows up in the telescopic lens, the sniper becomes a comedian and does funny things. Funny to them, not to the targets. An American sniper once told me he'd shot the hashish pipe out of an enemy soldier's mouth.

I thought about sharing these thoughts with my men, but if they hadn't figured it out already, then they didn't need to know, or they'd know soon enough.

Decision time. I said, "Okay, we've got to leave these guys for a body recovery detail. Strip the bodies, and let's get moving."

There wasn't a lot of enthusiastic movement until finally Sergeant Dawson stood and said, "You heard the lieutenant. Move it!"

Everyone got up slowly, heads and eyes darting around like cornered prey. The men stripped the bodies of the two dead radio operators, removing anything that could be of use to the enemy: rifles, ammo, canteens, dog tags, rations, compasses, boots, rucksacks, and so forth.

Dawson asked me, "How about the radios?"

"Let's take them," I replied. "Maybe we can make one good radio out of two."

We moved quickly out of the deforested area and into a thick growth of bamboo that offered some concealment, but gave us away by the movement of the tall, leafy shoots as we macheteed and moved our way through.

We spent the night in the bamboo, forming a defensive perimeter, and we allowed ourselves the belief that we'd shaken the sniper.

A few of the guys tried to make one live radio out of two dead ones, but the guys who knew about radios were six kilometers back and not in a position to help.

By dawn, we'd given up on the radios, and we buried them with our entrenching tools so as not to give anything up to the enemy.

We hadn't been able to call in our situation report during the night, so now our boss, Colonel Hayes, also known as Royal Duck Six, knew that his patrol, known as Black Weasel, had a problem. A radio problem, he was thinking, or maybe a got-captured problem, or a got-killed problem. These things happen with long-range recon patrols. One minute you're there, and the next you're gone forever.

We saddled up and moved toward the grid coordinates on the map that was Rendezvous Alpha.

We got out of the bamboo and into a nice thick growth of forest. We came to a rocky stream that we had to cross and we halted. Streambeds are like shooting galleries. Dawson volunteered to go first, and he bolted across the knee-high stream and scrambled up the opposite bank, dropping into a prone firing position, sweeping his M-16 rifle up and down the stream.

Two riflemen, Smitty and Johnson, went next and made it to the far side. Next, the medic, Garcia, carrying his big medical bag on his back, charged through the stream and was helped up by the other guys. The guy who carried the grenade launcher, Beatty, took a deep breath and moved so fast I thought he was walking on water. Another rifleman, Andolotti, waited five seconds, then ran so fast he almost caught up with Beatty.

Markowitz and I were left on the stream bank, and I said to him, "Your call."

He smiled and said to me, "He's waiting for *you*, Lieutenant. Your call."

I replied, "I'll bring up the rear. Good luck."

Markowitz said, "See you on the other side." He charged into the stream and about halfway across, he slipped and fell. I waited for him to get up and get going, but he didn't seem able to get his footing. Then I saw the water turning dark around him. He fell again and lay there, submerged, but still moving.

"Sniper!"

Garcia, the medic, and I charged simultaneously from opposite stream banks toward Markowitz. The guys on the far bank opened up with automatic weapon fire, raking and blasting the tree lines up and down the stream.

Garcia and I reached Markowitz at the same time, and we each grabbed an arm and dragged him as we ran toward the far bank. I glanced at the wounded man and saw white frothy blood running from his mouth.

We were about four meters from the trees growing along the bank when Markowitz's wrist jerked out of my hand. I turned and saw Garcia lying faceup in the rocky stream, a huge gaping hole in the left side of his head, meaning an exit wound, meaning the shot had come from the right.

I dropped face-first into the stream and scrambled to a small rock that gave me a little cover if I got real small.

I looked upstream in the direction the shot had come from, not expecting to see anything, but there, on a jutting bend in the stream about a hundred meters away, was a black-clad guy kneeling among the rocks. I stared, and the guy seemed to be staring back. From where my men were in the scrub brush, they couldn't see what I could see from the stream.

Slowly, I took my field glasses from their case and focused on the guy. He didn't seem to have a rifle, which was good, and he was wearing the traditional Vietnamese black silk pajamas. I focused in tighter and saw that it wasn't a guy; it was a woman with long black hair. A young woman, maybe early twenties, with high cheekbones and big unblinking eyes, looking right at me.

I had two totally contradictory thoughts: This was the sniper; this couldn't be the sniper. Just to be on the safe side, I unslung my rifle, but before I got it into a firing position, she shook her head and stood. I could now see a rifle in her hand, a long gun, probably a Russian Draganov sniper rifle, mounted with a telescopic lens.

I stared at her through my field glasses, and I knew if I moved myself or my rifle, that Draganov would be in both her hands, and I'd be dead. She had the range, as Markowitz or Garcia would attest to if they could, and she damned sure knew how to shoot.

The guys on the stream bank were still firing blindly, and through the fire I could hear them yelling at me, "Come on, Lieutenant! Get out of there! We got to get the hell out of here! Come on, come on!"

I looked one more time at the woman standing on the high bend in the stream, and she seemed very nonchalant. Maybe she was disappointed that we weren't much of a challenge to her.

I stared at her. She held up her hand with four fingers extended, then clenched her fist and pointed at me. My blood ran cold. She turned and disappeared into the brush behind her.

I jumped to my feet and ran through the stream and up the muddy bank, pulled along by outstretched hands into the brush.

I gasped, "Sniper! I saw her! Upstream. Let's go!" I began running on a path parallel to the winding stream toward where I'd last seen her.

Dawson ran up behind me and jerked me back by my rucksack. He said in a loud whisper, "What the hell are you talking about?"

"I saw her! It's a woman! She's upstream. About a hundred meters."

The other four guys caught up to us, and I explained quickly what I'd seen. I must have sounded a little nuts or something because they kept shooting glances at each other. Finally, they got it.

As I said, they're pros, and a pro's instinct for survival doesn't mean running away; it means running toward what's trying to kill you so you can kill it first.

In any case, we needed to run because we'd given away our positions with all that firing, and we were deep in enemy territory, so when you fire, you've got to get the hell away fast.

No one likes leaving dead guys behind, but this wasn't regular combat stuff where you recover dead and wounded at all costs; this was long-range recon and getting left behind is definitely a possibility.

We ran about a hundred meters along the path, and Andolotti called out, "We could be running right into an ambush."

Dawson replied through heavy breaths, "I'd rather do that than get picked off later. Move it!"

We came to the bend in the stream, and I ran out to the edge of the bank where I saw a brass cartridge sparkling in the sunlight. I picked it up and saw it was a 7.62 millimeter, most probably from a Draganov. I didn't need evidence, but somehow finding the cartridge made me more certain that I hadn't been hallucinating. I put the cartridge in my pocket.

We moved quickly back to the path, where we saw a few footprints in the damp soil. Reluctantly, but with the knowledge that it was her or us, we pressed on.

We moved at a half trot for about an hour, but by then, we knew we weren't going to find her. She would find us.

We'd been moving away from Rendezvous Alpha, which we could make in the three days left before our dawn rendezvous time, if nothing went wrong.

You never go back on the trail you took in, so we headed into the woods and chopped our way through brush until we intersected a trail that headed in the general direction we needed to go.

We moved as quickly as we could, but the heat and fatigue, and fifty pounds of gear, was slowing us down.

We took a few minutes' break every hour and pushed on until dusk, not saying much, but I'm sure everyone, myself included, was thinking about why the lady hadn't blown me out of the water. I had a few answers to that, and it had less to do with a sudden feeling of compassion on her part and more to do with fucking with our heads.

The sun had sunk into Laos, and the enemy moves at night.

We heard trucks and tanks rumbling somewhere to our right, then heard men chatting and laughing not far away. If I'd had a radio, I would have called in artillery on them. Actually, if I'd had a radio, I would have called in choppers to get us the hell out of there right after Muller and Landon got hit. But the lady had left us mute and deaf to the outside world.

We moved more quickly away from the enemy troop movements and about an hour later, we found a small hill covered with tall elephant grass where we set up a defensive perimeter, for what it was worth. We were six lightly armed guys, surrounded by massive numbers of enemy troops. Plus, one sniper, who knew we were there, but who wanted to keep us for herself.

We ate some dehydrated rations reconstituted in their pouches with tepid canteen water. No one said much.

About midnight, we took turns sleeping and keeping watch; two up, four down. But no one slept much. Near dawn, I was on guard duty with Sergeant Dawson, an old guy at thirty, who was on his second tour, and probably his last.

He said to me in a quiet voice, "You sure it was a woman?"

I nodded and grunted.

"You sure? You saw tits and stuff?"

I almost laughed. I replied, "I saw her in my field glasses. It was a woman." I added, "They make good snipers."

He nodded. "Had one in Quang Tri once. Killed four guys before we blew the shit out of her with rockets." He added, "We found her head."

I didn't reply.

He asked the obvious. "Why didn't she nail you?"

"Don't know."

"Maybe it's like . . . maybe there's a two-guy-a-day limit on her hunting permit."

"Not funny."

"No. Not funny." He asked, "You think we gave her the slip?"

"No."

"Me neither."

And that was the end of the conversation.

• • •

We moved out at first light and headed south toward Rendezvous Alpha.

About noon, we got to believing that we might make it. There were no more big streams to cross, just a few little brooks that were choked with good covering brush, and there were no open areas on the map that we couldn't avoid. But then we noticed that the trees and the brush started to look a little sick, and within half an hour, we realized we were in an Agent Orange defoliated area that wasn't marked on the map.

Pretty soon we were moving through a dead zone of bare trees and brown, withered brush that offered no concealment. Dawson said, "Lieutenant, we got to go back and around this defoliation."

I replied, "We don't know how big the area is. It might be a full day detour, then we're not going to get to Alpha."

He nodded and looked around. He said, "At least Charlie ain't around here. They don't like the defoliated areas."

"Neither do I."

We took a break, spread out, and got down, as per standard operating procedure when a patrol is stopped.

Smitty pulled a jungle bar out of his packet and bit off a piece of the chalky, so-called chocolate. He said, "That bitch." Meaning the sniper, of course. "That bitch could have wasted us all back there in that napalm area. She could've wasted at least you, Lieutenant, back at the stream, and maybe a few more of us. What's her fucking game?"

I didn't reply, and neither did anyone else.

I was getting a bad feeling about this place, so I stood, put on my rucksack, and said, "Saddle up and move out."

Everyone stood, and Andolotti unzipped his fly and said, "Hold up. Gotta take a quick piss."

About midstream, he pitched backward and landed with a thump on his back, still holding his thing, which was still streaming yellow piss.

We all hit the ground and lay frozen on the dead, chemical-smelling earth.

I called out, "Andolotti!"

No reply. I turned my head and eyes toward him. His chest was heaving, and I saw blood around his mouth. He gave a final heave and lay still.

From the way he'd been thrown backward, I knew he'd been hit square in the chest, so I knew where the shot had come from. Through the dead vegetation, I could see a slight rise in the land about a hundred meters due west. I called out, "Follow my tracers!" I took aim from my prone position and fired a long burst toward the rise. Every sixth round was a red, streaking tracer that looked like a laser beam pointing toward the suspected target.

Dawson, Smitty, and Johnson joined in with long bursts of M-16 fire, and we raked the hill, while Beatty, who had the grenade launcher, popped three phosphorous grenades at the hill, setting the dead vegetation ablaze.

I shouted, "Outta here!"

We moved back quickly in a crouch, firing to cover our retreat.

Beatty slipped another phosphorous round in his grenade

launcher and was about to get off a hip shot when the launcher flew out of his hands, and he went backward like he'd been hit by a truck.

Dawson yelled, "Beatty's hit!"

I shouted, "Move back! Move back!"

I was about ten meters from Beatty, and I could see he was still alive. I hit the ground and started crawling toward him, then saw his body jerk in three quick movements. A fourth shot hit his grenade launcher and a fifth shot threw dirt in my face. I got the message and got the hell out of there.

I joined up with Dawson, Smitty, and Johnson. We ran like hell until we came upon a dry gulley, which we dropped into. We moved in a crouch through the gulley for a few hundred meters until I gave the order to stop. This wasn't the direction we needed to go, so I ordered everyone out of the gulley, and we moved quickly due south, toward our rendezvous point, which was still about thirty kilometers away.

We got out of the defoliated area and entered a place that had been carpet-bombed by B-52s. The forest had been blasted to splinters by the five-hundred- and one-thousand-pound bombs, and craters as big as a house dotted the landscape.

All around us were twisted pieces of steel, almost unrecognizable as once being vehicles. Pieces of rotting corpses lay everywhere, and the surviving trees were draped with body parts. Some sort of carrion-eating birds were feasting and barely noticed us.

The sun was sinking, and we were near the end of our physical limits and our mental endurance, so I ordered everyone into a bomb crater. We lay along the sloping earth walls of the crater, caught our breaths, and drank from our canteens. The place stank of rotting flesh.

Dawson grabbed an arm and flung it out of the crater, and

then made the standard joke and said, "So, we count the arms and legs, divide by four, and we got a body count."

No one laughed.

He finished a canteen of water and informed us, "Two bad things about bomb strike zones. One, Charlie comes looking for salvage and pieces of people to bury. Two, the B-52s sometimes come back to the same place to get the guys looking for stuff." He added, unnecessarily, "We gotta get outta here."

I agreed and said, "Take five, then we move." I took out my map and studied it.

Smitty said to me, "Hey, Lieutenant, why's she always missing *you*?"

I didn't reply.

Johnson asked me, "You think she's still on us?"

I kept looking at the map and replied, "Assume she is."

I climbed to the rim of the crater and looked through my field glasses. I swept the area in a 360-degree circle, pausing every ten degrees to focus on any possible movement, any glint of metal, or a wisp of smoke, or anything that didn't look like it belonged in its surroundings.

I was a sitting duck, but I'd developed a fatalistic attitude in the last few days; she was saving me for last.

She'd get Smitty and Johnson in whatever order she wanted, then Sergeant Dawson, whom she had identified as a leader, then me.

I pictured her stalking us, like a big cat, slow and patient, then she struck. The survivors ran, and she ran after us. She was very fast, sure-footed, and quiet, and she knew just how close she could get without getting too close. The chances of us setting up an ambush were not good. All we could do now was run.

I slid back down into the crater and said, "Looks clear." I

checked my watch. "Thirty minutes until dark." I unfolded my map and studied it in the dim light. I said, "Okay, if we hustle, we can do five kilometers before dark and that will bring us to a rock slide area where we can spend the night."

Everyone nodded. Rocky areas were like natural fortifications, giving both cover and concealment, and usually good fields of fire. An added bonus was that Charlie avoided open rocky terrain because of our scout choppers so we weren't going to meet him there. And with luck, our guys might see us from the air.

The one downside was the lady with the gun. She had a map, or she knew the terrain, and she was smart enough to know where we'd be heading. Even if we'd lost her, she could guess where to find us. I mentioned this privately to Dawson.

He replied, "Maybe you're giving her too much credit."

"Maybe you're not."

He shrugged. "I like rocks around me, and I like choppers overhead who can see us and get us the fuck out of here."

"Okay . . . saddle up."

Everyone slipped on their rucksacks and in ten-second intervals, we climbed out of the crater at different points and assembled quickly on the south side of the hole, then began double-timing away from the bomb-blasted area.

A half-hour later, the ground began to rise, and flat white rocks stuck out of the damp brush-choked earth, like steps leading to an ancient jungle-covered temple.

Ten minutes later, we were in a rock slide area with sparse vegetation. To the west were high hills and a ridgeline that had collapsed some time ago and created the rock field.

We found a high point surrounded by good-sized slabs of stone and set up a small, tight defensive perimeter. Truly, you could hold off an army from here if you had enough food, water, and ammunition. We had extra food, water, and ammo, thanks to Muller and Landon.

We settled in for a long night. We couldn't light cigarettes, and we couldn't light heat tabs to boil water for the dehydrated rations. So we mixed the stuff with canteen water and Dawson and Johnson, who were smokers, got their fix by chewing the tobacco from their cigarettes.

About midnight, I took the first watch, and the other three guys slept.

I took my starlight scope from my rucksack and scanned the higher ground to the west where the ridgeline ended. The starlight scope is battery-powered, and it gives you a green-tinted picture by amplifying the ambient light of stars and moon.

I noticed a small waterfall cascading over the rocky ledge a hundred meters away. Then I saw a movement, and I focused tightly and held my elbows steady on the flat rock in front of me.

She was crouched on an outcropping beside the waterfall, and she was easy to see because she was completely naked. She was drinking from cupped hands, then moved closer to the waterfall, and let the cascading stream run over her body as she ran her hands through her hair, then down her sides and legs, then back up to her rear end, then her crotch.

I stared, transfixed at the sight. It was very sensual out of the context, but within the context it was grotesque, like watching a tiger languidly licking itself after a meal.

I reached behind me and pulled my M-16 rifle onto the rock, took one last look, then brought the starlight scope and rifle together. By feel, as I'd been taught, I mounted the scope on the rifle and took aim.

She was still there, and she had put her right foot under the stream of falling water and kept it there for a few seconds before switching to her other foot.

The four-power starlight scope made her look twenty-five meters away, but the actual distance of a hundred meters was a stretch for the M-16 rifle, which is made to spray bullets at shorter ranges.

I put her in my crosshairs and steadied my aim. I was only going to get one shot. A very loud shot, since I didn't have a silencer. Hit or miss, we'd have to get the hell out of there.

She turned from the waterfall, and I could tell she was slipping her feet into her sandals. She stood there full frontal nude, my crosshairs over her heart.

For some reason, I needed to look at her face again, to commit it to memory, to burn it into my mind. I looked slightly over the crosshairs at her face and saw that same disinterested, faraway look that I'd seen on the stream bank.

She reached back and brought her long black hair over her right shoulder and squeezed the water from it.

I focused again between her breasts and squeezed the trigger, just as she bent over to gather her black pajamas.

The blast of the rifle sounded very loud in the quiet night, and the report echoed through the stones. Night birds and animals started squawking, and the three guys behind me were on their feet before the sound of the shot faded into the distant hills.

I took a last look, but she was gone.

Dawson said excitedly, "What the hell—?"

"Her."

Smitty said, "Holy shit!"

Johnson asked, "You get her?"

"Maybe . . ."

"*Maybe?*" Dawson said. "*Maybe?* Maybe we should get the fuck out of here."

"Right. Saddle up."

We gathered our gear, and because we slept with our boots on, we were ready to move within a minute.

I led the way down the south slope of the rock field. The going was slow and treacherous in the dark. A sliver of moon dimly illuminated the white rocks, and also illuminated us. I didn't hear the shot because it was silenced, but I heard the ping of a ricochet against a nearby rock.

We hit the ground, then got into a low crouch and stumbled along, zigzagging, dropping, rolling, doing everything to make ourselves a difficult target.

Another shot ricocheted somewhere to our right, then another and another. I pictured her kneeling naked behind something, focused through her sniper scope, looking for movement and moon shadows, trying to guess our line of movement, and now and then popping off a round from her Russian rifle just to let us know she was thinking of us.

We came to a place where the rock slide entered a tree line, and we ran at full speed into the concealment of the forest.

I took the lead, and we moved as quickly as we could through the pitch-black woods.

We came to a wide trail over which a great many tires, tank treads, and rubber sandals had passed recently. Counterintuitively, I turned in the direction of the enemy troop movement, and we followed the trail south.

About an hour later, I could hear the throaty sound of a big diesel engine up ahead, and the clank of tank treads.

We slowed to a walk and followed at a distance, hoping they didn't stop for an unexpected break.

We traveled through the night, following the enemy army,

who kept up a moderate pace. Before dawn, I knew, those vehicles and men would scatter into the jungle to hide from our aircraft and helicopters. We needed to make a detour around their day camp so I led my patrol east through the forest. We found a trickling brook that flowed down from the hills toward the coast, and we followed it for an hour, then cut south again, hoping to skirt around the bad guys, who were by now scattering into the triple-canopy forest.

At dawn, we stopped in a bamboo thicket and rested. In fact, we were so exhausted, we just lay where we stopped and fell asleep among the bamboo and the bamboo vipers.

• • •

The midmorning sun and heat woke me, and I sat up, sweat running from my face and neck.

Sergeant Dawson was also awake and was drinking what looked like instant coffee from his canteen cup. He asked me, "How'd you miss her? And why'd you shoot?"

I replied, "I missed because I missed, and I shot because I made the decision to shoot. You got a problem with that?"

He shrugged.

I studied my terrain map, and Dawson asked me, "How far are we from Alpha?"

I put the map away and said, "I don't know where we are, so I don't know where Alpha is."

He didn't like that answer, so I said, "When we get moving, I'll find some terrain features and locate us. Don't worry about it, Sergeant."

"Yes, sir."

You need to establish who's in control if you're going to survive, so I said, "Get the men up and moving. Eat on the march. We've been here long enough."

"Yes, sir."

Sergeant Dawson got Smitty and Johnson up and within a minute, we were moving south through the bamboo, which gave way to scattered trees, then a thick subtropical growth of palm brush that cut our arms, hands, and faces.

Within an hour, I was able to locate us on the map, and I announced, "Rendezvous Alpha is about twenty kilometers south and west. We won't make it in the daylight, but we need to be there for our 0600 hours rendezvous."

Everyone nodded, if not enthusiastically, then at least with a little optimism. One more day and night of hell, and by first light, we'd be on the magic carpet, and half an hour later, we'd be in base camp on the coast, showering, eating real eggs and bacon, and getting debriefed, not necessarily in that order. Maybe all at once, if I had my way.

I had exactly twenty-nine days to go in this shithole, and by custom, you didn't go out on patrol with less than thirty to go. This was my last patrol, one way or the other.

We moved into a triple-canopy jungle where the lack of sunlight kept the brush at a minimum, and we should have been able to make good time, but we were barely able to put one foot in front of the other. We all had heat rash, crotch rot, jungle sores, festering cuts, and foot blisters big as onions. I had the sense that we were making barely two kilometers an hour.

It got darker in the triple canopy long before sunset and by 1900 hours, when it should have still been light, it was getting murky, though now and then sunlight would slant in from the west.

We pushed on, me, Sergeant Dawson, Smitty, and Johnson, the survivors of the radioless patrol known by the radio call sign of Black Weasel. We'd located troop movements, but were unable to report them. We'd evaded large numbers of the enemy, but couldn't evade a single woman who'd taken an obsessive interest in us. If, in fact, I found myself eating scrambled eggs while being debriefed by Royal Duck and the intelligence types, all I could think to say was that they'd better send a good antisniper team in before they sent anyone else. And don't be surprised if you never hear from the first couple of teams that go in.

We moved into a long patch of sunlight that was contrasted with a dark shadowy area up ahead, and my senses went into high gear. I was about to say, "Spread out and find shadow," when a movement up ahead caught my eye.

Even with her flash suppressor, I saw the spit of fire high up in the triple-canopy jungle, not more than seventy-five meters away. Johnson let out a loud grunt behind me, and I heard him hit the ground.

I dropped into a kneeling firing position and emptied a full magazine where I'd seen the muzzle flash.

As I was firing at where she was supposed to be, I caught another movement to my left and turned. I was aware of a long vine swinging in an arc back toward where I was spraying bullets. She wasn't on the vine, but she'd been on the vine and was now in a tree somewhere to my left.

Dawson and Smitty had been firing bursts where I'd directed my fire, and before I could shift my fire to where I thought she'd ridden the swinging vine, Smitty screamed out in pain, then stood, stumbled a few feet, and collapsed facedown. I saw his body jerk like he'd been hit again.

I shifted my fire to where I guessed she was, but Dawson kept firing at her last location, and I shouted to him, "Monkey vine!"

He got it and shifted his fire to intersect mine. Red tracers sliced through the jungle canopy, and leaves, branches, and palm fronds fell to the ground.

We backed out in a crouch, firing as we went, and regrouped about fifty meters back down the trail, then scrambled into a thicket of brush.

Dawson was visibly shaken for the first time since I'd known him. He kept saying, "Jesus Christ. Oh, God. Oh, God."

I said, "Quiet."

He sank cross-legged on the ground, then began rocking back and forth, mumbling something.

I said softly, "Get it together, Sergeant. Get it together now."

He didn't seem to hear me, then suddenly he brightened and said, "We got her. I know we got her. I saw her fall. We wasted that bitch."

I didn't think so, but it was a nice thought.

I said, "Get up."

He stood.

"Follow me."

I led us a hundred meters away, found another thicket of brush and said, "We stay here until midnight, then we move toward our rendezvous. Understand?"

He nodded.

We sat very still until dark, then drank some water and ate a few cookies from home that we'd found on Landon's body.

Sergeant Dawson had gotten himself under control and to make up for the lapse of cool, he said, "Let's go out and get her. You got the starlight scope. She don't have a nightscope. Right? We can see in the dark, she can't."

I listened, as though I was considering this insanity, then I replied thoughtfully, "I think our best course of action is to stay put for now. I think I can find Alpha from here even in the dark. If we go out after her, we'll get disoriented and miss our rendezvous. What do you think?"

He pretended to think about this, then nodded. "Yeah. We need to get back and report what happened. They need to get some antisnipers on this bitch."

"Right. Let the pros handle it."

"Yeah . . ."

"We can go along and give them some tips."

He didn't reply for a while, then said quietly, "We're not going to make it, Lieutenant. You understand? She's too good. She's not gonna let us make it."

I stayed silent for a while, then gave him some good news and some bad news that I knew I'd be sharing with him eventually. I said, "One of us is going to make it. She wants one of us, the patrol leader, me, or the patrol sergeant, you, to go back and tell them about her. Otherwise, all her fucking bullshit was for nothing. She could have wasted all of us at any point since day one, but she didn't. She made us piss our pants, tighten our assholes, sweat cold and run hot. She risked her own life to wow the shit out of us, and she didn't do that for a totally dead audience. One of us—you or me—is going to get on that chopper at dawn. And if it's you, I want you to report very accurately and very professionally what happened here. And you make sure you make the dead look good and bring honor on them. Then you—or me—volunteers to come back here and settle the score. Understand?"

He didn't reply for a long time, then said, "I understand."

"Good." I put out my hand, and we shook.

• • •

We moved through the night, and I navigated as best I could, using my compass and keeping track of our paces.

An hour before dawn, the land sloped steeply downward, and I knew we were in the vicinity of Rendezvous Alpha, which was a bowl-shaped depression about a kilometer across, thick with elephant grass.

We had less than twenty minutes to get to the approximate center of this place, and it should be easy, if we just kept going downhill until we started going uphill. Very simple, said Royal Duck. How can you miss the bottom of a bowl, even in the dark?

I looked at the luminescent glow of my watch. It was a few minutes to 0600 hours, and I didn't hear a chopper, and I didn't know if I was at the very bottom of this depression.

Normally, it wouldn't matter if we were even a hundred meters off because we could use a signaling mirror, or pop a smoke canister as a last resort. But the geniuses who picked this place hadn't taken into account the morning ground mist that had settled in the depression. The good news was that the lady with the gun, if she was anywhere on the rim of this depression, couldn't see us. We might both make it out.

Somewhere above the mist, the sun was rising and from the air, the terrain would be light enough for the choppers to find this bowl of pea soup.

Dawson and I decided we'd gotten to a place where the terrain was rising on all sides, so we stopped and listened for the beating chopper blades, which we hoped we could hear over our heavy breathing.

We waited. It was ten minutes after rendezvous time, but that wasn't a worry. The chopper pilots were always wary about these pickups in the middle of nowhere, and they tended to dally and recon a lot. There would be two Hueys to pick up ten men, though there were only two of us, and there'd be two or more Cobra gunships flying cover. If they drew fire, they'd try to suppress the fire, and sometimes they'd come in under fire. But not always.

It was now fifteen minutes past rendezvous time, and Dawson said, "They're not coming. They didn't hear from us, so they're not coming."

I replied, "We're here at the prearranged spot *because* they didn't hear from us."

"Yeah, but—"

"They're not going to leave us."

"Yeah, I know . . . but . . . maybe we're in the wrong place."

"I can read a fucking map."

"Yeah? Let me see the map."

I gave him the map, and he looked at it intently. Sergeant Dawson had a lot of good skills, but land navigation was not one of them.

He said, "Maybe we should go on to Bravo."

"Why?"

"Maybe the choppers saw gooks on the ground."

"Unless they're getting shot at, they're coming in. Take it easy."

We waited. Dawson asked, "You think she's out there?"

"We'll find out."

We waited and we listened. At 0630 hours, we heard the distinct beating of helicopter blades against the cool morning air. We looked at each other, and for the first time in a long time, we managed a smile.

We could hear the choppers get closer, and I knew the pilots were worried about putting down in a mist-shrouded area where they couldn't see the ground. But they'd been briefed that it was elephant grass, easy landing, and the downdraft would clear the mist for them. Still, we had no radio contact so they wouldn't know who was waiting for them on the ground.

I thought about popping a green smoke canister, which meant all clear, or a yellow that meant caution. That would tell them we were waiting, although it would also announce our presence to people who didn't need to know we were there.

Dawson said, "I'm gonna pop smoke. Pick a flavor."

"Wait. They need to get closer. They don't want more than three minutes between smoke and pickup, or they get pissed off and go home."

I listened to the approaching choppers, counted to sixty, then popped a yellow smoke canister. The billowy plume sat on the ground in the damp, windless air, then began to rise into the mist. At some point, it must have broken through the top of the gray fog because very quickly the sound of the choppers got very loud. A few seconds later, I could see a huge shadow overhead, and the mist started swirling like a tornado was coming through.

The first chopper was twenty meters away looking very ghostly in the gray mist as it settled toward the earth. The second was about twenty meters farther.

Dawson and I sprinted toward the first chopper, making hand signals toward the crew to make them understand there were only two of us, and waving the other chopper off. Someone understood because the second chopper lifted off before we reached the closest one. Our chopper hovered five feet off the ground, and I slapped Dawson's ass indicating he was first. He reached up and grabbed the hand of the crew chief. His feet found the chopper skid, and he was in the cabin in about two seconds. I was right behind him, and I think I actually high-jumped into the cabin, calling out above the noise of the blades and engine, "Only two! Eight dead! Go! Go!"

The crew chief nodded and spoke into his radio mouthpiece to the pilot.

I sat cross-legged on the floor as the chopper rose quickly through the mist.

I looked at Dawson, who was kneeling on the floor of the cabin and already had a cigarette lit. We made eye contact, and he gave me a thumbs-up. Just as the chopper lifted out of the misty depression, Dawson's cigarette shot out of his mouth, and he pitched forward, his face falling in my lap. I shouted, "Fire!" as I grabbed Dawson's shoulders and rolled him on his back.

He stared up at the ceiling of the cabin, blood running from the exit wound in his chest.

Both door gunners had opened fire with their machine guns raking the forest below as the Huey shot forward away from the area. The Cobra gunships fired their rockets and Gatling guns into the surrounding terrain, but it was mostly for show. No one knew where the shot had come from, though I did know who fired it.

I got down close to Phil Dawson, face to face, and we stared into each other's eyes. I said, "You're okay. You'll be fine. We'll go right to the hospital ship. Just hold on. Hold on. A few minutes more."

He tried to speak, but I couldn't hear him above the noise. I put my ear to his mouth and heard him say, "Bitch." Then he let go and died.

I sat beside him holding his hand, which was getting cold. The crew chief and the door gunners kept stealing glances at us, as did the pilot and copilot.

• • •

The magic carpet landed at the field hospital first, and medics took Sergeant Dawson's body away, then the chopper skimmed over the base camp and deposited me at the landing zone of the Lurp Headquarters.

The pilot had radioed ahead, and Colonel Hayes—Royal Duck—was there to meet me in his Jeep. He was alone, which I thought was a nice touch. He said, "Welcome home, Lieutenant."

I nodded.

He asked me to confirm that I was the only one left.

I nodded.

He patted my back.

We got in his Jeep, which he drove directly to his hootch, a little wooden structure with a tin roof. We went inside, and he passed a bottle of Chivas to me. I took a long swig, then he steered me to a canvas armchair.

He asked, "You feel like talking about it?"

"No."

"Later?"

"Yeah. Yes, sir."

"Good." He patted my shoulder and went toward the door of the single-room shack.

I said, "Woman."

He turned to me. "What's that?"

"Female sniper. A very dangerous woman."

"Right . . . take it easy. Finish the bottle. See you when you're ready. In my office."

"I'm going back to get her."

"Okay. We'll talk about it later." He gave me a concerned look and left.

I sat there, thinking about Dawson, Andolotti, Smitty, Johnson, Markowitz, Garcia, Beatty, Landon, and Muller, and finally about the sniper.

• • •

After I made my report, the Air Force carpet-bombed the area of my patrol for a week. The day the bombing ended, we sent three two-man antisniper teams into the area. I wanted to go back, but Colonel Hayes vetoed that. Just as well, since only one team made it back.

We kept people out of the area for a few weeks, then sent in an infantry company of two hundred men to locate and re-cover the bodies of the eight guys left behind, and also, of course, to look for the lady with the gun. They never found the bodies; maybe the bombs and artillery obliterated them. As for the lady, she, too, seemed to have vanished.

I went home and put the whole thing out of my mind. Or tried to.

I stayed in touch with a lot of the Lurp guys who were still in 'Nam when I left, and they'd write once in a while and an-swer the questions I always asked in my letters: Did you find her? Did she get anyone else?

The answer was always "No" and "No."

She seemed to have disappeared or gotten killed in subse-quent bombings or artillery strikes, or just simply quit while she was ahead. Among the guys who knew the story, she be-came a legend, and her disappearance only added to her al-most mythical stature.

To this day, I have no idea what motivated her, what secret game she was playing, or why. I speculated that probably she'd had family killed by the Americans, or maybe she'd been raped by GIs, or maybe she was just doing her duty to her country, as we did ours.

I still have the brass cartridge I'd picked up on the river-bank, and now and then I take it out of my desk drawer and look at it.

I didn't want to obsess on this, but as the years passed, I

began to believe that she was still alive and that I'd meet up with her someday, someplace, though I didn't know how or where.

I knew for certain I'd recognize her face, which I could still see clearly, and I knew she would recognize me—the guy she let get away, to tell her story. Now the story is told, and if we do ever meet, only one of us will walk away alive.

WHAT SHE OFFERED

THOMAS H. COOK

S ounds like a dangerous woman," my friend said. He'd not been with me in the bar the night before, not seen her leave or me follow after her.

I took a sip of vodka and glanced toward the window. Outside, the afternoon light was no doubt as it had always been, but it didn't look the same to me anymore. "I guess she was," I told him.

"So what happened?" my friend asked.

This: I was in the bar. It was two in the morning. The people around me were like tapes from *Mission Impossible*, only without the mission, just that self-destruction warning. You could almost hear it playing in their heads, stark and unyielding as the Chinese proverb: *If you continue down the road you're on, you will get to where you're headed.*

Where were they headed? As I saw it, mostly toward more of the same. They would finish this drink, this night, this week . . . and so on. At some point, they would die like animals after a long, exhausting haul, numb with weariness as they finally slumped beneath the burden. Worse still, according to me, this bar was the world, its few dully buzzing flies no more than stand-ins for the rest of us.

I had written about "us" in novel after novel. My tone was always bleak. In my books, there were no happy endings. People were lost and helpless, even the smart ones . . . especially the smart ones. Everything was vain and everything was fleeting. The strongest emotions quickly waned. A few things mattered, but only because we made them matter by insisting that they should. If we needed evidence of this, we made it up. As far as I could tell, there were basically three kinds of people, the ones who deceived others, the ones who deceived themselves, and the ones who understood that the people in the first two categories were the only ones they were ever like to meet. I put myself firmly in the third category, of course, the only member of my club, the one guy who understood that to see things in full light was the greatest darkness one could know.

And so I walked the streets and haunted the bars, and was, according to me, the only man on earth who had nothing to learn.

Then suddenly, she walked through the door.

To black, she offered one concession. A string of small white pearls. Everything else, the hat, the dress, the stockings, the shoes, the little purse . . . everything else was black. And so, what she offered at that first glimpse was just the old B-movie stereotype of the dangerous woman, the broad-billed hat that discreetly covers one eye, high heels tapping on rain-slicked streets, foreign currency in the small black purse. She offered the spy, the murderess, the lure of a secret past, and, of course, that little hint of erotic peril.

She knows the way men think, I said to myself as she

walked to the end of the bar and took her seat. She knows the way they think . . . and she's using it.

"So you thought she was what?" my friend asked.

I shrugged. "Inconsequential."

And so I watched without interest as the melodramatic touches accumulated. She lit a cigarette and smoked it pensively, her eyes opening and closing languidly, with the sort of world-weariness one sees in the heroines of old black-and-white movies.

Yes, that's it, I told myself. She is *noir* in the worst possible sense, thin as strips of film, and just as transparent at the edges. I looked at my watch. Time to go, I thought, time to go to my apartment and stretch out on the bed and wallow in my dark superiority, congratulate myself that once again I had not been fooled by the things that fool other men.

But it was only two in the morning, early for me, so I lingered in the bar, and wondered, though only vaguely, with no more than passing interest, if she had anything else to offer beyond this little show of being "dangerous."

"Then what?" my friend asked.

Then she reached in her purse, drew out a small black pad, flipped it open, wrote something, and passed it down the bar to me.

The paper was folded, of course. I unfolded it and read what she'd written: *I know what you know about life.*

It was exactly the kind of nonsense I'd expected, so I briskly scrawled a reply on the back of the paper and sent it down the bar to her.

She opened it and read what I'd written: *No, you don't. And you never will.* Then, without so much as looking up, she wrote a lightning-fast response and sent it hurtling back up the bar, quickly gathering her things and heading for the door as it went from hand to hand, so that she'd already left the place by the time it reached me.

I opened the note and read her reply: C+.

My anger spiked. C+? How dare she! I whirled around on the stool and rushed out of the bar, where I found her leaning casually against the little wrought-iron fence that surrounded it.

I waved the note in front of her. "What's this supposed to mean?" I demanded.

She smiled and offered me a cigarette. "I've read your books. They're really dreadful."

I don't smoke, but I took the cigarette anyway. "So, you're a critic?"

She gave no notice to what I'd just said. "The writing is beautiful," she said as she lit my cigarette with a red plastic lighter. "But the idea is really bad."

"Which idea is that?"

"You only have one," she said with total confidence. "That everything ends badly, no matter what we do." Her face tightened. "So, here's the deal. When I wrote, *I know what you know about life,* that wasn't exactly true. I know more."

I took a long draw on the cigarette. "So," I asked lightly. "Is this a date?"

She shook her head, and suddenly her eyes grew dark and somber. "No," she said, "this is a love affair."

I started to speak, but she lifted her hand and stopped me.

"I could do it with you, you know," she whispered, her voice now very grave. "Because you know almost as much as I do, and I want to do it with someone who knows that much."

From the look in her eyes I knew exactly what she wanted to "do" with me. "We'd need a gun," I told her with a dismissing grin.

She shook her head. "I'd never use a gun. It would have to

be pills." She let her cigarette drop from her fingers. "And we'd need to be in bed together," she added matter-of-factly. "Naked and in each other's arms."

"Why is that?"

Her smile was soft as light. "To show the world that you were wrong." The smile widened, almost playfully. "That something can end well."

"Suicide?" I asked. "You call that ending well?"

She laughed and tossed her hair slightly. "It's the only way to end well," she said.

And I thought, *She's nuts,* but for the first time in years, I wanted to hear more.

• • •

"A suicide pact," my friend whispered.

"That's what she offered, yes," I told him. "But not right away. She said that there was something I needed to do first."

"What?"

"Fall in love with her," I answered quietly.

"And she knew you would?" my friend asked. "Fall in love with her, I mean?"

"Yes, she did," I told him.

But she also knew that the usual process was fraught with trial, a road scattered with pits and snares. So she'd decided to forgo courtship, the tedious business of exchanging mounds of trivial biographical information. Physical intimacy would come first, she said. It was the gate through which we would enter each other.

"So, we should go to my place now," she concluded, after offering her brief explanation of all this. "We need to fuck."

"Fuck?" I laughed. "You're not exactly the romantic type, are you?"

"You can undress me if you want to," she said. "Or, if not, I'll do it myself."

"Maybe you should do it," I said jokingly. "That way I won't dislocate your shoulder."

She laughed. "I get suspicious if a man does it really well. It makes me think that he's a bit too familiar with all those female clasps and snaps and zippers. It makes me wonder if perhaps he's . . . worn it all himself."

"Jesus," I moaned. "You actually think about things like that?"

Her gaze and tone became deadly serious. "I can't handle every need," she said.

There was a question in her eyes, and I knew what the question was. She wanted to know if I had any secret cravings or odd sexual quirks, any "needs" she could not "handle."

"I'm strictly double-vanilla," I assured her. "No odd flavors."

She appeared slightly relieved. "My name is Veronica," she said.

"I was afraid you weren't going to tell me," I said. "That it was going to be one of those things where I never know who you are and vice versa. You know, ships that pass in the night."

"How banal that would be," she said.

"Yes, it would."

"Besides," she added. "I already knew who you were."

"Yes, of course."

"My apartment is just down the block," she said, then offered to take me there.

• • •

As it turned out, her place was a bit farther than just down the block, but it didn't matter. It was after two in the morning and

the streets were pretty much deserted. Even in New York, certain streets, especially certain Greenwich Village streets, are
never all that busy, and once people have gone to and from
work, they become little more than country lanes. That night
the trees that lined Jane Street swayed gently in the cool au-
tumn air, and I let myself accept what I thought she'd offered,
which, for all the "dangerous" talk, would probably be no more
than a brief erotic episode, maybe breakfast in the morning, a
little light conversation over coffee and scones. Then she
would go her way and I would go mine because one of us
would want it that way and the other wouldn't care enough to
argue the point.

"The vodka's in the freezer," she said as she opened the
door to her apartment, stepped inside and switched on the
light.

I walked into the kitchen while Veronica headed down a
nearby corridor. The refrigerator was at the far end of the
room, its freezer door festooned with pictures of Veronica and
a short, bald little man who looked to be in his late forties.

"That's Douglas," Veronica called from somewhere down
the hall. "My husband."

I felt a pinch of apprehension.

"He's away," she added.

The apprehension fled.

"I should hope so," I said as I opened the freezer door.

Veronica's husband faced me again when I closed it, the
ice-encrusted vodka bottle now securely in my right hand.
Now I noticed that Douglas was somewhat portly, deep lines
around his eyes, graying at the temples. Okay, I thought,
maybe midfifties. And yet, for all that, he had a boyish face. In
the pictures, Veronica towered over him, his bald head barely
reaching her broad shoulders. She was in every photograph,

his arm always wrapped affectionately around her waist. And in every photograph Douglas was smiling with such unencumbered joy that I knew that all his happiness came from her, from being with her, being her husband, that when he was with her he felt tall and dark and handsome, witty and smart and perhaps even a bit elegant. That was what she offered him, I supposed, the illusion that he deserved her.

"He was a bartender when I met him," she said as she swept into the kitchen. "Now he sells software." She lifted an impossibly long and graceful right arm to the cabinet at her side, opened its plain wooden doors and retrieved two decidedly ordinary glasses, which she placed squarely on the plain Formica counter before turning to face me. "From the beginning, I was always completely comfortable with Douglas," she said.

She could not have said it more clearly. Douglas was the man she had chosen to marry because he possessed whatever characteristics she required to feel utterly at home when she was at home, utterly herself when she was with him. If there had been some great love in her life, she had chosen Douglas over him because with Douglas she could live without change or alteration, without applying makeup to her soul. Because of that, I suddenly found myself vaguely envious of this squat little man, of the peace he gave her, the way she could no doubt rest in the crook of his arm, breathing slowly, falling asleep.

"He seems . . . nice," I said.

Veronica gave no indication that she'd heard me. "You take it straight," she said, referring to the way I took my drink, which was clearly something she'd noticed in the bar.

I nodded.

"Me, too."

She poured our drinks and directed me into the living room. The curtains were drawn tightly together, and looked a bit dusty. The furniture had been chosen for comfort rather than for style. There were a few potted plants, most of them brown at the edges. You could almost hear them begging for water. No dogs. No cats. No goldfish or hamsters or snakes or white mice. When Douglas was away, it appeared, Veronica lived alone.

Except for books, but they were everywhere. They filled shelf after towering shelf, or lay stacked to the point of toppling along the room's four walls. The authors ran the gamut, from the oldest classics to the most recent best sellers. Stendahl and Dostoyevsky rested shoulder to shoulder with Anne Rice and Michael Crichton. A few of my own stark titles were lined up between Robert Stone and Patrick O'Brian. There was no history or social science in her collection, and no poetry. It was all fiction, as Veronica herself seemed to be, a character she'd made up and was determined to play to the end. What she offered, I believed at that moment, was a well-rounded performance of a New York eccentric.

She touched her glass to mine, her eyes very still. "To what we're going to do," she said.

"Are we still talking about committing suicide together?" I scoffed as I lowered my glass without drinking. "What is this, Veronica? Some kind of *Sweet November* rewrite?"

"I don't know what you mean," she said.

"You know, that stupid movie where the dying girl takes this guy and lives with him for a month and—"

"I would never live with you," Veronica interrupted.

"That's not my point."

"And I'm not dying," Veronica added. She took a quick sip of vodka, placed her glass onto the small table beside the sofa, then rose, as if suddenly called by an invisible voice, and offered her hand to me. "Time for bed," she said.

"Just like that?" my friend asked.

"Just like that."

He looked at me warily. "This is a fantasy, right?" he asked. "This is something you made up."

"What happened next no one could make up."

"And what was that?"

She led me to the bedroom. We undressed silently. She crawled beneath the single sheet and patted the mattress. "This side is yours."

"Until Douglas gets back," I said as I drew in beside her.

"Douglas isn't coming back," she said, then leaned over and kissed me very softly.

"Why not?"

"Because he's dead," she answered lightly. "He's been dead for three years."

And thus I learned of her husband's slow decline, the cancer that began in his intestines and migrated to his liver and pancreas. It had taken six months, and each day Veronica had attended him. She would look in on him on her way to work every morning, then return to him at night, stay at his bedside until she was sure he would not awaken, then, at last, return here, to this very bed, to sleep for an hour or two, three at the most, before beginning the routine again.

"Six months," I said. "That's a long time."

"A dying person is a lot of work," she said.

"Yes, I know," I told her. "I was with my father while he died. I was exhausted by the time he finally went."

"Oh, I don't mean that," she said. "The physical part. The lack of sleep. That wasn't the hard part when it came to Douglas."

"What was?"

"Making him believe I loved him."

"You didn't?"

"No," she said, then kissed me again, a kiss that lingered a bit longer than the first, and gave me time to remember that just a few minutes before she'd told me that Douglas was currently selling software.

"Software," I said, drawing my lips from hers. "You said he sold software now."

She nodded. "Yes, he does."

"To other dead people?" I lifted myself up and propped my head in my hand. "I can't wait for an explanation."

"There is no explanation," she said. "Douglas always wanted to sell software. So, instead of saying that he's in the ground or in heaven, I just say he's selling software."

"So you give death a cute name," I said. "And that way you don't have to face it."

"I say he's selling software because I don't want the conversation that would follow if I told you he was dead," Veronica said sharply. "I hate consolation."

"Then why did you tell me at all?"

"Because you need to know that I'm like you," she answered. "Alone. That no one will mourn."

"So we're back to suicide again," I said. "Do you always circle back to death?"

She smiled. "Do you know what La Rouchefoucauld said about death?"

"It's not on the tip of my tongue, no."

"He said that it was like the sun. You couldn't look at it for very long without going blind." She shrugged. "But I think that if you look at it all the time, measure it against living, then you can choose."

I drew her into my arms. "You're a bit quirky, Veronica," I said playfully.

She shook her head, her voice quite self-assured. "No," she insisted. "I'm the sanest person you've ever met."

• • •

"And she was," I told my friend.

"What do you mean?"

"I mean she offered more than anyone I'd ever known."

"What did she offer?"

That night she offered the cool, sweet luxury of her flesh, a kiss that so brimmed with feeling I thought her lips would give off sparks.

We made love for a time then, suddenly, she stopped and pulled away. "Time to chat," she said, then walked to the kitchen and returned with another two glasses of vodka.

"Time to chat?" I asked, still disconcerted with how abruptly she'd drawn away from me.

"I don't have all night," she said as she offered me the glass.

I took the drink from her hand. "So we're not going to toast the dawn together?"

She sat on the bed, cross-legged and naked, her body sleek and smooth in the blue light. "You're glib," she said as she clinked her glass to mine. "So am I." She leaned forward slightly, her eyes glowing in the dark. "Here's the deal," she added. "If you're glib, you finally get to the end of what you can say. There are no words left for anything important. Just sleek words. Clever. Glib. That's when you know you've gone as far as you can go, that you have nothing left to offer but smooth talk."

"That's rather harsh, don't you think?" I took a sip of vodka. "And besides, what's the alternative to talking?"

"Silence," Veronica answered.

I laughed. "Veronica, you are hardly silent."

"Most of the time, I am," she said.

"And what does this silence conceal?"

"Anger," she answered without the slightest hesitation. "Fury."

Her face grew taut, and I thought the rage I suddenly glimpsed within her would set her hair ablaze.

"Of course you can get to silence in other ways," she said. She took a quick, brutal drink from her glass. "Douglas got there, but not by being glib."

"How then?"

"By suffering."

I looked for her lip to tremble, but it didn't. I looked for moisture in her eyes, but they were dry and still.

"By being terrified," she added. She glanced toward the window, let her gaze linger there for a moment, then returned to me. "The last week he didn't say a word," she told me. "That's when I knew it was time."

"Time for what?"

"Time for Douglas to get a new job."

I felt my heart stop dead. "In . . . software?" I asked.

She lit a candle, placed it on the narrow shelf above us, then yanked open the top drawer of the small table that sat beside her bed, retrieved a plastic pill case and shook it so that I could hear the pills rattling dryly inside it.

"I'd planned to give him these," she said, "but there wasn't time."

"What do you mean, there wasn't time?"

"I saw it in his face," she answered. "He was living like someone already in the ground. Someone buried and waiting for the air to give out. That kind of suffering, terror. I knew that one additional minute would be too long."

She placed the pills on the table, then grabbed the pillow upon which her head had rested, fluffed it gently, pressed it down upon my face, then lifted it again in a way that made me feel strangely returned to life. "It was all I had left to offer him," she said quietly, then took a long, slow pull on the vodka. "We have so little to offer."

And I thought with sudden, devastating clarity, *Her darkness is real; mine is just a pose.*

• • •

"What did you do?" my friend asked.

"I touched her face."

"And what did she do?"

She pulled my hand away almost violently. "This isn't about me," she said.

"Right now, everything is about you," I told her.

She grimaced. "Bullshit."

"I mean it."

"Which only makes it worse," she said sourly. Her eyes rolled upward, then came down again, dark and steely, like the twin barrels of a shotgun. "This is about you," she said crisply. "And I won't be cheated out of it."

I shrugged. "All life is a cheat, Veronica."

Her eyes tensed. "That isn't true and you know it," she said, her voice almost a hiss. "And because of that you're a liar, and all your books are lies." Her voice was so firm, so hard and unrelenting, I felt it like a wind. "Here's the deal," she said. "If you really felt the way you write, you'd kill yourself. If all that feeling was really in you, down deep in you, you wouldn't be able to live a single day." She dared me to contradict her, and when I didn't, she said, "You see everything but yourself. And here's what you don't see about yourself, Jack. You don't see that you're happy."

"Happy?" I asked.

"You are happy," Veronica insisted. "You won't admit it, but you are. And you should be."

Then she offered the elements of my happiness, the sheer good fortune I had enjoyed, health, adequate money, work I loved, little dollops of achievement.

"Compared to you, Douglas had nothing," she said.

"He had you," I said cautiously.

Her face soured again. "If you make it about me," she warned, "you'll have to leave."

She was serious, and I knew it. So I said, "What do you want from me, Veronica?"

Without hesitation she said, "I want you to stay."

"Stay?"

"While I take the pills."

I remembered the line she'd said just outside the bar only a few hours before, *I could do it with you, you know.*

I had taken this to mean that we would do it together, but now I knew that she had never included me. There was no pact. There was only Veronica.

"Will you do it?" she asked somberly.

"When?" I asked quietly.

She took the pills and poured them into her hand. "Now," she said.

"No," I blurted, and started to rise.

She pressed me down hard, her gaze relentlessly determined, so that I knew she would do what she intended, that there was no way to stop her.

"I want out of this noise," she said, pressing her one empty hand to her right ear. "Everything is so loud."

In the fierceness of those words I glimpsed the full measure of her torment, all she no longer wished to hear, the clanging daily vanities and thudding repetitions, the catcalls of the inferior, the trumpeting mediocrities, all of which lifted to a soul-searing roar the unbearable clatter of the wheel. She wanted an end to all of that, a silence she would not be denied.

"Will you stay?" she asked quietly.

I knew that any argument would strike her as just more noise she could not bear. It would clang like cymbals, only add to the mindless cacophony she was so desperate to escape.

And so I said, "All right."

With no further word, she swallowed the pills two at a time, washing them down with quick sips of vodka.

"I don't know what to say to you, Veronica," I told her when she took the last of them and put down the glass.

She curled under my arm. "Say what I said to Douglas," she told me. "In the end it's all anyone can offer."

"What did you say to him?" I asked softly.

"I'm here."

I drew my arm tightly around her. "I'm here," I said.

She snuggled in more closely. "Yes."

• • •

"And so you stayed?" my friend asked.

I nodded.

"And she . . . ?"

"In about an hour," I told him. "Then I dressed and walked the streets until I finally came here."

"So right now she's . . ."

"Gone," I said quickly, and suddenly imagined her sitting in the park across from the bar, still and silent.

"You couldn't stop her?"

"With what?" I asked. "I had nothing to offer." I glanced out the front window of the bar. "And besides," I added, "for a truly dangerous woman, a man is never the answer. That's what makes her dangerous. At least, to us."

My friend looked at me oddly. "So what are you going to do now?" he asked.

At the far end of the park a young couple was screaming at each other, the woman's fist in the air, the man shaking his head in violent confusion. I could imagine Veronica turning from them, walking silently away.

"I'm going to keep quiet," I answered. "For a very long time."

Then I got to my feet and walked out into the whirling city. The usual dissonance engulfed me, all the chaos and disarray, but I felt no need to add my own inchoate discord to the rest.

It was a strangely sweet feeling, I realized as I turned and headed home, embracing silence.

From deep within her enveloping calm, Veronica offered me her final words.

I know.

HER LORD AND MASTER

ANDREW KLAVAN

I t was obvious she'd killed him, but only I knew why. I'd been Jim's friend, and he'd told me everything. It was a shocking story in its way. I found it shocking, at any rate. More than once, when he confided in me, I'd felt the sweat gathering under my collar, on my chest. Goose bumps, and what in a more decorous age we would have called a "stirring in the loins." Nowadays, of course, we're supposed to be able to talk about these things, about anything, in fact. There are so many books and movies and television shows claiming to shatter "the last taboo" that you'd think we were in danger of running out of them.

Well, let's see. Let's just see.

• • •

Jim and Susan knew each other at work, and began a relationship after an office party, standard stuff. Jim was Vice President in charge of Entertainment at one of the larger radio networks.

"I don't know what my job is," he used to say, "but by gum I must be doing it." Susan was an Assistant Manager in Personnel, which meant she was the secretary in charge of scheduling.

Jim was a tallish, elegant Harvard grad, thirty-five. On the job, he had a slow, thoughtful manner, a way of appearing to consider every word he spoke. Plus a way of boring into your eyes when you spoke, as if every neuron he had was engaged in whatever tedious matter you'd brought before him. After hours, thankfully, he became more satirical, more sardonic. To be honest, I think he considered most people little better than idiots. Which makes him a cockeyed optimist, if you ask me.

Susan was sharp, dark, energetic, in her twenties. A little thin and beaky in the face for my taste, but pretty enough with long, straight, black, black hair. Plus she had a fine figure, small and compact and gracefully, meltingly round at breast and hip. Her attitude was aggressive, funny, challenging: You gonna take me as I am, pal, or what? Which I think disguised a certain defensiveness about her Queens background, her education, maybe even her intelligence. In any case, she could put a charge in your morning, striding by in a short skirt, or drawing her hair from her mouth with one long nail. A Watercooler Fuck, was the general male consensus. In those sociological debates in which gentlemen are prone to discuss how their various female colleagues and acquaintances should be coupled with, Susan was usually voted the girl you'd like to shove against the watercooler and take standing up with the overnight cleaning crew vacuuming down the hall.

So at a party one February at which we celebrated the launch and certain failure of some new moronic management scheme or other, we watched with glee and envy as Jim and Susan stood together, talked together, and eventually left together. And eventually slept together. We didn't watch that part, but I heard all about it later.

· · ·

I'm a news editor, thirty-eight, once divorced, seven years, two months and sixteen days ago. Sexually, I think I've pretty much been around the block. But we've all pretty much been around the block these days. They probably ought to widen the lanes around the block to ease the traffic. So, at first, what Jim was telling me brought no more than a mild glaze of lust to my eyes, not to mention the thin line of drool running unattended from the corner of my mouth.

She liked it rough. That's the story. Now it can be told. Our Susan enjoyed the occasional smack with her rumpty-tumpty. Jim, God love him, seemed somewhat disconcerted by this at first. He'd been around the block too, of course, but it was a block in a more sedate neighborhood. And I guess maybe he'd missed that particular address.

Apparently, when they went back to his apartment, Susan had presented Jim with the belt to his terrycloth bathrobe and said, "Tie me." Jim managed to follow these simple instructions and also the ones about grabbing her black, black hair in his fist and forcing her mouth down on what I will politely assume to be his throbbing tumescence. The smacking part came later, after he'd hurled her bellyward onto his bed and was ramming into her from behind. This, too, at her specific request.

"It was kind of kinky," Jim told me.

"Hey, I sympathize," I said. "What does this make you, only the second or third luckiest man on the face of the earth?"

Well, it was a turn-on, Jim admitted that. And it wasn't that he'd never done anything like it before. It was just that, in Jim's experience, you had to get to know a girl a little before you started clobbering her. It was intimate, fantasy stuff, not the sort of thing you did on a first date.

Plus, Jim genuinely liked Susan. He liked the tough, working-stiff jazz of her and the chip-on-the-shoulder wise-cracks with the vulnerability underneath. He wanted to get to know her, be with her awhile, maybe a long while. And if this was where they started, he wondered, where exactly were they going to go?

But any awkwardness, it turned out, was all on Jim's side. Susan seemed perfectly comfortable when she woke in his arms the next morning. "It was nice last night," she whispered, stretching up to kiss his stubble. And she held his hand as they hailed a cab to take her home for a change of clothes. And she wowed and charmed him with her office etiquette, giving not a clue to the world of their altered state, giving even him only a single token of it when they passed each other, nodding, in the hall, and she murmured, "God, we are *so* professional."

And they had dinner together up on Columbus at the Moroccan and she went on, hilarious, about the management types in her department. And Jim, who usually expressed amusement by narrowing his eyes and smiling thinly, fell back in his chair and laughed with his teeth showing, and had to wipe tears out of his crow's feet with the four fingers of one hand.

That night, she wanted him to thrash her with his leather belt. Jim demurred. "Don't we ever get to do it, just, the regular way?" he asked.

But she leaned in close and smoldered at him. "Do it. I want you to."

"You know, I'm a little concerned about the noise. The neighbors and everything."

Well, he had a point there. Susan went into the kitchen and

returned with a wooden spoon. They don't make quite the crack, apparently. Jim, always the gentleman, proceeded to tie her to the bedposts.

"The woman's killing me. I'm exhausted," he told me a couple of weeks later.

I put my hand under my shirt and moved it up and down so he could see my heart beating for him.

"I mean it," he said. "I mean, I'm up for this stuff sometimes. It's sexy, it's fun. But Jesus. I'd like to see her face from time to time."

"She'll calm down. You're just getting started," I said. "So she digs this stuff. Later, you can gently instruct her in the joys of the missionary position."

We had this conversation at a table in McCord's, the last unspoilt Irish bar on the gentrified West Side. The news team does tend to drift down here of an evening, so we were already speaking in undertones. Now, Jim leaned in toward me even closer. Our foreheads were almost touching and he glanced from side to side before he went on.

"The thing is," he said, "I think she's serious."

"What do you mean?"

"I mean, I'm all for fantasy stuff and all that. But I don't think she's kidding around."

"What do you mean?" I said again, more hoarsely and with a bead of sweat forming behind my ear.

It turned out their relationship had now progressed to the point where they were divvying up the household chores. Susan had doled out the assignments and it fell to her to clean Jim's apartment, cook his dinner, and wash the dishes. Naked. Jim's job was to force her to do these things and whip, spank or rape her if she showed reluctance or made, or pretended to make, some kind of mistake.

Now there's always an element of braggadocio when men

complain about their sex lives, but Jim really did seem troubled by this. "I'm not saying it doesn't turn me on. I admit, it's a turn-on. It's just getting kind of . . . ugly at this point. Isn't it?" he said.

I wiped my lips dry and dropped back in my seat. When I could finally stop panting and move my mouth, I said, "I don't know. To each his own. I mean, look, if you don't like it, eject. You know? If it doesn't work for you, hit the button."

Obviously, this thought had occurred to him before. He nodded slowly, as if considering it.

But he didn't eject. In fact, another week or so, and for all intents and purposes Susan was living with him.

• • •

At this point, my information becomes less detailed. Obviously, a guy's living with someone, he doesn't go on too much about their sex life. Everyone at the net knew the affair was a happening thing by now, but Susan and Jim remained entirely professional and detached on the job. They'd walk to work together holding hands. They'd kiss once outside the building. And after that, it was business as usual. No low tones in the hallway, no closed office doors. The few times we all went out drinking together after work, they didn't even sit next to each other. Through the bar window, when they left, we'd see Jim put his arm around her. That was all.

The last time Jim and I talked about it before he died was in McCord's again. I came in there one night and there he was sitting at a corner table alone. I knew by the way he was sitting—bolt upright with his eyes half open, staring, glazed—that he was drunk as God on Sunday. I sat down across from him and he made a sloppy gesture with his hand and said, "Drinks are on me." I ordered a scotch.

If I'd been smart, I would've stuck to sports. The Knicks were getting murdered, the Yanks, after a championship season, were struggling to keep pace with Baltimore as the new season got under way. I could've talked about all of that. I should've. But I was curious. If curious is the word I want. "Prurient," maybe, is the *mot juste.*

And I said, "So how are things going with Susan?"

And he said, as you will when you're serious about someone, "Fine. Things with Susan are fine." But then he added, "I'm her Lord and Master." Sitting bolt upright. Waving slightly like a lampost in a gale.

Susan had scripted their routines, but he knew them by heart now and ran through them without prompting. This was apparently more efficient because it left her free to beg him to stop. He would tie her and she would beg him and he would beat her while she begged. He would sodomize her and grab her hair, force her head around so she had to watch him while he did it. "Who's your Lord and Master?" he would say. And she would answer, "You're my Lord and Master. You are." Later she would do the chores, naked or in this lace and suspender outfit she'd bought. Usually she'd fumble something or spill something, and he would beat her, which got him ready to take her again.

After he told me this, his eyes sank closed, his lips parted. He seemed to sleep for a few minutes, then woke up with a slight start. But bolt upright always, always straight up and down. Even when he got up to leave, his posture was stiff and perfect. He wafted to the door as if he were one of those old deportment instructors. He was a funny kind of a drunk that way, even more dignified than when he was sober, a sort of exaggerated, comic version of his reserved, dignified sober self.

I watched him leave with a half-smile on my face. I miss him.

. . .

Susan stabbed him with a kitchen knife, one of those big ones. Just a single convulsive jab but it went straight in, severed the vena cava. He bled out lying on the kitchen floor, staring up at the ceiling while she screamed into the phone for an ambulance.

Jim being a bit of a muck-a-muck, it made the news. Then the feminists got a-hold of it, the real bully-girls who consider murdering your boyfriend a form of self-expression. They wanted the case dismissed out of hand. And a lot of people agreed they had a point this time. Susan, it was found, had bruises all over her torso, was bleeding from various orifices. And Jim had pretty clearly been wielding a nasty-looking sex store paddle when she went for the knife. According to the political dicta of the day, it was an obvious case of long-term abuse and long-delayed self-defense.

But the cops, for some reason, were not immediately convinced. In general, cops spend enough time in the depths of human depravity to keep a spare suit in the closet there. They know that even the most obvious political axioms don't always cut it when you're dealing with true romance.

So the Manhattan DA's office was caught between the devil and the deep blue sea. Susan had gotten a good lawyer fast and had said nothing to anyone. The police suspected they'd find evidence of consensual rough sex in Susan's life but so far hadn't produced the goods. The press, meanwhile, was starting to link Susan's name with the word "ordeal" a lot, and were running her story next to sidebars on sexual abuse, which was their way of being "objective" while taking Susan's side entirely. Anyway, the last thing the DA wanted was to jail the woman and then release her. So he waffled. Withheld charges for a day or two, pending further investigation. And, in the meantime, the prime suspect was set free.

• • •

As for me, all was depression and confusion. Jim wasn't my brother or anything, but he was a good buddy. And I knew I was probably the best friend he had at the network, maybe even in the city, maybe in the world. Still there were moments, watching the feminists on TV, watching Susan's lawyer, when I thought: How do I know? The guy says one thing, the girl says something else. How do I know everything Jim told me wasn't some kind of crazy lie, some sort of justification for the bad stuff he was doing to her?

Of course, all that aside, I called the police the day after the murder, Friday, the first I heard. I phoned a contact of mine in Homicide and told him I had solid information on the case. I think I half-expected to hear the whining sirens of the squaddies coming for me even as I hung up the phone. Instead, I was given a Monday morning appointment and asked to wander on by the station house to talk to the detectives in charge.

Which gave me the weekend free. I spent it anchored to the sofa by a leaden nausea. Gazing at the ceiling, arm flung across my brow. Trying to force tears, trying to blame myself, trying not to. The phone rang and rang, but I never answered it. It was just friends—I could hear them on the answering machine—wanting to get in on it: the sympathy, the grief, the gossip. Everybody craving a piece of a murder. I didn't have the energy to play.

Sunday evening, finally, there was a knock at my door. I'm on the top floor of a brownstone so you expect the street buzzer, but this was a knock. I figured it must be one of my neighbors who'd seen the story on TV. I called out as I put my shoes on. Tucked in my shirt as I went to the door. Pulled it open without even looking through the peephole.

And there was Susan.

A lot of things went through my mind in the second I saw her. As she stood there, combative and uncomfortable at once. Chin raised, belligerent; glance sidelong, shy. I thought: Who am I supposed to be here? What am I supposed to be like? Angry? Vengeful? Chilly? Just? Lofty? Compassionate? Christ, it was paralyzing. In the end, I just stood back and let her enter. She walked into the middle of the room and faced me as I closed the door.

Then she shrugged at me. One bare shoulder lifted, one lifted corner of her mouth, a wise guy smile. She was wearing a pale spring dress, the thin strings tied round her neck in a bow. It showed a lot of her dark flesh. I noticed a crescent of discolor on her thigh beneath the hem.

"I'm not too sure about the etiquette here," I said.

"Yeah. Maybe you could look under 'Entertaining the Girl Who Killed Your Best Friend.'"

I gave her back her wise guy smile. "Don't say too much, Susan, okay? I gotta go in to see the cops on Monday."

She stopped smiling, nodded, turned away. "So—what? Like, Jim told you everything? About us?" She toyed with the pad on my phone table.

I watched her. My reactions were subtle but intense. It was the way she turned, it was that thing she said. It made me think about what Jim had told me. It made me look, long and slow, down the line of her back. It made my skin feel hot, my stomach cold. An interesting combination.

I moistened my lips and tried to think about my dead friend. "Yeah, that's right," I said gruffly. "He told me pretty much everything."

Susan laughed over her shoulder at me. "Well, that's embarrassing, anyway."

"Hey, don't flirt with me, okay? Don't kill my friend and come over here and flirt with me."

She turned round again, hands primly folded in front of her. I looked so steadily at her face she must've known I was thinking about her breasts. "I'm not flirting with you," she said. "I just want to tell you."

"Tell me what?"

"What he did, that he beat me, that he humiliated me. He was twice my size. Think how you'd like it, think what you would've done if someone was doing that to you."

"Susan!" I spread my hands at her. "You asked him to!"

"Oh, yeah, like, 'She was asking for it,' right? Like you automatically believe that. Your buddy says it so it must be true."

I snorted. I thought about it. I looked at her. I thought about Jim. "Yeah," I said finally. "I do believe it. It was true."

She didn't argue the point. She went right on. "Yeah, well, even if it is true, it doesn't make it any better. You know? I mean, you should've seen the way it turned him on. I mean, he could've stopped it. I'd've stopped. He could've changed everything any time, if he wanted to. But he liked it so much . . . And then there he is, hurting me like that, and all turned on by it. How do you think that makes a person feel?"

I am not too proud to admit that I actually scratched my head, dumb as a monkey.

Susan ran one long nail over the phone table pad. She looked down at it. So did I. "Are you really going to the cops?"

"Yeah. Hell, yeah," I said. Then, as if I needed an excuse, "It's not like they won't find someone else. Some other guy you did this stuff with. He'll tell them the same thing."

She shook her head once. "No. There's only you. You're the only one who knows." Which left nothing to say. We stood there silent. She thinking, me just watching her, just watching the lines and colors of her.

Then, finally, she raised her eyes to me, tilted her head. She didn't slink toward me, or tiptoe her fingers up my chest. She didn't nestle under me so I could feel the heat of her breath or smell her perfume. She left that for the movies, for the femme fatales. All she did was stand there like that and give me that Susan look, chin out, dukes up, her soul in the offing, almost trembling in your hand.

"It gives you a lot of power over me, doesn't it?" she said.

"So what?" I said back.

She shrugged again. "You know what I like."

"Get out," I said. I didn't give myself time to start sweating. "Christ. Get the fuck out of here, Susan."

She walked to the door. I watched her go. Yeah, right, I thought. I have power over her. As if. I have power over her until they decide not to charge her, until the headlines disappear. Then where am I? Then I'm her Lord and Master. Just like Jim was.

She passed close to me. Close enough to hear my thoughts. She glanced up, surprised. She laughed at me. "What. You think I'd kill you too?"

"I'd always have to wonder, wouldn't I?" I said.

Still smiling, she jogged her eyebrows comically. "Whatever turns you on," she said.

It was the comedy that did it. I couldn't resist the impulse to wipe that smile off her murdering face. I reached out and grabbed her hair in my fist. Her black, black hair.

It was even softer than I thought it would be.

MR. GRAY'S FOLLY

JOHN CONNOLLY

I t was, said my wife, quite the ugliest thing she had ever seen.
I had to admit that she was correct in her assessment.
This was not, generally speaking, a typical occurrence in our
relationship. As she approached late middle age (with all the
grace and ease, it should be added, of a funeral party stumbling in a cemetery), Eleanor had grown increasingly intoler-
ant of views that diverged from her own. Inevitably, mine
appeared to diverge more often than most, so agreement in
any form was a cause for considerable, if muted, celebration.

Norton Hall was a wonderful acquisition, a late-eighteenth-
century country residence with landscaped gardens and fifty
acres of prime land. It was an architectural gem and would
make us a wonderful home, since it was simultaneously small
enough to be manageable yet spacious enough to permit us to
avoid each other for significant portions of the day. Unfortu-
nately, as my wife had duly noted, the folly at the end of the
garden was another matter entirely. It was ugly and brutal,

with unadorned rectangular pillars and a bare white cupola topped with a cross. There were no steps leading up to it and the only way of gaining access to the interior appeared to be by clambering over the base. Even the birds avoided it, preferring instead to take up positions in a nearby oak tree, where they cooed nervously amongst themselves like spinsters at a parish dance.

According to the agent, one of Norton Hall's previous owners, a Mr. Gray, had built the folly as a memorial to his late wife. It struck me that he couldn't have liked his wife very much if that was what he had built in her memory. I was not overly fond of my wife much of the time, but even I didn't dislike her enough to erect a monstrosity like that in her memory. At the very least, I would have softened some of the edges and stuck a dragon on the top as a reminder of the dear departed. A little damage to the base had been caused at some point by Mr. Ellis, the gentleman who had owned the house before us, but he seemed to have thought better of his original impulse and the area in question had since been repaired and repainted.

All things considered, it really was a frightful eyesore.

My first instinct was to have the blasted thing destroyed, but in the weeks that followed, I started to find the folly appealing. No, "appealing" isn't the right word. Rather, I began to feel that it had a purpose, which I had not yet surmised, and that it would be unwise to meddle until I knew more about it. How I came to feel that way, I can trace to one particular incident that occurred about five weeks after we took occupancy of Norton Hall.

I had taken a chair and placed it on the bare stone floor of the folly, as it was a beautiful summer's day and the folly offered the possibility of both shade and a pleasing aspect. I was

MR. GRAY'S FOLLY • 185

just settling down with the paper when the strangest thing happened: the floor moved, as if, for a single moment, it had somehow become liquid instead of solid and some hidden tide had caused a wave to ripple across its surface. The sunlight grew sickly and weak, and the landscape shrouded itself in drifting shadows. I felt as if a strip of gauze from a sick man's bed had been placed across my eyes, for I could faintly smell decay in the air. I stood up suddenly, experiencing a little lightness in the head, and saw a man standing among the trees, watching me.

"Hullo, there," I said. "Can I help you with something?"

He was tall and dressed in tweeds: a distinctly sickly-looking chap, I thought, with a thin face and dark, arresting eyes. And I swear that I heard him speak, although his lips didn't move. What he said was:

"Let the folly be."

Well, I found that a little rum, I have to admit, even in my weakened state. I'm not a man who is used to being addressed in such a way by complete strangers. Even Eleanor has the good grace to preface her orders with a "Would you mind . . . ?" followed by the occasional "please" or "thank you" to soften the blow.

"I say," I replied, "I own this land. You can't come in here telling me what I can and can't do with it. Who are you, anyway?"

But blast it all if he didn't repeat the same four words.

"Let the folly be."

And, with that, the fellow simply turned around and vanished into the trees. I was about to follow him and escort him off the property when I heard a movement on the grass behind me. I spun around, half-expecting him to have popped up there as well, but it was only Eleanor. For a moment, she was a part of the altered landscape, a wraith among wraiths, and then all gradually returned to normal and she was again my once-beloved wife.

"Who were you talking to, dear?" she asked.

"There was a chap hanging about, over there," I replied, indicating with my chin toward the trees.

She looked in the direction of the woods, then shrugged.

"Well, there's no one there now. Are you sure that you saw someone? Perhaps the heat is bothering you, or something worse. You should see a doctor."

And there it was. I was Edgar Merriman: husband, property owner, businessman, and potential lunatic in his wife's eyes. At this rate, it wouldn't be very long before a couple of strong men were sitting on my chest until the booby carriage arrived, my wife perhaps shedding a small crocodile tear of regret as she signed the committal papers.

It struck me, not for the first time, that Eleanor appeared to have lost some weight in recent weeks, or perhaps it was simply the way the light reflecting from the folly caught her face. It lent an air of hunger to her appearance, an impression reinforced by a brightness to her eyes that I had not seen before. It made me think of a rapacious bird and, for some reason, the thought caused me to shiver. I followed her back to the house for tea but I couldn't eat, partly because of the way she was looking at me over the scones like an impatient vulture waiting for some poor chap to give up the ghost, but also because she talked incessantly of the folly.

"When are you going to have it demolished, Edgar?" she began. "I want it done as soon as possible, before the bad weather sets in. Edgar! Edgar, are you listening?"

And damn it if she didn't grip my arm so tightly that I dropped my cup in shock, fragments of pale china littering the stone floor like the remnants of young dreams. The cup was part of our wedding china, yet its loss did not appear to trouble my wife as once it might have. In fact, she barely seemed to notice the broken cup, or the tea slowly seeping through the cracks in the floor. Her grip remained tight, and her hands were like talons, long and thin with hard, sharp nails. Thick blue veins coursed across the backs of her hands like serpents intertwining, barely restrained by her skin. A sour scent seeped from her pores, and it was all that I could do not to wrinkle my nose in disgust.

"Eleanor," I asked, "are you ill? Your hands are so thin, and I do believe you've lost weight from your face."

Reluctantly, she relinquished her grip upon my arm and turned her face away.

"Don't be silly, Edgar," she replied. "I'm fit as a fiddle."

But the question seemed to make her uncomfortable, because she immediately busied herself among the cupboards, making the kind of racket associated more with anger than purpose. I left her to it, rubbing my arm where she had gripped it and wondering at the nature of the woman to whom I was married.

• • •

That evening, for want of something better to do, I went to the library of the house. Norton Hall had been put on the market by some sister of the late Mr. Ellis, and the library and most of its furnishings were part of the sale. Mr. Ellis appeared to have met a bad end: According to local gossip, his wife left him and, in a fit of depression, he shot himself in a hotel room in London. His wife did not even turn up for his service, poor beggar. Actually, there was still some speculation among our more fanciful neighbors that Mr. Ellis had done away with his good lady wife, although the police were never able to pin anything on him. Whenever a particularly likely set of bones turned up on waste ground, or was found buried near a riverbank by an inquisitive dog, Mr. Ellis and his missing wife tended to receive a mention in the local newspaper reports, even though twenty years had passed since his death. A more superstitious man might have balked at buying Norton Hall under such circumstances, but I was not such a man. In any case, from what I knew of Mr. Ellis he appeared to have been an intelligent man and, therefore, if he had killed his wife he was unlikely to have left her remains lying about the house where someone might trip over them and think, "Hullo, that's not right."

I had only visited the library once or twice—I'm not much of a man for books, truth be told—and had done little more than glance at the titles and blow dust and cobwebs from the older volumes. It was a surprise to me, then, to find a book sitting on a small table by an armchair. I thought at first that Eleanor might have left it there, but she was even less of a reader than I was. I picked it up and opened it at random, revealing a page covered in elegant, closely written script. I flicked back to the title page and found the inscription: *A Middle-Eastern Journey by J. F. Gray*. A small, tattered photograph marked the page and, as I looked at it, I couldn't help but feel a nasty chill down my spine. The man in the photograph, obviously the titular J. F. Gray, looked uncannily like the chap who had been wandering around the grounds offering unsought-for advice about the folly. But that couldn't be possible, I thought: After all, Gray had been dead for almost fifty years now and probably had other things on his mind, like choirs eternal or heat rash, depending on the life that he had led on earth. I put the thought to the back of my mind and returned my attention to the book. It was, it emerged, much more than a journal of Gray's trip to the Middle East.

It was, in effect, a confession.

It seemed that, on a trip to Syria in 1900, John Frederick Gray had acquired, through theft, the bones of a woman believed to be Lilith, the first wife of Adam. According to Gray, who knew a little of the biblical apocrypha, Lilith was reputed to be a demon, the original witch, a symbol of the male fear of untapped female power. Gray heard the tale of the bones from some chap in Damascus who sold him a part of what he claimed was Alexander the Great's armor, and who subsequently directed him to a little village to the far north of the country where the bones were reputed to be kept in a locked crypt.

The journey was long and difficult, although such challenges always seem to be grist to the mill for chaps like Gray, who appear to regard a comfortable chair and a good pipe as vices on a par with the actions of the Sodomites. But when Gray reached the village with his guides he found himself made unwelcome by the natives. According to his journal, the villagers told him that entry to the crypt was forbidden to strangers, and most especially to women. Gray was asked to leave, but he set up camp for the night some small distance from the village and mulled over what he had been told.

It was after midnight when one of the local ne'er-do-wells made his way to the encampment and told Gray that, for a not insignificant fee, he was prepared to remove the casket containing the bones from its resting place and bring it to him. He was a man of his word. Within the hour he returned, and he brought with him an ornate, and clearly very ancient, casket, which he said contained the remains of Lilith. The box was about three feet long, two feet wide, and a foot high, and securely locked. The thief told Gray that the key remained always in the possession of the local imam, but the Englishman was unconcerned. The tale of Lilith was a myth, merely a creation of fearful men, but Gray believed he might be able to sell the beautiful casket as a curiosity when he returned home. He packed it away with his other acquisitions, and thought little more about it until he was back in England and reunited with his young wife, Jane, at Norton Hall.

Gray first began to notice a change in his wife's behavior shortly after the bones arrived in their home. She grew strangely thin, almost emaciated, and began to evince an unhealthy interest in the boxed remains. Then, one evening when he had thought her to be in bed asleep, Gray found her prying at the lock with a chisel. When he tried to take the tool away from her, she slashed at him wildly before making a final strike at the lock, shattering it so that it dropped to the floor in two pieces. Before he could stop her, she had wrenched open the lid and revealed its contents: old brown bones curled in on themselves, with patches of tattered skin still adhering, and a skull almost like that of a reptile or a bird, narrow and elongated while still retaining traces of a half-developed humanity.

And then, according to Gray, the bones moved. It was only the slightest thing at first, a rustling that might simply have been the bones settling after their sudden disturbance, but it quickly became pronounced. The fingers stretched, as if powered by unseen muscles and tendons, then the bones in the toes tapped softly against the sides of the casket. Finally, the skull swung on its exposed vertebrae and those beaklike jaws opened and closed with a faint click.

The dust in the casket began to rise and the remains were quickly surrounded by a reddish vapor. But the vapor came, not from the casket, but from Gray's own wife, emerging from her mouth in a torrent, as though her blood had somehow dried to powder and was now being wrenched from its veins. As he watched, she grew thinner and thinner, the skin on her face crumpling and tearing like paper, her eyes growing wider as the thing in the casket sucked the life from her. Through the mist, Gray caught a glimpse of the most terrifying face reconstituting itself. Round green-black eyes devoured him hungrily, the parchmentlike skin turned from gray to a scaly black, and the beaked jaws opened and closed with a sound like bones snapping as it tasted the air. Gray sensed its desire, its base sexual need. It would consume him, and he would be grateful for its appetites, even as its talons ripped into him and its beak blinded him and its limbs enfolded him in a final embrace. He felt himself responding, moving ever closer to the emerging being, just as a thin membrane slipped across the creature's eyes, like the blinking of a lizard, and its spell was briefly broken.

Gray recovered himself and dived at the casket, sending the lid shooting down hard on the creature's head. He could feel the foul being hammering and thrashing from within as he took the chisel and jammed it through the loop of the lock, locking and sealing the casket. The red vapor instantly disappeared, the thing's struggles eased and, as he watched, his beloved wife crumpled to the floor and breathed her last.

There was only one page remaining in the narrative, and it detailed the origins of the folly: the digging of its deep foundations, the placing of the casket at the very bottom, and the construction of the folly itself above it in an effort to restrain Lilith forever. It was a ridiculous tale, of course. It had to be. It was a fantasy, Gray's attempt to scare the servants or to earn himself a mention in some penny dreadful.

Yet when I lay beside Eleanor that night, I did not sleep and I sensed a wakefulness to her that made me uneasy.

• • •

The days that followed did little to calm my feelings of unhappiness, or to improve relations between my wife and me. I found myself returning again and again to Gray's tale, nonsense though it had initially seemed. I dreamed of unseen things tapping at our bedroom window and when, in my dream, I approached the pane to ascertain the cause of the noise, an elongated head would emerge from the darkness, its dark, predatory eyes gleaming hungrily as it broke through the glass and tried to devour me. As I fought it, I could feel the shape of its sagging breasts against me, and its legs wrapped around me in a mockery of a lover's ardor. Then I would awake to find a small smile on Eleanor's face, as though she knew of my dream and were secretly pleased at its effect upon me.

As we grew increasingly alienated from each other, I took to spending more time in the garden, or walking along the boundaries of my land, half hoping to catch some sight of the anonymous visitor who bore such a marked resemblance to the unfortunate J. F. Gray. It was on one such occasion that I spied a figure on a bicycle making laborious progress up the hill that led to the gates of Norton Hall. Constable Morris hove into view—quite literally, for he was a large man and his considerable girth, combined with the blurring effect of the day's heat, gave him the appearance of a great, black ship appearing slowly upon the horizon. Eventually he seemed to realize the futility of his continued effort to master the hill on two wheels when gravity appeared determined to frustrate him, and he duly dismounted and walked his bicycle along the remaining stretch until he came at last to the gates.

Constable Morris was one of two policemen assigned to the little station at Ebbingdon, the town nearest to Norton Hall. He and the local sergeant, Ludlow, had responsibility for maintaining order not only in Ebbingdon but in the nearby villages of Langton, Bracefield, and Harbiston, as well as their surrounding areas, a task that they accomplished using a combination of a single dilapidated police car, a pair of bicycles, and the vigilance of the local populace. I had spoken to Ludlow only on a handful of occasions, and had found him to be a rather taciturn man, but Morris was a regular sight on the road by our property and was more inclined to spend a spare moment talking (and catching his breath) than was his superior.

"Hot day," I remarked.

Constable Morris, red-faced from his exertions, wiped his shirtsleeve across his brow and concurred that, yes, it was indeed a devil of a day. I offered him a glass of homemade lemonade, should he choose to accompany me back to the house, and he readily agreed. We talked of local matters on the short walk from the gate, and I left him by the folly while I went into the kitchen to pour the lemonade. Eleanor was nowhere to be seen, but I could hear her moving about in the attic of the house, making a dreadful racket as she tossed aside boxes and scattered crates. I chose not to disturb her with news of Morris's arrival.

Outside, the policeman was walking idly around the folly, his hands clasped behind his back. I handed him his lemonade as I joined him, the ice cracking loudly in the glass, and watched as he took a deep draught. There were great sweat stains beneath his arms and upon his back, a deeper blue against the lighter shade of his shirt, like a relief map of the oceans.

"What do you think of it?" I asked him.

"It's good," he replied, believing me to be referring to the lemonade. "Just what the doctor ordered on a day like today."

I corrected him. "No, I meant the folly."

Morris shifted his feet slightly and lowered his head. "Not really for me to say, now, Mr. Merriman," he said. "I don't claim to be an expert on such matters."

"Expert or not, you must have an opinion on it."

"Well, frankly sir, I don't much care for it. Never have."

"You sound like you've been exposed to it on more than one occasion," I said.

"It's been a while," he said, a little warily. "Mr. Ellis . . ."

He trailed off. I waited. I was anxious to question him further, but I did not want him to think I was engaged merely in idle prying.

"I heard," I said at last, "that his wife disappeared, and that the poor man took his own life soon after."

Morris took another drink of lemonade and looked at me closely. It was easy to underestimate such a man, I thought: His awkwardness, his weight, his struggles with his bicycle, all were rather comical at first appearance. But Constable Morris was a shrewd man, and his lack of progress through the ranks was due not to any deficiencies in his character or his work, but to his own desire to remain at Ebbingdon and tend to those in his care. Now it was my turn to shift beneath his gaze.

"That's the story," said Morris. "I was going to say that Mr. Ellis didn't care much for the folly either. He wanted to demolish it, but then events took a turn for the worst and, well, you know the rest."

But, of course, I didn't. I knew only what I had heard through local gossip, and even that was meted out to me, as a new arrival, in carefully measured amounts. I told Morris that this was the case, and he smiled.

"Gossips with discretion," he said. "I never heard the like."

"I'm aware of how things stand in small villages," I said. "I expect that I could leave grandchildren behind me who would still be regarded with a certain amount of suspicion."

"You have any children then, sir?"

"No," I replied, unable to keep a twinge of regret from my voice. My wife was not particularly maternal, and nature appeared to have concurred in that assessment.

"It's an odd thing," said Morris, giving no indication that he had noticed the alteration in my tone. "It's been many years since children were heard in Norton Hall, not since before Mr. Gray's time. Mr Ellis, he was childless too."

It was not a topic I wished to pursue, but the mention of Ellis allowed me to steer the conversation into more interesting waters, and I jumped at the opportunity a little too eagerly.

"They say, well, they say that Mr. Ellis might have killed his wife."

I immediately felt embarrassed at speaking so bluntly, but Morris did not appear to mind. In fact, he seemed to appreciate my honesty at broaching the subject so openly.

"There was that suspicion," he admitted. "We questioned him, and two detectives came up from London to look into it, but it was as if she had disappeared off the face of the earth. We searched the property here, and all the fields and lands around, but we found nothing. There were rumors that she had a fancy man in Brighton, so we tracked him down and questioned him as well. He told us that he hadn't seen her in weeks, for all the trust you can put in the word of a man who would sleep with another man's wife. Eventually, we had to let the whole matter rest. There was no body, and without a body there was no crime. Then Mr. Ellis shot himself, and people came to their own conclusions about what might have happened to his wife."

He drained the last of his lemonade, then handed me the empty glass.

"Thank you," he said. "That was very refreshing."

I told him that he was most welcome, and watched as he prepared to mount his bicycle once again.

"Constable?"

He paused in his preparations.

"What do you think happened to Mrs. Ellis?"

Morris shook his head. "I don't know, sir, but I do know this. Susan Ellis doesn't walk this earth anymore. She lies beneath it."

And with that, he cycled away.

• • •

The following week I had business in London that could not be put off. I took the train down and spent most of a frustrating day discussing financial affairs, a frustration aggravated by a growing sense of disquiet, so that my time in London was spent with only a fraction of my attention concentrated on my finances and the remainder devoted to the nature of the evil that appeared to have tainted Norton Hall. Although not a superstitious man, I had grown increasingly uneasy about the history of our new home. The dreams had been coming to me with increasing regularity, accompanied always by the sound of talons tapping and jaws clicking and, sometimes, by the sight of Eleanor leaning over me when at last I awoke, her eyes bright and knowing, her cheekbones threatening to erupt like knife blades through the taut skin of her face. Gray's account of his travels had also unaccountably gone missing, and when I questioned Eleanor about it I sensed that she was lying to me when she denied any knowledge of its whereabouts. Both the attic and the cellar were a jumble of upturned boxes and discarded papers, the mess belying my wife's claims that she was merely "reorganizing" our surroundings.

Finally, there had been disturbing changes in the more intimate aspects of our married life. Such matters should remain between a man and his wife, but suffice it to say that our relations were of a greater frequency—and, at least on my wife's part, of a greater ferocity—than we had ever before known. It had now reached a point where I rather feared turning off the light, and I had taken to staying away from our bedroom until late into the night in the hope that Eleanor might be sleeping when at last I took my place beside her.

But Eleanor was rarely asleep, and her appetites were fearful in their insatiability.

• • •

It was dark when I got home that evening, but I could still see the marks of the vehicle tracks upon the lawn, and a gaping hole where the folly had once been. The remains of the construct itself lay in a jumble of concrete and lead on the gravel by the house, left there by the men responsible for its demolition, the paucity of its foundations now clearly revealed, for the structure itself was merely a feint, a means of covering up the pit that lay beneath. A figure stood at the lip of the hole, a lamp in her hand. As she turned to me, she smiled, a ghastly smile filled, it seemed to me, with both pity and malice.

"Eleanor!" I cried. "No!"

But it was too late. She turned and began to descend a ladder, the light quickly disappearing from view. I dropped my briefcase and dashed across the lawn, my chest heaving and a growing panic clawing at my gut, until I reached the lip of the hole. Below me, Eleanor was scraping at the dirt with her bare hands, slowly revealing the curled, skeletal figure of a woman, the remains still covered in a tattered pink dress, and I knew instinctively that this was Mrs. Ellis and that Constable Morris was right in his suspicions. She had not run away from her husband. Rather, she had been interred here by him, after she had dug her way beneath the folly and he had killed her, then himself, in a fit of horror and remorse. Mrs. Ellis's skull was slightly elongated around the nose and mouth, as though some dreadful transformation had been arrested by her sudden death.

By now, Eleanor's scratching had revealed a small coffin, dark and ornamented. I started down the ladder after her as she took a crowbar and tore at the great lock that Gray had placed on the casket before he buried it. I was on the final steps of the ladder when a wrenching sound came and, with a cry of triumph, Eleanor threw open the lid. There, just as Gray had described, lay the curled-up remains topped by a strange, elongated skull. Already, the dust was rising and a thin red trail of vapor seeped from Eleanor's mouth. Her body convulsed, as if it were being shaken by unseen hands. Her eyes bulged whitely in their sockets and her cheeks appeared to collapse into her open mouth, the lineaments of her skull clearly visible beneath the skin. The crowbar fell from her fingers and I grabbed it. Pushing her away, I raised the bar above my head and stood above the casket. A gray-black face with large, dark green eyes and hollows for ears looked up at me, and its sharp beaked jaws clicked as it rose toward me. Talons gripped the sides of its prison as it struggled to rise, and its body was a mockery of all that was beautiful in a woman.

Its breath smelled of dead things.

I closed my eyes, and struck. Something screamed, and the skull broke with a hollow, wet sound like the opening of a melon. The creature fell back, hissing, and I slammed down the lid. At my feet, Eleanor lay unconscious, the final traces of the red vapor coiling slowly between her teeth. Just as Gray had done years before, I took the crowbar and used it to jam the lock. From within the box came a furious hammering, and the crowbar jangled uneasily where it rested. The thing screamed repeatedly, a long high-pitched sound like the squealing of pigs in a slaughterhouse.

I placed Eleanor over my shoulder and, with some difficulty, climbed the ladder to the ground above, the thudding noises from the casket slowly fading. I drove her to Bridesmouth, where I placed her in the care of the local hospital. She remained unconscious for three days, and remembered nothing of the folly, or Lilith, when she awoke.

While she was in the hospital, I made arrangements for us to return permanently to London, and for Norton Hall to be sealed. And then, one bright afternoon, I watched as the hole in the lawn was lined with cement strengthened with steel. More cement was poured into the hole, three containers of it, until the maw was almost half full. Then the workmen began the task of building a second folly to cover the hole, larger and more ornate than its predecessor. It cost me half a year's income, but I had no doubt that it was worth it. Finally, while Eleanor continued to convalesce with her sister in Bournemouth, I watched as the last stones of the folly were set in place and the workmen set about removing their equipment from the lawn.

"I take it the missus didn't like the last folly, Mr. Merriman?" said the foreman, as we watched the sun set upon the new structure.

"I'm afraid it didn't suit her disposition," I replied.

The foreman gave me a puzzled look.

"They're funny creatures, women," he continued at last. "If they had their way, they'd rule the world."

"If they had their way," I echoed.

But they won't, I thought.

At least, not if I have anything to do with it.

A THOUSAND MILES FROM NOWHERE

LORENZO CARCATERRA

The tall man sat with his back resting against the thick glass window. His eyes were shut, three fingers of his right hand holding down a long-neck bottle of lukewarm beer. On a radio murmuring somewhere in the distance, the Dixie Chicks were working their way through "Give It Up or Let Me Go." The man took a deep breath and ran his free hand across the top of his left knee, trying to ease the pain that too many years of medication and three operations had failed to lessen. He was tired, lacking the patience to wait out yet another winter snowstorm, the din of what had, only hours earlier, been a bustling airport terminal, reduced now to the quiet scrapings of cleaning crews and the fitful sleep of stranded passengers.

He was supposed to have been in Nashville four hours ago, finished his job three hours ago and been halfway through a smoked rib and baked bean dinner by now. Instead, here he was, sitting in the back of a bar whose name he didn't know, manned by a middle-aged bartender who cared less about his next refill than he did about the tape-delayed lacrosse game coming down off the soundless TV above him. The tall man opened his eyes, turned his head and looked out through the steam-streaked glass. The snow was coming down at an angle, thick flakes building up on silent runways and against the wheels of stalled Boeing jets. An airport ground crew was spraying down an American Eagle jet with yellow foam, in a vain attempt to keep its engines from freezing in the midst of an unforgiving wind. The tall man turned away from the window and lifted his bottle of beer, finishing it off in two thick gulps.

There would be no flights tonight.

"You can blame me, if you want," the woman's voice said. "Happens every time I fly. I leave the house and the bad weather follows."

She stood facing the long window, watching the flakes land and slide down the thick glass, a gray satchel resting against the points of her black boots, long blonde hair shielding half her face. A black leather coat stopped at the knee and did little to disguise her slim, shapely body. Her voice was cotton soft and her white skin shimmered off the glow from the low-watt lights that lined the room and the heavy floods that lit the outside runways.

"Make it up to me," the tall man said to her.

She turned to look at him, her dark eyes giving off a glint of red, a cat caught in the glare of a flashlight. "How?" she asked.

"Let me buy you a drink," the tall man said. "Thanks to the weather you brought in, it looks like there's little else to do but wait. And I don't much feel like reading the paper—again."

The woman kicked aside her satchel and undid the buttons on her leather coat. She tossed the coat on an empty chair between them, swung aside strands of hair from her eyes, pulled back a chair and sat across from the tall man. "Bourbon," she said. "Glass of ice water with lemon on the side."

The tall man gave a hint of a smile, pushed his chair back, grabbed his empty beer bottle and walked toward the bar. The woman watched him leave and then turned her look to the raging storm, swirling gusts of powder and ice particles dancing in circles under the hot lights.

"You're gonna have to make do with lemon peel," the tall man said, resting the drinks on her side of the table. He sat back down and tilted a sweaty bottle of Heineken in her direction. "Cheers," he said with a smile and a wink and downed a long swallow from the cold beer.

The woman nodded and sipped her bourbon, the familiar burn in her throat and chest as welcome as an old friend. She sat back and looked across the table at the tall man. He was in his mid-forties and in shape, hard upper body chiseled by daily workouts, his white, button-down J. Crew shirt tight around the arms and neck. His face was tanned and handsome, set off by Greek olive eyes and rich dark hair. His gestures and movements were deliberate, never rushed, his body language calm and free of stress, the habits of a man at ease in his own skin. "What city aren't you going to tonight?" he asked.

"Los Angeles," the woman said, glancing down at the silver Tiffany watch latched around her thin wrist. "If the skies were clear, would have been in LAX twenty minutes ago."

"What's there?" he asked.

"Warm weather, palm trees, movie stars and an ocean you can swim in," the woman said.

"What's there for you?" he asked, leaning closer toward her, the beer bottle still in his right hand.

"All of that," she said. "Plus a home where I can walk to the beach, a car that loves winding hills and two cats that are always happy to see me."

"The beach, a car and two cats," the man said. "That usually means no kids and no husband."

"You can't have everything," the woman said.

"That depends on what you want everything to be," the man said.

"What's it for you?" the woman asked.

The man sipped his beer and shrugged. "This, right now," the man said. "Having a beer, sitting across from a beautiful woman in an empty airport. Being in the moment and enjoying it. Not having to huddle in a corner and burn out a cell phone battery to say goodnight to kids I never see enough to make a dent or listen to a wife complain about something I never even knew was a problem and could care less that it is. No mortgage, no bills, no worries. Live the way I travel. Light."

"You need money to live like that," the woman said. "And either a job or a rich father to hand it over. Which belongs to you?"

"If I'm going to open my heart, it'd be nice to know who it's going to," the man said, revealing a handsome smile.

"You could call me Josephine," the woman said. "But I wouldn't like it very much. Even when my mother used to use the name I'd cringe. Most of the people I talk to just call me Joey. It makes it easier for everyone that way."

"I knew a nun named Josephine once," the man said. "She didn't seem to like the name much either. So, Joey it is."

"And whose heart is it that's about to be opened up to Joey?" the woman asked, more a smirk than a smile crossing her lips, bourbon glass held close to her mouth.

"I'm Frank," the man said. "Same name as my father and grandfather. My family liked to keep things simple."

"So do you, based on what I've heard so far," Joey said.

"Pretty much," Frank said. "There usually isn't any kind of a payoff when you add in complications."

"That's not always easy to arrange," Joey said. "Sometimes complications just seem to happen."

"All the more reason not to toss our own into the mix," Frank said. "There's always somebody somewhere eager to make something simple hard. It's what they live for and it's what I do my best to avoid."

"In my line of work we call them defense attorneys and judges," Joey said.

"Is that what you do in L.A. when you're not at the beach or hanging around the house with the cats?" Frank asked. "Practice law?"

"I don't need to practice it all that much," Joey said. "I pretty much have cornered all I need to know."

"Which means you're good," he said.

"Which means I'm very good," Joey said.

"Which is bad news for the bad guys, I guess," Frank said, downing the last row of suds from his beer.

"Not if they cover their tracks," Joey said, her voice calm and matter-of-fact. "But most of them don't, which is how I get to meet them in the first place. Unless they commit the perfect crime, the absolute perfect crime, they'll get to stare at me talking about them in a courtroom."

"You ever see one?" Frank asked. "A perfect crime?"

"I've heard about a few," Joey said. She took a long drink of her bourbon, brushing the last drop off her lower lip with her tongue, and took a slow and quiet deep breath. "But I've seen only one."

"Was it one of yours?"

Joey shook her head. "I was still in law school," she said.

"My first year in. A young girl was found dead in her bedroom. Her apartment was on the second floor of a five-story walk-up. No break-in, not from the front door or from any of the windows. Nothing stolen, nothing missing, no prints, no DNA, no bullet casings. Just a dead girl and three bullets."

"And you think that's what made it perfect?" Frank asked, sitting up and leaning closer toward Joey. "You don't need to be a genius to know not to leave behind any prints, DNA or casings. Anybody who watches too many cop shows or reads too many legal thrillers can pick that up."

"You're right," Joey said. "What made it perfect was that he was never caught."

"Cops give a case as little or as much time as they think a case deserves," Frank said. "They're like car salesmen. They're not looking to sell every car on the lot, just as many as allows them to keep their job."

"Sounds like you've given this a lot of thought," Joey said.

"Not really," Frank said. "I'm just one of those people who watches too many cop shows and reads too many legal thrillers."

"I managed to get ahold of her case file," Joey said. "The cops did a pretty thorough job but they didn't have much to work with. The murder happened in the middle of the day, when most of the other tenants were out, either at work, at school, in a gym or shopping. She hadn't been living in the apartment very long, so didn't have many friends in the building."

"How'd he get in?" Frank asked. "Or I should ask, how do they think he got in?"

"You don't have to break in to get in," Joey said. "She might have known him, which I doubt. She might have let him in because he forced her to, but I don't think that's the case, either."

"And what does the Sherlock Holmes of Los Angeles think

happened?" Frank asked, his smile colder now, his eyes locked onto Joey's face.

"I think he knew her routine," Joey said. "What time she woke up. What time she went for her run and how long she ran. What her class schedule was and which buildings they were in. He studied her. He made it a point to get to know her, without ever having to meet her."

"If he did all that, he must have had a reason," Frank said. "Or been given one by somebody else."

"Reasons are always simple enough to find," Joey said. "Once you figure out the best place to look."

"And what did you get?" Frank asked. "Once you figured out where to look?"

"That somebody paid money to have her killed," Joey said, her fingers stroking at the sides of her water glass.

"If you dug deep enough to know that, then you know why he did it," Frank said. "What'd you find, personal or business?"

Joey finished her water and slid the empty glass toward Frank. "I'm always thirsty to begin with," she said. "Talking makes me even more so. You want another go-around? It's my treat."

"You're the one telling the story," he said, standing and turning toward the bar. "I'll supply the refreshments."

She watched him lean on the wood bar and wait while the bartender reached down for a fresh beer and then filled two empty glasses, one with bourbon and the other with ice and water. "She likes lemon in her water," she heard Frank say.

"And I'd like to get the hell home," the bartender said, dropping three lemon twists into the water glass. "This is last call. You want more than what I just gave you, order it now. I close up in twenty minutes."

"What's your rush?" Frank asked. "No plane is gonna pull outta here until the morning, if then."

"But my car is," the bartender said. "In twenty minutes."

Frank rested the glasses on the table. "Used to be a bartender was better than a shrink," he said. "Cared more or at least listened as if he did. I guess we found one that missed that part of bartending class."

"Maybe he's one of the lucky ones," Joey said. "Maybe he's got somebody somewhere waiting and worried."

Frank turned to look at the bartender, cradling the beer in both hands. "I don't think so," he said. "My guess is you and me are as close to company as he's gonna have tonight."

"Some people learn to live without company," Joey said. "Or family. Like you."

"It does help keep it all simple," Frank said, looking back at her, resting the beer on the edge of the table. "Things can get complicated real fast, pretty much for no reason, the second you let other people cross your radar."

"It doesn't bother you living the way you do?" Joey asked.

"I don't know," Frank said. "How is it you think I live?"

"You travel from city to city and from job to job," Joey said with an air of confidence. "The work pays pretty well, judging by the clothes you're wearing and the first-class ticket in your shirt pocket."

"If you're going to bother to put in the time on anything," Frank said, "make sure it at least pays you for the trouble."

"But yours is not a job for anyone," Joey said. "At least that's my guess."

"Few are," Frank said.

"But it must have its rewards," Joey said. "All good jobs do."

"What are yours?" Frank asked. "What is it about being a lawyer that makes you want to leave your bed in the morning?"

"That I can make it stop," Joey said. "If only just for a lucky few."

"Make what stop?"

"The evil at the other end of the table," Joey said. "And the pain felt by the innocent ones who sit behind me in the courtroom every day on every case. Their faces change with every trial, but they all look the same to me. I don't even need to see them to know what they're feeling, what they're thinking, all their regrets, all their wasted tears."

"Putting a guy in a cell makes them feel all better?" Frank asked.

"Not really," Joey said. "But I think it doesn't make the hurt they feel at losing someone they love get any worse to live with. A crime committed against one is always a memory shared by many."

"Spoken more like a victim than a lawyer," Frank said.

"Sometimes you can be both," Joey said.

"Do you ever think about the guy at that other end of the table?" Frank asked. "The one you seem so eager to put away?"

"Every day," Joey said. "The ones I helped convict and the ones that I couldn't and the one I never had a chance to bring to trial."

"What do you see when you look over there?" he asked. "Do you ever take the time to look beyond the hard eyes, the prison gym body and the hands resting flat on the wood table?"

"And if I did?" Joey said. "What is it I'd see?"

"Depends on who it is and what you're looking for," Frank said. "If you go in looking for pity, you'll get that soon enough. Every guy in an orange jumpsuit has a sad story he's eager to tell or sell. But if you go in search of the reasons a guy ends up sitting next to a lawyer he can't afford, then you might find something more than a sad story at the other end."

"Will it be enough to make me forget the victim?" Joey asked. "Or forgive what was done?"

"Not if you don't want to," Frank said.

"Aren't all those stories pretty much the same?" Joey asked. "Abusive childhood, parents not around, or on drugs if they are, crime the only door left open to them. Have I left anything out?"

"That's true nine out of ten times," Frank said.

"What is it that one other time?"

"It's a good cover for a guy who came from a solid home and a family that cared," Frank said. "He went to the best school in his area, played Little League baseball and flag football and sat next to his mother every Sunday at church service. He had good grades and a part-time job after school that kept him in comic books and trading cards."

"Sounds ideal," Joey said, holding her drink close to her face, elbow on the side of the table.

"It's the American way of life," Frank said. "But only if you judge it by what you see on the surface. You don't want to take it any lower than that."

"And if you do?" Joey asked. "What happens then?"

"Then you might see a set of pictures you won't like," Frank said. "You see a mother wearing too much makeup to a PTA meeting to cover the heavy drinking from the night before. You see a father who keeps odd hours and travels long distances on business trips that no one talks about. You see three loaded handguns kept in the middle drawer of his bedroom bureau and bags filled with neatly folded bills hidden in the attic under a small mountain of winter quilts."

"And how does any of that lead you to where you take someone else's life and not care about it?" Joey asked.

"That kind of living makes you hard," Frank said. "Teaches

you to keep buried anything that would even come close to where you'd care about anybody. Before your skin has a chance to clear up, you've already learned that people are never who they say they are and that even the most innocent person walking around is hiding some level of guilt underneath. In plain English, it makes it very easy not to care. About anything or about anybody."

"That include the victims that are left behind?" Joey asked.

"Especially them," Frank said. "They have to stay the way they were always meant to stay. Invisible. In fact, if you're really on your game, they disappear the second the job's done and they're outta your line of sight. And their name becomes as easy for you to forget as yesterday's weather. They become, out there on those streets, what the defendant becomes to somebody like you inside a courtroom. A face you try to put away and forget."

Joey drank down half the bourbon in one hard gulp, her right hand twitching slightly, unnerved for the first time since she sat down. It was so much easier for her to keep her emotions in check inside the courtroom. There, she was the one who held the controls, or at least she felt enough like she did. She asked the questions and expected to get the answers she wanted and needed to hear. But it was so much different inside the confines of a warm and stuffy bar, miles removed from any halls of justice. The hard-edged man across the table from her was a better-equipped foe than any that she had come across in all her years as a trial lawyer. He was quick to sense her raw points and even quicker to pounce on them. And more than anything else, he took pleasure from their give and take, fearless in the face of the questions and the answers they required.

Joey took another sip from her drink, rested the glass back on the table and rubbed the strain at the base of her neck. She looked up at Frank and caught him staring at her. "I guess this is what happens when you get snowed in," she said, looking to bring the mood up a notch, eager to once again wrest control of the conversation.

"Bad weather and cold beer," Frank said, holding up his close-to-empty bottle. "A lethal combination."

"You would have made a good lawyer," Joey told him.

"You couldn't have figured that from the way I dress," he said. "I must have done something foolish to give you that idea."

"You argue your case well," she said. "Make your points, but steer clear of any emotion. You keep it all in check. It's often the only way to walk away with a win."

"That's not true just of lawyers," Frank said. "It pretty much fits about any profession I can think of, good ones and bad. There are some lines of work where showing your emotions, letting your heart beat your brain to your mouth, can kill you faster than a stray bullet."

"But only the best can function at that high a level," Joey said, feeling like she was back on her offensive game, one leg crossed casually over the other. "And even the best lose that edge, even for just a minute. And that's when the price that's paid is always a steep one."

"If you're the best, I mean really are the best, not just think it or say it, then no matter what else you do you can't ever afford to lose," Frank said. "Not ever. In some lines of work, one loss is all you get."

"But it happens," Joey said. "No matter how much we plan, how much we prepare, no matter how ready we think we are, no matter how good we may be. It happens."

"Maybe in a courtroom or a boxing ring," Frank said. "Luck can sneak its way up on you inside those places. But in most other lines, you can't ever make room for either mistakes or luck."

"Unless the luck is good," Joey said, giving off a warm smile, once again at ease, working within her self-imposed comfort zone.

"I *never* count on luck," Frank said, index finger stabbing the edge of the table for emphasis. "It's not a risk worth the taking."

"What about this?" Joey asked. "You and me, sitting here, talking to each other. You take away the storm and two canceled flights and none of that ever happens. That sounds like luck. At least to me."

"Not luck," Frank said, shaking his head, managing a weak smile. "Destiny."

"That we would meet?" she asked.

"That you would find me," Frank said, his eyes telling her that he knew who she was even before she sat down.

Joey sat back in her chair, looked away from Frank and out toward the storm, its anger running now at full vent. "I always knew I would," she whispered, but in words loud enough for him to hear. "I never figured on *not* finding you."

"So did I," Frank said, staring at her, looking past the low glare of the table lamp. "I always knew you were out there, looking, asking questions, never more than one, two steps behind me."

Joey looked back at Frank and pushed aside her water glass. "You didn't make it easy," she said. "Every time I thought I was close, you would vanish, pop up again a few months later in some other city, leaving behind another trail to be followed."

"Part of what I do involves not getting caught," Frank said with a slight shrug. "Another part is knowing who it is that's out there looking for me."

"How long have you known?" she asked. "About me?"

Frank downed the remainder of his beer and laughed, low and quiet, his face barely creased. "Probably long before you knew about me," he said. "Number one in your class, both high school and college. Went through law school like flames through an old barn. Passed up the big firms and the bigger dollars, wanted no part of that world. It wasn't what you were about and wouldn't lead you to where you needed to go. Making partner didn't matter to you. Getting convictions was what you were chasing and you did get plenty of those."

"You could have brought it all to an end," she said. "Could have eased me out of your picture. Wouldn't have taken you much."

"There was no profit in it," Frank said. "And that made it not worth doing."

"And what was the profit in killing my sister?" Joey asked. She was surprised at how calm she felt, how relaxed her body and mannerisms were. She had always believed this moment would one day arrive, but had never allowed her thinking to take her beyond that point, to what she would do once it did present itself, what she would say.

"Someone thought she was a threat and paid to have that threat removed," Frank said. "It was nothing but a payout for me."

"How much?" Joey asked. "How much money did my sister put inside your pockets?"

"Fifteen thousand," Frank said. "Plus expenses. All in cash and all up front. That's about what you average in take home to nail a twenty-five-to-life sentence."

Joey took a deep breath, fighting off the visions of her sister's face, closing out the sounds of her happy laughter, erasing the sight of her paintings lining the entryway of her parents' home. She swallowed back the angry rumble in her stomach and the acid burn building in her throat. She had to keep herself emotionally detached from any and all feelings, ease her mind from the shadowed darkness of an empty bar and into the glaring light of an open courtroom. She had her prey in her sights, had him on the witness stand, had him where he could not ever run again. All she had left to do now, as she had done so many times before, across so many years, was to go in for the close. Nail the conviction and have the verdict rendered.

"They thought she was a witness to a hit and run," Joey said. "That she had seen enough to get a good look at a make and model, maybe even an outside chance at a partial plate number. But they were wrong. She was walking away from the accident, not toward it. By the time she heard the crash and turned around, the victim was down and dead and the car was one full block away."

"She was on that block," Frank said. "And the only person near the scene that the cops even bothered to talk to. That was all they needed to put a call in to me."

"It was a call that never needed to be made," Joey said. "All they had to do was get their hands on the police report. My sister was what the cops call a DE. A dead end. She gave them nothing because she had nothing to give. But that nothing was more than enough to have her stamped for death. Some innocent girl was fingered and killed all because some New York gangster wanted his drug-addicted son to get away with a murder."

"I don't pick who I work for," Frank said. "They pick me."

"They pick you because they know the job will get done," Joey said. "It'll be clean and quiet. And almost impossible to trace, either back to you, or the money or to the voice at the other end of the telephone."

"Not so impossible," Frank said. "Or you wouldn't be sitting here."

"I made it my business to find you," she said. "I made it my life."

"I always knew you would," Frank said. "All these years I knew you were out there and I knew you would never stop."

"There were times I wished you would have stopped me," Joey said, sadness etching her words. "Brought it all to an end. For you and for me."

"I never gave it any thought," Frank said.

Joey took a deep breath and closed her eyes for a brief moment. This was always the hardest part of the Q&A for her, asking the short, direct queries that were designed to bring a victim's face to the jury. Keeping the victims alive, making them a presence in a courtroom often dominated by a charming, well-mannered and well-behaved defendant, was always the most painful part of a prosecution. "The victim is the one person they never see that they *need* to see," an old judge had once told her. "It is so easy for the jury to forget. It is the prosecutor's job to keep that victim alive. Full closure can only come with a guilty verdict and a conviction. Nothing else will do."

The bartender turned off the silent television and pulled the switch on the blue-glow lights behind the rows of whiskey bottles. He stared over at Frank and Joey, his middle-aged face weary and void of any expression. He was short, with a squat frame that was balanced by two broad arms, a long line of aging purple tattoos running down their fleshy side. His bald head glistened with tiny sweat beads and slivers of scalp oil. Ralph Santo was the kind of man who went into life expecting little in return and he walked away never disappointed.

"Why did she let you into her apartment?" Joey asked.

"What story did you tell her that made her trust you enough to do that?"

"Why don't you call her by her name?" Frank asked, returning the question with one of his own. "She's not just another victim. She's your sister."

"You don't deserve to hear her name," Joey said, her low voice a venomous hiss.

"She had a good heart," Frank said. "Like a lot of kids her age. I told her I had lost my wallet and needed to make a phone call. Try to reach my girlfriend and have her come pick me up."

"She trusted you," Joey said.

"Most people do," Frank said. "You would have, too."

"What if she didn't have a good heart?" Joey asked. "What if she had just said no and kept walking or offered to give you money for a cab? What would have happened then?"

"It never got to that," Frank said. "It seldom does."

"What if it had?" Joey asked. "Would you have killed her on the street?"

"Only if I was really eager to get caught," Frank said. "Which I wasn't."

"When did she know?" Joey asked. "That a phone call wasn't what you were after."

"Why are you doing this?" Frank asked. "You know everything you need to know. Skip the details. It'll make it easier to live with yourself. No matter how tonight ends up being played out."

"When did she know?" Joey asked, her question now more pointed and direct, her anger residing just below the surface.

"We were in the apartment and she led me to the small dining room, turned to me and pointed out the phone," Frank said. "That was the first time she saw the gun."

"Did she cry?" Joey asked. "Or scream for help?"

"No," Frank said.

"Did she say anything to you at all?"

"She asked me not to rape her," Frank said.

"And that's why you didn't?"

"You know better than to ask that," Frank said. "I didn't rape her because I don't rape anybody. I was there to do a job. I did it and then I left. If it means anything, I wasn't looking to cause her any great pain. I did it the best I could and as fast as I could."

"She say anything before she died?" Joey asked.

"No," Frank said. "She just closed her eyes and waited for it to happen."

"Did you ever think of not doing it?" Joey said. "Didn't seeing that sweet, innocent girl, shivering on a bed, waiting for you to pump bullets into her body, not make you just want to walk away from it all?"

"What difference would my answer to that make to you?" Frank said. "It doesn't matter what I thought or how I felt. All that matters is what I did."

"You made a name for yourself off that murder," Joey said. "It put you in demand. The calls came in steady after that, the work more than you could handle."

"Let's just say it got easier after that," Frank said.

"And you only got better," Joey said. "Here it is more than twenty years later and no one has even come close to putting handcuffs on you."

"Is that what you're waiting to see?" Frank asked.

"Maybe that would have been enough twenty years ago," Joey said. "But not now. I need more than that."

"If you were going to kill me you would have done it when you had the chance," Frank said. "And that chance was when you first walked in and right before you ordered that first drink."

"I wish I could kill you," Joey said. "I wish I could pull out a gun and shoot you until you were dead. I wish I could do to you what you did to my sister. But we both know that I can't and talking about it is just a waste of time."

"You came a long way and waited through a lot of years just to hear me say I did it," Frank said. "Is that going to be enough for you?"

"You can't get a conviction without a guilty plea," Joey said. "I didn't have that until tonight."

"Well then, you got what you came for," Frank said. "I'm guilty as charged, Counselor. Which leaves you where? Calling the cops won't do you much good. It's going to take a terrorist attack to get them out in this weather, not a twenty-year-old murder case none of them even remember. And airport security couldn't catch their ass with both hands, let alone someone who's been running for as long as me."

"There's just one more thing left for me to do," Joey said. "And I don't need the cops, or security to get that done."

"Do I need to guess?" Frank asked. "Or you going to spoil the suspense and tell me?"

"It's what I've been waiting more than twenty years to do," Joey said. "I get to sentence you."

"That's a judge's job," Frank said. "You get promoted and not tell me about it?"

"In this case, I'm one-stop shopping," Joey said. "Prosecutor, jury and judge."

"I hope it's not community service," Frank said. "I would really hate that."

"And it's not life in prison, either," Joey said. "I don't have the power to do that. Or for that matter, the desire."

"Which leaves what?"

Joey pushed her chair back and stood, her eyes glaring down at Frank. "The death penalty," she said. "I sentence you to die for the murder of my sister. There will be no appeals filed and the twenty years that have passed since the crime was committed take care of any stays of execution you might have earned."

"I've only had a couple of beers," Frank said, smiling and brushing off the harshness of her words. "That's not much of a last meal."

"You picked the place," Joey said, picking up her black leather coat. "Not me. But I'll get the tab. A condemned man shouldn't have to pay for anything other than for his crime."

"You're really not following proper procedure," Frank said. "I always had you pinned as a stickler for details. But here I am sentenced to die and no last shower and no fresh batch of clothes. That's not like you to be sloppy, Counselor."

"I have to use what's available to me," Joey said, tossing the coat on and reaching for her bag. "Besides, you don't look like you need either a shower or new clothes. But I did make arrangements for your remains."

"Buried or burned?" he asked.

"That's at the discretion of the executioner," Joey said. She picked up her bag, took one final look at Frank and turned to leave the bar.

"If he's a pro, he'll probably do both," Frank said, his eyes not moving from the table.

"You would know that better than I would," Joey said, her head down, walking toward the open entrance to the bar.

"Hope to run into you again, Counselor," Frank said, raising his voice one notch, looking at her back.

Joey stopped and dropped her bag; its low-impact thud

echoed inside the silent and empty bar. She lowered her head and closed her eyes, her two hands balled into tight fists. "I'm afraid not, Frank," she said, calling him by his name for the only time that night. "This was our first and last meeting. It's all over between us. This case is now closed."

Frank nodded. He didn't need to turn around to know that he'd been locked into the perfect setup from the time he walked into the bar. He didn't need to hear the muted footsteps coming his way or the click of the nine-millimeter that was sure to be aimed at the back of his head. He knew his run was over.

He glanced up at Joey, her back to him, her body still, her head hanging low. He knew she'd been on his tail all these years and wondered why they had both waited until this night to bring the chase to an abrupt end. He was relaxed and relieved in those few silent moments before the first bullet hit. He had chosen the life and now had chosen his own way out of it. He was glad that Joey had been the one, knew she would eventually find the courage to take it to the next step. In that sense, there were two people in that bar on that snowy night that felt a burden lifted.

Joey heard the three muted shots and then heard Frank utter a low, guttural moan and then heard a thud as his upper body fell face forward on the small table, an empty beer bottle smashing to the floor. She stayed frozen in place, waiting with her head bowed as the footsteps now came walking in her direction.

"It's done," she heard the bartender say as he stood next to her. "He's dead."

"Thank you," she said.

"I'll clean the place up and get rid of the body," he told her. "By the time the storm clears, he'll be gone for good."

"And so will you," she said.

"No profit in sticking around," the bartender said. "I hate bars and I hate airports. This is definitely not the place for me."

Joey reached down and picked up her bag. "How good was he?" she asked. "Do you know?"

"Frank Corso was the best," the bartender said. "None better. There are enough stories about him to fill a dozen books."

"But you got to him," she said. "Does that make you better than him now?"

"I got to him because he wanted me to," the bartender said. "Believe me, if he didn't want to go down, it would have been my body being left under a mound of snow."

"Why would he do that?" she asked. "Give up the way he did?"

"Maybe he just got tired of the game," the bartender said. "It's been known to happen sometimes. Or maybe, he felt he owed you. That happens, too. Or maybe it was something else. Something a guy like him could never allow to happen."

"What?"

"Maybe Frank fell in love with you," the bartender said. "You chasing him all these years, he ended up knowing as much about you as you did about him. You get close to a person that way, closer even than to somebody you see every day of your life. You end up feeling for that person. Usually it's hate. But, on a one-in-a-million shot, it does roll out as love."

"We'll never know then," Joey said.

"You can catch a cab if you need one on the lower level," the bartender said. "There are buses, too, but you might have to wait the rest of the night for one to take you back to the city."

"I'm not in any hurry," Joey said, walking slowly out of the darkness of the bar and into the soft glare of the terminal, lined on both sides by shuttered stores. "I have nowhere else to go."

WITNESS

J. A. JANCE

What are you going to do about it?" I asked.

Refusing to meet my gaze, Mindy Harshaw poked at her salad with her fork but ate nothing. Her lower lip trembled. "What can I do?" she asked hopelessly.

A year ago I'd been matron of honor at Mindy's wedding. She had been radiant then. A few months later, when she and our other pal, Stephanie, and I met for coffee at Starbucks, she had definitely lost her glow. She had been uncharacteristically quiet then and had hidden out behind a pair of enormous sunglasses, claiming she had an infection related to pinkeye. Now, having heard what she had to say, I suspected the pinkeye story was just that—a story. And the woman sitting across from me bore no resemblance to my lifelong friend who had been a beaming bride only a few months earlier.

I had been shocked when she slipped into the booth across from me. She looked wan and pale, and I thought she had lost more weight than she could afford to lose. I didn't say, "My

God, Min! You look like hell!" although I probably should have. But now, after she had told me at least some of what had been going on, I wasn't the least bit shy about offering my opinion.

"What you do is blow the whistle on the jerk," I said. "You're not the first Cinderella who woke up after the honeymoon to discover she had married a frog instead of Prince Charming."

Mindy sighed. "It didn't turn out that way for you and Jimmy."

That was true. I had been a thirty-eight-year-old "old maid" when I was introduced to James Drury in the lobby before a performance of *Angry Housewives*, an original Seattle-based musical about a group of frustrated mothers who start a rock band and end up with an unlikely hit entitled, "Eat Your Fucking Cornflakes." Not being a housewife at the time, I hadn't much wanted to go, but a friend from school had dragged me along. James Drury had been bullied into going to the play by a friend from the bank where he worked. The moment Jimmy and I met, we clicked. Just like that. Neither one of us had been married before, and our whirlwind courtship had left our friends, Mindy included, shaking their heads. Jimmy and I had enjoyed eleven glorious years together before a drunk driver, going the wrong way on the I-90 bridge, had snuffed out Jimmy's life and dismantled mine.

It was now three years later. The ache of losing him was still there, but his death was long enough in the past that when Mindy asked me to be her matron of honor, I had been glad to do so. I had known Mindy Crawford since grade school. In high school and college she had always gone for the wrong guys—for the wild ones, the ones living on the edge, for the muscle-bound jocks who played sports, looked great in jeans and T-shirts but had nothing whatsoever going on upstairs. But in the days and weeks leading up to Mindy's wedding to Lawrence Miles Harshaw III, I thought for sure she had come up with a winner.

Larry had money, looks and brains, and not necessarily in that order. Obviously, having money isn't everything, but I was grateful that, after years of hardscrabble existence, Mindy would finally be in a situation where she wouldn't be living hand-to-mouth. As far as I could see, Larry was crazy about her. Which is one of the reasons I was so provoked with him right now. Larry Harshaw had pulled the wool over Mindy's eyes and mine as well. She had an excuse—she was in love with the guy. I've spent the last twenty-five years working as a high school guidance counselor, and I resented the hell out of being duped. Two and a half decades of working with troubled kids has taught me way more than I ever wanted to know about the realities and pervasiveness of domestic violence. It worried me that Mindy seemed totally oblivious about what was in store for her.

"What do you think I should do?" she asked.

"Let's go over what you just told me," I said. "He reads your mail, checks your e-mail. He monitors your telephone calls and checks the mileage on the odometer whenever you use the car. What does this sound like to you?"

"He wants me all to himself?" Mindy asked meekly.

"It's a lot more serious than that," I told her. "It's called isolation. He's cutting you off from your support network. I'm surprised he let you meet me for lunch."

"It was spur of the moment," Mindy admitted. "I didn't exactly tell him."

Or ask permission, I thought.

Suddenly I felt much older and wiser than my fifty-two

years, and Mindy seemed like an innocent—a babe in the woods. Trying to guide recalcitrant teenagers has taught me that I'm not going to get far by telling anybody what they need to do. If I really want to help, I have to get the students who come to my office to see their problems and difficulties for themselves. Mindy wasn't one of my students, but the same thing was true for her. If she was going to save herself, she would have to come to terms with what was happening in her life and marriage on her own. Comprehending the existence of a problem is the first essential step in solving it.

"I've seen how Larry Harshaw acts," I said. "In public, he's the perfect gentleman. What's he like in private?" My question was followed by a long, awkward silence. "Well?" I prodded finally. "Are you going to tell me?"

"He's not very nice," Mindy said in a small voice.

"How so?" I asked. "Does he tell you you're stupid, for example?"

Mindy nodded. "Yes, and that I'm not good with money."

"Because . . . ?"

"Because I don't balance my checkbook."

"Min, I've never known you to balance a checkbook—not once in forty years. But have you ever bounced a check?"

"No."

"Well then? So much for the money-handling problem. What else?"

"There's more to it than just the checkbook," Mindy said. "Even though it's not true, I'm worried that he thinks I married him for his money. When we were engaged, all his friends kept telling him we needed to have a prenup. I told him at the time that I'd be happy to sign one, but he said not to be silly. That he loved me and that whatever he had he was willing to share."

Up to a point, I thought.

"Okay," I said. "He treats you like a prisoner in your own home. He checks on your comings and goings. He belittles you. What else?"

"What do you mean?" Mindy asked,

"Has he ever hurt you?"

"He's hurt my feelings," she replied.

"Has he ever hit you or hurt you physically?" I insisted.

"Not really."

"What does that mean?"

"We were cross-country skiing out by Lake Kachess a couple of weeks ago," she said slowly. "A storm was coming, and I had this terrible feeling that he was going to drive off and leave me out there all alone. That he was going to leave me to freeze to death."

"What did you do?" I asked.

"I told him that I'd hurt my ankle and wouldn't get out of the car."

An involuntary chill swept up my spine. I had no doubt that some subliminal sense of self-preservation was what had kept Mindy off her skis that day and kept her alive long enough to tell her hair-raising tale to me.

"But he's never struck you?" I asked. "Bruised you or pushed you around?"

Mindy shook her head. "No," she said. "Nothing like that."

But she was wearing a turtlenecked sweater. With long sleeves. I know how domestic violence works. I know how cagey abusers can be in making sure none of the bruising shows. I also know how hard it is for women to admit they've been hit. They think that somehow they've caused this terrible calamity to befall them, and by admitting what's happened they're also confessing their own implicit culpability.

"You need to get out," I said quietly. "You need to get out now, before it gets worse. Because it will get worse."

"I can't," she said. "I mean, I just barely finished sending the thank you notes for the wedding presents."

"Screw the wedding presents," I said. "Don't let them stand in the way . . ."

Mindy's cell phone rang, and she fumbled it out of her pocket. "Hi, hon," she said too brightly. "Yes. I stopped to grab some lunch. I'll be home in a few." She ended the call and then added, "Sorry. I've gotta go." She pulled a twenty-dollar bill out of her wallet and dropped it on the table next to her mostly uneaten salad.

"He's pulling your leash," I said. "Bringing you to heel."

"I know," she said. "Still, I need to go." And she left.

I sat there for a few minutes longer before paying the bill and heading home. Earlier that gloomy Saturday morning, when Mindy had called to invite me to a spur-of-the-moment lunch, I had been out in the garage sorting Jimmy's stuff. It was a task that I had delayed time and again. At first I had put it off because it was too painful. And then I put it off because I was too tired. But now, three years later, it was time. I was planning on doing some traveling this coming summer. That meant I needed to reclaim enough room in the garage to park my shiny new Beetle inside.

But now, burdened with what I'd learned from Mindy, I went back to the task with a heavy heart. Jimmy had bought the small Capitol Hill fixer-upper five years before I met him and had set about transforming it. He had stripped and refurbished the fine old hardwood floors. He had repainted and installed crown moldings everywhere. He had ripped out the old plumbing and cabinets and replaced them with updated plumbing fixtures and cabinets of his own design and making.

When we married, I had sold my downtown condo and moved in with him. Disposing of all his woodworking tools was part of the job ahead of me. Sorting his clothing was another.

My folks had come back to Seattle months after the funeral. My mother had insisted on boxing up Jimmy's clothing and having my father cart it out to the garage. "It's part of moving on," she said. She would have taken it to Goodwill right then, but I told her I wanted to sort through it myself And I did, want to sort it, that is. The plastic bag containing the tux Jimmy wore at our wedding was the topmost item in the second box I opened. Seeing it was too much. I broke down and cried. Again. But then I steeled myself to the task. I put it in the Goodwill pile and went on.

There was nothing James Drury did that he didn't do right. As I went through his clothing, much of it still in bags fresh from the cleaners, I missed him anew. It wasn't until after he was gone that I discovered how much he had cared. There were the insurance policies I hadn't known existed. One meant that the mortgage was now paid in full. Another had left a sizeable enough nest egg that I'd be able to retire from teaching as soon as I was eligible rather than having to work any longer than I wanted to.

And that was exactly the kind of stability I had wanted for Mindy as well. I'd really believed that at last she'd found someone who would truly love her and give her a lasting sense of security. The contrast between my situation and hers was striking—and terribly sad.

So often, anticipating doing something proves to be far worse than simply digging in and doing it. By six o'clock that evening, the job I had put off for years because it was impossible was pretty well done. I had loaded my trash can with as much as it could hold and had a pile of a dozen bulging black plastic trash bags sorted and ready to go to Goodwill. A single call to Don Williams, a shop teacher and fellow faculty member at Franklin High School, had elicited the excited promise that he'd come by the next day with a pickup truck to collect any of the tools I wanted to dispose of. It was as I hung up the phone after talking to Don that I remembered the guns. Not Jimmy's guns, because he didn't own any. Larry Harshaw's guns.

I'd seen them the evening of their engagement party. Larry had been showing me through his spacious house overlooking Elliott Bay in Magnolia, one of Seattle's fine old neighborhoods. He had led me into his wood-lined study where an extensive collection of weapons was visible in a locked display case. On his desk was a picture frame. Inside it was a letter of appreciation from the National Rifle Association lauding Larry for his many years of loyal membership. It was signed in unwavering penmanship by former NRA president Charlton Heston himself.

Back then I had only just met Larry Harshaw. He was engaged to one of my best friends. I had wanted to make a good impression, so I feigned far more interest in his gun collection than I had felt. Since that night, I'd had no occasion to return to Larry's study. Now, though, I remembered the ominous presence of all those guns. The likelihood that there were others that I hadn't seen left me with a terrible sense of dread. What if . . . ?

I grabbed the phone and dialed Mindy's cell phone. She didn't answer, and I didn't leave a message. For the next half-hour I paced around my house, trying to decide what to do. Should I call the cops? And tell them what? That I was afraid something had happened to a friend—that her husband might be trying to do her harm—when I had no proof at all that was the case?

Finally, unable to let it go, I got into my VW and drove there. Like waterfront homes the world over, the front of the house was primarily there for the view. Visitors actually entered the house through a backyard gate that opened on a small alley. As soon as I stepped out of the car, I heard voices coming from the open door of the garage. Leaving my car door ajar, I stood and listened.

"Come on, Wes," Mindy was saying. "You've got to do better than that. Grab both my upper arms and squeeze as hard as you can. We need bruises—clearly visible bruises. And then backhand me—right on the lip. Fortunately, Larry's left-handed and so are you."

I cringed when I heard the dull thwack as flesh pounded flesh, but the blow evidently wasn't enough to satisfy Mindy.

"Again," she ordered. "You need to draw blood."

I heard another blow followed by a man's voice. "Aw, geez. Now I've got it all over my shirt."

"My God, Wes. I never would have thought you'd be so damned squeamish. It's a good thing you're not the one who has to pull the trigger. I'll be sure there's plenty of my blood on Larry's shirt, too. Now get the hell out of here. He's due home in a few minutes. I don't want you anywhere near here when he shows up."

"You're sure this is going to work?"

"Of course, it's going to work," Mindy replied. "As soon as the cops come looking for me, I'll send them straight to Francine. After that load of shit I laid on her this afternoon, it'll be self-defense for sure."

Francine! Me! I was the one who'd had a load of shit laid on me. Larry Harshaw wasn't getting ready to kill Mindy. It was the other way around, and I was going to be a prime witness—for the defense.

For a few seconds, I stood rooted to the spot. Finally I managed to will myself to move. I jumped into the car, slammed the door, started the engine and raced to the bottom of the hill. Afraid Wes might have followed me, I ducked into a driveway two houses up from the intersection. Seconds later the Dodge Ram pickup that had been parked next to the garage came roaring down the hill. The driver paused at the bottom of the alley and seemed to look both ways. I held my breath, but he must not have seen what vehicle I was in when I took off. Or else he didn't see me parked there. After what seemed like a very long time, he finally pulled into the street and drove off. From where I was, I wasn't able to make out his license number, and I sure as hell wasn't going to follow him hoping to get a closer look.

I was getting ready to call 9-1-1 when another car came down the street, signaling to turn into the alley. With a sinking heart, I realized I was looking at the headlights of Larry Harshaw's Cadillac. I turned the key in the ignition and slammed my VW into reverse. Flashing my headlights on and off, I followed Larry up the hill. He stopped halfway to the top and got out of the car.

"Can I help you?" he called back to me. "Is something wrong?"

"Yes," I said. "Something's terribly wrong. It's Francine, Francine Drury. I've got to talk to you, Larry. It's important."

"Well, come on up to the house," he said. "We can talk there."

"No," I said desperately. "We can't go to the house."

"Why not? What's wrong? Has something happened to Mindy? My God, is she all right?"

"You've got to listen to me, Larry. Mindy's fine, but she's got a boyfriend. They're planning to kill you and make it look like self-defense. I heard the two of them talking about it just now."

"Kill me?" Larry said. "Are you kidding? Mindy loves me, and she wouldn't hurt a flea. That's the most preposterous thing I've ever heard. Where did you come up with such an outrageous idea? You haven't been drinking, have you, Francine?"

"Of course I haven't been drinking," I said. "I was standing outside the gate. I heard them talking inside the garage—Mindy and somebody named Wes."

"Wes Noonan, no doubt," Larry said confidently. "I'll have you know Wes is a very good friend of mine. I'm sure all of this is just some silly misunderstanding. Come on up to the house now, Francine. We'll talk this over, have a drink or two and a good laugh besides when we finally get to the bottom of whatever's going on."

"Didn't you hear what I said?" I insisted desperately. "Mindy's going to kill you and try to make it look like you attacked her."

"She'll do no such thing," Larry Harshaw told me. "Now come on. It's starting to rain. I have no intention of standing here, getting wet and arguing about this. Are you coming or not?"

"Not," I said. "But please don't go."

"I'm going," he said. And he did.

I scrambled into my car, grabbed my cell phone, and dialed 9-1-1. "Washington State Patrol," a voice said. "What is the nature of your emergency?"

"My name's Francine Drury," I said. "I'm on Magnolia, in Seattle. And someone's about to be murdered."

I was still on the phone, giving them Mindy's address, when I heard the distinctive pop, pop of gunfire. There was a pause and then a third pop. "Oh, my God!" I exclaimed into the phone. "Please hurry. She already did it. She shot him. Send an ambulance, too!"

I stood there shaking, leaning against the roof of my Beetle for support as two blue police cars and an ambulance, lights flashing and sirens blaring, went screaming up the hill past me. I've never felt more useless. If only I could have made him believe me . . .

A third cop car pulled up behind me and a uniformed officer stepped out. "Ms. Drury?" he asked. "Are you the one who placed the first 9-1-1 call?"

"Yes," I managed. "Yes, I am." Then I burst into tears. "It's all my fault," I blubbered. "I heard her say she was going to kill him. I tried to warn him, but he wouldn't listen to me, and now he's dead."

Something came in over the officer's radio. I heard a garbled voice, but I couldn't make out the words. "Sit down, please," the officer urged me. "Let me get you some water."

I did. I was too weak to object or do anything other than what I'd been told. I sat where he told me. There were other people on the street now, streaming out of neighboring houses, trying to figure out what had happened and what was going on.

Moments later the ambulance came roaring back down the hill. The onlookers parted to let it through.

"That's the male vic," the officer explained, handing me a bottle of water. His name tag said he was Sergeant Lowrey. "She winged him. Superficial wound to the shoulder. They're taking him to Harborview. He's going to be fine."

"And Mindy?" I asked. "What about her?"

Sergeant Lowrey took out a small notebook. "That's her name? Mindy what?"

"Mindy Harshaw," I answered. "What about her?"

Lowrey shook his head. "When it didn't turn out the way she expected, she turned the gun on herself."

"You mean she's gone?" I stammered. "She's dead?"

Sergeant Lowrey nodded. "I'm afraid so," he answered. "I hope she wasn't a friend of yours."

"I thought she was," I said quietly, fighting back more tears. "But I guess she wasn't anymore."

SOFT SPOT

IAN RANKIN

Most evenings, Dennis Henshall took his work home with him.

Not that anyone knew. He reckoned most of his fellow prison warders wouldn't care one way or the other. As far as they were concerned, Dennis was a bit on the odd side anyway, sitting most of the day in his office, poring over correspondence, ruler and razor blade at the ready. He had to be careful with those blades: one of the rules of the job. Kept them under lock and key, away from deft fingers. Each morning, he would unlock his desk drawer and count them, then remove one, only ever the one. When that got blunt, he'd take it home with him, dump it in the kitchen bin. The desk drawer back in his office stayed locked the rest of the day, and mostly his door was kept locked, too, except when he was inside. A two-minute break to go pee, still he locked the door behind him, the blade back in its drawer, that drawer locked, too.

You could never be too careful.

His filing cabinet was secured with a vertical metal bar connecting all four drawer handles. The first time the Governor had visited, he'd made no comment about this added precaution, but hadn't been able to stop himself glancing over at the tall green cabinet throughout his conversation with Dennis.

The other warders, they reckoned Dennis was hiding stuff; porn mags and whiskey. Hid himself in his office, one hand around the bottle neck, the other busy in his trousers. He did little to dispel the myth, quite liked the fact that this other life was being invented for him. In point of fact, the cabinet contained nothing but alphabetized correspondence: letters connecting inmates to their friends and loved ones on the outside. These were the letters that had been deemed UTF: Unable to Forward. A letter could be deemed UTF if it gave away too much information about prison routine, or if it seemed threatening. Swearing and sexual content were fine, but most letters remained coy, once it was realized that Dennis, as prison censor, would be reading any correspondence first.

This was his job, and he carried out the work diligently. His ruler would underline a contentious sentence, and he would get to work with the razor blade. Excised sections were kept in the filing cabinet, glued to a sheet of stationery with typed comments including date, the inmate's identity, and reason for excision. Each morning a fresh delivery of mail awaited him; every afternoon, he checked the outgoing post. These envelopes were prestamped and addressed, but not stuck down until Dennis had authorized their contents.

He opened incoming mail with a wooden letter opener he'd bought from a curio shop on Cockburn Street. It was African, the handle carved to resemble an elongated head. This, too, he kept locked away whenever he vacated his office.

His room hadn't always been an office. He guessed it had started life as some sort of store. Maybe eight feet square, with two small, barred windows high up on one wall. There were metal pipes in the corner opposite the filing cabinet, and sounds from outside seemed to travel through them: distorted voices, barked orders, clanging and rattling. Dennis had taped a couple of posters to his walls. One showed the somber emptiness of Glencoe—a place he'd never been, despite regular promises to himself—while the other was a photograph of one of the East Neuk's fishing villages, taken from the harbor wall. Dennis liked them both equally. Staring at one or the other, he could transport himself to Highland wilderness or coastal haven, providing the briefest of respites from the sounds and smells of HMP Edinburgh.

The smells were worst in the morning: unaired cells thrown open, the great unwashed scratching and belching as they slouched toward breakfast. He seldom had contact—actual contact—with these men, yet he felt he knew them. Knew them through their letters, filled with clumsy sentences and spelling mistakes, yet eloquent for all that, and sometimes even poignant. *Give the kids a big hug from me . . . I try to think about the good times only . . . Every day I don't see you, a bit more of me crumbles away . . . When I get out, we'll start over . . .*

Getting out: A lot of the letters spoke of this magical time, when past mistakes would be erased and fresh beginnings made possible. Even old lags, the ones who'd contrived to spend more of their life in prison than out, promised that they'd never stray again, that they'd make everything all right. *I'll be missing our anniversary again, Jean, but you're never far from my thoughts . . .* Small comfort for the wives like Jean, whose own letters ran to ten or twelve sides, crammed with the daily agonies of life without a breadwinner. *Johnny's running wild, Tam. The doctor says it's what's contributing to my condition. He needs a dad, but all I get are more of the tablets.*

Jean and Tam: Their life apart had become a sort of soap opera to Dennis. Every week they exchanged letters, even though Jean visited her husband almost as regularly. Sometimes Dennis watched the visitors as they arrived, trying to identify letter writers. Then he'd study them as they made their way to this table or that, helping him match inmate and correspondent. Tam and Jean always squeezed hands, never hugged or kissed, seeming almost embarrassed at the less restrained behavior of couples around them.

Dennis seldom censored their letters, even on the odd occasions when something contentious cropped up. His own wife had left him a decade ago. He still kept some framed photos of her on the mantelpiece. In one of them, she was holding his hand, smiling for the camera. He might be watching TV, seated with a can of beer in his hand, and suddenly his eyes would start drifting toward that picture. Like Glencoe and the harbor, it took him to a different place. Then he would get up and cross to the dining table, where he'd have laid out the letters.

He didn't take every last piece of correspondence home, just those concerning relationships that interested him. He'd bought a fax machine that doubled as a copier—cheaper, the shop assistant had informed him, than buying an actual photocopier. He would take the letters from his leather satchel and feed them into the machine. Next morning, the originals went back into the office with him. He knew he was doing something he shouldn't, knew the Governor would be angry with him, or at the very least dismayed. But Dennis couldn't see what harm he was doing. No one else was going to read them. They were for him alone.

One recent inmate was proving an intriguing specimen. He wrote a couple of times a day—obviously had plenty of money for stamps. His girlfriend was called Jemma, and she'd been pregnant but had lost the baby. Tommy was worried that he was to blame, that the shock of his conviction had caused her to abort. Dennis had yet to lay eyes on Tommy, knew he could say a few reassuring words to the kid.

But he wouldn't. Wouldn't get involved.

Another inmate, first name of Morris, had interested Dennis a few months previously. Morris had written one or two letters a week—steamy love letters. Always, it seemed to Dennis, to a different woman. Morris had been pointed out to him in the breakfast queue. The man looked nothing special: a scrawny specimen with a lopsided grin.

"He ever get visitors?" Dennis had asked the warder.

"You're joking, aren't you?"

And Dennis had just shrugged, puzzled. The women Morris wrote to, they lived in the city. No reason for them not to visit. His address and prisoner number were printed at the top of each letter.

And then the Governor had asked Dennis to "nip along" to his office, informing him that Morris was banned forthwith from sending letters. Turned out, the sod was picking names out of the phone book, writing to complete strangers, sending detailed accounts of his fantasies.

The warders had laughed about it afterward: "Reckoned if he sent out enough of them, he'd get lucky eventually," one had explained. "Maybe he would have, too. Some women on the outside go for the hardened con . . ."

Ah, yes, the hardened con. Plenty of those in HMP Edinburgh. But Dennis knew who really ran the show: Paul Blaine. Blaine was a cut above the muggers and junkies whose orbit around him he managed to ignore. When he walked through the prison halls, it was as if he'd surrounded himself with some invisible force field, so that no one came within several feet of him, unless he wanted them there. He had a "lieutenant" called Chippy Chalmers, whose lurking presence acted as a reminder of the force field. Not that anyone reckoned Blaine needed a minder. He was six three, thick-shouldered, and kept his hands half-clenched. Everything he did, he did slowly, with deliberation. He wasn't here to make enemies or rub the warders up the wrong way. He just wanted to serve his time and head on out to where his empire still awaited.

Nevertheless, from the moment he'd walked in, he'd been the jail's natural leader. The gangs and factions tiptoed around him, showing respect. Six years he was serving, having finally been nabbed on tax evasion, deception and fraud—probably out in a little over three, a couple of months already under his belt. He'd lost some weight since arriving, but looked the better for it, despite the gray tinge to his cheeks—same chalky look all cons ended up with, "prison tan," they called it. When Blaine's wife came visiting, more warders than normal crowded into the hall, not because anything was going to happen, but because Blaine had married well.

"Achingly well," one warder had whispered to Dennis with a wink.

Her name was Selina. At twenty-nine, she was ten years Blaine's junior. When the warders discussed her over breaktime tea and sandwiches, Dennis had to lock his mouth shut. Thing was, he knew more about her than they did.

He knew just about everything.

She lived at an address in Bearsden, on the posh outskirts

of Glasgow, visited her husband every fortnight rather than weekly, even though she was only forty-odd miles away. But she did write. She wrote four or five letters to every one of his. And the things she said . . .

I miss your hard-ons! See, Paul, I'm totally, absolutely lovestruck. If you were here, I'd straddle you till morning . . .

Whole passages like this were intertwined with gossip and the everyday: *I'm helping Elaine at Riddrie tomorrow. Perhaps ring our Bill, lift Elaine's morale?*

These snippets appealed to Dennis every bit as much as the more personal stuff, giving him a feel for Selina's life. In one of her early letters, she'd even included a Polaroid of herself, posed in short skirt and halter top, head tilted, hands on hips. More photos had followed. Dennis had tried copying them, but they wouldn't fit into his fax machine, so he'd gone to a newsagent's instead and used the machine there. The copies were grainy, far from perfect. Still, they went into his collection.

I tried satisfying myself in bed last night, but it wasn't the same. How could it be? I had a photo of you on the pillow beside me, a far cry from the real thing. Hope the pics I'm sending are cheering you up. Not much else to report. Fred's off up north. (Denise isn't talking to him—and not keeping sober!)

At other times, she spoke of how difficult it was, making ends meet. She hadn't found a job yet, but was looking. Dennis had done a bit of digging, finding newspaper reports that suggested that police had "failed to find missing Blaine millions." Millions? Then what was Selina complaining about?

Last time she'd visited, Dennis had asked a warder to let him know. He'd been a bit nervous—no idea why—as he'd walked into the hall. And there she was, seated with her back to him, one leg crossed over the other, skirt high up on her thighs, showing a tanned, muscular calf. Tight white T-shirt with a pink cashmere jersey buttoned over it. Blonde hair, lots of it, cascading down one shoulder.

"Isn't she something?" the warder had grinned.

Even better than her photos, Dennis felt like saying. Then he'd noticed Blaine's eyes on him, and averted his gaze just as Selina was turning in her seat to check what had distracted her husband's attention from her.

Dennis had hurried back to his office. But a few days later, while passing through one of the halls, he'd found Blaine and Chalmers walking in his direction.

"Lovely, isn't she?" Blaine had said.

"What's that?"

"You know what I mean." Blaine stopped directly in front of him, looking him up and down. "I suppose I should say thanks."

"For what?"

A shrug. "I know how screws can be. Some of them would keep the photos to themselves . . ." Now a pause. "I'm told you're the quiet type, Mr. Henshall. That's good. I respect that. The letters . . . nobody else sees them but you?"

Dennis had managed to shake his head, holding Blaine's gaze.

"That's good," the gangster had repeated.

And he'd walked off, Chalmers half a step behind him, casting a baleful look back in Dennis's direction.

• • •

More digging: Blaine in and out of trouble since he was at school. Gang leader at sixteen, terrorizing Glasgow's concrete suburbs. Jail time for the stabbing of a rival, then narrowly escaping the same fate for his role in the murder of another gangster's son. Growing wise by now, starting to assemble that force field. A whole regiment of "soldiers" who'd do the time on his behalf. His reputation solidifying, so that he no longer needed to maim or threaten: Others were there to do it for him, leaving him to wear a respectable suit, working each day in an actual office, fronting a taxi firm, a security firm and a dozen other enterprises.

Selina had arrived on the scene as his receptionist, then secretary, elevated to P.A. before marrying him in front of a congregation like something out of *The Godfather*. But she was no dumb blonde: came from a good family, had studied at college. The more Dennis considered her, the harder he found it to conceive of her as "totally, absolutely lovestruck." This, too, had to be a front. She wanted Blaine kept docile, feeding him fantasies. Why? One tabloid hack had suggested an answer: *With her winning combination of brains and beauty—and the past guidance of a master manipulator—might this be one moll capable of running the whole shooting match, without getting caught in the cross fire?*

Seated at his dining table, Dennis pondered this. Then he pored over her photographs and wondered some more. His food grew cold on its plate, the TV stayed off, and he reread her letters in sequence . . . saw her in his mind's eye, tanned legs, hair swept over one ear. Clear, innocent-looking eyes, a face that drew to it every stare available.

Brains and beauty. Put her together with her husband and you had Beauty and the Beast. Dennis forced himself to eat some of the congealing fry-up, and started counting down to the weekend.

Saturday morning, he parked his car curbside, across the road from her house. He'd been expecting something better. The papers had called it a "mansion," but in reality it was a plain two-story detached house, maybe dating back to the 1960s. The front garden had been paved over to create a couple of parking spaces. A sporty-looking silver Merc sat on display. Beside it, a larger car had had a tarpaulin thrown over it. Dennis guessed this was Blaine's, kept under wraps until his return. There were net curtains covering every window, no sign of life behind them. Dennis checked his watch: not quite ten. He'd assumed she would sleep late at the weekend; most people he knew seemed to. For himself, he was always awake before dawn, never could get back to sleep again. This morning, he'd gone to a café near his home, reading the paper at a table as he sipped his tea, washing down the toast and jam. Now that he was here, he felt thirsty again, and realized he should have brought a flask with him, maybe some sandwiches and something to read. His wasn't the only car on the street, but he knew people would start wondering about him if he sat for a whole morning. Then again, they were probably used to it: reporters and such like.

For want of anything else to do, he switched on the radio, tried eight or nine stations—Medium Wave and VHF—before settling on one that had a lot of classical music and not much talk between the tunes. It was another hour before anything happened. A car drew to a stop outside the house, horn blaring three times. It was an old Volvo, its color fading. The man who got out was medium height and medium build, hair slicked back from his forehead. He wore a black polo-neck, black denims, three-quarter-length black leather coat. And sunglasses, despite the slate-gray sky. Tanned, too, probably courtesy of one of the city's tanning parlors. He pushed open the gate and walked up to the house, thumped on the door with his fist. There was something protruding from his mouth. Dennis thought it might be a cocktail stick.

Selina already had her coat on: a denim jacket with silver studs. Her white trousers were skin-tight. She pecked her visitor on the cheek, wriggled when he tried sliding his arms around her waist. She looked stunning, and Dennis realized he'd stopped breathing for a moment. He tried not to grip the steering wheel too tightly, wound his window down to try to catch what they were saying as they came down the path toward the waiting car.

The man leaned in toward Selina and whispered something. She thumped him on the shoulder.

"Fred!" she squealed. The man called Fred chuckled and smiled to himself. But now Selina was looking at his car and shaking her head.

"We'll take the Merc."

"What's wrong with mine?"

"It looks like shit, Fred, that's what. You want to take a girl shopping, you need a classier set of wheels."

She went back into the house for her keys, while Fred opened the gates. Then the pair of them got into Selina's car. Dennis didn't bother trying to hide. Maybe part of him wanted her to see him, to know she had an admirer. But it was as if he was invisible, she was talking to Fred.

Fred?

Fred's off up north. Denise isn't talking to him . . .

But Fred wasn't up north; he was right here. Why had she lied? Maybe so her husband wouldn't suspect.

"Naughty girl," Dennis muttered to himself as he followed the small silver car.

Selina drove like a demon, but the traffic heading into the city was sluggish: all those Saturday shoppers. Dennis had little trouble keeping the Merc in view, and followed it into one of the multistories behind Sauchiehall Street. Selina waited on level three, while a woman backed out of the last empty bay. Dennis took a chance and headed up to the next level, where there were plenty of spaces. He locked his car and walked back down the ramp, just as Selina and Fred were heading into the shopping center.

They were like boyfriend and girlfriend: Selina trying on various permutations of clothes while Fred gave a nod or a shrug, growing fidgety and fed up after an hour. They'd moved from the center to an array of designer shops the other side of George Square. By now, Selina was carrying three bags, Fred a further four. She'd tried cajoling him into a brown suede jacket, but he'd bought nothing. So far, all the purchases were hers, and, Dennis noticed, paid for with her own cash. Several hundred pounds, by his estimate: peeled from rolls of notes in her jacket pockets.

So much for her complaints to Blaine about not having any money.

They settled on an Italian restaurant for lunch. Dennis decided he had time for a break. Ran into a pub to use the toilet, then into a shop for a sandwich and bottle of water, plus the early edition of the evening paper.

"What the hell am I doing?" he asked himself as he unwrapped the sandwich. But then he smiled, because he was enjoying himself. In fact, enjoying this Saturday more than any in recent memory. When they emerged from the restaurant, it looked as if Fred had been refreshed by more than an odd glass of wine. He had his free arm around Selina's shoulders until he dropped some of the shopping. After that, he concentrated on carrying the bags. They headed back to the multistory. Dennis followed the Merc, realizing soon enough that it was headed for Bearsden and expedition's end. The Merc was in the driveway as he drove past. Glancing to his left he was startled to find

Selina staring at him as she closed her driver's-side door. Her eyes narrowed, as if trying to place him. Then she turned and helped the still-groggy Fred into the house.

• • •

The Governor's secretary, Mrs. Beeton, was good as gold when Dennis explained why he wanted the file.

"Recent letters have been mentioning someone called Fred. I want to check if he's someone we should know about."

This was good enough reason for Mrs. Beeton to seek out and hand over the file on Paul Blaine. Dennis thanked her and retreated to his office, locking his door behind him. The file was bulky; too much for him to think about photocopying. Instead, he sat down to read. He found Fred soon enough: Frederick Hart, nominally in charge of a taxi firm that was actually owned by Blaine. Hart had been in trouble for intimidating the competition, fighting over pitches and routes. Prosecuted but not convicted. There was nothing about a wife called Denise, but Dennis found what he was looking for in one of the newspaper cuttings. Fred was married with four teenage kids. Lived in an ex–council house with an eight-foot wall around it. There was even a grainy photo of the man, looking considerably younger, scowling as he left a court building

"Hello, Fred," Dennis whispered.

When Selina's next letter arrived, Dennis felt his heart pounding, as if it were meant for him rather than her husband. He sniffed the envelope, studied the handwritten address, took his time opening it. Unfolded the paper—just a single sheet, written on both sides.

Started to read.

It gets a bit lonely here with you not around. Denise drops in sometimes to go shopping.

Liar.

I go whole days on end and never set foot out of the house, so I know what it's like to be banged up!

And Dennis reckoned he knew who was doing the banging.

He started taking evening drives to Bearsden. Sometimes he would park a few streets away and pretend he was a local out for a walk, managing to pass her house a couple of times, maybe pausing to check his watch, tie a shoelace, or answer an imaginary call on his cell phone. If the weather wasn't great, he would sit in the car, or simply drive around. He got to know her estate, could even recognize one or two of the neighbors. And they, in turn, got to know him; or at least they knew his face. No longer a stranger, and therefore not suspicious. Maybe they reckoned he'd just moved into the area. He got nods and smiles and the occasional bit of chat. And then one evening, as he was driving into her street, he saw the For Sale sign. His first thought was: I could buy it! Buy it and be near her! But then he saw that the sign was firmly planted in Selina's own driveway. Did Blaine know about this? Dennis didn't think so; nothing had been mentioned in the correspondence. Of course, it might have been discussed during one of her visits, but he got the feeling this was yet another secret she was keeping from her husband. But why sell the house? Did it mean she really did have money worries? If so, what was she doing with pocketfuls of cash? Dennis stopped curbside and jotted down the phone number on the sign, tried calling on his cell phone, but was advised by a message that the solicitor's office opened at nine in the morning.

He called again at nine the following morning, explaining that he was interested in the house. "Is the seller after a quick sale, do you think?" he asked.

"How do you mean, sir?"

"I just wondered if the price might be negotiable, say if someone came along with a solid offer."

"It's fixed price, sir."

"That usually means they're in a hurry to sell."

"Oh, it'll sell all right. I'd suggest that you arrange a viewing for this week, if you're interested."

"A viewing?" Dennis gnawed his bottom lip. "Maybe that's an idea, yes."

"I've got a cancellation this evening, if that suits."

"This evening?"

"Eight o'clock."

Dennis hesitated. "Eight o'clock," he repeated.

"Excellent. And it's Mr. . . ."

He swallowed hard. "Denny. My name's Frank Denny."

"And do you have a contact number, Mr. Denny?"

Dennis was sweating. He offered his cell phone number.

"Terrific," the woman said. "You'll be shown round by a Mr. Appleby."

"Appleby?" Dennis frowned.

"He works for us," the woman explained.

"The owner won't be there, then?" Dennis asked, starting to relax a little.

"Some owners prefer it that way."

"All right . . . that's fine. Eight o'clock, then."

"Good-bye, Mr. Denny."

"Thanks for all your help . . ."

He spent the rest of the day in a daze. In a final effort to clear his head, he went for a walk around the prison—the yard first, and then the halls. Some of the men knew him—he hadn't always been a censor. Time was, he'd been a lockup, same as the others: working shifts and weekends, having to live with the smells of slopping-out and the kitchens. Some of his colleagues said he was daft for taking the vacant post of censor—it meant no chance of overtime.

"It suits me," he'd explained at the time. The Governor had agreed. But now Dennis was beginning to wonder. His head was still swimming as he climbed the metal stairs to the upper level . . . he knew where he was headed, couldn't seem to stop himself. Chalmers was resting his considerable weight against a whitewashed brick wall, guarding the open doorway next to him. Inside, Blaine was stretched out on a bed, head lying on his clasped hands.

"How are you today, Mr. Henshall?" he called, and Dennis realized he had come to a stop in the doorway. He folded his arms, as if there might be some reason for his visit.

"I'm all right. How about you?"

"Not feeling too great actually." Blaine removed one hand slowly and patted his chest with it. "The old ticker isn't what it used to be. Mind you, whose is?" Blaine smiled, and Dennis tried not to. "Must be nice for you, finishing your shift, getting to walk out of here. Down the pub for a pint . . . or is it straight home to a nice, warm missus?" Blaine paused. "Sorry, I forgot. Your wife left you, didn't she? Was it another man?"

Dennis didn't answer. Instead, he asked a question of his own: "What about your own wife?"

"Selina? Good as gold, she is. You know that . . . you read everything she gets up to."

"She doesn't visit as often as she could."

"What's the point? I'd rather she stayed away. This place clings to you—ever noticed when you go home at night, the way the smell's still in your nostrils? Would you want a woman you love coming to a place like this?" He rested his head back down, staring at the ceiling of his cell. "Selina likes nothing better than sitting at home with her puzzles. Magazines full of them. Crosswords . . . that's what she likes."

"Really?" Dennis tried not to smile at this image of Selina.

"What-d'you-call-thems . . . acrobatics?"

"She likes acrobatics?" Dennis was betting she did.

Blaine shook his head. "A word like that. Good as gold, she is, you mark my words."

"I'll do that."

"What about you, Mr. Henshall? Been a while since your wife scarpered—any women in your life?"

"That's none of your business."

Blaine chuckled. "I've never met a man yet who hasn't had a soft spot for her," he called out, as Dennis turned to go.

Dennis thinking: *I'll bet you haven't.* Maybe it wasn't just Fred. Maybe there were others, fueling her shopping trips. Or she was spending her husband's loot without his knowledge. And now was about to do a runner, taking it with her. Dennis realized something: He had power over her now, knew things about her she wouldn't want Blaine to find out. Power over Fred, too, if it came to it. The thought warmed him during the rest of his walk.

• • •

"Mr. Denny?"

"That's right," Dennis said. "And you must be Mr. Appleby?"

"Come in, come in."

Mr. Appleby was a short, overweight man in his late sixties, smartly attired and businesslike. He made Dennis add his name to a list on the table in the narrow hallway, then asked him if he needed a schedule. Dennis replied that he did, and a printed brochure was handed over: four pages of color photos of the house, along with details of the accommodation and grounds.

"Would you like the tour, or are you happy to look around by yourself?"

"I'll be fine," Dennis replied.

"Any questions, I'll be right here." And Mr. Appleby sat himself down on a chair, while Dennis pretended to be studying the schedule. He made his way into the living room, checked he wasn't visible from the hall. Then he looked. The furniture was new-looking but gaudy: vivid orange sofa, a large TV and even larger cocktail cabinet. Magazines and newspapers had been crammed into a rack. Dennis noted that some of them were puzzle magazines, so maybe Blaine hadn't been too wrong about Selina after all. There were no photos on display, no mementoes of foreign holidays. A mixture of ornaments, looking like a job lot from one of the bigger, trendier stores: narrow vases, paperweights, candlesticks. Heading back into the hall, he smiled at Mr. Appleby before making for the kitchen. A wall had been knocked through so that glass doors now led to a dining room with French doors leading out into the back garden. "Fitted kitchen units by Nijinsky," the brochure said, adding that all appliances, curtains and floor coverings were included in the sale. Wherever Selina was headed, she was taking none of this with her.

The two final downstairs rooms were a cramped cloakroom/w.c. and what was described as "Bedroom 4" but was currently being used for storage: cardboard boxes, racks of women's clothes. Dennis ran a hand down one of the dresses, rubbing the hem between finger and thumb. Then he pressed his nose to it, picking up the faintest trace of her perfume.

Upstairs, there were three bedrooms off the landing, the "master" featuring an "en suite by Ballard." The master was the largest room by far, and the only one being used as a bedroom. Dennis slid the drawers open, touching her clothes. Pulled open the wardrobe, drank in the sight of her various dresses, skirts and blouses. There were more of Blaine's clothes, too, of course: a few expensive-looking suits, striped shirts with the cuff links already attached. Would she dump them before leaving, Dennis wondered?

The other bedrooms seemed to comprise "his" and "hers" studies. In his: shelves of books—mostly crime and war novels, plus sports biographies—a desk covered in paperwork, and a music center with albums by Glen Campbell, Tony Bennett and others.

Selina's study was something else again: more puzzle magazines, but everything kept neat. There was an unused knitting machine in one corner, a rocking chair in another. Dennis pulled a photograph album out from a shelf and flicked through it, stopping at a beach holiday, Selina in a pink bikini, a coy smile for the camera. Dennis glanced out into the hall, heard Mr. Appleby stifle a sneeze downstairs and then removed one of the photos, slipping it into his pocket. As he descended the staircase, he was reading the brochure again.

"A delightful family home," Mr. Appleby told him.

"Absolutely."

"And fixed price. You'll need to be quick. I'd bet a pound to a penny, this'll be gone by four o'clock tomorrow."

"You think so?"

"Pound to a penny."

"Well, I'll sleep on it," Dennis said, realizing that his hand was resting against his jacket pocket.

"You do that, Mr. Denny," his guide said, opening the door for him.

• • •

When Dennis woke up next morning, he was surrounded by her.

He'd stopped at a late-opening shop and used their color copier. Decided not to stint: printed twenty slow copies. He could see that the shopkeeper wanted to ask him about the photo and the quantity, but the man knew better than to pry.

Pictures of her on his bed, on the sofa, laid out on his dining table. Even one on the floor of the hallway, left there when he'd dropped it. The original, he took to work with him, locking it in his desk. At visiting time that afternoon, there was a knock at his door. He unlocked it. One of the warders stood there, arms folded.

"You coming for a butcher's?"

"I take it Mrs. Blaine is in the building," Dennis commented, managing to sound calm while his heart pounded.

The warder spread his hands in front of him. "Showtime," he said with a grin.

But, to Dennis's surprise, Selina was not alone. She'd brought Fred with her. The pair of them sat opposite Blaine, Selina doing most of the talking. Dennis was appalled and impressed in equal measure. You're about to leave your husband, and the last time you see him, you bring along the man who's been keeping you warm at nights. But it was a dangerous game she was playing. Blaine would be furious when he found out, and he had plenty of friends on the outside. Dennis doubted he'd want Selina hurt: Blaine obviously loved her to bits. But Fred . . . Fred was another matter entirely. Killing would be too good for him. Yet there he sat, one arm slung over the back of the chair, casual as anything. Just visiting his old employer, his mate, nodding whenever Blaine deigned to speak to him, managing to keep just enough distance between Selina and him, so Blaine couldn't read anything into the body language. Maybe he'd been explaining his fictitious jaunt "up north," his return to Denise.

Dennis realized that he hated Fred, even without really knowing him. He hated who and what he was, hated the fact that he obviously made money yet drove a clapped-out car. Hated the way he'd put his arm around Selina that time in Glasgow. Hated that he had more money and probably more women than Dennis ever would have.

What the hell was Selina doing, wasting herself on him? It didn't make sense. Except . . . except, she would need someone to take the blame when she fled, someone Blaine could take his anger out on. Dennis allowed himself a smile. Could she be so calculating, so clever? He didn't doubt it, not for one second. Yes, she was playing with Fred, same as she was with her own, duped husband. It was perfect.

Apart from the one detail: Dennis himself, who felt he knew everything now. He realized that he had allowed his eyes to drift out of focus. When he blinked them clear, he saw that Selina had turned her head to look at him. Her eyes narrowed as she gave the briefest of smiles.

"Which one of us was that for?" the warder next to Dennis asked. Dennis himself had no doubt. She'd recognized him, maybe placed him as the man she'd seen driving past her house. She turned to say something to her husband, and Fred snapped round, glaring at the warders.

"Ooh, I'm scared," the warder beside Dennis muttered, before starting to chuckle. But it wasn't him Fred was looking at: It was Dennis.

Blaine himself just stared at the tabletop, nodding slowly, then said a few words to his wife, who nodded back. When it came time to leave, she gave Blaine a more effusive embrace than usual. *It's called the kiss-off*, Dennis thought. She even waved at her husband as she walked away on her noisy two-inch heels. Blew him another kiss, while Fred allowed himself a glance around the room, sizing up the other women on display and rolling his shoulders, as if content that he was leaving with the classiest of the bunch.

Dennis walked back to his office and made a phone call.

"I'm afraid you're too late," he was told. "That property was sold this morning."

He replaced the receiver. She was on her way . . . he might never see her again. And there was nothing he could do about it, was there?

Maybe not.

Half an hour later, he left his room, locking it behind him as usual. His walk through the prison took him right past Blaine's open cell door. Chalmers was on guard duty as usual.

"Visitor, boss," he growled. Blaine had been seated on his bed, but rose to his feet, facing Dennis.

"What's this I hear about you, Mr. Henshall? Seems you've taken a right shine to Selina. She saw you driving past the house." Blaine took a step closer, his tone jocular but face set like stone. "Now why would you do a thing like that? Can't think your employers would be too thrilled . . ."

"She must've made a mistake."

"That right? She got the make of car and the color: green Vauxhall Cavalier. Ring any bells?"

"She's made a mistake."

"So you keep saying. I know I told you plenty of men come to fancy her, but they don't all go to your extremes, Mr. Henshall. You been following her? Watching the house? That's *my* house, too, you know. How many times you done it? Cruising past . . . peeking through the curtains . . ." Blood had risen to Blaine's cheeks, a tremble entering his voice. Dennis realized that he was sandwiched between these two men, Blaine and Chalmers. No other warders around.

"You a bit of a perv, Mr. Henshall? Locked in that room of yours, reading all those love letters . . . give you a hard-on, does it? No wife to go home to, so you start sniffing around other men's. What's the Governor going to think about that, eh?"

Dennis's face creased. "You thick bastard! Can't even see what's under your nose! She's out there spending all your loot, shacking up with your pal Fred. I've seen them. Now she's sold the house and she's clearing off. You just had your last conjugal visit, Blaine, only you're too stupid to see it!"

"You're lying." Beads of sweat had appeared on Blaine's forehead. His face was almost puce, and his breathing sounded ragged.

"She's been conning you from the minute you walked in here," Dennis rushed on. "Telling you she's hard up when she spends rolls of cash in every clothes shop in town. Goes shopping with Fred, in case you didn't know. He carries her bags, carries them all the way into the house. He's in there for *hours*."

"Liar!"

"We'll soon find out, won't we? You can call home, see if the line's been disconnected yet. Or wait for her next visit. Trust me, it'll be a while coming . . ."

Blaine's hands went out, and Dennis flinched. But the man was hanging on to him, not attacking him. All the same, Dennis cried out, just as Blaine slumped to his knees, hands still gripping Dennis's uniform. Chalmers was yelling for help, running feet approaching. Blaine choking, clutching at his chest now as he fell onto his back, legs writhing. Then Dennis remembered: *old ticker isn't what it used to be . . .*

"I think it's a coronary," he said, as the first of the warders rushed in.

• • •

The Governor had asked for Dennis's version, which he'd had time to think about. Just passing . . . stopped to chat . . . next thing, Blaine's collapsing.

"Seems to tie in with Chalmers's version," the Governor had said, to Dennis's relief. Of course, Blaine might have other ideas, always supposing he made it.

"He going to be all right, sir?"

"The hospital will tell us soon enough."

Rushed to the Western General, leaving Chalmers in the doorway of the cell, looking stunned. His only words: "I might not be seeing him again . . ."

Dennis retreated to his office, ignoring knocks at the door: other warders, wanting to hear the story. He took out the photograph of Selina in her pink bikini. Maybe she'd get away with it now, get everything she wanted. And Dennis would have helped.

And she might never know.

It was nearly going-home time when another call summoned him to the Governor's office. Dennis knew it would be bad news, but when his boss spoke, he got the shock of his life.

"Blaine's escaped."

"Sorry, sir?"

"He's fled the hospital. Looks like it was a setup. A man and a woman were waiting for him, one dressed as a nurse, the other an orderly. One of the escort team has a concussion, another's lost a couple of teeth." The Governor looked up at Dennis. "He tricked you, tricked all of us. Bastard wasn't having a heart attack. His wife and another man came visiting today. Probably making final preparations."

"But I . . ."

"You entered the picture at the wrong moment, Henshall. Because an officer was there at the time, we took it that bit more seriously." The Governor returned to some paperwork. "Just a bit of bad timing on your part . . . but a major bloody headache for the rest of us."

Dennis staggered back to his office. It couldn't be . . . it couldn't be. What the hell . . . ? He sat dazed until well past going-home time. Drove home as if by remote control. Slumped into his chair. The story was on the evening news: dramatic escape from hospital trolley. So that had been the plan all along . . . sell the house and make a clean break, either as a couple or with Fred in tow. Fred. accomplice rather than lover. Scheming with Selina to set her husband free. He took out the copies of her correspondence with Blaine, reading each one through, looking to see if there was anything he'd missed.

No, of course there wasn't. They could have made plans each time they met. Always the chance of being overheard, of lips being read. But that had to be the way it was. Nothing more or less to it . . . Dennis couldn't face sitting here a moment longer, surrounded by her letters, her photos, his senses flooded by memories of her: the shopping trip, her house, her clothing . . .

He walked to his local bar and ordered a whiskey with a lager chaser. Downed the whiskey in one gulp, shaking the remnants into the beer glass.

"Hard day, Dennis?" one of the regulars asked. Dennis knew him; knew his first name anyway. Tommy. He'd been drinking here for as many years as Dennis had. All Dennis really knew about him were his first name and the fact that he worked as a plumber. It was amazing how little you could know about someone.

But there was a third thing: Tommy liked quizzes. Quizzes and puzzles. He was captain of the bar's Pub Quiz team, and there were trophies behind the bar as proof of his prowess. He was busy right now: tabloid open at the "Coffee-Break Page." He'd completed both crosswords and was working away at something else. Selina and her crossword puzzles.

Crosswords . . . and what was the other thing Blaine had said: acrobatics?

"Tommy," Dennis said, "is there a word puzzle called an acrobatic?"

"Not that I know of." Tommy hadn't bothered looking up from his paper.

"A word like that then."

"Acrostic, maybe."

"And what's an acrostic?"

"It's when you've got a string of words and you take the first letter from each one. The cryptics use them a lot."

"The first letter from . . . ?"

Tommy looked ready to explain further, but Dennis was already heading for the door.

• • •

I miss your hard-ons. See, Paul, I'm totally, absolutely lovestruck!

And embedded in it, the word "hospital." Dennis stared at his work, the work of several hours. Many of her letters contained no hidden messages. Those that did hid them within raunchy passages, presumably to stop anyone noticing them because—as Dennis had been—they'd be too busy reading and rereading the saucy bits.

Helping Elaine at Riddrie tomorrow. Perhaps ring our Bill, lift Elaine's morale?

While Dennis had been wondering about the identities of

Elaine and Bill, speculating on their relationship, Selina had been sending another message: "heart problem." She'd suckered him. He'd never suspected a thing.

Fred's off up north. (Denise isn't talking to him—and not keeping sober!)

"Found it. Thanks."

Found what? The cash, of course: another bundle of Blaine's cash. He eked it out to her a bit at a time, his way of ensuring she stuck around, or didn't blow it all at once. His letters to her contained messages showing where the money was hidden. Little stashes all over the place. Blaine's were clumsier than Selina's. Maybe Dennis would have spotted them, if he hadn't been more interested in her.

Infatuated with her. Those photos . . . all the little sexy bits . . . all there to stop him spotting the code.

And now she was gone. Really was gone. She'd finished the game, stopped playing with him. He'd have to go back to Jean and Tam and all the other letter writers, back to the real world.

Either that or try to follow her trail. The way she'd smiled at him . . . almost in complicity, as if she'd been enjoying his part in the charade. Would she send another letter, to him this time? And if she did, would he head off in pursuit of her, solving the clues along the way?

All he could do now was wait.

THIRD PARTY

JAY McINERNEY

Difficult to describe precisely, the taste of that eighth or ninth cigarette of the day, a mix of ozone, blond tobacco and early evening angst on the tongue. But he recognized it every time. It was the taste of lost love.

Alex started smoking again whenever he lost a woman. When he fell in love again he would quit. And when love died, he'd light up again. Partly it was a physical reaction to stress; partly metaphorical—the substitution of one addiction for another. And no small part of this reflex was mythological—indulging a romantic image of himself as a lone figure standing on a bridge in a foreign city, cigarette cupped in his hand, his leather jacket open to the elements.

He imagined the passersby speculating about his private sorrow as he stood on the Pont des Arts, mysterious, wet and unapproachable. His sense of loss seemed more real when he imagined himself through the eyes of strangers. The pedestrians with their evening baguettes and their Michelin guides and their umbrellas, hunched against the March precipitation, an alloy of drizzle and mist.

When it all ended with Lydia he'd decided to go to Paris, not only because it was a good place to smoke, but because it seemed like the appropriate backdrop. His grief was more poignant and picturesque in that city. Bad enough that Lydia had left him; what made it worse was that it was his own fault; he suffered both the ache of the victim and the guilt of the villain. His appetite had not suffered, however; his stomach was complaining like a terrier demanding its evening walk, blissfully unaware that the household was in mourning. Ennobling as it might seem to suffer in Paris, only a fool would starve himself there.

Standing in the middle of the river he tried to decide which way to go. Having dined last night in a bistro that looked grim and authentic enough for his purposes but that proved to be full of voluble Americans and Germans attired as if for the gym or the tropics, he decided to head for the Hotel Coste, where, at the very least, the Americans would be fashionably jaded and dressed in shades of gray and black.

The bar was full and, of course, there were no tables when he arrived. The hostess, a pretty Asian sylph with a West London accent, sized him up skeptically. Hers was not the traditional Parisian hauteur, the sneer of the maître d'hôtel at a three-star restaurant; she was rather the temple guardian of that international tribe which included rock stars, fashion models, designers, actors and directors—as well as those who photographed them, wrote about them and fucked them. As the art director of a boutique ad agency, Alex lived on the fringes of this world. In New York he knew many of the doormen and maître d's, but here the best he could hope was that he looked the part. The hostess seemed to be puzzling over his claims to membership;

her expression slightly hopeful, as if she was on the verge of giving him the benefit of the doubt. Suddenly her narrow squint gave way to a smile of recognition. "I'm sorry, I didn't recognize you," she said. "How are you?" Alex had only been here twice, on a visit a few years before; it seemed unlikely he would have been remembered. On the other hand, he was a generous tipper and, he reasoned, not a bad-looking guy.

She led him to a small but highly visible table set for four. He'd told her he was expecting someone in the hopes of increasing his chances of seating. "I'll send a waiter right over," she said. "Let me know if there's anything else I can do for you." So benevolent was her smile that he tried to think of some small request to gratify her.

Still feeling expansive when the waiter arrived, he ordered a bottle of champagne. He scanned the room. While he recognized several of the patrons—a burly American novelist of the Montana school, the skinny lead singer of a Brit Pop band—he didn't see anyone he actually *knew* in the old-fashioned sense. Feeling self-conscious in his solitude, he studied the menu and wondered why he'd never brought Lydia to Paris. He regretted it now, for her sake as well as his own; the pleasures of travel were less real to him when they couldn't be verified by a witness.

He'd taken her for granted—that was part of the problem. Why did that always happen?

When he looked up a young couple was standing at the edge of the room, searching the crowd. The woman was striking—a tall beauty of indeterminate race. They seemed disoriented, as if they had been summoned to a brilliant party that had migrated elsewhere. The woman met his gaze—and smiled. Alex smiled back. She tugged on her companion's sleeve and nodded toward Alex's table.

Suddenly they were approaching.

"Do you mind if we join you for a moment?" the woman asked. "We can't find our friends." She didn't wait for the answer, taking the seat next to Alex, exposing, in the process, a length of taupe-colored, unstockinged thigh.

"Frederic," the man said, extending his hand. He seemed more self-conscious than his companion. "And this is Tasha."

"Please, sit," Alex said. Some instinct prevented him from giving his own name.

"What are *you* doing in Paris?" Tasha asked.

"Just, you know, getting away."

The waiter arrived with the champagne.

Alex requested two more glasses.

"I think we have some friends in common," Tasha said. "Ethan and Frederique."

Alex nodded noncommittally.

"I love New York," Frederic said.

"It's not what it used to be," Tasha countered.

"I know what you mean." Alex wanted to see where this was going.

"Still," Frederic said, "it's better than Paris."

"Well," Alex said. "Yes and no."

"Barcelona," Frederic said, "is the only hip city in Europe."

"And Berlin," said Tasha.

"Not anymore."

"Do you know Paris well?" Tasha asked.

"Not really."

"We should show you."

"It's shit," Frederic said.

"There some new places," she said, "that aren't too boring."

"Where are *you* from?" Alex asked the girl, trying to parse her exotic looks.

"I live in Paris," she said.

"When she's not in New York."

They drank the bottle of champagne and ordered another. Alex was happy for the company. Moreover, he couldn't help liking himself as whoever they imagined him to be. The idea that they had mistaken him for someone else was tremendously liberating. And he was fascinated by Tasha, who was definitely flirting with him. Several times she grabbed his knee for emphasis and at several points she scratched her left breast. An absentminded gesture, or a deliberately provocative one? Alex tried to determine if her attachment to Frederic was romantic. The signs pointed in both directions. The Frenchman watched her closely and yet he didn't seem to resent her flirting. At one point she said, "Frederic and I used to go out." The more Alex looked at her the more enthralled he became. She was a perfect coctkail of racial features, familiar enough to answer an acculturated ideal and exotic enough to startle.

"You Americans are so puritanical," she said. "All this fuss about your president getting a blow job."

"It has nothing to do with sex," Alex answered, conscious of a flush rising on his cheeks. "It's a right-wing coup." He'd wanted to sound cool and jaded. Yet somehow it came out defensive.

"Everything has to do with sex," she said, staring into his eyes.

Thus provoked, the Veuve Clicquot tingling like a brilliant isotope in his veins, he ran his hand up the inside of her thigh, stopping only at the border of her tight short skirt. Holding his gaze, she opened her mouth with her tongue and moistened her lips.

"This is shit," said Frederic.

Although Alex was certain the other man couldn't see his

hand, the subject of Frederic's exclamation was worrisomely indeterminate.

"You think everything is shit."

"That's because it is."

"You're an expert on shit."

"There's no more art. Only shit."

"Now that *that's* settled," said Tasha.

• • •

A debate about dinner: Frederic wanted to go to Buddha bar, Tasha wanted to stay. They compromised, ordering caviar and another bottle of champagne. When the check arrived Alex remembered at the last moment not to throw down his credit card. He decided, as a first step toward elucidating the mystery of his new identity, that he was the kind of guy who paid cash. While Alex counted out the bills Frederic gazed studiously into the distance with the air of a man who is practiced in the art of ignoring checks. Alex had a brief, irritated intuition that he was being used. Maybe this was a routine with them, pretending to recognize a stranger with a good table. Before he could develop this notion Tasha had taken his arm and was leading him out into the night. The pressure of her arm, the scent of her skin, were invigorating. He decided to see where this would take him. It wasn't as if he had anything else to do.

Frederic's car, which was parked a few blocks away, did not look operational. The front grille was bashed in; one of the headlights pointed up at a forty-five-degree angle. "Don't worry," Tasha said. "Frederic's an excellent driver. He only crashes when he feels like it."

"How are you feeling *tonight*?" Alex asked.

"I feel like dancing," he said. He began to sing Bowie's "Let's

Dance," drumming his hands on the steering wheel as Alex climbed into the back.

Le Bain Douche was half-empty. The only person they recognized was Bernard Henri Levy. Either they were too early, or a couple of years too late. The conversation had lapsed into French and Alex wasn't following everything. Tasha was all over him, stroking his arm and, intermittently, her own perfect left breast, and he was a little nervous about Frederic's reaction. At one point there was a sharp exchange that he didn't catch. Frederic stood up and walked off.

"Look," Alex said. "I don't want to cause any trouble."

"No trouble," she said.

"Is he your boyfriend?"

"We used to go out. Now we're just friends."

She pulled him forward and kissed, slowly exploring the inside of his mouth with her tongue. Suddenly she leaned away and glanced up at a woman in a white leather jacket who was dancing beside an adjoining table.

"I think big tits are beautiful," she said before kissing him with renewed ardor.

"I think *your* tits are beautiful," he said.

"They are, actually," she said. "But not big."

When Frederic returned his mood seemed to have lifted. He laid several bills on the table. "Let's go," he said.

• • •

Alex hadn't been clubbing in several years. After he and Lydia had moved in together the clubs had lost their appeal. Now he felt the return of the old thrill, the anticipation of the hunt—the sense that the night held secrets that would be unveiled before it was over. Tasha was talking about someone in New York that Alex was supposed to know. "The last time I saw him he just kept banging his head against the wall, and I said to him, Michael, you've really got to stop doing these drugs. It's been fifteen years now."

· · ·

First stop was a ballroom in Montmartre. A band was onstage playing an almost credible version of "Smells Like Teen Spirit." While they waited at the bar, Frederic played vigorous air guitar and shouted the refrain. "Here we are now, entertain us." After sucking down their cosmopolitans they drifted out to the dance floor. The din was just loud enough to obviate conversation.

The band launched into "Goddamn the Queers." Tasha divided her attentions between the two of them, grinding her pelvis into Alex during a particularly bad rendition of "Champagne SuperNova." Closing his eyes and enveloping her with his arms, he lost track of his spatial coordinates. Were those her breasts, or the cheeks of her ass in his hands? She flicked her tongue in his ear; he pictured a cobra rising from a wicker basket.

When he opened his eyes he saw Frederic and another man conferring and watching him from the edge of the dance floor.

Alex went off to find the men's room and another beer. When he returned, Tasha and Frederic were slow dancing to a French ballad and making out. He decided to leave and cut his losses. Whatever the game was, he suddenly felt too tired to play it. At that moment Tasha looked across the room and waved to him from the dance floor. She slalomed toward him through the dancers, Frederic following behind her.

"Let's go," she shouted.

· · ·

Out on the sidewalk, Frederic turned obsequious. "Man, you must think Paris is total shit."

"I'm having a good time," Alex said. "Don't worry about it."

"I do worry about it, man. It's a question of *honor*."

"I'm fine."

"At least we could find some drugs," said Tasha.

"The drugs in Paris are all shit."

"I don't need drugs," Alex said.

"*Don't want to get stoned*," Frederic sang. "*But I don't want to not get stoned.*"

They began to argue about the next destination. Tasha was making the case for a place called, apparently, Faster Pussycat, Kill Kill. Frederic insisted it wasn't open. He was pushing L'Enfer. The debate continued in the car. Eventually they crossed the river and later still lurched to a stop beneath the Montparnasse tower.

The two doormen greeted his companions warmly. They descended the staircase into a space that seemed to glow with a purple light, the source of which Alex could not discern. A throbbing drum and bass riff washed over the dancers. Grabbing hold of the tip of his belt, Tasha led him toward a raised area above the dance floor that seemed to be a VIP area.

Conversation became almost impossible. Which was kind of a relief. Alex met several people, or rather, nodded at several people who in turn nodded at him. A Japanese woman shouted into his ear in what was probably several languages and later returned with a catalogue of terrible paintings. He nodded as he thumbed through the catalogue. Apparently it was a gift. Far more welcome—a man handed him an unlabeled bottle full of clear liquid. He poured some into his glass. It tasted like moonshine.

Tasha towed him out to the dance floor. She wrapped her

arms around him and sucked his tongue into her mouth. Just when his tongue felt like it was going to be ripped from his mouth she bit down on it, hard. Within moments he tasted blood. Perhaps this was what she wanted, for she continued to kiss him as she thrust her pelvis into his. She sucked hard on his tongue. He imagined himself sucked whole into her mouth. He liked the idea. And without for a moment losing his focus on Tasha, he suddenly thought of Lydia and the girl before Lydia, and the girl after Lydia, the one he had betrayed her with. How was it, he wondered, that desire for one woman always reawakened his desire for all the other women in his life?

"Let's get out of here," he shouted, mad with lust. She nodded and pulled away, going into a little solipsistic dance a few feet away. Alex watched, trying to pick and follow her rhythm until he gave up and captured her in his arms. He forced his tongue between her teeth, surprised by the pain of his recent wound. Fortunately she didn't bite him this time; in fact she pulled away. Suddenly she was weaving her way back to the VIP area, where Frederic seemed to be having an argument with the bartender. When he saw Tasha he seized a bottle on the bar and threw it at the floor near her feet, where it shattered.

Frederic shouted something unintelligible before bolting up the stairs. Tasha started to follow.

"Don't go," Alex shouted, holding her arm.

"I'm sorry," she shouted, removing his hand from her arm. She kissed him gently on the lips.

"Say good-bye," Alex said.

"Good-bye."

"Say my name."

She looked at him quizzically, and then, as if she suddenly

got the joke, she smiled and laughed mirthlessly, pointing at him as if to say—you almost got me.

He watched her disappear up the steps, her long legs seeming to become even longer as they receded.

Alex had another glass of the clear liquor but the scene now struck him as tawdry and flat. It was a little past three. As he was leaving the Japanese woman pressed several nightclub invitations into his hand.

• • •

Out on the sidewalk he tried to get his bearings. He started to walk toward St. Germain. His mood lifted with the thought that it was only ten o'clock in New York. He would call Lydia. Suddenly he believed he knew what to say to her. As he picked up his pace he noticed a beam of light moving slowly along the wall beside and above him; he turned to Frederic's bashed-in Renault cruising the street behind him.

"Get in," said Tasha.

He shrugged. Whatever happened, it was better than walking.

"Frederic wants to check out this after-hours place."

"Maybe you could just drop me off at my hotel."

"Don't be a drag."

The look she gave him awoke in him the mad lust of the dance floor; he was tired of being jerked around and yet his desire overwhelmed his pride. After all this he felt he deserved his reward, and he realized he was willing to do almost anything to get it. He climbed in the backseat. Frederic gunned the engine and popped the clutch. Tasha looked back at Alex, shaping her lips into a kiss, then turned to Frederic. Her tongue emerged from her lips and slowly disappeared in Frederic's ear. When Frederic stopped for a light she moved around to kiss him full on the mouth. He realized that he was involved—that he was part of the transaction between them. And suddenly he thought of Lydia, how he had told her his betrayal had nothing to do with her, which was what you said. How could he explain to her that as he bucked atop another woman it was she, Lydia, who filled his heart.

Tasha suddenly climbed over the backseat and started kissing him. Thrusting her busy tongue into his mouth, she ran her hand down to his crotch. "Oh, *yes*, where did that come from?" She took his earlobe between her teeth as she unzipped his fly.

Alex moaned as she reached into his shorts. He looked at Frederic, who looked right back at him . . . who seemed to be driving faster as he adjusted the rearview mirror. Tasha slid down his chest, feathering the hair of his belly with her tongue. A vague intuition of danger faded away in the wash of vivid sensation. She was squeezing his cock in her hand and then it was in her mouth and he felt powerless to intervene. He didn't care what happened, so long as she didn't stop. At first he could barely feel the touch of her lips, the pleasure residing more in the anticipation of what was to follow. At last she raked him gently with her teeth. Alex moaned and squirmed lower in the seat as the car picked up speed.

The pressure of her lips became more authoritative.

"Who am I?" he whispered. And a minute later: "Tell me who you think I am."

Her response, though unintelligible, forced a moan of pleasure from his own lips. Glancing at the rearview mirror, he saw that Frederic was watching, looking down into the backseat, even as the car picked up speed. When Frederic shifted abruptly into fourth, Alex inadvertently bit down on his own tongue as his head snapped forward, his teeth scissoring the fresh wound there.

On a sudden impulse he pulled out of Tasha's mouth just as Frederic jammed on the brakes and sent them into a spin.

. . .

He had no idea how much time passed before he struggled out of the car. The crash had seemed almost leisurely, the car turning like a falling leaf until the illusion of weightlessness was shattered by the collision with the guardrail. He tried to remember it all as he sat, folded like a contortionist in the backseat, taking inventory of his extremities. A peaceful, Sunday silence prevailed. No one seemed to be moving. His cheek was sore and bleeding on the inside where he'd slammed it against the passenger seat headrest. Just when he was beginning to suspect his hearing was gone he heard Tasha moaning beside him. The serenity of survival was replaced by anger when he saw Frederic's head moving on the dashboard and remembered what might have happened.

Hobbling around to the other side of the car, he yanked the door open and hauled Frederic roughly out to the pavement, where he lay blinking, a gash on his forehead.

"What was that about?" Alex said.

The Frenchman blinked and winced, inserting a finger in his mouth to check his teeth.

In a fury, he kicked Frederic in the ribs. "Who the hell do you think I am?"

Frederic smiled and looked up at him. "You're just a guy," he said. "You're nobody."

. . .

Walking back to his hotel, he found himself thinking of Lydia. His cheek was sore and bruised; when Frederic finally hit the guardrail he'd slammed it against the window. And the smoke from his cigarette made him all the more aware of the cuts on his tongue. But he was grateful to have escaped with these superficial wounds. The car had spun 180 degrees and popped a tire on the curb before coming to rest on the sidewalk. Alex had left them there, walking away without a word as Tasha called after him.

When he'd been caught, when his tryst with Tracey had become impossible to deny, he'd told Lydia it had nothing to do with her—what one always said—but that wasn't true. It was all about her. Although he'd lied and tried to hide his transgression, in the end, he realized now, he needed her to know. It was all about betrayal, that most intimate of transactions between two people. She was part of the equation. How could he explain to her that as he bucked atop another woman it was she, Lydia, who filled his heart. That it was like racing one's car at a tree. How the moment before impact would be vivid with love of the very thing you were about to lose.

THE LAST KISS

S. J. ROZAN

Washing her blood off his hands (sticky and clinging, then hot and slippery, red trails swirling, pink clouds rushing away), he thought of their first kiss. Not until then, and strange, that was: He'd burned for her so, and that kiss had ignited him. Different from all the others after, because unfamiliar; electrifying not just with her heat and the spicy salt taste of her but with newness, the nearly uncontainable excitement of the threshold.

The softness and sting of that kiss had returned at odd times in the past months, when he was not with her but also when he was, sometimes even as he was kissing her, that kiss overlaid on others; he could summon the memory, and often did, but the thrill was far greater when it ambushed him, as now. Sometimes its impact was so great that he stumbled, had to reach out and hold something to keep from falling.

"Not tonight," she'd said that first night, butterfly fingertips inflaming his skin, lips grazing his, then flitting away; then melting into him with a rush so urgent he thought she'd changed her mind and it would be tonight. But she released him and smiled and didn't say, "No," only, "Not tonight."

She thought she was denying him, that she had control. No. He'd waited not because she wanted it, but because waiting tightened the wire, drove the fever up.

And it must have been waiting that made this happen: that kiss—for a few days, all he had—flowed through his memory and flesh, saturated him. And then, at moments he couldn't predict, it concentrated, rose and crashed over him like a wave.

Moments like this.

With it now, for the first time, came an ache. Not entirely unpleasant, it added sweetness, softened the edges. The ache was regret: Memory, all he'd had at first, was all he was left with, now that she was gone.

As she had to be.

As she'd wanted to be.

That was what he'd seen, though none of the others had. She'd declared it clearly, and if to him, then surely to each. But he'd thought it wild exaggeration, and no doubt they thought the same. Only later, when she'd pulled the single string that dropped the web over him and stood back smiling, did he realize who the true quarry was intended to be.

Not him, but she herself.

He wished he'd seen it earlier, but he couldn't claim that. He was smarter than the others, and certainly smarter than she was, but he was only a man. When she'd come to him, he'd wanted her. When she'd leaned into him for that first kiss he'd felt only promise and pride.

She'd come to him as a client. The way, he'd understood later, she'd come to them all, but at the time he hadn't known that.

"Jeffrey Bettinger's been my attorney until now." She'd spoken crisply, settling in his office chair. She wore a soft wool suit the mahogany color of her hair, a blouse a shade darker than her ivory skin. Her cheeks glowed from the cold. As she crossed her legs, a gem of melting ice slid from her boot to his carpet. He molded his features into a mask of polite interest, his true attention riveted by the wool and silk, the mounds and hollows and the darkness beneath.

He'd noticed her with Bettinger, of course, been as amazed as anyone to see the oil-painting richness of her sharing a drink with the faded snapshot that was Bettinger. He hadn't known she was a client and he hadn't known about Cramer or Robbins or Sutton, then, either. He hadn't known what she wanted, or what she'd done. Though when he discovered the truth of that, he couldn't honestly say he'd have done anything in any different way.

With her to that first meeting she'd brought a kidskin portfolio with a tiny silver lock. Valuable papers, she told him. As her new attorney, he need not execute any of the papers, except in the event of her death, in which case she was hereby instructing him to break the lock and follow the wishes expressed inside. Right now he need merely lock the portfolio in his office safe. He did have a safe, of course?

Of course. He'd taken the portfolio, allowing his fingers to linger on hers, breathing slowly her rich summery scent.

From the first he'd been a completely professional lawyer. What happened between them—first in his imaginings, then, soon, in nights and days—never distracted him from his duties, as it would a weaker man. Probably, he told himself, that was why she'd left Bettinger: The man was a wimp. He'd likely never advised her, just let her lead him around with a ring through his nose. Himself, he wasn't like that: He'd objected, argued, offered alternatives each time she'd instructed him to sell a property at a hopelessly low price, to draft a codicil to her will leaving a bequest to some suspect cause. She was a rich woman, he told her, but there was an end to wealth if unhusbanded.

The phrase unexpectedly drew from her a bitter laugh: the word "husband," she explained. Hers had been a lawyer, a cold, vile man who'd forbidden her children or friends, beaten and bound her, made living an unending hell. More than once he'd threatened to kill her if provoked, and she despised herself for the cowardice that stopped her from forcing his hand, or from performing the act herself. She'd plotted against him in dark, secret fantasy; she thought, she admitted without blinking, that she might have actually been insane for a time, driven mad by isolation, pain and fear.

"Did you try?" he asked, feeling desire grow as she spoke, seeing behind his eyes visions of her shivering and bruised, cowering below a looming shadow.

"To kill him? He died." She spoke contemptuously. "Before I worked up the courage to kill either of us."

Her husband's sudden death, she said, had been a surprise, and the wealth she was left with was her only source of pleasure. (When he heard that his face blazed, his mind racing to the night before, the heat of their kisses, the crescendo of their rocking, together, together.) She paused a deliberate moment. With a smile, and with no amendment or exception to her statement, she went on to say that she would spend his money how and where she liked.

He didn't answer. He crossed the room and closed the door, and took her right there on his office carpet.

When their flesh intertwined she did whatever he asked, however odd, painful or humiliating. In the light of the business day, on the other hand, he was entirely unsuccessful in persuading, cajoling, insisting. But he tried each time, because there was no ring through his nose.

Now, as he worked, the memory of that first kiss flooding through him, he found himself awash in other memories also, unlooked-for but welcome. Swaddling her body in blankets for the trip to the hillside where he'd leave her, a place she'd shown him and told him she loved, he heard her voice, the breathy whisper that slithered like ice along his spine. The coppery smell of blood metamorphosed to the jungle blossoms of her perfume as he cleaned the room. No one would look here for her, or come here for any other reason, to this gloriously isolated, derelict house across the river. But he was by nature careful. He washed away the bloodstains, turned the mattress over.

They'd had no need to slip away to this secret spot, except for the shiver it gave them both. They were single, they were adults, they could have carried on their affair at high noon on Main Street. But she'd found the house, and when she told him about it over a roadhouse table, her stockinged toes trailing along his calf, they'd agreed to agree that it was best to be seen together only as attorney and client.

The heat in his palms as, his work finished, he toweled dry, made him think of her skin, pale velvet always warmer than his, as though she lived in a feverish cloud, a torrid private tropics out of which she reached for him.

At the time he'd thought, *to* him, she was reaching out *to* him. But he was mistaken.

Last week she'd come to his office unannounced, and, sitting in that same chair (glowing this time with sweat: the day was damp and hot), declared she was not satisfied. Not satisfied? Then what were the moans, the crashing heartbeat, the soft sighs?

"I'm firing you," she said. "Your services are no longer required."

"What's wrong with you?" he hissed fiercely, striding across the room to close the door.

She rose immediately and opened it again. "I'll take my papers, please." She remained standing and nodded pointedly at the safe.

"Are you—?"

"I have an appointment with Mr. Dreyer. Of Dreyer and Holt." Ice dripped from her words; he thought of her boots, that first morning. She looked at her watch. "If you choose not to return my papers I'll have no choice but to add that to my complaint to the police and the Ethics Commission."

He tried to grasp hold. "Complaint?"

"Yes, and retaining my papers will compound it. I imagine there's a distinction, even among lawyers, between taking sexual and professional advantage of a client, and outright theft."

Astonished, he stood mute.

She raised her eyebrows. "Making love to a widow to distract her from bad advice bordering on malfeasance? That's grounds for complaint, wouldn't you say? Some of the transactions you handled for me lost thousands. I'm firing you. I'll be filing professional and criminal complaints a week from today."

In their nights she'd cooed obscenities. The filthy words her hot breath tipped into his ear had exhilarated but never shocked him. But the abstract phrases she coolly spoke now stunned him with their indecency.

"Those deals. They were your idea, all of them. I objected every time. I have memos, letters in the file—"

"Postdated, no doubt."

"No! You know—"

"What I know is, regardless of whether you're convicted of anything, no wealthy widow will ever come to you again, after I'm through with you."

The intercom buzzed; his secretary told him his ten o'clock appointment had arrived. Bewildered, disoriented, he opened the safe and gave her the kidskin portfolio.

She turned and left.

He slept badly that night and the one that followed. Longing for her, confusion about her, and this new fear of her roiled his attempts at oblivion. Two days later he was still in shock.

And lucky, that had turned out to be.

He'd done something rare, left the office in the early afternoon—on what could he possibly concentrate?—to head to the oak-paneled tavern where lawyers met to bargain, to dispute and to forget.

"You don't look good," Sammy, the bartender, had said, as though he needed to be told. He'd shaken his head, given no explanation. Sammy knew his job: he poured a drink and proffered consolation. "At least you're not Bettinger." Sammy lifted his chin toward a crumpled form in the corner. "He's being investigated, did you know that? The Ethics Commission, and the police."

A long look at the unmoving Bettinger; the slow fire of scotch burning his way to clarity. He slid his second drink from the bar and crossed the room. He bought Bettinger a drink and another, and morose Bettinger, in slurred and garbled half-sentences, staring into his gin, muttering "black widow bitch," cast light on his darkness.

She'd set them up. Bettinger was the one before him, but before that had come Cramer, and Robbins, and Sutton. Every one her hero, saving her from the incompetence of the attorney before (the formal complaints and charges she'd filed being something she mentioned to none). Every one instructed to make bad business deals, to sell low and buy high. Every one's objections quieted with the generosity of her body, in the deserted house.

Every one ruined.

Bettinger, sloppy with brotherhood, offered him sympathy, claimed revulsion, pretended to fury and swore revenge. But he could see—anyone could see—that if she walked in right then to the tavern where they sat, Bettinger would follow her out on his hands and knees.

He left Bettinger in his pool of self-pity and walked through the fading day to think. The gray of the sky went to black and he considered this: Each complaint had been filed, as she'd said the one against him would be, a full week after she'd dropped her bombshell and changed attorneys. Stars pricked holes in the sky and he thought about this: the self-loathing in her voice when she talked about her failure to rescue herself from her husband's brutality by taking her own life. The city streets quieted around him as he heard her say spending her inheritance was her only pleasure.

And he saw what the others hadn't: who the trap was really set for, who the intended victim was.

So he did as she wanted. He called her, and asked her whether she had filed the charges and complaints against him yet. She had not. He asked her to meet him at the house that was theirs, across the river. "To talk about it," he said. And he heard a shiver of anticipation in her voice as she agreed.

And now, tonight, he'd given her what she'd hoped for, fulfilled her desire.

Desires. The sweep of her car's headlights had brought him to the door. As she stepped onto the porch where he waited, he felt her heat. They stopped still and time stopped with them, until, without speaking, she pressed her body, her lips, on his. He led her to the bed. He undressed her slowly, her blouse, her skirt, her silken slip, and tethered her to the bed with the silver handcuffs she'd brought him in their first days. With his hands, with his lips and tongue he took time, made slow love to her, built her toward the peak and reached it with her. After, he didn't unlock the cuffs, nor did she ask him to. He held her gently, stroking her hair as she lay motionless, eyes closed, lips parted.

Then he rose, and blindfolded her. She smiled softly. He kissed her a last time. The tastes, the scents, the thrills of the first kiss rushed in and rolled over him like a wave. Then they subsided, revealing the satin finality of this last one.

The last one.

She'd tried, he understood now, to drive each of them, Bettinger and the others, to this, hoping for one to release her. The disasters that befell them were punishment for being weak.

He was strong.

The blade glittered as he slid it into her heart.

She arched toward him as in pleasure. She didn't scream, but gave the same small cry he'd heard not long before, at the height of her joy.

He burned her clothes in the fireplace, wrapped her purse with her body, laid her across the rear seat of her own car. He drove to the hillside overlooking the town, dug her a grave among the trees, and, under a sky dotted with stars, he said farewell.

Abandoning her car far into the woods, he hiked back to the house for his own, drove home and slept soundly.

At the office the next day his morning was productive and his afternoon was the same. He decided to go down to the tavern and buy Bettinger a drink. Bettinger, after all, had done him a great favor. Of course, he'd done Bettinger one, Cramer and Robbins and Sutton, too, though they'd never know whom to thank. With the complainant gone, the cases against them would never be made. He'd freed them, too.

He was about to leave when the police arrived. They wasted no time, but arrested him for her murder.

"We got a call from her attorney."

He searched for his voice. "Paul Dreyer?"

The lead detective explained. She'd left Dreyer a message last night that she'd call in the morning, before ten. If she didn't, he was to open a kidskin portfolio in his safe. She hadn't called, so, acting on instructions, Dreyer had broken the lock. Inside were directions to the house and the hillside, and a note asking that the authorities examine transactions her previous attorney had conducted for her. She wasn't sure, the note said, but she believed she'd been cheated. She was going to confront the attorney, who'd also been her lover. And, the note said, she was afraid.

The attorney was not named.

But she had told the attorney she was using now who her previous attorney had been.

The cops had had a busy morning. They'd found the house, her body, her car. They'd found her blood on the turned-over mattress. They'd found his fingerprints.

They led him away.

As he stepped onto the sidewalk, the tastes, scents, thrills of their first kiss waited in ambush. They crashed so hard over him that he stumbled, and because he was handcuffed and could not reach out to hold anything, he fell.

SNEAKER WAVE

ANNE PERRY

Tonia was driving and Kate was in the front seat beside her, talking about the route, which left Susannah free to gaze at the sublime coastline stretching in brilliant blue to the western horizon. Not that the route needed any discussing. They were simply following the rim of the ocean south from Astoria the twenty miles or so to the beach house where they were going to spend a few days together.

It was spring 1922, and they had seen little of each other in the last few years since the war. Of course, America had been involved in it only toward the end, but it had still brought tremendous changes into their lives. Even as far west as the Oregon coast they had felt the reverberations of the conflict in Europe. Society could never be the same again with the return of peace.

Was "peace" the right word? Susannah looked at the shining width of the Pacific spread out before her as the car eased speed, climbing up the gradient. There were pine trees to the left, forests stretching inland with a wealth of timber that made families like hers rich, and north was the vast Columbia River with its seemingly inexhaustible salmon, supplying canneries that exported to the world. But "peace"? That was an inner quality, and as she watched her elder sisters in front— Tonia polite, proud, all her hurt suppressed under careful control; Kate, her grief exploding now and then into scalding temper—peace did not seem the word to use.

"We can't expect this perfect weather to last," Kate said, turning in her seat to stare out to sea. The coastline was dazzling, cliffs and rocky promontories jagged, waves crashing in and white surf shining in the sun.

"Of course not," Tonia agreed, her voice edged with emotion. "Nothing ever does."

Kate kept her face turned away. "Then we'd better make the best of it while we can. A little rain won't hurt—it's only the endless gray days I really mind. I don't even care if there's a storm—they can be magnificent."

"You wouldn't," Tonia replied, taking her hand off the wheel for a moment to push her hair back. She had it aggressively short in the new fashion. It was dark, and beautiful, emphasizing the strength of her features.

"What is that supposed to mean?" Kate said suspiciously.

"That you like storms, of course," Tonia answered with a tiny smile. "Thunder, lightning and the closeness of danger. Don't you? The electricity in the air?"

"I like the wind and the sea," Kate said, as if she were measuring her words, sensing that she needed to be careful.

Tonia smiled, a secret expression, knowing more than she was saying.

"I wonder if we'll see any whales," Susannah put in. "They go north about this time of the year."

"If you are prepared to stand and watch long enough, I daresay you will," Tonia answered her. "You were always good at watching." She seemed about to add something, then changed her mind.

It left Susannah feeling uncomfortable without knowing why. She had always regarded Tonia with admiration and some awe. She was beautiful, clever, thirty-three years old to Kate's twenty-nine and Susannah's twenty-five. It was Tonia who had married the brilliant, charming Ralph Bessemer. What a wedding that had been! All Astoria that mattered had been there, happy, showing off, touched with envy, but hiding it for the most part. It was money marrying more money. What else did anyone expect? And Antonia Galway was the perfect bride for him, with her looks, her poise, her heritage, she would be all he wished, not only to answer his love, but to help achieve his ambitions.

But that had been years ago. Now Ralph was dead, and neither Kate nor Susannah had married, at least not yet.

They were nearly there. The beach house had belonged to the family for years. Before the war their parents had come here often. It was full of memories, most of them happy. After their deaths the sisters had come less often, but only because other aspects of life had taken up too much time.

Tonia swerved the car off the road onto the track and five minutes later they pulled up in front of the small wooden house, less than a hundred yards from the edge of the shingle, and then the long slope down to the hard sand. There were a few trees close by, single, wind-bent pines, brave enough to stand alone against the winter. Farther up the slope were rhododendrons in scarlet and amethyst profusion right into the shade of the forest canopy. They were wild now, but someone had planted them once.

"Don't sit there, Susannah!" Tonia said briskly. "We've got to unpack!"

Susannah snapped out of her daydream and obeyed. They had one suitcase each for clothes, heavy skirts and jackets against the wind, strong shoes, warm woollens and night clothes. Added to that, of course, there were boxes of food, bed linen, towels, cleaning materials. They would leave the place as they found it! And books to read, a jigsaw puzzle and a little hand work, Kate's embroidery, Tonia's crocheting, Susannah's sewing. They might never touch them; it depended on the weather. Miserable thought, but it could rain for a week, quite easily.

They carried the boxes in, unpacked and put away, made up the beds and lit the fire in the sitting room and the pot-bellied iron stove in the kitchen, for cooking and hot water. Fuel had never been a problem, there was driftwood enough to last a lifetime. Carrying it in and sawing it to manageable lengths was really a man's job, but as many people had discovered since the war, women could do most things, if they had to.

"I'd like to go along the beach before we eat," Kate said, standing at the big window in the sitting room and staring across the rough grass to the shore. She could see the curve of the point to the south, and the long sweep of the bay to the north, and the calm water of an inland lagoon, where a small river emptied out into a natural basin before finding its way to the sea. That was motionless now, and two blue herons made an elegant, sweeping pattern across the pale sky before landing somewhere out of sight.

"Good idea," Susannah agreed, longing to feel the hard sand under her feet, and stride out before settling for the night. Astoria was on the water, but it was the river, and mighty as the Columbia was, for her it had always lacked the sheer, unfettered power and vitality of the ocean. On this particular shore the waves broke incessantly, even on a windless day. There was something in the formation of the land that caused the water to crest and break in white spume, gather and break again, and again, so that as far as the eye could see along the shore white water was hurled high against the blue sky, and crashed in boiling foam to race up the beach. If ever the ocean were alive, it was here.

Tonia gathered her coat in silent agreement, and the three of them set out, walking abreast over the grass then picking their way with care down the drop to the stones, through the washed-up driftwood, and then at last to the sand. The tide was out and there was plenty of room to walk. The wind was soft, and the fall of the waves had a steady, comforting boom and roar.

Kate lifted her face to the wind, her dark auburn hair blowing off her face, showing the lines of her cheek and brow clear, and yet oddly vulnerable, as if she had known too much pain, and still carried it with her.

Tonia was walking a little ahead now, looking toward the sea. Susannah wondered if Tonia saw in Kate any of the same things that she did. Did she sense the guilt, or only the anger? Had she even the remotest idea how much of it was grief? Ralph had been dead for over a year now, but of course the pain was older than that. There had been the two years before, when he had been in prison. How the world could shatter in one short week! At least it had for Kate, and for Tonia.

For Susannah it had broken slowly, like a creeping decay, getting worse a day at a time, until it had become unbearable. But they didn't know that. They were striding out now ahead of her, hair blowing, skirts molded against their bodies by the wind, no more than a breeze really, but nothing to soften it between here and Japan!

She bent and picked up a sand dollar, a perfect one. How few things were as perfect as they seemed. She had thought Ralph was perfect once. But then so had Tonia, and Kate. Had he laughed at that—all three sisters?

She used to think he had the best, the most robust and individual sense of humor, that his laughter healed all the little scrapes and abrasions of life, made them stop mattering and sink into things worthy only of jokes—and then forgetting. But she used to think a lot of silly things, once.

She put the sand dollar down again, gently, so it would not break. There were other shells also, most of which she did not know the names for. She did know the razor shells, and knew to be careful touching them; the edges could gash deep. In fact you could pretty well cut someone's throat with the big ones, the sort you found in rock pools at the point, when the tide was low.

They were about twenty feet from where the waves finally stopped, hesitated, and then sucked back and under into the deep water again. The sand was wet, but she was not quite sure whether the tide was going in or out. Kate was nearest the sea, Tonia next to her. The light was lengthening, the air a little cooler, the mountains of white foam more luminous.

Then suddenly one wave didn't stop, it kept on coming, surging farther up the sand, swift and deep, and Kate was in it up to her calves, her boots and skirt soaked, and Tonia only just escaped because she saw it in time and ran, skirts flying.

The wave sucked back again, almost knocking Kate off balance, drawing the sand from under her, and she gasped with the shock and the cold. Then she started stumbling up, wet skirt slapping around her ankles.

Tonia looked at her with wide eyes, her expression unreadable. "Forgot about the sneaker waves, eh?" she observed.

"I'm sodden!" Kate said in fury. "My boots, my skirt, everything! For heaven's sake, you could have warned me! Or at least got out of my way!"

Tonia's eyebrows shot up. "Warned you? My dear, you know the Oregon coast as well as I do! If you didn't see a sneaker wave coming, then you weren't paying attention, your mind was somewhere else. And I am not in your way. The beach is wide enough for all of us."

"You saw it in time to run!" Kate accused, her anger still clear in her face. "I would have warned you!"

Something close to a smile touched Tonia's mouth. "Would you?" she asked. "Would you really, Kate?"

"What kind of a question is that?" Kate shouted at her. "Of course I would!"

"I wonder." Tonia turned away.

Susannah waited for Kate to retaliate, then saw her standing still, the wet skirt clinging around her legs, ice cold in the wind. She was watching Tonia walk away, and there was embarrassment in her expression and even a touch as if it were the beginning of fear.

Susannah caught her breath, and felt her heart pounding. As clearly as if she had heard words, she knew what was in Kate's mind, the horror and the shame. And yet she had gone on doing it, as if she couldn't stop. Ralph had been Tonia's husband, charming, witty, ambitious, bound for the State Senate, and perhaps the governor's mansion one day not too far away.

Now she was terrified that Tonia knew, or at least suspected. Did she? Was that the hidden meaning behind her words? Or was it just bereavement in Tonia, loneliness and crushed pride, because Ralph had fallen so far? And in Kate the guilty fleeing where no man pursued, because she had the taste of her own betrayal always in her mouth?

Tonia bent and picked up a shell. It must have been a good one, because she put it in her pocket, then looked back at Kate. She barely seemed to notice Susannah, as if she had been a seagull, or some other natural thing that belonged here, but was of no importance.

Susannah was not offended past the first moment of feeling excluded. After that it was relief. If Tonia did at last suspect something, it was Kate she was thinking of. Kate's betrayal of her was wrong, in anyone's eyes. One might understand it—oh, so very easily! Memory of Ralph filled her and surrounded her, like the sweep of the salt air enclosing her in its arms, filling her senses and burning into her mouth, her lungs, even her mind. Except that it was clean and sweet, and it was boundless, enough for every living thing. For one to take it did not rob another. Yes, she could understand Kate, any woman might, however they condemned.

Would they condemn Susannah? Would they see it as the act of a woman scorned, used and cast aside, a petty act of jealousy and revenge?

It hadn't been. But it would still cut deep, right to the bone, if it were thought to be. It would help little if strangers knew it had been so desperately difficult, an act of terrible decision, fought and struggled over, the choice between betrayal of others, or of self and all she knew to be right. She needed that understanding from those she cared for.

But in her heart she knew Tonia at least would never understand. She had loved Ralph with a consuming devotion. Perhaps some of it had been ambition, seeing his possibilities, and his hunger to achieve them, and maybe more than a little of it had been the pride of ownership. The most charming, intelligent, polished man in Astoria had been hers. Of all the well-bred and elegant young women who had chased him, she had been the one he chose. But there had been a good deal of plain human passion as well, the laughter, the warmth, the ache to love and be loved, the pounding heart at his step, the happiness when he smiled, the sound of his voice even when he wasn't there, the perfect memory of his smile. No, Tonia would not understand or forgive anything that Susannah had done. Thank God she did not know.

For that matter, Kate would not forgive it either. That was as certain as nightfall. Her rage would be absolute, in spite of her own betrayal. She would not see it as passion, and therefore wrong, but so very pardonable. She would see it as cold-hearted vengeance—which it was not! In the end it had been her only choice!

But thank God Kate did not know either. This was the first time the three of them had been alone together since Ralph's death, and they were going to spend five days here, each guarding their secrets. They would smile and talk as if there were nothing to pretend about, no lies, no hidden rage or pain. It would be the ultimate test!

They were making their way back toward the house, the wind behind them now, cooler as the sun was lower on the horizon, spilling a bright path across the water and tipping the great curling heads of the waves with pale fire. The thunder of them breaking never ceased, yet it was an oddly peaceful sound, like the breathing of the earth. This time they did not walk close enough for a sneaker wave to catch them.

Susannah could not get the thought of that out of her mind as she watched Kate struggle against the close, wet fabric. It must be horribly cold against her legs, but she did not speak of it again.

. . .

The next morning was warm and fair. At this time of the year it could not be taken for granted that it would last, so when Tonia suggested that they drive south along the coast road, and walk around the next cape under the pine trees, both Kate and Susannah accepted the idea.

After breakfast they set out, Tonia driving as usual. It was half an hour's journey. They made trivial conversation about mutual friends, the condition of the road, even political subjects such as the situation in Europe in the attempt to rebuild after the devastation of over four years of war that had taken the lives of more than ten million men, and maimed or crippled God knew how many more. It was a grim thing to think of, but it was safe. There was nothing personal in it, nothing to dig up their own still festering wounds.

They parked the car and walked in the sun up the steep footpath out above the sea. They heard the sharp, clear song of a red-winged blackbird, and a moment later saw it sitting on a branch, its brilliant patches of scarlet easily visible. The wild honeysuckle was in bloom, and the scent of pine needles gave the air a pungency that seemed to wash away every sour thought or memory, as the sight of the sea took it from the mind.

They watched in the distance for the sight of whales breaching, the white spout of water against the blue that would give away their position. Below them the white ranks of waves broke endlessly on the sand, dazzling the eye, the offshore wind carrying the spray back like smoke from their crests.

"This is perfect," Kate said with a smile. "I can't think of anything more beautiful."

"It looks it," Tonia agreed. "Especially from up here. But looks can deceive, can't they, Kate. You should know that."

Kate was startled. "What's that supposed to mean? Just because I got caught by the wave yesterday evening! Whoever was walking closest to the water could have been caught. It just happened to be me."

"Is that how you see life?" Tonia' s smile was cold. "Nothing is cause and effect, no responsibility? It just happens to be you?"

A flick of temper lit in Kate's eyes. "Isn't that rather a stretch? I got my feet wet by a sneaker wave, so my whole life's philosophy is irresponsible? I could just as easily say that you ran up the shore without warning me, so your whole life is to run away from things and leave other people to suffer!"

"By other people, you mean you?" Tonia asked, a mild humor in her voice. "Are you sure you mean me? Susannah didn't get wet either. She walked well away from the water all the time."

"Oh, good for Susannah!" Kate said sarcastically. "How wise! How brave!"

Were they talking about the wave, or something else? Susannah was cold in the sun. Did Tonia know, and this was her way of telling Kate? She intended to make those needle-sharp remarks all week, until Kate's hot, wild temper broke and there was a real fight between them, which somehow Tonia would win.

Somehow! Tonia had been Ralph's wife! Kate had been his mistress. There could be no justification for that, no moral or social right. They would both say bitter things, and the freeing of the anger might be momentarily a relief, but there would be no forgetting, no going back to where they had been before. Tonia would call Kate a thief, even a whore, and a betrayer of everything that family meant.

Kate would point out that Ralph had married Tonia, but had grown tired of her, and in the end preferred Kate. It was Kate he had loved. Nothing could change, or heal that now. Tonia would have no charge to counter with. It was the truth.

Susannah was twisted with sorrow for them both. They had both loved him, in their ways, and believed he had loved them.

Of course they were wrong! The difference was that Tonia knew it, however she had learned! Kate still didn't. She didn't know that Ralph Bessemer had loved no one. He had been an arrogant, ambitious man who used people to satisfy his own appetites, physical, yes, but mostly for power, admiration, money and to be endlessly admired.

Susannah knew that! She knew beyond doubt it was the truth. Perhaps Tonia still believed somewhere in her heart that the trial had been unjust, there had been no theft, no long, careful corruption so Ralph could gain the political office he hungered for so intensely. Perhaps that was his only real hunger. Women were a pleasant route to its achievement, like a good meal to sustain you on a journey.

Had he ever loved Tonia? Or was she simply an advantageous marriage? Had he loved Kate, or was she just entertaining, and fun to take, so he could deceive the bossy, possessing Tonia, and laugh behind her back?

Susannah knew perfectly well why he had come after her! At least she knew now! At first she had imagined he had loved her. Standing here in the bright air above the roar of the waves, smelling the pine and the honeysuckle, she could remember how sweet had been the few, intoxicating weeks when his smile had lit her daydreams, his voice wakened her imagination, the touch of his hand sent her heart pounding, blood racing in her veins.

But he had been too sure of himself! He had asked for her help too soon. Two sisters won, he had taken the third for granted. She was to be of use, no more. She was in the perfect position, trusted by bank officials, to pass him the information he wanted. But she had used it to trap him instead.

No one else knew that, of course. Tonia had no idea it was Susannah who had told the police where to look, and had in effect put the pieces together for them. She thought it was that clever detective, Innes. She had blamed him, and he had been happy enough to be credited with the downfall of a figure as prominent as Ralph Bessemer, and as corrupt! The State Senate had been saved from profound damage, and he had been promoted.

Naturally Kate had believed the same. Kate was passionate, funny, hot-tempered, softhearted at times, often thoughtless. But above all she was uncomplicated. She would not look behind the obvious.

They were walking slowly back into the shade of the pines. There were wild brambles at the side of the track.

"There'll be fruit to pick in the fall," Tonia observed. "You'll like that, Kate! Just be careful you don't get caught on the thorns. You can get nasty scratches, very deep. And they can get infected, if you're really unlucky."

"I'll be careful," Kate replied a little tersely.

"Oh—so you've learned, have you?" Tonia turned for a moment to glance behind her, her face cold, delicate arched eyebrows high.

"I've always been careful picking berries," Kate retorted.

"So you have," Tonia agreed. "Or any other fruit. You've managed to get in and out without a scratch at all, and take the prize with you." She turned back to look where she was going again.

Kate hesitated in her stride. By now she had to be as sure as Susannah was that Tonia knew. She was playing a game, saying, and not saying, pricking the skin with wounds until Kate lost her temper and provoked an open quarrel!

What then? Shouting, accusation, misery, guilt? Was that what Tonia wanted, that Kate should feel that bitter, corroding shame of the betrayer exposed? It would do no good. Nothing Ralph had said or done would be changed, and above all he would not be brought back to love or cheat either of them!

But she could not tell Tonia that without giving away that she knew!

They reached the car in silence and got in. The drive back in the dappled sunlight should have been wonderful, but the outward beauty of the day was already clouded over for all of them. All the way back, and through lunch in the house, Tonia made double-edged remarks, and Kate got angrier and angrier. Twice she hit back, but the sharpness of it was tempered by the knowledge of her own guilt. Susannah could see it in her face, the flare of temper, the perfect answer in her eyes, then the tight control because she remembered all the reasons why Tonia was riddled with hurt, why at least in one respect she had every right to retaliate.

But shame would not bridle her tongue forever. Susannah knew that without a second's hesitation. Surely Tonia did as well?

After lunch there were chores to do, dishes, preparation for the evening meal, wood to collect and a little to cut. In the middle of the afternoon Kate announced that she would go for a walk around the inland water, preferably alone, and look for the blue herons.

Susannah turned to Tonia. "I'd like to go along the beach again. Will you come with me?" Perhaps she could persuade her out of the quarrel.

"Of course," Tonia agreed. "That's an excellent idea."

Susannah was pleased, and surprised. Maybe it was not going to be so difficult after all.

It was a little cooler than yesterday, but still pleasant, and the tide was even farther out, leaving them plenty of room to walk along the sand below the stones.

Tonia was smiling. Her shoulders were tense and she walked with purpose rather than ease, but still it was a great improvement on the morning. Perhaps she had gone as far as she meant to?

Susannah was undecided whether to say anything or not. Now might be her only chance. Three more days of this bitter innuendo would be unbearable. How could she do it without betraying herself?

"Tonia?"

"Yes?" They had stopped walking and were staring at the tumbling water.

"Do you have to go on making such a point of Kate getting caught in the wave? Does it really matter?"

Tonia bit her lip thoughtfully, then she looked sideways back at Susannah. "Do you mean that I should forget all the past, and think only of the moment now, and the future?" she asked. Her eyes were narrowed a little, intent on the answer, her expression completely unreadable.

"I didn't mean anything so sweeping," Susannah replied, and then knew instantly that it was a lie, and not a good one. Tonia did not believe it. That was exactly what she had meant. She stumbled to retrieve it. "Just not the wave, the . . . the brambles. It sounds as if . . ."

She did not know how to finish.

Tonia was smiling, not with warmth but with amusement, an inner anticipation as if she foresaw exactly where they were going, and intended it. "Yes?"

"As if you're deliberately trying to provoke her," Susannah finished lamely.

"Oh? Why on earth do you imagine I would want to do that?" Tonia asked. She looked absolutely innocent, but in that instant Susannah knew with an ice-cold certainty that Tonia was perfectly aware of the love affair between Ralph and Kate, and that she intended to exact her revenge for it, slowly, drop by drop if necessary. It was in her eyes, like a hard, bright edge, and in her smile.

Susannah drew in her breath. Dare she say it, openly? There was something in Tonia that made her hesitate, a power, and memory of the days when she had been the eldest sister, to be admired, obeyed, whose praise mattered most.

"Because you're grieving for Ralph, and you want to hurt her," she said aloud. It was a compromise, half of the truth.

"My grieving for Ralph makes me want to hurt Kate?" Tonia asked. "Or are you suggesting his death has unhinged my mind?"

"No! Of course not!" Susannah protested.

"It might have," Tonia replied, her eyes narrowed against the sharp, afternoon sun reflected off the white water. "After all, to have your husband sent to prison for five years, subjected to the vile life inside such a place, forced to mix with the worst people in our state, and then finally driven into a corner by them, and murdered like an animal—don't you think that could be enough to drive some women out of their senses?"

She knew! It was a sick certainty twisting like a knife in the pit of Susannah's stomach. Tonia knew that it was she who had told the police about Ralph. Did she also know that Ralph had tried to make love to her, not because he cared for her, or even was attracted to her, but in order to use her in his corruption? No, probably not. She opened her mouth to defend herself, and realized there was no defense. Tonia did not care why; the fact was all that mattered. She did not want reason; she wanted pain in payment for her own.

Susannah gulped, her mouth dry, her legs suddenly weak. She was afraid, and furious with herself for it. Had it been any-one except Tonia she might have been able to face them. She was not wrong! What else could she have done? Sleep with Ralph, betray the bank so he could use the money to win a Senate seat? Was that what Tonia would have wanted?

Yes, probably. Ralph didn't love her! He was arrogant enough to think a smile from him, a little passion that would pass for love, and she would do whatever he wanted. He would throw her away afterward, and she would be too mortified, too ashamed to tell anyone.

"Yes," she said aloud, looking back at Tonia. "I suppose it might be enough to drive some people mad—but you're not 'some people.' You won't lose sight of reality. It was a tragedy Ralph was murdered. It wasn't his fault, and it wasn't Kate's fault either. They got the man who did it, and he's been exe-cuted."

"Oh, yes," Tonia agreed. "He's dead." There was a look of momentary, intense satisfaction in her face, almost joy. "Did I suggest it was Kate's fault? I didn't mean to. No, Kate would never have hurt Ralph, I know that. And she wouldn't have wanted him in prison either." Her voice was laden with mean-ing, her face hard, the wind whipping her dark hair across it.

They were twenty yards from where the breaking water reached, and as they stood there another sneaker wave came racing up the sand and stopped only a couple of feet short of Tonia's shoes. She ignored it, as if she knew she were impervious to such things. There was something frightening in her calm, the sense of complete control in her eyes, her face, even the way her body braced against the wind.

Susannah was as certain as she was of nightfall that Tonia intended to take her revenge, her own concept of justice, for Kate's betrayal of her, and for Susannah's. She could do it here, away from Astoria, where no one else would see her, and she would do it slowly, carefully and completely. What she did not know was how.

Tonia was smiling at her, a cruel, half-excited smile that finally hid nothing. All her hurt and fury were in it, her knowledge of Kate and Ralph, and the way they had laughed and loved behind her back, and that Ralph had made the fatal mistake of trying the same trick, but without the heart, on Susannah as well—not for lust but for profit. But she could not be wooed or flattered into corruption. She had turned him in, which had ultimately cost him his life, and so finally stolen him from both Tonia and Kate.

How would Tonia do it? Poison in the food, or the water? A pillow over her face when she slept, and blame Kate for it? An accident of some sort, a slip in the bath, perhaps, and drown in the hot, soapy water? A fall somewhere, even over the cliff. One would not have to go more than ten or twelve feet onto the rocks; that would be enough.

Or the sea? Something to do with those magnificent, pounding waves with their terrifying, exhilarating beauty, and the power of a thousand miles of ocean behind them, sucking back under, dragging in with the undertow, those hungry, unpredictable sneaker waves that reached out farther than the rest, and pulled the unwary, even off dry land.

"You look as if you have been caught with your hand in the cookie jar, Susannah!" Tonia said with only the slightest sneer in her voice. "Are you afraid of being sent to bed without any supper?"

Susannah spread her hands wide. "I haven't taken any cookies!"

"Oh you did, my dear! You just couldn't hold on to them!" Tonia answered. "No cookies for anyone now. But let's go back and have supper. I promise you can have a share of everything!" She started to walk back along the sand, striding out easily, her arms loose at her sides and her steps graceful.

Susannah stumbled behind, her feet sinking in the sand, fear making her awkward, anger at the injustice of it tripping her, and helplessness robbing her of breath, of strength, even the ability to see clearly and choose her path up through the stones.

• • •

Dinner was a nightmare for Susannah. Tonia was charming. She smiled at both her sisters, told entertaining stories from events in Astoria society to which she had been, and they had not. The food, which she had insisted on cooking alone, was delicious, fresh fish in a delicate sauce, and vegetables chopped and steamed to exactly the right consistency. She also served it herself, and passed the plates.

"Aren't you hungry?" she inquired solicitously as Susannah poked one thing with her fork, and then another without eating. "I'd have thought the walk along the beach would have given you an appetite. It has me." And she proceeded to eat with relish.

Kate had no idea. Susannah knew that as she saw her begin to eat hungrily as well. She might be aware of Tonia's knowledge of her love affair with Ralph, even how far it had gone, but she was not afraid. Was she blind? Did she really not understand Tonia at all, for all the years they had known each other, growing up, and after?

"Aren't you feeling well?" Tonia asked with concern, looking at Susannah still probing at the food rather than eating it. "Shall I get you something else?"

The moment froze. Incredibly, Kate was not looking at her, but Tonia was, mockery in her eyes. She knew Susannah was afraid, and she was enjoying it.

"No . . . no thank you." Susannah made the decision from reflex, not judgment. "This is fine. I was just thinking." She took a deliberate mouthful.

"Something interesting?" Tonia inquired.

Susannah made up a quick lie. She wished she could have thought of something useful, something defensive, or at the very least, warning. "Only about what we might do tomorrow, if the weather is fine, of course."

"Ah, the future!" Tonia rolled the words around her tongue. "I was quite wrong. You see I imagined you were thinking of the past. It's wonderful to be here, free as the wind, with tomorrow, and the day after, and the day after that, in which to do whatever we please—isn't it, Susannah!"

"To choose among options, anyway," Susannah replied.

Tonia looked surprised. "You feel limited? What is there you would like to do, and can't? Is there something you want? Something you can't have?" She turned slightly. "And what about you, Kate? Is there anything you want, and can't have?"

Kate looked up, puzzled. "Not more than anyone else. Why?" She glanced at Susannah. "What do you want to do?"

Leave, but she could not say that, and she could not do it without Tonia. She had the car, and the keys to it. And anyway, if she did run, it would seem like the confession of a guilty conscience. She had nothing to be guilty about. Ralph was a thief, planning to buy his way to state office with corruption. The fact that he was her brother-in-law excused nothing.

"I really don't care," she replied awkwardly.

"We could climb round the point," Tonia suggested. "When the tide's out, the rock pools are full of all sorts of things—sea anemones, urchins, razor shells, starfish." She smiled. "It's beautiful."

And dangerous, Susannah thought with an inward clenching of her stomach. One slip and you could break a leg, cut your arm open on one of the razor shells, even, at the right tide, fall off an edge high enough, deep enough, and drown. Out on the farthest edge, even get taken off by a wave.

"I'd rather walk along the beach," she replied. "Or up in the woods for a change."

Tonia smiled. "Whatever," she said with quiet satisfaction. "Would you like coffee? Or tea, perhaps? That would be better in the evening. Or how about hot chocolate? Shall I make hot chocolate for all of us?" She half-rose as if it had already been accepted.

Kate said "yes," and Susannah "no" at the same moment. Tonia chose to hear the "yes." Susannah said "no" again, and Tonia ignored her. "It'll be good for you," she said over her shoulder. "Help you sleep."

"What's the matter with you?" Kate asked. "Anyone would think she was going to poison you!"

The evening passed so slowly it assumed the proportions of a nightmare. They sat around the fire facing each other, sipping chocolate after the dishes were washed. The air had chilled considerably, and the wind had risen.

"I think there could be a storm," Kate remarked, a smile on her lips.

"Oh yes," Tonia agreed. "I'm quite sure there will be."

There were several moments of silence except for a low moan outside and the rattling in the eaves where a tile was loose.

"Ralph used to like storms," Tonia went on.

"No he didn't!" Kate said instantly, then almost bit her tongue. "Did he?" she added, too late.

Tonia looked wide-eyed. "My dear, are you asking me?"

Kate flushed pink. "Perhaps I misunderstood," she said lamely.

"Who? Me, or Ralph?" Tonia inquired.

"I really don't remember. It hardly matters!" Kate snapped.

But Tonia would not let it go. "Did you have a particular storm in mind?"

"I told you!" Kate was angry now, and guilty. Susannah could see the shame in her eyes, and she was absolutely certain Tonia could. "I don't remember! It was a misunderstanding."

"About likes and dislikes?" Tonia went on. "Or love and hate? How can you mistake one for the other . . . do you suppose?" She looked as if she were intensely interested, without emotion, until one saw the clenched fist by her side, and the rigid line of her back.

"Maybe the difference between fear and excitement," Kate responded, staring at her, meeting the challenge at last.

"Oh yes!" Tonia agreed with satisfaction. "Excitement, the fear of danger, the roar of thunder and the chance of being struck by lightning. You mistook the fear for love?"

Kate's face was scarlet.

Susannah sat, her muscles locked as if any moment the explosion would come. She dreaded it, but she knew now that it was inevitable. It would happen some time, tonight, tomorrow, the day after, but before they went home, that was certain.

"Or the love for fear?" Kate met the challenge squarely.

Tonia shook her head. "Oh no," she said with a tight little smile. "One knows love, believe me, dear. If you ever meet it, you'll understand." And she stood up, smiled at each of them in turn, and wished them goodnight. She went to the door and added, "Sleep soundly," and went out.

Kate turned to Susannah. She seemed about to ask her something, then realized she could not afford to raise the subject with her. She had no idea how much she knew, or where her loyalties would lie. She let out her breath again with a sigh, and they spent another miserable half-hour, then went to bed also.

•   •   •

Susannah took a long time to go to sleep, in spite of the comfortable sounds of wind and rain outside. She woke with a violent start, crying out in fear.

Tonia was sitting on the end of her bed, one of the pillows in her hands. For a freezing instant pure tension gripped Susannah and she scrambled to sit upright, throwing the entangling bedclothes off her legs so she could fight freely.

Tonia looked amazed. "That must have been some nightmare!" she said with a shadow of amusement in her face.

"N . . . nightmare?" Susannah stammered.

"Yes. You were crying out in your sleep. That's why I came."

Susannah realized it was still dark, the bedroom light was on, but beyond the curtains it was black. She could not take her eyes off Tonia to look at the clock on the bedside table. She had not been dreaming, she was absolutely certain of that. She always remembered her dreams. "What's the pillow for?"

she demanded, her voice dry and a little wobbly. Had she only just avoided being suffocated in her sleep?

"You knocked it onto the floor," Tonia replied.

She hadn't. It was extra. She already had two on the bed. Her heart was beating wildly, pounding in her chest, her pulse racing. Should she challenge Tonia now, tear it out into the open and face it? Dare she? That would make it irrevocable. Then what? What was left of their relationship after that?

"No, I didn't," she said breathlessly. "I've still got two!"

Tonia smiled, as if that were exactly what she had wanted her to say. "You had three, dear. One to prop you up if you wished to read." She gave a very slight laugh, dry and brittle. "Did you think I brought it in here to suffocate you with? Why on earth would I do that? Have you done something dreadful that I don't know about? Is that why you don't eat well, and wake up screaming in the night?" She stood up, still holding the extra pillow in her arms.

"No, of course it isn't!" Susannah snapped. Then she looked straight at Tonia. "You already know all there is to be known!"

"Yes," Tonia agreed softly. "Yes . . . I do!" And still carrying the pillow, she went out and closed the door silently, as totally silently as she had come.

• • •

Breakfast was miserable. Susannah had a nagging headache, Kate looked tense and also seemed unable to eat. Only Tonia was relentlessly cheerful and apparently full of energy. She cooked and served, asking both the others solicitously if they had slept, if they were well, if she could do anything more for them.

"You look hungover," she said briskly to Susannah. "A good

walk around the point would make you feel far better. And you too, Kate. We should go now. The weather's cleared and the tide's just right. And I'd enjoy it as well. Get your coats and come." She did not wait for them but grasped her own coat off the peg by the door and, putting one arm through the sleeve, went outside into the windy sunshine.

Kate was undecided.

"Come on!" Tonia called. "It's a wonderful morning! Crisp and sweet, and I can hear a blackbird singing. The wind's coming in off the sea, and it smells like heaven."

Susannah suddenly made up her mind. She would face it, even provoke it if necessary, but she was not going to spend the rest of the week, let alone the rest of her life, being afraid of Tonia and letting her manipulate her into guilt and wild idiotic imaginings every time she felt like it. It was not her fault Ralph had had an affair with Kate, or that he'd tried to use her. It was not her fault he was corrupt, or that the court had found him guilty and sent him to jail. He was guilty! And it was not her fault one of the other prisoners had killed him. That last might not have been deserved, it might have been as tragic and unjust as Tonia believed, but Susannah was not going to take the blame for it.

But she would rather not face it alone. "Come on, Kate!" she added with decision. "A big clean wind blowing through everything will do us a lot of good!"

Kate obeyed, reluctantly, and the three of them walked abreast up to the rise at the edge of the grass, over the heavy stones and at last onto the thin rim of hard sand at the edge of the tide. All of them were watching for the odd big waves, and ran very smartly up the stones when they came, always just avoiding getting wet.

They went toward the rocky point where the tidal pools

were full of treasures. They reached the beginning of the outcrop and started to climb carefully, watching every foothold, Tonia first, then Kate, Susannah last. They went as far out as there was a decent place to stand, Susannah the lowest and closest to where the deep water rushed past, white spume hurling in over the teeth of the rocks, and sucking back, dragging the sand and stones and shells. Farther out, beyond the very edge of the point, five ranks of waves, one beyond the other, roared in, heads bent, foam and spray flying, boiling over to cover the whole face of the sea with white.

It was a time when no words were necessary, but Tonia spoke.

"Magnificent, isn't it? Elemental, like the great passions of life."

Kate looked away. "I suppose so." She was staring along the shore at the curve of the beach and the miles of coast with rocks and spurs and jagged standing outcrops as far as the eye could see.

"Oh, yes," Tonia went on. "I can understand passion, even the lust that's so strong it overtakes all morality, and you want something so badly you just take it, even if it belongs to someone else. Can't you, Kate?"

Kate swung around, the wind blowing her hair across her face. She pushed it back impatiently. She was close to Tonia, but about three feet lower. "For God's sake shut up about it!" she shouted. "You knew Ralph and I were in love! I'm sorry! He was your husband, and he loved me. I loved him too! We couldn't both have him. You lost."

"Both?" Tonia laughed, and control of it escaped her, her voice rising high and wild. "He's dead, Kate! He died in a toilet in the state prison! He was stabbed in the belly, and bled to death there on the floor! Nobody near him! Not you, not me, not even dear Susannah!"

Kate swayed as if she would lose her balance. "What do you mean, Susannah? He wasn't in love with her! He didn't even like her!"

"Of course he didn't like her!" Tonia shouted back, her eyes narrowed, her lips drawn tight over her teeth. "But he knew she was clever! He tried to use her, at the bank. But our dear little Susannah didn't want to be used. She wanted to have him, and if she couldn't, she'd rather destroy him. She doesn't take rejection well, our little sister! When he asked for her help, and she wished him to become her lover as the price, and he brushed her off, she took her revenge. And perfect it was! She betrayed him to the police—got together all the evidence, created any that was lacking, and set him up! There was no way he could escape it. Poor Ralph! He had no idea what jealousy and rejection would do to her. She might just as well have stuck the knife into him herself!"

Kate wheeled around, almost overbalancing, her face white, eyes blazing with a passion of rage. She started down toward Susannah, covering the few yards between them, jumping, scrambling, incredibly not slipping.

"I didn't!" Susannah yelled, stepping backward, toward the edge of the rocks and the racing sea. "I didn't make up anything! Everything I gave the police was exactly what he was doing!"

"You gave him up!" Kate said with incredulous fury. "It was you who betrayed Ralph!" But it was not a question. She had heard the knowledge in Tonia's voice, and the guilt in Susannah's. She launched herself at Susannah and flung both of them backward onto the rocks. The next wave roared past them, knocking the breath out of their bodies, ice cold, and leaving them struggling on the shelf of the rock to the edge where it fell straight down.

"I didn't betray him!" Susannah gasped, trying to throw Kate off her and scramble back up again. "He was going to steal money to finance his run for the Senate! I stopped him. Damn it, get off me! Ralph was playing you both for fools! He was corrupt as hell!"

Kate hit her, hard, across the side of the face, hurling her off balance backward to the rock shelf again.

"You killed him!" she cried in a howl of anguish. "He loved me! I could have prevented him from doing that! If you'd come to me, I'd have saved him!" She was sobbing as memory, broken dreams and unbearable loneliness swept over her. "I loved him! I could have . . ."

"I know you loved him!" Susannah put her hand up to her burning face and crawled sideways to where the shelf was wider. "But he didn't love anyone, not you, not Tonia, not anyone at all! Kate! The man you loved never existed!"

"Yes he did! He could have . . ."

"He could have . . . but he didn't! He chose not to!"

"No he didn't!" Tonia shouted, coming down toward them. "It's not true, Kate. She took the chance from him! She killed him! Go on!"

Kate hesitated. She could push Susannah back off the edge, hard down into the water.

"Go on!" Tonia screamed. "She killed Ralph! She betrayed him, sent him to that filthy place to be murdered! On the toilet floor! Ralph . . . beautiful, happy, magical Ralph! Susannah destroyed him!" She was just behind Kate now, only feet away.

Susannah could hear the waves crash in behind her, then crunch on the stones, draw in and suck back. How many had there been while she was crouched here? Three, four, five?

Kate turned from Tonia to Susannah, and back.

"Do it!" Tonia cried again. "If you loved Ralph, do it! She took him from you! He didn't want her, so she smashed everything."

"He didn't want any of us!" Susannah shouted desperately. "He only wanted the Senate—the power and the money!"

Kate swiveled back to Susannah and took another step toward her, her skin whipped by the wind, eyes wide.

Susannah saw Tonia just beyond her, the hatred naked in her face. "Haven't you the guts to do it yourself?" she shouted. "No wonder Ralph wanted Kate! At least she has her own passions, not someone else's! You coward!" She was crouching now, balanced.

Tonia's lips pulled back in a snarl of anger and she lunged forward, knocking aside Kate, who slipped and fell, grasping onto the weed to save herself.

Susannah moved sideways, twisting her leg and falling as Tonia landed. Now they were side by side, only feet apart. Susannah started to crawl back up the slope again, her leg stabbing with pain.

"That's right!" Tonia called with searing derision. "Crawl away! D'you think I can't catch you?" She started forward, slowly, spinning it out.

Susannah heard the wave before she saw it, taller, heavier than the others, the sneaker wave with all the hungry power of the ocean within.

"The wave!" she called out. She did not want to warn Tonia, but the words were out before she thought. "Look out!"

Tonia was laughing. She did not believe her.

"Look out!" Susannah screamed.

The wave broke, high and white, pouring over rocks with an obliterating roar. It was only up to Tonia's knees, but the strength of it tore away her feet from the ground and pulled her into its cauldron.

Kate was soaked, but she clung onto the weed and was left gasping.

Susannah was blinded for a moment, her clothes drenched with the spray, but she pushed the wet hair out of her eyes to see Tonia struggle, arms and legs flailing for a moment, then swallowed up, no more than a dark mass in the heart of the wave as it sucked back into the ocean and folded into itself back again into deep water.

Kate was sobbing, trying to stand up, her face ashen.

"You can't do anything," Susannah said quietly. "We'd better climb higher, there'll be another one, there always is."

"Did you . . . did you tell the police about Ralph?" Kate stammered.

"Yes." She turned and met her eyes directly. "He was a thief, and he was going to be a corrupt senator. You think I should have helped him to do that?"

"But he . . . and you?" Kate said with disbelief.

"A cheat," Susannah said for her. "Has it not occurred to you that if he would cheat on Tonia with you, then he would cheat on you with me—or anyone who would serve his cause?"

Kate looked crushed.

Susannah held out her hand. "Come on. We need to go higher, above all the waves, not just most of them."

Kate clung onto her. "But . . . what about Tonia?"

"An accident," Susannah replied. "Sneaker waves get people every year. I guess it's not enough to get it right most of the time, it's the weakness you didn't think of that'll destroy you."

Kate put her hands up to her face. "She wanted me to kill you!"

"I know." Susannah put her arm around her. "Come on."

LOULY AND PRETTY BOY

ELMORE LEONARD

Here are some dates in Louly Ring's life from 1912, the year she was born in Tulsa, Oklahoma, to 1931, when she ran away from home to meet Joe Young, following his release from the Missouri State Penitentiary.

In 1918 her daddy, a Tulsa stockyard hand, joined the U.S. Marines and was killed at Bois de Belleau during the World War. Her mom, sniffling as she held the letter, told Louly it was a woods over in France.

In 1920 her mom married a hardshell Baptist by the name of Otis Bender and they went to live on his cotton farm near Sallisaw, south of Tulsa on the edge of the Cookson Hills. By the time Louly was twelve, her mom had two sons by Otis and Otis had Louly out in the fields picking cotton. He was the only person in the world who called her by her Christian name, Louise. She hated picking cotton but her mom wouldn't say anything to Otis. Otis believed that when you were old enough to do a day's work, you worked. It meant Louly was finished with school by the sixth grade.

In 1924, that summer, they attended her cousin Ruby's wedding in Bixby. Ruby was seventeen, the boy she married, Charley Floyd, twenty. Ruby was dark but pretty, showing Cherokee blood from her mama's side. Because of their age difference Louly and Ruby had nothing to say to each other. Charley called her kiddo and would lay his hand on her head and muss her bobbed hair that was sort of reddish from her mom. He told her she had the biggest brown eyes he had ever seen on a little girl.

In 1925 she began reading about Charles Arthur Floyd in the paper: how he and two others went up to St. Louis and robbed the Kroger Food payroll office of $11,500. They were caught in Sallisaw driving around in a brand-new Studebaker they bought in Ft. Smith, Arkansas. The Kroger Food paymaster identified Charley saying, "That's him, the pretty boy with apple cheeks." The newspapers ate it up and referred to Charley from then on as Pretty Boy Floyd.

Louly remembered him from the wedding as cute with wavy hair, but kind of scary the way he grinned at you—not being sure what he was thinking. She bet he hated being called Pretty Boy. Looking at his picture she cut out of the paper Louly felt herself getting a crush on him.

In 1929, while he was still in the penitentiary, Ruby divorced him on the grounds of neglect and married a man from Kansas. Louly thought it was terrible, Ruby betraying Charley like that. "Ruby don't see him ever again going straight," her mom said. "She needs a husband the same as I did to ease the burdens of life, have a father for her little boy Dempsey." Born in December of '24 and named for the world's heavyweight boxing champ.

Now that Charley was divorced Louly wanted to write and sympathize but didn't know which of his names to use. She had heard his friends called him Choc, after his fondness for Choctaw Beer, his favorite beverage when he was in his teens and roamed Oklahoma and Kansas with harvest crews. Her mom said it was where he first took up with bad companions, "those drifters he met at harvest time," and later on working oil patches.

Louly opened her letter "Dear Charley," and said she thought it was a shame Ruby divorcing him while he was still in prison, not having the nerve to wait till he was out. What she most wanted to know, "Do you remember me from your wedding?" She stuck a picture of herself in a bathing suit, standing sideways and smiling over her shoulder at the camera. This way her fourteen-year-old breasts, coming along, were seen in profile.

Charley wrote back saying sure he remembered her, "the little girl with the big brown eyes." Saying, "I'm getting out in March and going to Kansas City to see what's doing. I have given your address to an inmate here by the name of Joe Young who we call Booger, being funny. He is from Okmulgee but has to do another year or so in this garbage can and would like to have a pen pal as pretty as you are."

Nuts. But then Joe Young wrote her a letter with a picture of himself taken in the yard with his shirt off, a fairly good-looking bozo with big ears and blondish hair. He said he kept her bathing-suit picture on the wall next to his rack so he'd look at it before going to sleep and dream of her all night. He never signed his letters Booger, always, "With love, your Joe Young."

Once they were exchanging letters she told him how much she hated picking cotton, dragging that duck sack along the rows all day in the heat and dust, her hands raw from pulling the bolls off the stalks, gloves after a while not doing a bit of good. Joe said in his letter, "What are you a nigger slave? You don't like picking cotton leave there and run away. It is what I done."

Pretty soon he said in a letter, "I am getting my release sometime next summer. Why don't you plan on meeting me so we can get together." Louly said she was dying to visit Kansas City and St. Louis, wondering if she would ever see Charley Floyd again. She asked Joe why he was in prison and he wrote back to say, "Honey, I'm a bank robber, same as Choc."

She had been reading more stories about Pretty Boy Floyd. He had returned to Akins, his hometown, for his daddy's funeral—*Akins only seven miles from Sallisaw*—his dad shot by a neighbor during an argument over a pile of lumber. When the neighbor disappeared there were people who said Pretty Boy had killed him. Seven miles away and she didn't know it till after.

There was his picture again. PRETTY BOY FLOYD ARRESTED IN AKRON for bank robbery. Sentenced to fifteen years in the Ohio State Penitentiary. Now she'd never see him but at least could start writing again.

A few weeks later another picture. PRETTY BOY FLOYD ESCAPES ON WAY TO PRISON. Broke a window in the toilet and jumped off the train and by the time they got it stopped he was gone.

It was exciting just trying to keep track of him, Louly getting chills and thrills knowing everybody in the world was reading about this famous outlaw she was related to—by marriage but not blood—this desperado who liked her brown eyes and had mussed her hair when she was a kid.

Now another picture. PRETTY BOY FLOYD IN SHOOTOUT WITH POLICE. Outside a barbershop in Bowling Green, Ohio, and got away. There with a woman named Juanita—Louly not liking the sound of that.

Joe Young wrote to say, "I bet Choc is threw with Ohio and will never go back there." But the main reason he wrote was to tell her, "I am getting my release the end of August. I will let you know soon where to meet me."

Louly had been working winters at Harkrider's grocery store in Sallisaw for six dollars a week part-time. She had to give five of it to Otis, the man never once thanking her, leaving a dollar to put in her running-away kitty. From winter to the next fall, working at the store most of six months a year, she hadn't saved a whole lot but she was going. She might have her timid-soul mom's looks, the reddish hair, but had the nerve and get-up-and-go of her daddy, killed in action charging a German machine gun nest in that woods in France.

Late in October, who walked in the grocery store but Joe Young. Louly knew him even wearing a suit, and he knew her, grinning as he came up to the counter, his shirt wide open at the neck. He said, "Well, I'm out."

She said, "You been out two months, haven't you?"

He said, "I been robbing banks. Me and Choc."

She thought she had to go to the bathroom, the urge coming over her in her groin and then gone. Louly gave herself a few moments to compose herself and act like the mention of Choc didn't mean anything special, Joe Young staring in her face with his grin, giving her the feeling he was dumb as dirt. Some other convict must've wrote his letters for him. She said in a casual way, "Oh, is Charley here with you?"

"He's around," Joe Young said, looking toward the door. "You ready? We gotta go."

She said, "I like that suit on you," giving herself time to think. The points of his shirt collar spread open to his shoulders, his hair long on top but skinned on the sides, his ears sticking out, Joe Young grinning like it was his usual dopey expression. "I'm not ready just yet," Louly said. "I don't have my running-away money with me."

"How much you save?"

"Thirty-eight dollars."

"Jesus, working here two years?"

"I told you, Otis takes most of my wages."

"You want, I'll crack his head for him."

"I wouldn't mind. The thing is, I'm not leaving without my money."

Joe Young looked at the door as he put his hand in his pocket saying, "Little girl, I'm paying your way. You won't need the thirty-eight dollars."

Little girl—she stood a good two inches taller than he was, even in his run-down cowboy boots. She was shaking her head now. "Otis bought a Model A Roadster with my money, paying it off twenty a month."

"You want to steal his car?"

"It's mine, ain't it, if he's using my money?"

Louly had made up her mind and Joe Young was anxious to get out of here. She had pay coming, so they'd meet November first—no, the second—at the Georgian Hotel in Henryetta, in the coffee shop around noon.

The day before she was to leave Louly told her mom she was sick. Instead of going to work she got her things ready and used the curling iron on her hair. The next day, while her mom was hanging wash, the two boys at school and Otis was out in the field, Louly rolled the Ford Roadster out of the shed and drove into Sallisaw to get a pack of Lucky Strikes for the trip. She loved to smoke and had been doing it with boys but never had to buy the cigarettes. When boys wanted to take her in the woods she'd ask, "You have Luckies? A whole pack?"

The druggist's son, one of her boyfriends, gave her a pack

free of charge and asked where she was yesterday, acting sly, saying, "You're always talking about Pretty Boy Floyd, I wonder if he stopped by your house."

They liked to kid her about Pretty Boy. Louly, not paying close attention, said, "I'll let you know when he does." But then saw the boy about to spring something on her.

"The reason I ask, he was here in town yesterday, Pretty Boy Floyd was."

She said, "Oh?" careful now. The boy took his time and it was hard not to grab him by the front of his shirt.

"Yeah, he brought his family down from Akins, his mama, two of his sisters, some others, so they could watch him rob the bank. His grampa watched from the field across the street. Bob Riggs, the bank assistant, said Pretty Boy had a Tommy gun, but did not shoot anybody. He come out of the bank with two thousand five-hundred and thirty-one dollars, him and two other fellas. He gave some of the money to his people and they say to anybody he thought hadn't et in a while, everybody grinning at him. Pretty Boy had Bob Riggs ride on the running board to the end of town and let him go."

This was the second time now he had been close by: first when his daddy was killed only seven miles away and now right here in Sallisaw, all kinds of people seeing him, damn it, but her. Just yesterday . . .

He knew she lived in Sallisaw. She wondered if he'd looked for her in the crowd watching.

She had to wonder, too, if she *had* been here would he of recognized her, and bet he would've.

She said to her boyfriend in the drugstore, "Charley ever hears you called him Pretty Boy, he'll come in for a pack of Luckies, what he always smokes, and then kill you."

• • •

The Georgian was the biggest hotel Louly had ever seen. Coming up on it in the Model A she was thinking these bank robbers knew how to live high on the hog. She pulled in front and a colored man in a green uniform coat with gold buttons and a peaked cap came around to open her door—and saw Joe Young on the sidewalk waving the doorman away, saying as he got in the car, "Jesus Christ, you stole it, didn't you. Jesus, how old are you, going around stealing cars?"

Louly said, "How old you have to be?"

He told her to keep straight ahead.

She said, "You aren't staying at the hotel?"

"I'm at a tourist court."

"Charley there?"

"He's around someplace."

"Well, he was in Sallisaw yesterday," Louly sounding mad now, "if that's what you call *around*," seeing by Joe Young's expression she was telling him something he didn't know. "I thought you were in his gang."

"He's got an old boy name of Birdwell with him. I hook up with Choc when I feel like it."

She was almost positive Joe Young was lying to her.

"Am I gonna see Charley or not?"

"He'll be back, don't worry your head about it." He said, "We got this car, I won't have to steal one." Joe Young in a good mood now. "What we need Choc for?" Grinning at her close by the car. "We got each other."

It told her what to expect.

Once they got to the tourist court and were in No. 7, like a little one-room frame house that needed paint, Joe Young took off his coat and she saw the Colt automatic with a pearl grip stuck in his pants. He laid it on the dresser by a full quart of whiskey and two glasses and poured them each a drink, his bigger than hers. She stood watching till he told her to take off her coat and when she did told her to take off her dress. Now she was in her white brassiere and panties. Joe Young looked her over before handing the smaller drink to her and clinking glasses.

"To our future."

Louly said, "Doing what?" Seeing the fun in his eyes.

He put his glass on the dresser, brought two .38 revolvers from the drawer and offered her one. She took it, big and heavy in her hand and said, "Yeah . . . ?"

"You know how to steal a car," Joe Young said, "and I admire that. But I bet you never held up a place with a gun."

"That's what we're gonna do?"

"Start with a filling station and work you up to a bank." He said, "I bet you never been to bed with a grown man, either."

Louly felt like telling him she was bigger than he was, taller, anyway, but didn't. This was a new experience, different than with boys her age in the woods, and she wanted to see what it was like.

Well, he grunted a lot and was rough, breathed hard through his nose and smelled of Lucky Tiger hair tonic, but it wasn't that much different than with boys. She got to liking it before he was finished and patted his back with her rough, cotton-picking fingers till he began to breathe easy again. Once he rolled off her she got her douche bag out of Otis's grip she'd taken and went in the bathroom, Joe Young's voice following her with, "Whoooeee . . ."

Then saying, "You know what you are now, little girl? You're what's called a gun moll."

Joe Young slept awhile, woke up still snookered and wanted to get something to eat. So they went to Purity, Joe said was the best place in Henryetta.

Louly said at the table, "Charley Floyd came in here one time. People found out he was in town and everybody stayed in their house."

"How you know that?"

"I know everything about him was ever written, some things only told."

"Where'd he stay in Kansas City?"

"Mother Ash's boardinghouse on Holmes Street."

"Who'd he go to Ohio with?"

"The Jim Bradley gang."

Joe Young picked up his coffee he'd poured a shot into. He said, "You're gonna start reading about me, chile."

It reminded her she didn't know how old Joe Young was and took this opportunity to ask him.

"I'm thirty next month, born on Christmas Day, same as Baby Jesus."

Louly smiled. She couldn't help it, seeing Joe Young lying in a manger with Baby Jesus, the three Wise Men looking at him funny. She asked Joe how many times he'd had his picture in the paper.

"When I got sent to Jeff City they's all kinds of pictures of me was in there."

"I mean how many different times, for other stickups?"

She watched him sit back as the waitress came with their supper and he gave her a pat on the butt as she turned from the table. The waitress said, "Fresh," and acted surprised in a cute way. Louly was ready to tell how Charley Floyd had his picture in the Sallisaw paper fifty-one times in the past year, once for each of the fifty-one banks robbed in Oklahoma, all of them claiming Charley as the bank robber. But if she told him, Joe Young would say Charley couldn't of robbed that many since he was in Ohio part of '31. Which was true. An estimate said he might've robbed thirty-eight banks, but even that might cause Joe Young to be jealous and get cranky, so she let it drop and they ate their chicken-fried steaks.

Joe Young told her to pay the bill, a buck-sixty for everything including rhubarb pie for dessert, out of her running-away money. They got back to the tourist court and he screwed her again on her full stomach, breathing through his nose, and she saw how this being a gun moll wasn't all a bed of roses.

• • •

In the morning they set out east on Highway 40 for the Cookson Hills, Joe Young driving the Model A with his elbow out the window, Louly holding her coat close to her, the collar up against the wind, Joe Young talking a lot, saying he knew where Choc liked to hide. They'd go on up to Muskogee, cross the Arkansas and head down along the river to Braggs. "I know the boy likes that country around Braggs." Along the way he could hold up a filling station, show Louly how it was done.

Heading out of Henryetta she said, "There's one."

He said, "Too many cars."

Thirty miles later leaving Checotah, turning north toward Muskogee, Louly looked back and said, "What's wrong with that Texaco station?"

"Something about it I don't like," Joe Young said. "You have to have a feel for this work."

Louly said, "You pick it." She had the .38 he gave her in a black and pink bag her mom had crocheted for her.

They came up on Summit and crept through town, both of them looking, Louly waiting for him to choose a place to rob. She was getting excited. They came to the other side of town and Joe Young said, "There's our place. We can fill up, get a cup of coffee."

Louly said, "Hold it up?"

"Look it over."

"It's sure a dump."

Two gas pumps in front of a rickety place, paint peeling, a sign that said EATS and told that soup was a dime and a hamburg five cents.

They went in while a bent-over old man filled their tank, Joe Young bringing his whiskey bottle with him, almost drained, and put it on the counter. The woman behind it was skin and bones, worn out, brushing strands of hair from her face. She placed cups in front of them and Joe Young poured what was left in the bottle into his.

Louly did not want to rob this woman.

The woman saying, "I think she's dry."

Joe Young was concentrating on dripping the last drops from his bottle. He said, "Can you help me out?"

Now the woman was pouring their coffee. "You want shine? Or I can give you Kentucky for three dollars."

"Gimme a couple," Joe Young said, drawing his Colt, laying it on the counter, "and what's in the till."

Louly did not want to rob this woman. She was thinking you didn't *have* to rob a person just 'cause the person had money, did you?

The woman said, "Goddamn you, mister."

Joe Young picked up his gun and went around to open the cash register at the end of the counter. Taking out bills he said to the woman, "Where you keep the whiskey money?"

She said, "In there," despair in her voice.

He said, "Fourteen dollars?" holding it up, and turned to Louly. "Put your gun on her so she don't move. The geezer come in, put it on him, too." Joe Young went through a doorway to what looked like an office.

The woman said to Louly, pointing the gun from the crocheted bag at her now, "How come you're with that trash? You seem like a girl from a nice family, have a pretty bag . . . There something wrong with you? My Lord, you can't do better'n him?"

Louly said, "You know who's a good friend of mine? Charley Floyd, if you know who I mean. He married my cousin Ruby." The woman shook her head and Louly said, "Pretty Boy Floyd," and wanted to bite her tongue.

Now the woman seemed to smile, showing black lines between the teeth she had. "He come in here one time. I fixed him breakfast and he paid me two dollars for it. You ever hear of that? I charge twenty-five cents for two eggs, four strips of bacon, toast and all you want of coffee, and he give me two dollars."

"When was this?" Louly said.

The woman looked past Louly trying to see when it was and said, "Twenty-nine, after his daddy was killed that time."

They got the fourteen from the till and fifty-seven dollars in whiskey money from the back, Joe Young talking again about heading for Muskogee, telling Louly it was his instinct told him to go in there. How was this place doing business, two big service stations only a few blocks away? So he'd brought the bottle in, see what it would get him. "You hear what she said? 'Goddamn you,' but called me 'Mister.' "

"Charley had breakfast in there one time," Louly said, "and paid her two dollars for it."

"Showing off," Joe Young said.

He decided they'd stay in Muskogee instead of going down to Braggs and rest up here.

Louly said, "Yeah, we must've come a good fifty miles today."

Joe Young told her not to get smart with him. "I'm gonna put you in a tourist cabin and see some boys I know. Find out where Choc's at."

She didn't believe him, but what was the sense of arguing?

•   •   •

It was early evening now, the sun going down.

The man who knocked on the door—she could see him through the glass part—was tall and slim in a dark suit, a young guy dressed up, holding his hat at his leg. She believed he was the police, but had no reason, standing here looking at him, not to open the door.

He said, "Miss," and showed her his I.D. and a star in a circle in a wallet he held open, "I'm Deputy U.S. Marshal Carl Webster. Who am I speaking to?"

She said, "I'm Louly Ring?"

He smiled straight teeth at her and said, "You're a cousin of Pretty Boy Floyd's wife, Ruby, aren't you?"

Like getting ice-cold water thrown in her face she was so surprised. "How'd you know that?"

"We been making a book on Pretty Boy, noting down connections, everybody he knows. You recall the last time you saw him?"

"At their wedding, eight years ago."

"No time since? How about the other day in Sallisaw?"

"I never saw him. But listen, him and Ruby are divorced."

The marshal, Carl Webster, shook his head. "He went up to Coffeyville and got her back. But aren't you missing a automobile, a Model A Ford?"

She had not heard a *word* about Charley and Ruby being back together. None of the papers ever mentioned her, just the woman named Juanita. Louly said, "The car isn't missing, a friend of mine's using it."

He said, "The car's in your name?" and recited the Oklahoma license number.

"I paid for it out of my wages. It just happens to be in my stepfather's name, Otis Bender."

"I guess there's some kind of misunderstanding," Carl Webster said. "Otis claims it was stolen off his property in Sequoyah County. Who's your friend borrowed it?"

She did hesitate before saying his name.

"When's Joe coming back?"

"Later on. 'Cept he'll stay with his friends he gets too drunk."

Carl Webster said, "I wouldn't mind talking to him," and gave Louly a business card from his pocket with a star on it and letters she could feel. "Ask Joe to give me a call later on, or sometime tomorrow if he don't come home. Y'all just driving around?"

"Seeing the sights."

Every time she kept looking at him he'd start to smile. Carl Webster. She could feel his name under her thumb. She said, "You're writing a book on Charley Floyd?"

"Not a real one. We're collecting the names of anybody he ever knew that might want to put him up."

"You gonna ask me if I would?"

There was the smile.

"I already know."

She liked the way he shook her hand and thanked her, and the way he put on his hat, nothing to it, knowing how to cock it just right.

· · ·

Joe Young returned about 9:00 a.m. making awful faces working his mouth, trying to get a taste out of it. He came in the room and took a good pull on the whiskey bottle, then another, sucked in his breath and let it out and seemed better. He said, "I don't believe what we got into with those chickens last night."

"Wait," Louly said. She told him about the marshal stopping by, and Joe Young became jittery and couldn't stand still, saying, "I ain't going back. I done ten years and swore to Jesus I ain't ever going back." Now he was looking out the window.

Louly wanted to know what Joe and his buddies did to the chickens, but knew they had to get out of here. She tried to tell him they had to leave, *right now*.

He was still drunk or starting over, saying now, "They come after me they's gonna be a shoot-out. I'm taking some of the scudders with me." Maybe not even knowing he was playing Jimmy Cagney now.

Louly said, "You only stole seventy-one dollars."

"I done other things in the State of Oklahoma," Joe Young said. "They take me alive I'm facing fifteen years to life. I swear I ain't going back."

What was going *on* here? They're driving around looking for Charley Floyd—the next thing this dumbbell wants to shoot it out with the law and here she was in this room with him. "They don't want *me*," Louly said. Knowing she couldn't talk to him, the state he was in. She had to get out of here, open the door and run. She got her crocheted bag from the dresser, started for the door and was stopped by the bullhorn.

The electrified voice loud, saying, "JOE YOUNG, COME OUT WITH YOUR HANDS IN THE AIR."

What Joe Young did—he held his Colt straight out in front of him and started firing through the glass pane in the door. People outside returned fire, blew out the window, gouged the door with gunfire, Louly dropping to the floor with her bag, until she heard a voice on the bullhorn call out, "HOLD YOUR FIRE."

Louly looked up to see Joe Young standing by the bed with a gun in each hand now, the Colt and a .38. She said, "Joe, you have to give yourself up. They're gonna kill both of us you keep shooting."

He didn't even look at her. He yelled out, "Come and get me!" and started shooting again, both guns at the same time.

Louly's hand went in the crocheted bag and came out with the .38 he'd given her to help him rob places. From the floor, up on her elbows, she aimed the revolver at Joe Young, cocked it and *bam*, shot him through the chest.

•   •   •

Louly stepped away from the door and the marshal, Carl Webster, came in holding a revolver. She saw men standing out in the road, some with rifles. Carl Webster was looking at Joe Young curled up on the floor. He holstered his revolver, took the .38 from Louly and sniffed the end of the barrel and stared at her without saying anything before going to one knee to see if Joe Young had a pulse. He got up saying, "The Oklahoma Bankers Association wants people like Joe dead, and that's what he is. They're gonna give you a five-hundred-dollar reward for killing your friend."

"He wasn't a friend."

"He was yesterday. Make up your mind."

"He stole the car and made me go with him."

"Against your will," Carl Webster said. "Stay with that you won't go to jail."

"It's true, Carl," Louly said, showing him her big brown eyes. "Really."

• • •

The headline in the Muskogee paper, over a small photo of Louise Ring, said SALLISAW GIRL SHOOTS ABDUCTOR.

According to Louise, she had to stop Joe Young or be killed in the exchange of gunfire. She also said her name was Louly, not Louise. The marshal on the scene said it was a courageous act, the girl shooting her abductor. "We considered Joe Young a mad-dog felon with nothing to lose." The marshal said that Joe Young was suspected of being a member of Pretty Boy Floyd's gang. He also mentioned that Louly Ring was related to Floyd's wife and acquainted with the desperado.

The headline in the Tulsa paper, over a larger photo of Louly, said GIRL SHOOTS MEMBER OF PRETTY BOY FLOYD GANG. The story told that Louly Ring was a friend of Pretty Boy's and had been abducted by the former gang member, who, according to Louly, "was jealous of Pretty Boy and kidnapped me to get back at him."

By the time the story had appeared everywhere from Ft. Smith, Arkansas, to Toledo, Ohio, the favorite headline was GIRLFRIEND OF PRETTY BOY FLOYD GUNS DOWN MAD-DOG FELON.

The marshal, Carl Webster, came to Sallisaw on business and stopped in Harkrider's for a sack of Beechnut scrap. He was surprised to see Louly.

"You're still working here?"

"I'm shopping for my mom. No, Carl, I got my reward money and I'll be leaving here pretty soon. Otis hasn't said a word to me since I got home. He's afraid I might shoot him."

"Where you going?"

"This writer for *True Detective* wants me to come to Tulsa. They'll put me up at the Mayo Hotel and pay a hundred dollars for my story. Reporters from Kansas City and St. Louis, Missouri, have already been to the house."

"You're sure getting a lot of mileage out of knowing Pretty Boy, aren't you?"

"They start out asking about my shooting that dumbbell Joe Young, but what they want to know, if I'm Charley Floyd's girlfriend. I say, 'Where'd you get that idea?'"

"But you don't deny it."

"I say, 'Believe what you want, since I can't change your mind.' What I wonder, you think Charley's read about it and seen my picture?"

"Sure he has," Carl said. "I imagine he'd even like to see you again, in person."

Louly said, "Wow," like she hadn't thought of that before this moment. "You're kidding. Really?"

BORN BAD

JEFFERY DEAVER

Sleep, my child and peace attend thee, all through the night. . . .

The words of the lullaby looped relentlessly through her mind, as persistent as the clattering Oregon rain on the roof and window.

The song that she'd sung to Beth Anne when the girl was three or four seated itself in her head and wouldn't stop echoing. Twenty-five years ago, the two of them: mother and daughter, sitting in the kitchen of the family's home outside Detroit. Liz Polemus, hunching over the Formica table, the frugal young mother and wife, working hard to stretch the dollars.

Singing to her daughter, who sat across from her, fascinated with the woman's deft hands.

I who love you shall be near you, all through the night.
Soft the drowsy hours are creeping.
Hill and vale in slumber sleeping.

Liz felt a cramp in her right arm—the one that had never

healed properly—and realized she was still gripping the receiver fiercely at the news she'd just received. That her daughter was on her way to the house.

The daughter she hadn't spoken with in more than three
years.

I my loving vigil keeping, all through the night.

Liz finally replaced the telephone and felt blood surge into
her arm, itching, stinging. She sat down on the embroidered
couch that had been in the family for years and massaged her
throbbing forearm. She felt light-headed, confused, as if she
wasn't sure the phone call had been real or a wispy scene from
a dream.

Only the woman wasn't lost in the peace of sleep. No, Beth
Anne was on her way. A half-hour and she'd be at Liz's door.

Outside, the rain continued to fall steadily, tumbling into
the pines that filled Liz's yard. She'd lived in this house for
nearly a year, a small place miles from the nearest suburb. Most
people would've thought it too small, too remote. But to Liz it
was an oasis. The slim widow, midfifties, had a busy life and
little time for housekeeping. She could clean the place quickly
and get back to work. And while hardly a recluse, she preferred
the buffer zone of forest that separated her from her neighbors. The minuscule size also discouraged suggestions by any
male friends that, hey, got an idea, how 'bout I move in? The
woman would merely look around the one-bedroom home
and explain that two people would go crazy in such cramped
quarters; after her husband's death she'd resolved she'd never
remarry or live with another man.

Her thoughts now drifted to Jim. Their daughter had left
home and cut off all contact with the family before he died. It
had always stung her that the girl hadn't even called after his
death, let alone attended his funeral. Anger at this instance of

the girl's callousness shivered within Liz but she pushed it aside, reminding herself that whatever the young woman's purpose tonight there wouldn't be enough time to exhume even a fraction of the painful memories that lay between mother and daughter like wreckage from a plane crash.

A glance at the clock. Nearly ten minutes had sped by since the call, Liz realized with a start.

Anxious, she walked into her sewing room. This, the largest room in the house, was decorated with needlepoints of her own and her mother's and a dozen racks of spools—some dating back to the fifties and sixties. Every shade of God's palette was represented in those threads. Boxes full of *Vogue* and Butterick patterns too. The centerpiece of the room was an old electric Singer. It had none of the fancy stitch cams of the new machines, no lights or complex gauges or knobs. The machine was a forty-year-old, black-enameled workhorse, identical to the one that her mother had used.

Liz had sewed since she was twelve and in difficult times the craft sustained her. She loved every part of the process: buying the fabric—hearing the *thud thud thud* as the clerk would turn the flat bolts of cloth over and over, unwinding the yardage (Liz could tell the women with near-prefect precision when a particular amount had been unfolded). Pinning the crisp, translucent paper onto the cloth. Cutting with the heavy pinking shears, which left a dragon-tooth edge on the fabric. Readying the machine, winding the bobbin, threading the needle . . .

There was something so completely soothing about sewing: taking these substances—cotton from the land, wool from animals—and blending them into something altogether new. The worst aspect of the injury several years ago was the damage to her right arm, which kept her off the Singer for three unbearable months.

Sewing was therapeutic for Liz, yes, but more than that, it was a part of her profession and had helped her become a well-to-do woman; nearby were racks of designer gowns, awaiting her skillful touch.

Her eyes rose to the clock. Fifteen minutes. Another breathless slug of panic.

Picturing so clearly that day twenty-five years ago—Beth Anne in her flannel 'jammies, sitting at the rickety kitchen table and watching her mother's quick fingers with fascination as Liz sang to her.

Sleep, my child, and peace attend thee . . .

This memory gave birth to dozens of others and the agitation rose in Liz's heart like the water level of the rain-swollen stream behind her house. Well, she told herself now firmly, don't just sit here . . . do something. Keep busy. She found a navy-blue jacket in her closet, walked to her sewing table, then dug through a basket until she found a matching remnant of wool. She'd use this to make a pocket for the garment. Liz went to work, smoothing the cloth, marking it with tailor's chalk, finding the scissors, cutting carefully. She focused on her task but the distraction wasn't enough to take her mind off the impending visit—and memories from years ago.

The shoplifting incident, for instance. When the girl was twelve.

Liz recalled the phone ringing, answering it. The head of security at a nearby department store was reporting—to Liz's and Jim's shock—that Beth Anne had been caught with nearly a thousand dollars' worth of jewelry hidden in a paper bag.

The parents had pleaded with the manager not to press charges. They'd said there must've been some mistake.

"Well," the security chief said skeptically, "we found her

with five watches. A necklace too. Wrapped up in this grocery bag. I mean, that don't sound like any mistake to me."

Finally, after much reassurance that this was a fluke and promises she'd never come into the store again, the manager agreed to keep the police out of the matter.

Outside the store, once the family was alone, Liz turned to Beth Anne furiously. "Why on earth did you do that?"

"Why not?" was the girl's singsong response, a snide smile on her face.

"It was stupid."

"Like, I care."

"Beth Anne . . . why're you acting this way?"

"What way?" the girl'd asked in mock confusion.

Her mother had tried to engage her in a dialogue—the way the talk shows and psychologists said you should do with your kids—but Beth Anne remained bored and distracted. Liz had delivered a vague, and obviously futile, warning and had given up.

Thinking now: You put a certain amount of effort into stitching a jacket or dress and you get the garment you expect. There's no mystery. But you put a thousand times *more* effort into raising your child and the result is the opposite of what you hope and dream for. This seemed so unfair.

Liz's keen gray eyes examined the wool jacket, making sure the pocket lay flat and was pinned correctly into position. She paused, looking up, out the window toward the black spikes of the pine, but what she was seeing were more hard memories of Beth Anne. What a mouth on that girl! Beth Anne would look her mother or father in the eye and say, "There is no Goddamn way you're going to make me go with you." Or, "Do you have *any* fucking clue at all?"

Maybe they should've been stricter in their upbringing. In

Liz's family you got whipped for cursing or talking back to adults or for not doing what your parents asked you to do. She and Jim had never spanked Beth Anne; maybe they *should've* swatted her once or twice.

One time, somebody had called in sick at the family business—a warehouse Jim had inherited—and he needed Beth Anne to help out. She'd snapped at him, "I'd rather be dead than go back inside that shithole with you."

Her father had backed down sheepishly but Liz stormed up to her daughter. "Don't talk to your father that way."

"Oh?" the girl asked in a sarcastic voice. "How *should* I talk to him? Like some obedient little daughter who does everything he wants? Maybe that's what he wanted but it's not who he got." She'd grabbed her purse, heading for the door.

"Where are you going?"

"To see some friends."

"You are not. Get back here this minute!"

Her reply was a slamming door. Jim started after her but in an instant she was gone, crunching through two-month-old gray Michigan snow.

And those "friends"?

Trish and Eric and Sean . . . Kids from families with totally different values from Liz's and Jim's. They tried to forbid her from seeing them. But that, of course, had no effect.

"Don't tell me who I can hang out with," Beth Anne had said furiously. The girl was eighteen then and as tall as her mother. As she walked forward with a glower, Liz retreated uneasily. The girl continued, "And what do you know about them anyway?"

"They don't like your father and me—that's all I need to know. What's wrong with Todd and Joan's kids? Or Brad's? Your father and I've known them for years."

"What's *wrong* with them?" the girl muttered sarcastically. "Try, they're losers." This time grabbing both her purse and the cigarettes she'd started smoking, she made another dramatic exit.

With her right foot Liz pressed the pedal of the Singer and the motor gave its distinctive grind, then broke into *clatta clatta clatta* as the needle sped up and down, vanishing into the cloth, leaving a neat row of stitches around the pocket.

Clatta, clatta, clatta . . .

In middle school the girl would never get home until seven or eight and in high school she'd arrive much later. Sometimes she'd stay away all night. Weekends too she just disappeared and had nothing to do with the family.

Clatta clatta clatta. The rhythmic grind of the Singer soothed Liz somewhat but couldn't keep her from panicking again when she looked at the clock. Her daughter could be here at any minute.

Her girl, her little baby . . .

Sleep, my child . . .

And the question that had plagued Liz for years returned now: What had gone wrong? For hours and hours she'd replay the girl's early years, trying to see what Liz had done to make Beth Anne reject her so completely. She'd been an attentive, in-volved mother, been consistent and fair, made meals for the family every day, washed and ironed the girl's clothes, bought her whatever she needed. All she could think of was that she'd been too strong-minded, too unyielding in her approach to raising the girl, too stern sometimes.

But this hardly seemed like much of a crime. Besides, Beth Anne had been equally mad at her father—the softie of the parents. Easygoing, doting to the point of spoiling the girl, Jim was the perfect father. He'd help Beth Anne and her friends with their homework, drive them to school himself when Liz was working, read her bedtime stories and tuck her in at night. He made up "special games" for him and Beth Anne to play. It was just the sort of parental bond that most children would love.

But the girl would fly into rages at him too and go out of her way to avoid spending time with him.

No, Liz could think of no dark incidents in the past, no traumas, no tragedies that could have turned Beth Anne into a renegade. She returned to the conclusion that she'd come to years ago: that—as unfair and cruel as it seemed—her daughter had simply been born fundamentally different from Liz; something had happened in the wiring to make the girl the rebel she was.

And looking at the cloth, smoothing it under her long, smooth fingers, Liz considered something else: rebellious, yes, but was she a *threat* too?

Liz now admitted that part of the ill ease she felt tonight wasn't only from the impending confrontation with her wayward child; it was that the young woman scared her.

She looked up from her jacket and stared at the rain spattering her window. Her right arm tingling painfully, she recalled that terrible day several years ago—the day that drove her permanently from Detroit and still gave her breathless nightmares. Liz had walked into a jewelry store and stopped in shock, gasping as she saw a pistol swinging toward her. She could still see the yellow flash as the man pulled the trigger, hear the stunning explosion, feel the numbing shock as the bullet slammed into her arm, sending her sprawling on the tile floor, crying out in pain and confusion.

Her daughter, of course, had nothing to do with that tragedy. Yet Liz had realized that Beth Anne was just as willing and capable of pulling the trigger as that man had done during the robbery; she had proof her daughter was a dangerous woman. A few years ago, after Beth Anne had left home, Liz had gone to visit Jim's grave. The day was foggy as cotton and she was nearly to the tombstone when she realized that somebody was standing over it. To her shock she realized it was Beth Anne. Liz eased back into the mist, heart pounding fiercely. She debated for a long moment but finally decided that she didn't have the courage to confront the girl and decided to leave a note on her car's windshield.

But as she stepped to the Chevy, fishing in her handbag for a pen and some paper, she glanced inside and her heart shivered at the sight: a jacket, a clutter of papers and half-hidden beneath them a pistol and some plastic bags, which contained white powder—drugs, Liz assumed.

Oh, yes, she now thought, her daughter, little Beth Anne Polemus, was very capable of killing.

Liz's foot rose from the pedal and the Singer fell silent. She lifted the clamp and cut the dangling threads. She pulled it on and slipped a few things into the pocket, examined herself in the mirror and decided that she was satisfied with the work.

Then she stared at her dim reflection. Leave! a voice in her head said. She's a threat! Get out now before Beth Anne arrives.

But after a moment of debate Liz sighed. One of the reasons she'd moved here in the first place was that she'd learned her daughter had relocated to the Northwest. Liz had been meaning to try to track the girl down but had found herself oddly reluctant to do so. No, she'd stay, she'd meet with Beth Anne. But she wasn't going to be stupid, not after the robbery. Liz now hung the jacket on a hanger and walked to the closet. She pulled down a box from the top shelf and looked inside. There sat a small pistol. "A ladies' gun," Jim had called it when he gave it to her years ago. She took it out and stared at the weapon.

Sleep, my child . . . All through the night.

Then she shuddered in disgust. No, she couldn't possibly use a weapon against her daughter. Of course not.

The idea of putting the girl to sleep forever was inconceivable.

And yet . . . what if it were a choice between her life and her daughter's? What if the hatred within the girl had pushed her over the edge?

Could she kill Beth Anne to save her own life?

No mother should ever have to make a choice like this one.

She hesitated for a long moment, then started to put the gun back. But a flash of light stopped her. Headlights filled the front yard and cast bright yellow cat's eyes on the sewing room wall beside Liz.

The woman glanced once more at the gun and, rather than put it away in the closet, set it on a dresser near the door and covered it with a doily. She walked into the living room and stared out the window at the car in her driveway, which sat motionless, lights still on, wipers whipping back and forth fast, her daughter hesitating to climb out; Liz suspected it wasn't the bad weather that kept the girl inside.

A long, long moment later the headlights went dark.

Well, think positive, Liz told herself. Maybe her daughter had changed. Maybe the point of the visit was reaching out to make amends for all the betrayal over the years. They could finally begin to work on having a normal relationship.

Still, she glanced back at the sewing room, where the gun sat on the dresser, and told herself: Take it. Keep it in your pocket.

Then: No, put it back in the closet.

Liz did neither. Leaving the gun on the dresser, she strode to the front door of her house and opened it, feeling cold mist coat her face.

She stood back from the approaching silhouetted form of the slim young woman as Beth Anne walked through the doorway and stopped. A pause, then she swung the door shut behind her.

Liz remained in the middle of the living room, pressing her hands together nervously.

Pulling back the hood of her windbreaker, Beth Anne wiped rain off her face. The young woman's face was weathered, ruddy. She wore no makeup. She'd be twenty-eight, Liz knew, but she looked older. Her hair was now short, revealing tiny earrings. For some reason, Liz wondered if someone had given them to the girl or if she'd bought them for herself.

"Well, hello, honey."

"Mother."

A hesitation then a brief, humorless laugh from Liz. "You used to call me 'Mom.'"

"Did I?"

"Yes. Don't you remember?"

A shake of the head. But Liz thought that in fact she did remember but was reluctant to acknowledge the memory. She looked her daughter over carefully.

Beth Anne glanced around the small living room. Her eye settled on a picture of herself and her father together—they were on the boat dock near the family home in Michigan.

Liz asked, "When you called you said somebody told you I was here. Who?"

"It doesn't matter. Just somebody. You've been living here since . . ." Her voice faded.

"A couple of years. Do you want a drink?"

352 • JEFFERY DEAVER

"No."

Liz remembered that she'd found the girl sneaking some beer when she was sixteen and wondered if she'd continued to drink and now had a problem with alcohol.

"Tea, then? Coffee?"

"No."

"You knew I moved to the Northwest?" Beth Anne asked.

"You always talked about the area, getting away from . . . well, getting out of Michigan and coming here. Then after you moved out you got some mail at the house. From somebody in Seattle."

Beth Anne nodded. Was there a slight grimace too? As if she was angry with herself for carelessly leaving a clue to her whereabouts. "And you moved to Portland to be near me?"

Liz smiled. "I guess I did. I started to look you up but I lost the nerve." Liz felt tears welling in her eyes as her daughter continued her examination of the room. The house was small, yes, but the furniture, electronics and appointments were the best—the rewards of Liz's hard work in recent years. Two feelings vied within the woman: She half-hoped the girl would be tempted to reconnect with her mother when she saw how much money Liz had but, simultaneously, she was ashamed of the opulence; her daughter's clothes and cheap costume jewelry suggested she was struggling.

The silence was like fire. It burned Liz's skin and heart.

Beth Anne unclenched her left hand and her mother noticed a minuscule engagement ring and a simple gold band. The tears now rolled from her eyes. "You—?"

The young woman followed her mother's gaze to the ring. She nodded.

Liz wondered what sort of man her son-in-law was. Would he be someone soft like Jim, someone who could temper the

girl's wayward personality? Or would he be hard? Like Beth
Anne herself?

"You have children?" Liz asked.

"That's not for you to know."

"Are you working?"

"Are you asking if I've changed, Mother?"

Liz didn't want to hear the answer to this question and
continued quickly, pitching her case. "I was thinking," she said,
desperation creeping into her voice, "that maybe I could go up
to Seattle. We could see each other . . . We could even work together. We could be partners. Fifty-fifty. We'd have so much
fun. I always thought we'd be great together. I always
dreamed—"

"You and me working together, Mother?" She glanced into
the sewing room, nodded toward the machine, the racks of
dresses. "That's not my life. It never was. It never could be.
After all these years, you really don't understand that, do you?"
The words and their cold tone answered Liz's question firmly:
No, the girl hadn't changed one bit.

Her voice went harsh. "Then why're you here? What's your
point in coming?"

"I think you know, don't you?"

"No, Beth Anne, I *don't* know. Some kind of psycho revenge?"

"You could say that, I guess." She looked around the room
again. "Let's go."

Liz's breath was coming fast. "Why? Everything we ever did
was for you."

"I'd say you did it *to* me." A gun appeared in her daughter's
hand and the black muzzle lolled in Liz's direction. "Outside,"
she whispered.

"My God! No!" She inhaled a gasp, as the memory of the

shooting in the jewelry store came back to her hard. Her arm tingled and tears streaked down her cheeks.

She pictured the gun on the dresser.

Sleep, my child . . .

"I'm not going anywhere!" Liz said, wiping her eyes.

"Yes, you are. Outside."

"What are you going to do?" she asked desperately.

"What I should've done a long time ago."

Liz leaned against a chair for support. Her daughter noticed the woman's left hand, which had eased to within inches of the telephone.

"No!" the girl barked. "Get away from it."

Liz gave a hopeless glance at the receiver and then did as she was told.

"Come with me."

"Now? In the rain."

The girl nodded.

"Let me get a coat."

"There's one by the door."

"It's not warm enough."

The girl hesitated, as if she was going to say that the warmth of her mother's coat was irrelevant, considering what was about to happen. But then she nodded. "But don't try to use the phone. I'll be watching."

Stepping into the doorway of the sewing room, Liz picked up the blue jacket she'd just been working on. She slowly put it on, her eyes riveted to the doily and the hump of the pistol beneath it. She glanced back into the living room. Her daughter was staring at a framed snapshot of herself at eleven or twelve standing next to her father and mother.

Quickly she reached down and picked up the gun. She

could turn fast, point it at her daughter. Scream to her to throw away her own gun.

Mother, I can feel you near me, all through the night . . .

Father, I know you can hear me, all through the night . . .

But what if Beth Anne *didn't* give up the gun?

What if she raised it, intending to shoot?

What would Liz do then?

To save her own life could she kill her daughter?

Sleep, my child . . .

Beth Anne was still turned away, examining the picture. Liz would be able to do it—turn, one fast shot. She felt the pistol, its weight tugging at her throbbing arm.

But then she sighed.

The answer was no. A deafening no. She'd never hurt her daughter. Whatever was going to happen next, outside in the rain, she could never hurt the girl.

Replacing the gun, Liz joined Beth Anne.

"Let's go," her daughter said and, shoving her own pistol into the waistband of her jeans, she led the woman outside, gripping her mother roughly by the arm. This was, Liz realized, the first physical contact in at least four years.

They stopped on the porch and Liz spun around to face her daughter. "If you do this, you'll regret it for the rest of your life."

"No," the girl said. "I'd regret *not* doing it."

Liz felt a spatter of rain join the tears on her cheeks. She glanced at her daughter. The young woman's face was wet and red too, but this was, her mother knew, solely from the rain; her eyes were completely tearless. In a whisper she asked, "What've I ever done to make you hate me?"

This question went unanswered as the first of the squad cars pulled into the yard, red and blue and white lights igniting the fat raindrops around them like sparks at a Fourth of July celebration. A man in his thirties, wearing a dark windbreaker and a badge around his neck, climbed out of the first car and walked toward the house, two uniformed state troopers behind him. He nodded to Beth Anne. "I'm Dan Heath, Oregon State Police."

The young woman shook his hand. "Detective Beth Anne Polemus, Seattle PD."

"Welcome to Portland," he said.

She gave an ironic shrug, took the handcuffs he held and cuffed her mother's hands securely.

•   •   •

Numb from the cold rain—and from the emotional fusion of the meeting—Beth Anne listened as Heath recited to the older woman, "Elizabeth Polemus, you're under arrest for murder, attempted murder, assault, armed robbery and dealing in stolen goods." He read her her rights and explained that she'd be arraigned in Oregon on local charges but was subject to an extradition order back to Michigan on a number of outstanding warrants there, including capital murder.

Beth Anne gestured to the young OSP officer who'd met her at the airport. She hadn't had time to do the paperwork that'd allow her to bring her own service weapon into another state so the trooper had loaned her one of theirs. She returned it to him now and turned back to watch a trooper search her mother.

"Honey," her mother began, the voice miserable, pleading.

Beth Anne ignored her and Heath nodded to the young uniformed trooper, who led the woman toward a squad car. But Beth Anne stopped him and called, "Hold on. Frisk her better."

The uniformed trooper blinked, looking over the slim, slight captive, who seemed as unthreatening as a child. But, with a nod from Heath, he motioned over a policewoman, who expertly patted her down. The officer frowned when she came to the small of Liz's back. The mother gave a piercing glance to her daughter as the officer pulled up the woman's navy-blue jacket, revealing a small pocket sewn into the inside back of the garment. Inside was a small switchblade knife and a universal handcuff key.

"Jesus," whispered the officer. He nodded to the police-woman, who searched her again. No other surprises were found.

Beth Anne said, "That was a trick I remember from the old days. She'd sew secret pockets into her clothes. For shoplifting and hiding weapons." A cold laugh from the young woman. "Sewing and robbery. Those're her talents." The smile faded. "Killing too, of course."

"How could you do this to your mother?" Liz snapped viciously. "You Judas."

Beth Anne watched, detached, as the woman was led to a squad car.

Heath and Beth Anne stepped into the living room of the house. As the policewoman again surveyed the hundreds of thousands of dollars of stolen property filling the bungalow, Heath said, "Thanks, Detective. I know this was hard for you. But we were desperate to collar her without anybody else getting hurt."

Capturing Liz Polemus could indeed have turned into a bloodbath. It had happened before. Several years ago, when her mother and her lover, Brad Selbit, had tried to knock over a jewelry store in Ann Arbor, Liz had been surprised by the security guard. He'd shot her in the arm. But that hadn't stopped her from grabbing her pistol with her other hand and killing him and a customer and then later shooting one of the responding police officers. She'd managed to escape. She'd left Michigan for Portland, where she and Brad had started up her operation again, sticking with her forte—knocking over jewelry stores and boutiques selling designer clothes, which she'd use her skills as a seamstress to alter and then would sell to fences in other states.

An informant had told the Oregon State Police that Liz Polemus was the one behind the string of recent robberies in the Northwest and was living under a fake name in a bungalow here. The OSP detectives on the case had learned that her daughter was a detective with the Seattle police department and had helicoptered Beth Anne to Portland airport. She'd driven here alone to get her mother to surrender peacefully.

"She was on two states' ten-most-wanted lists. And I heard she was making a name for herself in California too. Imagine that—your own mother." Heath's voice faded, thinking this might be indelicate.

But Beth Anne didn't care. She mused, "That was my childhood—armed robbery, burglary, money laundering . . . My father owned a warehouse where they fenced the stuff. That was their front—they'd inherited it from his father. Who was in the business too, by the way."

"You *grandfather*?"

She nodded. "That warehouse . . . I can still see it so clear. Smell it. Feel the cold. And I was only there once. When I was about eight, I guess. It was full of perped merch. My father left me in the office alone for a few minutes and I peeked out the door and saw him and one of his buddies beating the hell out of this guy. Nearly killed him."

"Doesn't sound like they tried to keep anything very secret from you."

"Secret? Hell, they did everything they could to get me *into* the business. My father had these special games, he called them. Oh, I was supposed to go over to friends' houses and scope out if they had valuables and where they were. Or check out TVs and VCRs at school and let him know where they kept them and what kind of locks were on the doors."

Heath shook his head in astonishment. Then he asked, "But you never had any run-ins with the law?"

She laughed. "Actually, yeah—I got busted once for shoplifting."

Heath nodded. "I copped a pack of cigarettes when I was fourteen. I can still feel my daddy's belt on my butt for that one."

"No, no," Beth Anne said. "I got busted *returning* some crap my mother stole."

"You what?"

"She took me to the store as cover. You know, a mother and daughter wouldn't be as suspicious as a woman by herself. I saw her pocket some watches and a necklace. When we got home I put the merch in a bag and took it back to the store. The guard saw me looking guilty, I guess, and he nailed me before I could replace anything. I took the rap. I mean, I wasn't going to drop a dime on my parents, was I? . . . My mother was so mad . . . They honestly couldn't figure out why I didn't want to follow in their footsteps."

"You need some time with Dr. Phil or somebody."

"Been there. Still am."

She nodded as memories came back to her. "From, like, twelve or thirteen on, I tried to stay as far away from home as I could. I did every after-school activity I could. Volunteered at a hospital on weekends. My friends really helped me out. They were the best . . . I probably picked them because they were one-eighty from my parents' criminal crowd. I'd hang with the National Merit scholars, the debate team, Latin club. Anybody who was decent and normal. I wasn't a great student but I spent so much time at the library or studying at friends' houses I got a full scholarship and put myself through college."

"Where'd you go?"

"Ann Arbor. Criminal justice major. I took the CS exam and landed a spot on Detroit PD. Worked there for a while. Narcotics mostly. Then moved out here and joined the force in Seattle."

"And you've got your gold shield. You made detective fast." Heath looked over the house. "She lived here by herself? Where's your father?"

"Dead," Beth Anne said matter-of-factly. "She killed him."

"*What?*"

"Wait'll you read the extradition order from Michigan. Nobody knew it at the time, of course. The original coroner's report was an accident. But a few months ago this guy in prison in Michigan confessed that he'd helped her. Mother found out my father was skimming money from their operation and sharing it with some girlfriend. She hired this guy to kill him and make it look like an accidental drowning."

"I'm sorry, Detective."

Beth Anne shrugged. "I always wondered if I could forgive them. I remember once, I was still working Narc in Detroit. I'd just run a big bust out on Six Mile. Confiscated a bunch of smack. I was on my way to log the stuff into Evidence back at the station and I saw I was driving past the cemetery where my father was buried. I'd never been there. I pulled in and walked up to the grave and tried to forgive him. But I couldn't. I realized then that I never could—not him or my mother. That's when I decided I had to leave Michigan."

"Your mother ever remarry?"

"She took up with Selbit a few years ago but she never married him. You collared him yet?"

"No. He's around here somewhere but he's gone to ground."

Beth Anne gave a nod toward the phone. "Mother tried to grab the phone when I came in tonight. She might've been trying to get a message to him. I'd check out the phone records. That might lead you to him."

"Good idea, Detective. I'll get a warrant tonight."

Beth Anne stared through the rain, toward where the squad car bearing her mother had vanished some minutes ago. "The weird part was that she believed she was doing the right thing for me, trying to get me into the business. Being a crook was her nature; she thought it was my nature too. She and Dad were born bad. They couldn't figure out why I was born good and wouldn't change."

"You have a family?" Heath asked.

"My husband's a sergeant in Juvenile." Then Beth Anne smiled. "And we're expecting. Our first."

"Hey, very cool."

"I'm on the job until June. Then I'm taking an LOA for a couple of years to be a mom." She felt an urge to add, "Because children come first before anything." But, under the circumstances, she didn't think she needed to elaborate.

"Crime Scene's going to seal the place," Heath said. "But if you want to take a look around, that'd be okay. Maybe there's some pictures or something you want. Nobody'd care if you took some personal effects."

Beth Anne tapped her head. "I got more mementos up here than I need."

"Got it."

She zipped up her windbreaker, pulled the hood up. Another hollow laugh.

Heath lifted an eyebrow.

"You know my earliest memory?" she asked.

"What's that?"

"In the kitchen of my parents' first house outside of Detroit. I was sitting at the table. I must've been three. My mother was singing to me."

"Singing? Just like a real mother."

Beth Anne mused, "I don't know what song it was. I just remember her singing to keep me distracted. So I wouldn't play with what she was working on at the table."

"What was she doing, sewing?" Heath nodded toward the room containing a sewing machine and racks of stolen dresses.

"Nope," the woman answered. "She was reloading ammunition."

"You serious?"

A nod. "I figured out when I was older what she was doing. My folks didn't have much money then and they'd buy empty brass cartridges at gun shows and reload them. All I remember is the bullets were shiny and I wanted to play with them. She said if I didn't touch them she'd sing to me."

This story brought the conversation to a halt. The two officers listened to the rain falling on the roof.

Born bad . . .

"All right," Beth Anne finally said, "I'm going home."

Heath walked her outside and they said their good-byes. Beth Anne started the rental car and drove up the muddy, winding road toward the state highway.

Suddenly, from somewhere in the folds of her memory, a melody came into her head. She hummed a few bars out loud but couldn't place the tune. It left her vaguely unsettled. So Beth Anne flicked the radio on and found Jammin' 95.5, filling your night with solid-gold hits, party on, Portland . . . She turned the volume up high and, thumping the steering wheel in time to the music, headed north toward the airport.